RACHEL DE QUEIROZ was born in Ceará, in the northeast of Brazil. She made her debut in the literary world with the novel, O QUINZE in 1930, and further established her literary reputation with JOÃO MIGUEL, CAMINA DE FEDRAS and AS TRÊS MARIAS. Rachel de Queiroz has also written children's literature, drama and television scripts. She is a member of the Brazilian Academy of Letters and lives in Ceará and Rio with her husband.

DORA, DORALINA
RACHEL DE QUEIROZ
Translated by Dorothy Scott Loos

 A BARD BOOK/PUBLISHED BY AVON BOOKS

Dora, Doralina was first published in Portuguese by Jose
Olympio Editora, 1975.

AVON BOOKS
A division of
The Hearst Corporation
1790 Broadway
New York, New York 10019

OYAMA!

I
SENHORA'S BOOK

AND SO, AS THE CAPTAIN USED TO SAY, IT'S NATU-ral to be in pain. I was always in pain. Pain always hurts, and the only time it doesn't is when you are dead.

It's worst when the pain lies dormant. There's no pain that doesn't die down, and most of the time it burns itself out. What kills you today is forgotten tomorrow. I don't know if this is true or false because all that's real for me is remembrance. That goodness and happiness are snuffed out the same as evil seems unjust to me: The good things in life occur less often, the evil ten times more. What actually ought to happen is that evil should fade away and allow the good to remain in hearts longing for happiness.

More than once I said that if I had a daughter I would name her Alegria. But I had no daughter. I knew a lady in Rio named Alegria: Dona Alegria, a neighbor in our *vila* house in Catete. Very early in the morning I would get my bread—in those days bread was delivered at the entrance gate—and she got hers at the same time. I would say good morning, and in her rundown mules and with matted curly hair she would sourly mutter her good morning in return. Dona Alegria! From then on I shied away from the name although I might still think about a daughter.

Well, I had neither daughter nor son. The child I had was born dead: They put me to sleep and cut it away from me. It was dead inside me. No one saw it. But I'll speak of all this later when it pains less, or at least not so much.

Happily that was long ago. I thought I was going to narrate these remembrances in anger, but I was wrong. Pain dissipates. Also anger and even hate. Happiness also dissipates—didn't I just say so? My child, my child! Frankly, I hardly remember my lost son. But I envy other women with their children, grandchildren, and spouses of these children.

Fortunately we renew ourselves, like everything else in this world that never repeats itself. It may seem that everything remains the same but of course everything changes—

3

the leaves of the plants, the birds, the fish, the flies. We look upon nature as a partial proof of eternity—there are always fish, birds, flies, and leaves. Only people die and go away and never come back. In fact, nothing ever comes back. Not even the waves of the sea. The water is different in each wave: The water at high tide soaks into the sand that filters it and the new wave is new water, fallen from the rain clouds. Yesterday's leaves turn yellow, become dust, and return to earth. Today's are new, made from new sap, sucked from soil watered by new rains. The birds are also new, sons and grandsons of those nestmakers which sang during the past year; and so it is with the fish, the rats in the pantry, and the fryers—everything. Not to speak of the flies, crickets, and mosquitoes. Everything.

This is also true of other persons who come to replace those who are leaving, but all too often people think that the young have no right to take the places of the old, as if each human being had his place reserved and no one could ever again put someone else in his niche.

That is the real error—no one wants to accept substitutes; people receive the newcomers and even like them but without letting go of the old ones. But this isn't possible; the world being as it is, won't it change? God knows what He is doing. What is important is that even if we despair—as it is in my case, or was—one day our time finally comes and we go away in our turn, and let those who remain despair. If they despair. Because there are possibly those who go away and only leave behind a sense of relief. Just imagine what it would be like if they remained forever. Thank God! even those who stayed too long have gone.

Ah, Senhora. Sometimes I spend a month, even a month and a half—and if no one speaks of her, I spend many months, indeed could spend even years, without thinking of her at all. But there was a time when she pained me and hurt me—when I burned like an open knife wound.

Senhora. Gradually, almost against my wishes, I became accustomed to say the name that everyone else used; I tried to call her mother, but she didn't respond. Even if she had forced it on me—she never did—even if I had been obliged to use it and had forced myself to say it, the word would have stuck in my throat. There she was with those catlike eyes—neither blue nor green—her very white skin, her

4

flushed face, her firm bosom, her sturdy walk on thick legs. Even when still young not only did her hands begin to age somewhat, knotted as they were with blue veins: Marks already cut and crisscrossed on her neck, wrinkling the skin. Her voice was clear as a bell and her teeth were white. I bet she died without ever losing a single one of those white teeth.

This then was Senhora herself, Senhora whom I thought I would have to carry nailed to me for time everlasting. Actually she didn't have to die in order to pass out of my life. For me she gradually faded away, bit by bit every day: and when I read her death notice I almost sighed with relief: for now all was definite, our accounts settled.

The bruises that remained and perhaps some remorse—all were soon buried. There had been a time when I thought her death would be like someone lifting a one-hundred-kilo rock off me; but curiously enough the rock crumbled away, without my ever noticing its gradual disappearance. Perhaps properly speaking it wasn't a rock: Who knows, perhaps it was a block of ice slowly melted by time, leaving only cold water. Cold, cold water.

And Laurindo. In those days I didn't talk much about him and hardly ever thought of him. But one day the Captain suddenly had who knows what pangs of jealousy, and asked me about Laurindo. I hated for anyone to ask about him, and it was even worse for the Captain to do so. I was thinking flippantly: Who? The dead Laurindo? Or who, Laurindo, my husband? Who, my cousin, Laurindo?

He was all that: the dead Laurindo, my late husband, my cousin. He deserved all my forgetfulness and flippancy. But the Captain in no way merited such an answer. I was engulfed with that half-bitter taste of gut and blood that the name of Laurindo still made rise up in me, from throat to mouth.

We—the Captain and I—our heads bent over the rail, were on the ferry bound for Niteroi. I looked down at the blue-brown water which rose and fell like something alive. I breathed in the salt air, trying to get the bad taste out of my mouth. I glanced at him, standing a little behind me, and put my hand lovingly on his arm.

"Laurindo? Today Laurindo seems to me a name out of a story told by someone else."

5

So it seemed then. But not always. When Laurindo was alive, he was very much alive: flesh, bones, warm blood. Entering and leaving, asking for things, engaging people. To tell the truth, he even liked to sing. He would play some old waltzes on the player piano—"Skaters" and "When Love Dies." I still remember these. From time to time the old piano would miss a note. After Laurindo died Senhora sold that piano to Maria Mimosa, professor and choir director of the church in Aroeiras.

And this, mind you, was after I had left the fazenda. During the brief time I stayed after his death she didn't bother me. I think she wished that everything should end with his death: The sun shouldn't rise or the wind blow. She was pained even if they swept the house. If a child ran along the corridor, she would slam the door and lock herself up in the oratory. People thought she was praying, but I knew better. And perhaps Xavinha suspected.

By the way, have I mentioned Xavinha? Xavinha was an old maid, a distant relative, fair with freckles and blue eyes the color of faded indigo, a protruding jaw, with one yellow prominent pointed tooth jutting out over her thin upper lip. Xavinha had always been there in the Soledade fazenda, sewing on the New Home machine. I remember when I had learned to read the name for her and pointed out that this machine was all wrong and very stupid: The word should not be *Home* but *Homem*—man—a child's typical misunderstanding. When I was even younger, I liked to call out to show off before the kitchen women:

"Xavinha, is your name *Chave*—key?"

She always blew up when teased; and if I were near, she would pinch me.

"My name is Francisca Xavier Miranda. Xavinha is my nickname." Xavinha meant *apelido* for nickname but she always said *apelidio*. She liked to use highfalutin words like *o filho de arame* (literally, the son of wire) instead of *o fio de arame* (the wire thread). As a child I detested Xavinha. This loathing was another thing that time erased. Senhora tolerated her; incidentally, the word toleration can well sum up Senhora's character: In general she let things pass, she stood aside. She only stepped on what got directly in her way.

On that New Home machine Xavinha sewed my every-day clothes, the children's undergarments, the humble work clothes of the women who worked in the fazenda, and Senhora's petticoats with their openwork lace-trimmed ruffles. Afterwards she had to sew Laurindo's shorts and pajamas, but she hated to sew men's clothing, especially men's drawers.

"I'm a nice girl, Godmother, a virgin. I never thought I would have to sew men's underwear. Drawers!"

Senhora would rivet those cold, catlike eyes on her: "Puling. Don't say drawers. Say shorts. People don't wear drawers anymore. Get back to work."

One might even call this an old maid's puling, and deep down Xavinha loved it. She was particularly careful about Laurindo's pajamas: the collar sewed in French overstitching, the trouser fly with a backstitch so fine that it couldn't be seen, the buttonholes embroidered. After she put in the string, she washed and ironed them herself and begged permission to enter the *alcova* to put his clothing in the drawer.

The *alcova* was the master bedroom that had been closed off for years after my father died. It had a turned spool bed, wardrobe, and a chest of drawers. It stayed locked up tight and was opened only to be cleaned. The servant girls were afraid to enter there at night because of my father's soul. It made me mad when they said this. I found it disrespectful of them to speak of "your father's soul." All the same, I didn't enter at night either; but in the daytime I liked to shut myself up in that bedroom, all alone, and think about my father. At the same time I thought about how he looked in the portrait in the parlor, with his curled mustache and his wide tie with the stickpin of coral surrounded by tiny diamonds. One day Senhora gave that stickpin to Laurindo as a surprise, saying that it was a man's jewel. I didn't like that: The stickpin had been my father's, why didn't she give it to me? But I said nothing: The time had come when I no longer bothered to oppose her.

During the week of my marriage festivities I myself prepared the *alcova* for us. Senhora wanted to get the cottage at the Umbuzal place ready, saying it was more suitable for the honeymoon. When she said "honeymoon" her lips tightened, as if that word made her bitter. But I said I wouldn't leave my house. Bats were in the cottage, the red glass in the windows was broken, and there was still the smell of rats, fried chicken, and the old pipe of Neném Sampaia who took care of the house after Aunt Iaiá and Uncle Doctor had died of old age within two months of each other. First Aunt Iaiá, then Uncle Doctor. It has been so long since that time that all I remember about them is having seen them leaving for Sunday mass in the cabriolet. He wore a gold chain on his vest, and she had on *tamancos* (clogs), in case the cabriolet got stuck in the mud when fording the creek, and she would have to get out; she wore the old shoes in order not to muddy the chamois-skin shoes polished with shoe white. But she never had to get out; for the little animal that pulled the cabriolet would sigh but always got through the wet mud. So I could never see Aunt Iaiá in her beat-up old shoes and elegant straw silk dress which was her Sunday-go-to-meeting outfit.

As I said before to Senhora, "I'm staying here because this is my house. I'm going to get the *alcova* ready."

Senhora was astonished. Perhaps it never occurred to her that I could possibly want the *alcova*. But she didn't resist my plan.

The floor was scoured with sand from the river. The broken pane of the guillotine window, which looked out on my garden full of tuberoses, jasmine, and carnations, was replaced. The wall was whitewashed, and then the entire house was whitewashed, even the kitchen. Seu Alvino, the saddlemaker from Aroeiras, agreed to make over the horse-hair mattress on which I had been born, according to Xavinha. And where I was conceived, I thought to myself, because nice girls didn't say such things out loud.

The young Alvino came with a donkey to fetch the mattress. He rolled it up like a cadaver, tied it in the middle, and put it on his load. But after the renovation he didn't roll it up again, and the mattress was returned on a street cart, wrapped in newspaper and covered with oilcloth so that the new blue-striped cover wouldn't get dirty.

I had ordered my new *cumaru* (tonka bean) perfumed wood trunk, lined with cretonne, to be taken to the *alcova*. The trunk was where we had been keeping the clothing which Xavinha and her two nieces, called in for that purpose, had been spending the six months of my engagement

8

sewing by hand and on the New Home machine: the camisoles, pajamas, embroidered slips with openings of Valenciennes lace, panties, and the three nightgowns—one of fine pink silk, one of blue satin, and the third of white voile, sleeveless, with open lacework and tucking. The voile was so pretty I put it aside for the first night.

When she saw the servant girls going by with the trunk, Senhora said, "Whoever heard of keeping clothes in a trunk? Why not put them in the wardrobe?"

"The wardrobe is for the groom's things," I replied. "I'm leaving the chest of drawers for my trousseau."

Senhora picked up the pencil from the account book and asked, as if she didn't understand, "The trousseau linens?"

I said that since bed and table linens hadn't been made for me, I had assumed that her trousseau linens, still laid away, were to be mine: the hand-embroidered linen sheets, the lace pillowcases, the openwork cambric and lace face towels, and the white damask tablecloth with its twenty-four napkins. I wanted them all.

Senhora closed the account book and slowly got up. "I thought that since you would be living here, you wouldn't wish to separate your linens from the house linens."

But she pulled from her dress pocket the key ring which shone like silver (the metal objects she always handled were never tarnished or rusted) and went to the trunkroom, a little room which had only one door and a glass and tile roof that hardly lighted it.

Senhora opened the large cedar chest that was lined with an antique paper with a small flower pattern.

One by one she pulled out the linen sheets which had been kept among sachets of *capim-santo:* it appeared as if some had never been used and the creases were yellow. Then followed the square pillowcases, the hand towels, the fine cotton linens for the head table, and that damask tablecloth with its two dozen napkins.

At the bottom of the chest was an embroidered lingerie set, the most beautiful I had ever seen, which I had coveted since childhood. Seeing that Senhora was closing the lock of the trunk and turning the key, I asked about the lingerie set; but Senhora gave the key another turn, lifted her head above her shoulders and said, looking up at the glass and tile roof: "That I will not give up. It was for my first night, when I married your father."

9

I was furious. "So, is it to be put in your coffin when you are dead?"

Senhora kept the keys in her pocket, reached the door, but before leaving, looked me in the face for the first time. "Perhaps."

I had told the Captain that Laurindo was my cousin, which was a manner of speaking. At least he wasn't a first cousin, or even a cousin-in-law, or a kissing cousin as they sometimes say, or a second or third cousin, but a very distant relative. When Dr. Fenelon, the owner of the Arabia fazenda which adjoined ours, brought Laurindo, an agricultural engineer, to survey the lands along a half-league of the river, Laurindo said to Senhora with his innocent air and half-whispered way of talking:

"My mother always said that we are cousins—distant to be sure—she being the daughter of Francisca Helena, nicknamed Neném. She married Major Quirino, owner of that place in the serra, Bom Recreio, in Mulungu. . . ."

Oh, yes, Senhora remembered Cousin Neném and Major Quirino very well—he was close-shaven like a priest when everybody else sported mustaches. As a child, a very young child, she had gone to the wedding of one of the Bom Recreio girls. There had been three days of festivities; this must have been Leonila's wedding.

"They were grown-up girls and I was so very young. . . ."

At that Laurindo broke into smiles—he had a fugitive smile. "Well, Leonila is my mother."

Senhora also smiled and half-closed her eyes, which were fixed on the young man's face. "Heavens, so you are Leonila's son, imagine that!"

"I am the youngest. My mother already has a passel of grandchildren. Moreover, she lives with my married sister in São Luis de Maranhão."

Senhora never ceased to be amazed. "In Maranhão! I never knew. With time people gradually lose contact with their relatives. . . ."

Then he addressed her as "Cousin Senhora," but she told him he should use "aunt," that an old cousin from whom one received the blessing is called "aunt." She was in such full bloom that she didn't look her forty years, with her beautiful half-golden hair twisted into a bun held with tortoise hairpins, and the linen dress with short sleeves revealing the rounded arms, the bared shoulders and the soft neck. Aunt indeed!

Laurindo's smile lit up again. "I find it more to my taste to say Cousin Senhora."

I thought about his receiving the blessing from Senhora. I for my part had long since dropped this custom. One time after I had slept late, awakened and passed by Senhora, I gave her a good morning, and she didn't protest; when it was time to go to bed I said good night. Only the next day when we were at the table and she was stirring her coffee did she ask: "What's this good morning about? What about the blessing?"

I looked Senhora straight in the eyes and knew I was being insolent. I paused for a moment, then lowered my eyes to the plate of corn.

"Maria Milagre talks about how to be a captive slave by definition meant he had to receive the blessing morning and night. If the slaves didn't do it they were beaten."

"And you conduct yourself by what an old black woman tells you?"

"Also in the books. I've never read in any book about girls receiving the blessing. They might be talking with father, mother, or grandparent—even godmother—and they simply say good morning or good night."

Xavinha, who wanted to get in Senhora's good graces, asked if they also didn't say good afternoon. But Senhora didn't hear and answered in that distant manner of hers, talking to the walls, table, china, or any other objects, without ever looking anyone in the face.

"Oh, I was surely wrong to have wasted the money I spent putting you in the *Colégio* where you learned such absurdities."

I wanted to say, "Your misfortune is one only: that I was ever born, and after I was born that you had to bring me up." But I was afraid. By that time I had already stopped calling Senhora "Mama." I still didn't have the courage to say "Senhora" to her face. I said "A Senhora" (the Lady) which was different. But I refused to call her mother. I don't know if she noticed. In her absence, when I gave her messages to others or when there was something in which Senhora was involved, I would say "she." Everybody would understand. I think Senhora also knew that the house servants, whom she had taught to call her "My Godmother," also called her "she" behind her back. The old *caboclas,* (Tr. note: the term *caboclo* usually refers to a person of mixed white and Indian blood. The author affirms that now in Ceará it means an ordinary person, more generally of the working class with no reference to race), when they didn't use Godmother, said "Dona." But old Maria Milagre, who came from slavery times, called her Mistress. Maria also gave me the name of Missy and I would command her to stop all of that nonsense: For they might even pin on me the nickname of Missy, just imagine. Dôra was already bad enough for me. When I was about fourteen years old, I wanted to have the name of Isolde. But just see if Senhora would ever give me the name of Isolde. My father might have, I don't know. He died so early that I don't know if he would have liked it or not. I was doomed to know nothing about him. But I was capable of swearing—and I did in fact swear—that it couldn't have been my father who chose for his darling little daughter that horrible name of Maria das Dores.

My name was another topic of discussion at the table. I believe it even anticipated the "blessing" incident. Now I know it was indeed so. It was. It was the same all my life during the invariable bickering at the breakfast table between Senhora and me. Sometimes I, or she, or we both woke up cross. Sometimes when I had had a bad dream I would recall it in a way to provoke her ill humor. And she—will anyone ever know what she dreamed—would come to the table all fragrant and rosy, sometimes even with her hair loose, in a ruffled kimona which she dragged along the floor. After coffee she took her bath, put on some low-heeled shoes and one of her linen dresses—either white or blue and green print—never red, pink, or yellow because they weren't colors a widow would wear. She adored lilac, but I don't ever remember that she had any lilac housedresses—most likely she found the color so beautiful that she reserved it for her street dresses.

Xavinha made by the half dozen all those housedresses for Senhora and me; she copied patterns in magazines. Using this sort of pattern for me was wishful thinking because my dresses, at least, never bore the slightest resemblance to them. Even Senhora's were more or less of the same style: the neck line cut low because of the heat and buttoned from top to bottom. Senhora's came out perfectly, but when it came to trying on mine that sycophant Xavinha would complain with a mouth full of pins, "Put some stuffing into that chest, child. How can I fit a blouse on such a flat thing?"

I would answer furiously: "I am not a freshened milch cow to have udders."

Eyeing her on the sly in her severe blouses with the closed collars and the pleated skirt she always wore, I would venture: "Look who's talking, that old skinny rail of a thing."

Xavinha didn't wear brassieres like everybody else but a *corpete* (a quilted breast binder) laced up like a corset. She liked to show off at night parading along the corridor in *corpete* and white petticoat.

"I don't have to go around showing off my bosom to everybody. . . ."

And Maria Milagre would hiss with ill humor: "And so someone might even die of passion seeing so much beauty!"

When it came time to offer proof, Xavinha would end the discussion with the only reply that she had for everything: "But I don't count. I'm not rich!"

When Senhora installed the radio with a truck battery in the parlor, Xavinha didn't seem to care much for the concert singing; but she was mad about those soap operas. She was so much in love with the actor Celso Guimarães that she cried and stamped her feet when an important visitor arrived, and Senhora didn't turn the radio on.

"They do this to me only because I'm not rich!"

The invention of the transistor was years away. It's a pity that Xavinha couldn't have had her own at that time. (Much later she did get one from the Captain when I told him about her passion for the artists, but by then her passion was spent, poor thing.) If transistors had existed when César Ladiera and Ismênia dos Santos were at the height of their popularity, Xavinha would have gone to sleep with the transistor in her hammock instead of with some man she might pick up. Oh, she would have died to spend the entire night listening to the soothing and insinuating carioca voice of the announcer who whispered the violent scenes from the soap operas.

But, as I was saying, that morning when we were at the breakfast table I remember that I had before me a plate of *sequilhos* (little tapioca cakes made with coconut milk). As I was stirring the sugar with a little spoon in the café au lait and listening to the cardinal which came every day at that hour to the branch of the juca tree near our window to sing, I was startled to hear Senhora's voice: "Wake up, Maria das Dores. Eat!"

I trembled with rage.

"I don't know which of the names you call me is the more terrible: Dôra or Maria das Dores. If a name were merely a sign pasted on the skin, I would peel mine off even if it caused my blood to flow."

Xavinha delicately licked the butter off the tip of her knife and interjected, "If it were I, I would consider Dorita. I think that Dorita is pretty."

Senhora was impatient with Xavinha and cut her short. "Come now, don't be an idiot. Dorita, Ninita—those are names for lap dogs. Just imagine a daughter of mine called Dorita! Only if she leaves my roof and becomes a whore."

I was all the more angry because I didn't wish to confess that the idea of Dorita appealed to me very much; moreover, if I chose it now, Xavinha would feel more important. Clearly Dorita was now out of the question since Senhora said that it was a name for lap dogs or whores.

I pushed away the still full cup and stained the tablecloth—I knew nothing irritated Senhora more! I put my elbows on the table and my face in my hands. "I hate, oh how I hate my name and all its variations: Maria das Dores, Dôra, Dasdores, Dorinha, Dorita. If I could I would go to the registrar's office and erase it; I would go to the baptistry and tear it out of the book where my baptism was recorded."

Senhora didn't reply. She bit her lips and, looking at me, seemed to be hoping that I would sink even lower so she could then punish. And I risked further: "That name—that name—Senhora gave it to me only to punish me. MARIA DAS DORES! As if to say that I am the cause of your sorrows."

Senhora spoke softly, which amazed me because her voice was more sad than angry. "I made a promise to your patron saint to give you her name as I have already told you many times. I prayed to Our Lady of Sorrows to keep me from dying in childbirth. I don't know if you are aware of it, but you almost killed me."

14

I drew back and she continued. "In my fear of death I reached out to the saint and she gave me her protection. I escaped eclampsia almost by a miracle!"

I still didn't know what to say, and Senhora concluded in her normal voice: "Moreover, Maria das Dores is a very pretty name for a young girl."

"I detest it! And Dôra is even worse!"

"My wishes were that you be called by your baptismal name. The one who invented Dôra was your grandmother. And I never argued with my mother-in-law."

"And my father, what did he call me?"

Suddenly I had to know what my father called me; it would be my father's against my mother's word.

But Senhora didn't answer. I was already getting up and preparing to say—oh, I don't know anymore what I was preparing to say—when from the end of the table once more came Xavinha's voice: "Your father used to lift you up in his arms, and he called you Doralina—'Doralina, my little flower'—he would tickle you, and you would break into smiles. You were so small that you were still babbling, '*Angu, angu*—mush, mush.' Your father made you jump into his hands and shouted: 'Run, everybody! Doralina wants *angu!* '"

My eyes filled up and I sat down again so as not to interrupt Xavinha's story, but Senhora's voice lashed out: "Go kneel down in the oratory and ask Our Lady of Sorrows, your Godmother, to forgive you. Pray the 'I sinner,' and three 'Hail Mary's.' "

I wasn't about to confess. There wasn't even a priest to make me ask forgiveness. Senhora didn't raise her voice, she only repeated, "Go on, go on. The 'I sinner' and three 'Hail Mary's.' And add 'Our Lady of Sorrows, my holy Godmother, pardon my heresies for I don't know what I say.' "

I went but I didn't pray. I knelt looking at the saint. All in all I didn't like the new Our Lady which Senhora had acquired less than two years ago in Fortaleza. It was a plaster of Paris bust painted pink, blue, and gold; and from the moment it was taken out of the box I thought it looked like Senhora. The old Our Lady was now on a shelf in Xavinha's room: small and in dark wood, and from the sword which crossed her heart dripped blood—dark blood, not gold. It almost seemed a real heart. As for myself, Senhora had

15

exchanged—(*exchanged?*—no, *bought; why not say the exact word?*)—had bought a new saint because it looked like her. It touched her vanity. So I didn't pray. I kept on saying: "Doralina, Doralina, my little flower," as my father used to call me. If I didn't say also *"angu, angu"* as I had as a little girl with my father, it was only because I was ashamed.

About that time, one afternoon Dr. Fenelon brought Laurindo to the house for the first time.

Dr. Fenelon's fazenda, Arabia, and our Soledade had some boundary disputes which had been handed down from grandparents and great-grandparents. In the legal documents the "half league" began at the bank of the river with the east-west dividing line extending from there until it met at the other side of the south side. But it happened that one year when there was a heavy winter the river changed its bed. This created a disputed no-man's-land. (This was during the time of the rich old man Raimundo Cirilo, the father of that baroness, the grand aunt of Senhora, to whom she alluded at times and from whom had come the inheritance.) Those on one side wanted the dividing line to begin in the new river since the legal documents stipulated that the dividing line should begin in the river, right? But those on the other side wanted the boundary to remain at the foot of the old riverbed. That was where the boundary line had been drawn ever since the date of *sesmaria*, when all in the stream was conceded to D. Emerenciana, from the principal branch of the old Cirilo family; for that reason those lands are still called "the inheritance of Emerenciana."

Dr. Fenelon, seated in a rope hammock on the porch, traced with the tip of his whip on the tile floor the horizontal line of the old river, and the course of the new river; his idea was to make the boundary on the vertical line some one hundred *braças* between the new and old rivers. For years and years Senhora didn't accept the compromise—she said she was obeying her father's logic: If the river marked the boundary, where the river was, there the land was.

Today Senhora gave in—no one could understand what had caused such a turnabout in her heart. Perhaps because Dr. Fenelon helped in the assessment of my father's estate—with his marriage my father had acquired a half and upon his death his heirs would share in this part; Dr. Fenelon gave the opinion that as there was a family—meaning me—the daughter would inherit all and no other relatives had any rights. Dr. Fenelon's opinion was sustained by law.

Of that particular story I only enjoyed knowing that I was already the heiress of the half belonging to my father—the lawful heiress. I found that word *lawful* beautiful and spent hours thinking about all the Soledade fazenda that was mine. Senhora always explained that when the assessment was made, they had agreed to pull out my part in the mata—forest and lake—lands and a small extension on the farthest borders to the west; but whenever I heard this I cried hysterically and raved and screamed that I didn't accept this little old part of the land at that faraway site. I wanted half of the entire estate, of the house, of the reservoir—I wanted to select trees I liked; the bits of road, the shady places, and the streams I loved. I wanted half of the orchard and half of the vegetable garden, half of the cane brake. Senhora wasn't irritated, which was surprising, but then again, it wasn't—I understood this only later.

"If you question this, it can remain undivided. On my death it will all be yours."

"But when I marry, what will happen?"

At that Senhora sized me up and down—my skinny legs, my thin ankles, flat chest and long hair pulled back tightly:

"*If* you marry."

Well, I must confess, I didn't have great hopes of marrying. When I would go to the city for an appointment with the doctor or dentist, I never found a boyfriend. True, I never went alone. Moreover, I stayed in the pension of Dona Loura, a respectable widow with a young daughter. She said she was a relative of ours and Senhora confirmed this. Some years before, shortly after her husband died, Dona Loura developed a lung congestion, spat blood, and in terror wrote to Senhora:

Dear friend and relative, it is with my heart in my hands that I dare to ask you to let me and my little daughter spend two winter months in your fazenda where I can have plenty of milk so I can gain a little

17

weight. I have been very ill, but thanks to God I have escaped death. But the doctor feels that I need to complete the cure by spending some time in a good climate and by eating the good food of the *sertão* . . .

After the signature she added a P.S. "I beg you not to be afraid of catching anything because my lungs are now all right even if I have a congestion. I have the doctor's statement to this effect. Yours . . ."

Senhora sent a telegram—I must say I was astonished—but she sent it, telling Cousin Loura to come. She had a cow set aside for the visitors' milk and advised Dr. Fenelon in the event of a relapse.

That was a happy time at Soledade. Xavinha and I took care of the little girl who, incidentally, was very skinny, with no appetite, and badly spoiled. We bathed her and put loops of ribbon in her hair, but the perverse little creature tattled to her mother that we pulled her hair. In spite of her illness, Dona Loura was an amusing woman. She knew how to sing all sorts of Argentinian tangos; she taught me *Mano a Mano* and *Muchacho de Oro*; even today I still remember the words—and in Spanish, too!

She asked Senhora for permission to play the gramophone, a machine we had acquired when my father was alive.

"These records are as old as Methuselah"—and so it happened that when Cousin Loura returned to the city she sent me three new records with music of Mario Reis whom she adored, but which otherwise wouldn't be played on this gramophone.

She showed me how to cut clothes that were stylish, freeing me from the tyranny of Xavinha's ruffles. She combed my hair, put some powder on me—even a bit of mandarin rouge!—and to console me, said: "Senhora, put five kilos on this child and see what a beautiful girl you'll have!"

Senhora looked at me with her cold eyes and said discreetly, "Let whoever can put even a half-kilo on her. I have already lost hope—she takes after her father's family."

Well, to resume, it was after this time at the fazenda that Dona Loura returned to the city with color in her cheeks and opened the boardinghouse. She rented a big house on

Tristão Gonçalves Street and used up the few resources that she had left after liquidating her deceased husband's assets.

When Senhora had to go to the city, she accepted D. Loura's hospitality with pleasure.

"Now we have a place to stay; and it's much better to pay than receive free hospitality in a relative's house."

D. Loura that first time refused to accept a penny.

"That makes no sense! The house is yours, Senhora. The house, the owner, and the owner's daughter are at your disposal! I owe you much more for I didn't pay you a cent. Have pity!"

Senhora accepted, but with that style of hers of doing what she wanted and assuming others would agree.

"This time it's all right. But in the future you must accept pay whether it be I or the child."

And as D. Loura didn't wish to promise, she replied, "Remember, Senhora, all that I owe you for the good treatment, affection, and the freedom of your house—for so many months!"

"But this is your livelihood. There in my house it cost me nothing for what you ate and drank. It was all off the land and I paid no rent. Here you pay for everything, even water! Affection, yes, that you may give freely and that is already much."

It was Senhora herself who told us this at the table, explaining that we now had a stopover in the city. She imitated D. Loura's speech with its little affectations. Senhora could imitate anyone when she wished, but it was very rare for her to make jokes, at least in my presence.

Xavinha added, "If it were I, I would accept nothing, not even under pressure! After all she enjoyed her stay for months!"

But Senhora cut her off impatiently. "Don't give me any of your silly ideas. Don't you know what it costs to live in the city?"

On that day of Laurindo's first visit no one spoke of my father's estate. Only about the changes in the old riverbed. I had no reason to be angry and said nothing. I was all taken up with looking at Laurindo seated on the wicker chair in riding breeches and boots, an American khaki shirt, and a lit cigarette constantly in his hand. A cigarette was already an integral part of his body: the smell wasn't only on his breath and in his mouth, but on his hands, clothing, and skin; perhaps one can say even mixed with his blood. After his death he still smelled of cigarettes—I myself smelled it.

The two older ones kept on debating, tracing the river on the floor. Laurindo looked and listened, but he didn't say anything: his drawing of the line would be decisive. But before having done the measurement he couldn't take the side of one or the other.

Today, after so many years, I ask myself if Laurindo had even that delicate handsomeness that I thought I saw. No, he didn't have it, or perhaps on the other hand he did, because in the end who can say what the rules are for judging people handsome. A person isn't a house or church for which the plan is drawn on paper, measured by the ruler, the meters and centimeters counted, adorned with marble and carved wood and finally gilded so that it can be beautiful. A person may even have the mouth, nose and ears in their proper places; but it doesn't mean that any one of the features is more handsome than another and determines the overall beauty. Each feature can be correct and the whole not be handsome. As in the case of Laurindo, for example, who was neither very tall, nor his chest large; nor did he have green or black eyes which could be called pretty, nor the quality of rugged skin like certain men who are considered handsome. With him, it was more the posture of the body, a dry skin, and an air of style and cleanliness, the fugitive smile. But at that time I had seen no portrait of any movie star who surpassed him in handsomeness. Moreover his voice, never out of control, seduced me; with other people around he seemed to be speaking only to you, and even when he had been drinking—and on how many later occasions I saw Laurindo drunk—and got angry, he didn't shout: He spoke even lower, more softly, until at times what he said was almost a sort of sob.

They set the day and hour of the following week for the opening of the trails into the *caatinga* (the scrub forest). Only then did they consult Laurindo, who took a little notebook out of his pocket, read some dates, and said this was all fine. Senhora didn't plan to go with them; in her place she would send Antônio Amador.

"Do you need me these first days?"

Dr. Fenelon assured her that they would not; they would first go alone to open up the trails.

Senhora made a gesture. "In all of this I ask that you remember that I don't have anyone to speak up for me: I am a lone widow."

(And I? I was already twenty-two years old, but she didn't count me. She was a *lone widow!*)

At this point Dr. Fenelon laughed, looked Senhora up and down (which I found even daring) as if he were sizing up the woman. "A widow you may be, Senhora, but if you are alone it is because you wish it so. And you still have your bodyguards; that cowhand Amador will kill and die for Senhora . . . not to speak of Dr. Laurindo here who has just discovered that he is your cousin." He broke into a coarse laugh. "If I had any sense, I would do well to get myself another surveyor."

Then the men got up; and when they had already passed from the parlor to the porch, Dr. Fenelon asked for a word with Senhora in private. It must have been about money for the beginning of the work, and Dr. Fenelon never joked about money matters.

"Pardon me, Laurindo, it's just for a minute."

Senhora took Dr. Fenelon into the small office where there was a secretary which had belonged to my father. It had secret drawers which were used by Senhora to keep money and jewelry. I continued walking to the porch and garden, in the direction of the horses waiting below at the nearby mulungu tree.

Laurindo walked behind me, and with each step I took I sensed that he was walking in my footsteps. He was easily a meter behind me, but I had the impression that his breath caressed my hair. He suddenly stopped in the garden close to the *rosa-amélia* that had four half-opened buds. He spoke my name, and I stopped. (At that precise instant I heard, there in the counting room, the sound of the bell for the secret lock which opened my father's secretary. It was money, all right, which Dr. Fenelon wished.)

I faced Laurindo who, extending his hand in one of those unexpected gestures to which I was to get thoroughly accustomed later, broke the stem of the most beautiful bud; and then he handed it to me, all serious and without saying a word. I tried to smile sweetly because I didn't know what else to do. I ended up taking the rose bud and putting it

21

quickly into the neck opening of my dress, and immediately I felt a rose thorn scratching the skin of my neck.

I kept that rose bud he had given me as though it were a golden bud or as one would keep a ring with a stone—an engagement ring perhaps?

Only much later, when nothing was left of the rose bud, I noted: He had taken the rose bud from my garden; so the first present Laurindo gave me was something that was already mine!

I was twenty-two years old, she was forty-five—Laurindo married me. One day, before the announcement of my engagement, I came along the hall and heard one of the women in the kitchen saying:

"The widow set her cap for him but the girl caught the man."

Xavinha, who was drinking eggnog from a porringer while perched on a tall stool, gave a little laugh. "Heavens, pardon me!"

But even today I can't swear that Senhora really wanted to marry him. I think most probably not. After experiencing the power of widowhood she never wanted to marry again. She would often complain, but I knew she was only flaunting her power:

"A widowed woman is the man of the house; a widowed mother is both mother and father."

I took such remarks personally. Today I think she was speaking in generalities, for everybody. In our slave quarters she wanted to be *Sinhá* as well as *Sinhô*—mistress as well as slave master.

Laurindo—had he thought about all of this? One day, two months after the wedding, Xavinha went shopping in Aroeiras and scarcely had she returned when you could see she was dying to tell something.

"For this reason I'm angry with those people in Aroeiras. I never saw people who liked to meddle so much, and they don't even respect decent people!"

Senhora turned her head toward Xavinha and waited for more information. "Yes, and what were they saying today?"

Xavinha, however, turned red, didn't answer directly

and dissembled. "Nothing, only the usual things. I'm going to take my bath!"—and she left for the kitchen.

Senhora commented that the worst thing about old maids was their vapors, their fanciful ideas. They would make mountains out of molehills.

I don't know, but I suspect that Senhora didn't wish to speculate in my presence on Xavinha's new report. It was as though she already knew about the gossip and wished to divert my attention.

I let the supper hour pass. Senhora went to her room, and I crossed the hall to Xavinha's room and opened her door slowly. (She always left the door ajar when she slept.) She used to say that she never barred the door because she was afraid the little lamp might set fire to the mosquito netting of her hammock; and if the door were barred, no one could enter to help her, and she would die barbecued.

Xavinha was seated on the hammock in her long unbleached muslin gown which was closed up tight at the neck. Her braided hair fell in two rat-tails on her shoulders. Over there in the corner on a table the little lamp was lit. She had the rosary in her hands and was praying, moving her lips silently.

I entered quietly, but even so I frightened Xavinha.

"My goodness, child! What's the matter? Aren't you well?"

I said that I had gone to get a drink of water and saw the gleam of light from the lamp under her door and suddenly remembered the gossip of Aroeiras. "What exactly were they saying? And why were you afraid to tell Senhora?"

She gave a few rocks in the hammock and licked her lips with pleasure. "Well, I don't think Godmother would like it. Those people in Aroeiras don't even respect the rich anymore. Before they attacked only their own low-class people. . . ."

"But what was the story, Xavinha? Did it have anything to do with me?"

Little by little, with much biting of lips and whispered words, the story came out. Just think—she met D. Dagmar in the pharmacy—she met, no, the woman was already there because the pharmacy belonged to her. Her husband lived in the street because he didn't want to have anything to do with the business.

"When I asked for a bottle of paregoric, she at once asked

23

if it was for 'the little bride'—if the little bride was already beginning to have a queasy stomach. . . .''

From that point on Xavinha didn't like it. They insisted on speculating about goings-on at the fazenda, and she hated people who speculated; and so she answered in all seriousness that at Soledade, at least for the time being, no one was talking about any new child. Then D. Dagmar said that the people in the street were much surprised about the marriage. There were people in Aroeiras who even made bets that the old girl and not the young one would land the catch. Mr. Carmelio de Paula was one. But the Notary Public, that Esmerino, had said right there at the display counter of the pharmacy that he bet no matter what, it would be the young girl and he collected his bet: Laurindo married the girl.

''Didn't he see that if he married the widow he would get only half of her half of the estate because the other half was the daughter's inheritance? But by marrying the girl he would have access to the inheritance from her father and in addition there would be the inheritance from her mother, coming directly without any division. . . .''

Seu Carmelio said that it could be so, that he knew nothing about inheritances, but that he did know people, and anyway, he very much doubted if the *engineer* could get his hands on whatever it might be before the death of the old lady.

I turned my back and went out without waiting for Xavinha to finish the gossip; half-trembling and with a bad taste in my mouth I walked toward my room. I entered the *alcova* very slowly, but my concern not to awaken Laurindo was needless. Laurindo still hadn't gone to bed; he was in the parlor playing patience under the Belgian lamp.

Ours had been a strange love affair ever since the incident of the rose bud. Laurindo would come to Soledade with Dr. Fenelon, and they would stay for lunch; or at other times he would come alone to dine.

He would sit at the table in front of me; Senhora was at the head and he talked with her almost exclusively. Xavinha found the young man most elegant—what breeding—and it almost seemed as if he had come from Rio.

He would bring the letters which Cousin Leonila wrote from São Luis. I never thought that a mother so far away

24

could write such letters. There was one which said: "My son, I hope that you will work hard and succeed in life: make a fortune and realize my hopes for you because I have sacrificed so much for your education." If I had been in Laurindo's place, I wouldn't have shown that letter; moreover, I don't know if he was aware of what he was doing. Senhora read those lines out loud, Laurindo got red in the face and said quickly: "No, the message for you is lower down."

Senhora found the line and read:

Say to Cousin Senhora that I thank her very much for having received my son in her home and that if I could I would go to Ceará to visit her and embrace her lovely daughter.

I was somewhat embarrassed and asked, half jokingly, whether he had told his mother all that he was doing.

"I write her every week," Laurindo replied. "I'm very much attached to my mother. As soon as I can arrange it she will come to live with me."

Well, that might be his idea but it wasn't mine. One mother was enough for me, and how! If she is happy, let her stay where she is. Didn't Cousin Leonila always say in her letters that the best place for her to live was in São Luis and that she hardly felt the heat?

Senhora returned the letter, commenting that Cousin Leonila had a good handwriting, by which one could recognize the students from the Colégio das Irmãs. Laurindo put the envelope back in his pocket, agreeing that his mother indeed had a beautiful handwriting.

As for him, his handwriting was not only not elegant, it was even difficult to read, as was evident in those pencilled notes which he threw into my room through the window or gave to some servant boy to deliver to me on the sly. They didn't bear my name at the top or his signature below. They didn't even begin with "My beloved" or "Dear one." Only one of them ended with "a kiss," and that one he handed me himself one night on the dark porch.

I know of persons who love openly, frankly, and even arrogantly. I loved secretly and jealously, thus fitting in with Laurindo's hidden ways. Did anyone imagine I would share love or Laurindo with Senhora or anyone else? It was

25

the first time in my life that I had something for nothing, with no strings attached, without having to fight for it, since it all came from him: It was he who sought me out with his hands and eyes—always on the sly, but constantly. It was he who came to visit me in the house, every day now. It was he who gave me his promises and his person of his own free will without my having to compete or beg.

As for Senhora, ever since I was young it always seemed that I had to fight with her about everything, even about the bedtime hour; she didn't even serve me at the table—everyone served himself. When I was a child she would command someone else to bathe me, dress me, and comb my plain braids. But she ordered just any old person—I never had a nursemaid who was my very own. I remember that one day I complained about this and Senhora railed:

"None of this! A nursemaid only instills bad habits in children."

To tell the truth, I never felt that I owned anything in Soledade. I was more like a guest left to herself who had nothing of her own. Everyone, everything belonged to Senhora—the servants, the goats, the cattle, the house—all were Senhora's. Moreover, it was common practice for those in the fazenda family no longer to use "Senhora"— but "Dona." "Dona wishes," "Dona commands."

I didn't have father, grandfather, grandmother, godmother, uncle, brother, or sister. Every day I went to school in a buggy—in those days the buggies still didn't have rubber-tired wheels. It was a cabriolet with big iron wheels like the one that belonged to Uncle Doctor. Who knows but that it was the very same one? It could have been inherited since I believe that when I reached school age Aunt Iaiá and Uncle Doctor had already died.

Compadre Antônio Amador would take me and bring me back along with the brass containers of milk which he sold to the sisters. According to him it was this milk which paid for my education at the Colégio.

I remained there until I was seventeen years old, and I was always the youngest in the class, skinny and withdrawn; almost all the others were already developed young women and ready for marriage. In the first year one girl left to marry a widower; the last year, the fourth, there was an epidemic of marriages when three students left the school before receiving the diploma—those engaged found that they already knew enough and anyway who needs a degree to raise children.

I never did well in the Colégio and I didn't like it there. Perhaps if I had boarded in I would have adapted myself to it, but Senhora didn't wish that. One Sunday in the middle of the year the sisters brought some students to Soledade for a picnic. It was an agony for me—I wanted to shut myself up in my room, but Senhora was screaming that I wasn't doing the honors of the house. There was a girl with a bouquet of flowers who recited some verses which called Senhora our "benefactress." But I already knew those verses that had been applied to so many other persons; and they were always the same, or almost so, only the girl who recited them changed. Later, on another day, I reported this fact at the table—I pretended I was talking to Xavinha, but I intended for Senhora to hear; and I saw that she didn't like it one bit. At least I got some satisfaction from this conversation, which spared us another such visit.

I must have been almost fourteen years old when a man appeared at Soledade, a stranger by the name of Raimundo Delmiro.

However, he had another name which he revealed to me only much later and then in whispers. I swore never to reveal it to anyone—I swore it and kept my oath. His second name was Lua Nova, but that is another story about which more shall be said later.

Raimundo Delmiro arrived at the house in bad shape, mounted on an old donkey to which a halter made with a piece of thin rope was badly secured. Dirty, ragged shirt and pants and without a hat. The *alpagatas* with quilted soles and edged with eyelets which he wore were much better. He halted the donkey in the yard, and gave greetings; I was on the porch idling away my time making lace. The lace edging was already turning yellow. Senhora had a mania about forcing me to make lace during vacations—"a suitable occupation for a white girl instead of running around in the bushes with the barefoot half-breeds."

Yes, it was vacation time in the middle of December, and the sun drew fire from the stones. One couldn't know if it was the intensity of light which made the apparition shimmer in the sun or if it was the man who was swaying. But it

27

was he, yes, because he suddenly fell on the neck of the donkey; and the halter slipped from his hands. Then he began to slide slowly, and finally dropped to the ground where he stretched out.

Two servant girls, Luzia and Zeza, and I ran toward him but we stopped after a short distance, fearful that he was dead. No, he wasn't dead. He breathed heavily, groaned, and changed color. He had fallen on his left side; the right sleeve of his shirt had been pulled out, and his arm was folded inside a stained, colored handkerchief which served as a sling. From the shoulder to the elbow that arm was a dark mass of blood and sweat; it was dressed with pieces of castor-oil bean leaves, badly fastened with strips of rags.

I looked around to see if perhaps Senhora mightn't be near, but I saw no sign of her. There was only Antônio Amador, who came from drinking his cup of coffee at the kitchen window which he did at all moments of the day. Amador also saw the man fall. He came at once and we arrived at the same time. He crouched down and looked closely at the distorted face with several days' growth of beard and felt his head.

"He's burning up with fever."

"Let's pull this poor man out of the sun," I begged. The Indian girls helped Amador, and they half-carried, half-dragged the man and laid him on the pavement in the shade of the wall.

The hoarse words which passed through the swollen lips seemed to ask for "water, water." I sent Luzia to get a cupful in the kitchen and with my own hands I poured the cool water very slowly into the poor thing's open mouth; but he couldn't swallow, and the water trickled down his neck. The poor man could hardly lick a few drops off his lips. Antônio Amador asked my permission, held him up by the nape of his neck, and put the cup to his mouth; then he drank a small swallow, then a large swallow, and finally he held the cup in his left hand and drank all the rest. He gave a sigh of relief and then said something which I understood to be "that's enough," and Amador stretched him out on the ground again.

His main problem was the arm bone. An ugly bruise went from the elbow to the hand—and the swelling enlarged his neck and chest which the torn sleeve laid bare.

Any girl in a fazenda had been trained in nursing. As a

little girl she sees her mother and aunts curing the *caboclos*—cuts, small wounds, a tumor that needs lancing, a poisonous thorn or splinter to extract.

Senhora had introduced me to my duties as fast as I could handle them and so even when I was very young I treated the navels of the newborn with Mercurochrome before the *comadres* could apply the tobacco leaves and cobweb paste. From girlhood I had treated small wounds, knife cuts, cuts from broken glass, and that sort of thing. Somewhat later, Senhora having been away, I gave first aid and then afterwards treated for two weeks the foot of Luis Chagas, who had his little toe cut off by an unfortunate blow of the scythe. I took care of Luis so well that the scar where the toe had been was smooth and clean and he would laugh out loud and show off the foot. Even Senhora praised me.

So in that hour I calmly assumed authority and said to Amador that it was necessary to put the man in a hammock and to treat that shoulder.

Instinctively I sent Luzia to the house to fetch a colored hammock, one of those separated from the rest, ready to be loaned to some passerby who might seek hospitality at Soledade and hadn't brought his own. I told her to ready the last room in the corridor of the storage house that was some distance from the wall at the right of the big house.

I myself went to the storage room to get the little white enamel basin and asked Zeza, the other girl, to bring a pitcher of warm water. I took from the medicine cabinet cotton, sterilized water, iodine, and some bandages of old linen sheets which Senhora had torn into strips for that purpose after having had them boiled, dried in the sun, and stored in a little tin canister.

When I returned, Amador already had put the man in the hammock and had torn away the rest of the dirty shirt. I put warm water in the basin and Amador washed the creature's face, neck, and chest—all encrusted with black blood.

The patient began taking on a more healthy color, more that of a mulatto than of a *caboclo*. He wasn't a young man—perhaps already in his fifties. He had a big bull neck, a large chest, and arms corded with veins and muscles. His hair was already peppered with gray.

After the face came the wounded shoulder: I myself untied the knot of the sling; and when the arm fell loose, the man let out a hoarse cry. I folded the arm again gently over

29

his chest; I examined the bone of the arm below the shoulder, and it seemed to me that nothing was broken there. But on the shoulder, God, one could hardly know where anything was under the dry, crusted blood. I patiently cut away the strips of cloth and took out the pieces of the castor-oil bean leaves. Then I saw the wound, small at the entrance but the flesh torn and ragged at the socket and the ribs where it ended. Since it was all swollen and purple red, one couldn't see the tip of the bone—something inside was fractured. I bathed that torn flesh with sterilized water, squeezed dry the white bubbling liquid, wet the cotton pads with iodine, and cleansed the wound. Everything was now so swollen—and perhaps numb—that the man didn't appear to feel even the sting of the iodine. Afterwards I bandaged the chest and shoulder with the clean cloths.

In agony, the man began to complain again and plead for water. Amador suggested that we give him warm milk with sugar, and I dissolved an aspirin in the milk because of the fever. The poor thing swallowed it all in a gulp: He must have been very hungry. Then we repeated the dose of milk.

But he took only one or two swallows, let his head fall, and closed his eyes.

Standing over us, Zeza asked in terror: "Is he dead?"

Antônio Amador reassured us. "No, he is overcome by weakness and has fallen asleep. Now he will probably sleep for several hours."

This all took place a long time ago; but it seems to me that I still see plainly everything that happened then. I have never been able to forget. Remember, believe me, that I have treated many sick people since then. But it was my first important case if you don't count Luis Chagas's little toe—but it wasn't only because of this: There were other reasons for remembering so vividly, as I'll explain later.

Of course Senhora wasn't pleased to learn that I had dared to aid that faceless and nameless passerby, put him up in a room, and doctor him—all without her orders.

And when I came from the little room with the medical things in my hands she said to me, "So, you are now giving asylum to any wandering gypsy who appears without even asking my permission?"

I passed her without answering, for this was now becoming my custom. As I turned my back on her, she looked to Antônio Amador.

"So, it was you who picked up the character and carried him inside? Who is he?—Some drunkard?"

I entered the house to wash my hands without waiting to hear the rest. Let Antônio Amador make the explanations.

For three weeks I nursed the stranger. Antônio Amador, on Senhora's orders, undressed him and searched him. He found nothing in his pockets except a dirty bill of little value and a bundle of aluminum medallions—all with Father Cicero, the miracle worker, on the front and Our Lady of Sorrows (my patron saint!) on the back.

The donkey on which he arrived stayed for a while in the yard with the halter dragging; later in the midst of the confusion it just walked away and disappeared.

After three weeks the wounds were closed and the fever subdued. At the end of that third week I said at the table—it was really Xavinha who brought up the subject—that Mr. Raimundo Delmiro considered himself well but that he was still a little weak. The shoulder was still stiff, but the arm could move from the elbow down.

Some days later, when Senhora went to the front yard after her bath, as was her custom, she threw open the door of the storage house without asking permission, which was also her habit. She treated everything there as her possession: neither a member of the Soledade household nor any dweller there had the right to a closed door.

At first I thought about not expressing an opinion and not following her as she hadn't called me; but at the same time I couldn't withdraw my protection from the unfortunate one—with Senhora one could never be sure what she'd do. Since he was my ward, I ran after her.

Raimundo Delmiro was seated in the hammock, and to all appearances was praying. A small holy picture card of Our Lady of Sorrows which Zeza had loaned him was on top of a small table, and he was moving his lips; his head was lowered, the injured arm was in his lap, and he was beating on his chest with his left hand. When he saw the door opening he stood up, but Senhora didn't even allow him time to say good morning.

"So you're well? Then are you ready to start your journey?"

Delmiro, dazed, looked at Senhora as if hypnotized. It was I who walked in front of her, made the man sit down again in the hammock and thus take the weight off his trembling legs. And I said, "The shoulder has mended, but Mr. Delmiro is still very weak."

Senhora crossed her arms on her chest and looked at me. *"You* know his name, but you haven't said a word to me about anything yet."

She turned her attention to the man and spat out: "Where do you come from and who shot you in the shoulder? Was it a dispute? Were you alone or in a band? And what about your companions?"

And I dared to reply: "His name is Raimundo Delmiro, and he is from Riacho do Sangue. He was wounded in a dispute—"

But Senhora cut me off as always. "He has a tongue. Let him speak."

Then Delmiro, half stammering, told Senhora what he had already told me: He was a native of Riacho do Sangue where he was born and raised. He worked with animals and cattle. It had been a year and a half since he went to Picos with a herd of donkeys, when the revolutionaries passed by Piaui and ran across him. He was duped by the rebels' proposals; they swore to him that the government had already lost the war, that the revolution was victorious, and that even Father Cicero had sent his people to fight on the side of the Prestes rebellion. He even became enthusiastic, handed over his donkeys (he received a requisition); they gave him arms and ammunition, and he joined the band. But during the trip and when he arrived at Ceará, he discovered the lies: Prestes wasn't winning anything at all, but on the contrary, was being pursued; and Juarez, in whom everyone had faith, had been taken prisoner, and now all was hopeless. The worst thing was that Father Cicero was against the rebels and had even given his blessing to the government's provisional soldiers to fight Prestes.

Delmiro became disgusted and unhappy about all of this; finally he decided to escape. On a certain evening he checked in but by morning he had disappeared. The sergeant took the escape as his personal responsibility and sent a patrol after him—for almost a week they tracked the deserter—and he, who had fled without arms lest he be taken for a rebel, couldn't even fight back when overtaken. So he was captured because the donkey could hardly walk at all; and those in the patrol shot him, beat him with their guns, left him for dead, and carried away his donkey.

Regaining his senses sometime later, God knows when, he was dazed, aching all over, the shoulder throbbing and the arm dead. Since he was wounded in the right arm, it was fortunate he was left-handed. All he could do was make a sling with his neckerchief and put castor-oil bean leaves on the wound. He passed by a house, asked for water and it was given him, but the people were frightened and slammed the door in his face. He couldn't possibly think of remaining in any one place for fear of the rebels. He walked without food for two days; then he slept, but he didn't know for how long due to the fever. After that he didn't know the number of days he walked toward the border.

At one house a girl gave him a plate of beans. He even had the good luck to find that old donkey loose in the middle of the road: he mounted, but it was difficult to make the animal go without reins or halter. Passing by a closed-up house he came across two little pieces of cord hanging from a metal hook, and with them he made a crude halter. He let the donkey go wherever it chose. At times he would fall on the donkey's neck, and he continued along in this manner. Once the animal stopped on the bank of a reservoir to drink and he, too, drank—and it was very painful to remount. He didn't know how long he had been traveling when he arrived at the patio of the fazenda, and the donkey stopped at the foot of the mulungu tree. He sensed that he was sliding to the ground. He fainted, and when he came to an angel of Our Savior was helping him.

Senhora listened to all of this silently, with only a short question now and then—" . . . and from where? . . ." "Where exactly?"—"Why?"—then she crossed her arms.

"What angel? That one over there? She's my daughter, and you're at my fazenda, Soledade."

But she spoke without anger, which amazed me. Only afterwards did I remember that Senhora hated the rebels when she learned that they came to the fazendas, requisitioning fowl and cattle, leaving the so-called "requisition

33

receipt" to be repaid "after the victory of the revolutionary army." But neither did she like the government and always encouraged her electors to vote for the opposition for fear they might dare to give a vote to our enemy, the prefect of Aroeiras. Senhora even used to send messages to the man: "The revolution is coming!"

But if anyone wanted to take what was hers, she was against the world: She wanted no part of the government or of the revolution. She would say that if one or the other came to occupy her land, they wouldn't get it if she were alive—she preferred to set fire to the house, clearing, and mata.

Well, that was the "official" story of Delmiro. The other version I learned before winning my big battle with Senhora and had succeeded in giving the stranger a place to stay in the old house of the late João de Deus.

(That old João de Deus was a quack and goat thief according to the rumors about him after his death: His only son disappeared right after the burial and Senhora had someone take charge of the deceased's house and clearing. Then, well disguised in a *mafumbo* thicket, enclosed in the planting, were discovered five pens where they hid the stolen goats which the son would carry away on a Saturday night to sell at the fair. For this reason the old João had made his home in that harsh place, almost in the middle of the forest; and after he died and the son had disappeared that remote spot took on a frightening character. . . .)

One morning when I accompanied Luzia with the plate of cuscus with milk for my patient, Delmiro told me that he felt almost well.

"As for the future, my chances are limited. It's now time for me to leave, find some place where I can plant a little corn, a bit of beans, and throw up a cabin to await death— the lady can plainly see—with this broken arm what other future could I have?"

Then I remembered the abandoned *tapera* of João de Deus and suggested that he should go there to live.

I went on horseback at a slow pace to show him the place because Delmiro still wasn't steady on his legs, nor did he have his breathing under control. When we arrived at the abandoned dwelling, covered with jitirana plants in a veritable explosion of blooms, the place was so calm, so beautiful and sad that it made the heart contract. Delmiro asked permission to sit down on a tree trunk in the middle of the yard. He looked around him and took stock for a while. Then he lifted his eyes to me—I was still on horseback—and said that he had had a vision.

In this vision he had seen this old house exactly as it was, with its walls falling down and the roof tiles clogged up, and now he realized that he had been brought from far away to come live here.

But in the vision, a voice also told him that he couldn't continue with lies and deceptions and that it was necessary to make a complete confession as if he were at the feet of a priest. If he were pardoned he would stay. If not, he would be on his way. If the latter he would have to go on wandering sadly along the roads, eating by begging, until the hour of death and Judgment Day.

So, beating on his breast, groaning and crying, he vowed to tell me all, God willing.

The story he had told Senhora was accurate in almost all its details, except one or two. Yes, he had been pursued, wounded and ill-treated, and left for dead on the highway. But he hadn't come alone, he had come with three companions. Of these three, one had been killed and the other two taken prisoner, one having been wounded in a shoot-out with the police. When the soldiers took the prisoners away, he, Delmiro, remained by the dead one, overlooked since he was thought to be dead also. When the police returned to bury the dead, they couldn't find him because he had already regained consciousness and fled.

On that day, the following night, and the day after that, he remained in hiding, taking refuge in a hole under a hedge. The shoulder didn't pain too much but was quiet; perhaps the worst thing was the thirst.

On the second night he dragged himself from under the hedge, decided to leave, and walked until dawn. From then on all happened as he had told Senhora: the castor-oil bean leaves, the cup of water, the plate of beans, the stolen donkey.

But the crucial point: Those companions of his *were not* rebel soldiers—Delmiro, himself, had never laid eyes on a rebel; all he knew about them was through speaking with people who were frightened by the Prestes Column. The group to which he was attached, it's true, were army recruits; but they quickly became bandits, taking advantage of the situation. They began by stealing horses and then went on to steal cattle. But when the pursuit got hot they had to free the animals and go by foot in the *caatinga*. The police formed a patrol for the express purpose of hunting them down. They had many fights with the soldiers, and they managed to escape but always losing a companion; and finally of the nine who started out only four remained.

The patrol sergeant besides being very perverse was also opinionated; before entering the police force he had been an outlaw in *cangaço*; he was captured and in order to be pardoned he had enlisted. He was meaner than the devil. In those forays with him Delmiro's band pushed ever farther away from familiar terrain, and without friends or anyone to hide them—and the sergeant wished it that way—they ended up getting wiped out.

However, I needn't have feared that a police patrol might show up at Soledade. No one in the band or outside of it knew Delmiro by name; within the band he had a code name: he was called Lua Nova—New Moon—because of his reticence and his scowling face; on a night of new moon all is paradoxical and mysterious, not even a rooster crows.

Before the final encounter with the police they cut each other's hair, up to that time worn shoulder length. They were already trying to disguise themselves and catch a train back to their own territory. But Delmiro never intended to return to Riacho do Sangue since he had left there because of some affair of vengeance.

No one had seen his face clearly. The assault on the saloon had taken place at night, and they had by then learned a way to put their hair over their faces, thus covering up their features and at the same time making themselves even more frightening.

Upon leaving the two dead men on the road—one really dead, the other pretending to be dead—the police soldiers carried away their arms—rifles, cartouches, the long *rabo-de-galo* knives and even a small dagger which Delmiro carried stuck in his belt. And together with the guns, of course, the swordbelt where he kept his money. The money added up to hardly more than three *contos de reis*. Money was what they were seeking and they never overlooked it.

Now, repentant and maimed, he wanted with God's help to remain in the *tapera* of João de Deus—he swore he wanted nothing else in this world. He had made his confession in conformity with what he thought was required. He put his fate into my hands.

If I had wished, I could have denounced him to Senhora, who would have turned him over to the authorities. He promised to leave without causing any trouble in our house, even while knowing that if he went thinly disguised along the road the soldiers would kill him for ''resisting arrest.''

If I would leave him his life, he swore never to touch arms again and to do penance as if the Lord had ordered it.

He was old without any relatives—no father, mother, or wife; only his enemies scattered here and there remembered him. It wasn't the fear of death which obliged him to ask my protection: His fear was to die like an animal without having been purged of his sins, and thus in the hereafter doomed to burn in hell for centuries and centuries.

And so Raimundo Delmiro, nicknamed New Moon, fell on his knees and lifted his eyes to me. I listened to him while still mounted on my horse.

''Here I am at your feet like a lamb, and I accept whatever you order because I hold you as my savior angel; and any word from your lips is a word from heaven. I swear to abandon my old name and way of life; I promise never to touch arms again, unless it be on your orders and for your protection. May Jesus Christ, the Messiah and our Lady of Sorrows, protector of Juazeiro and our holy Father Cicero, together with you here, keep me in your hands and have mercy on me. Amen. Amen. Amen!''

I had the fight with Senhora, and I succeeded in guaranteeing the *tapera* for Delmiro. The old man moved in at once, taking with him the hammock which I had given him, a small earthen jar with the mouth broken which I had arranged for with Maria Milagre, an aluminum plate, a cup, and a spoon. Zeza thought of the knife only when he was some distance away, and we ran to give him an old knife; but Delmiro would accept it only from my hands, not from the girl's, in order not to break his oath because the knife was a weapon.

Working slowly with his left arm Delmiro built up the abandoned *tapera* little by little, repaired a good piece of

João de Deus' fence and thus made a small clearing. He tore up the coop and burned the mato brush over again; when the rains came he asked me for seeds and made a small planting of tobacco and beans, two liters of corn, and some handfuls of manioc. (Since he had nothing to start with, it was I who maintained him, stealing things from the pantry with Maria Milagre's help. I don't know what Senhora thought about all of this, as to how Delmiro managed to eat, for example.) He cultivated everything in his field so well that when the harvest came his planting produced much more than others with larger clearings.

He lived alone without friends or wife or even a dog. The people of the fazenda, and even Senhora, got used to him. One day when Dr. Fenelon commented on the presence of that "loner" and asked why he shouldn't be sent away—"Nobody knows him and he is of no use, is he?"—Senhora answered brusquely:"Oh, my land is full of foxes and snakes. Leave the old man alone, he won't harm anyone."

Finally it ended up with people having doubts about passing his place. Delmiro didn't seek out anyone, and each year he raised a little higher the interwoven fence lacking any gate that enclosed his clearing and his house. He let his beard grow and it was now getting white. He dressed in some old pants that were more like a loincloth, and went naked from the waist up.

Some days I would steer my horse in that direction, lean against the fence, and shout for him. After a while, Delmiro would appear, bringing some little present that he had for me—a rooting of a flower that he had in a little pot, a pair of gourds tied with a *malva* braid like water wings so I could swim in the dammed-up lake; or a small ceramic bucket for "when I had my clabber." It was the size of a porringer and had been polished so thin with a cashew leaf that it was almost transparent.

When I had more time he would lift up the fence to give passageway for my horse and would show me the birds. Along the foundation under the house hung some gourds with little window openings like the mud birdhouses where the birds came to nest. Others made their nests on their own—I only know that every conceivable type of bird came there, redheads, canaries, nightingales, and even song-birds.

Delmiro planted a little strip of rice just to feed the birds; and once he raised a wild duck which had fallen wounded into the lake, and he nursed and tamed it. Some time before he had raised an abandoned fawn which returned to the wilderness after it grew up. I asked him why he didn't tie up the deer—I asked because I thought he wanted me to do so. I knew very well that Delmiro had a horror of making a prisoner of any living thing, however wild it might be—he didn't even catch armadillos. The birds came and went as they pleased, as did the small lizards which lived in the cracks of the mud wall; there were even monkeys.

With time Delmiro grew more eccentric and solitary. Whoever might pass by his house, especially at night, was frightened, hearing that voice, hoarse like an animal's, singing his hymns, each one more dolefully than the last.

One day, when I was around the kitchen, I heard the women gossiping and laughing about an incident: just imagine, Neném Sampaia, that half-crazy woman who lived in the cottage at the Umbuzal place and who was our local prostitute, mother of two sons to whom she claimed as father all the men of the vicinity—well, that crazy Neném Sampaia bet five mil-reis that she could seduce Delmiro.

And so one morning she leaned on his fence, shouting and crying: "Help me, Mr. Delmiro, help me! I bumped into a beehive and those creatures attacked me, they are killing me! Help me!"

And as soon as Delmiro's head appeared over the fence Neném roared: "They got into my clothes!"—and she took off her skirt and blouse. Completely naked she began rubbing her hands over her body as though she were trying to rid herself of the insects.

Then Delmiro spoke: "Wait there and I'll get something."

Neném continued scratching herself and crying, her body exposed all the while until he returned with an old broom that he had wet and put on the fire and which now gave off steam and smoke. And he said: "Insects are frightened away by smoke." He put the broom next to the woman's body which was enveloped in the smoke as in a cloud. Suffocating and coughing, Neném gave up and put on her skirt.

"Enough, Mr. Delmiro, enough, the insects have all gone!"

Delmiro jumped over the fence once again and without saying a word or looking back, went off with the still smoking broom like a rifle on his shoulder as if nothing had happened.

About every seven weeks after that he would appear at the fazenda during the siesta hour when Senhora was asleep. He brought a half sack of beans or corn and a rope of tobacco for which I made an exchange for provisions like matches, salt, and raw sugar. Antônio Amador gave him a little old donkey to carry away his cargo. On feast days I had Xavinha make him some clothes and from time to time I gave him a hammock.

But I was always careful to weigh what he brought and note the agreed-upon price in anticipation of Senhora's claims. She never failed to demand payment. I matched account against account and the balance was always in Delmiro's favor. Senhora would say acidly: "And who pays me for the land?"

One day I summoned up my courage: "He doesn't owe you anything. He lives and plants on what is mine."

"Yours—yours? Where is yours?"

But for some time now I had the reply ready: "Senhora agreed to leave the estate undivided. So then, mine is whatever I say is mine."

After I married, Delmiro stopped appearing at the fazenda during the daytime. He still brought the corn and beans for the exchange but came late at night; he left the sack at the warehouse door. The following night I had Amador place the coffee, salt and raw sugar in the foliage of the mulungu tree to protect them from the insects (that same mulungu tree under which Delmiro fell, half-dead, so many years ago). On the following day the food was gone.

Laurindo wanted to know Delmiro better since he was intrigued by the stories which circulated about the foolish, solitary old man, my protégé. So I took my husband to the fence, but Delmiro didn't appear. I called and called, but he pretended not to hear. Laurindo became impatient and wanted to jump the fence, but I warned him not to do so.

"You can see that he has gone out—perhaps to fetch water with his burro. It's best that you don't enter alone—with his mania for animals he just might be raising a cobra."

I knew that Laurindo was afraid of cobras. He killed them only when he had to and from a distance with a shot.

He didn't jump the fence but he would take walks in the direction of the clearing and almost always came back with a *rolinha* or *juriti* bird in his saddlebag.

Later on I went alone to visit Delmiro. I called and he appeared at once. Afterwards he went back to look for a honeycomb which he brought wrapped up in some leaves and said: "Tell your husband to have pity on my little animals."

Upon arriving home I delivered the message and Laurindo laughed.

"Your mother says that old man is your bodyguard."

At that I was furious.

"Until today I have had no need for a bodyguard. But who knows . . . if it's necessary? Even if he's old . . ."

"With his right arm maimed?"—and Laurindo left whistling.

At nighttime in Soledade it was an old custom for the men to gather on the porch of the fazenda for coffee and conversation. The cowhands would give an account of the day's happenings: the cow that was missing, the sheep that had disappeared, the opening in the fence, the mooing of the new calf. Senhora would distribute her orders for the following day, and I would listen silently, balancing myself in the rope hammock.

With Laurindo's arrival the conversation lasted longer, now that there was a master in the house and the men felt less shy than when only in the presence of Senhora as heretofore. In my father's time, according to Maria Milagre, the conversation went on until very late at night, each one telling about his case of terror which the "beloved master" appreciated very much. Scary ghosts, strange animals—all made their appearance. That nightly visit was the recreation of the fazenda family. The women with the children sought the kitchen and the men scattered about on the benches of the porch. Whoever wished to join the group came, and there was never a small audience. Almost always more

41

room was needed on the benches and some men perched on the bannisters.

Senhora sat in her hammock and Laurindo took mine at my father's old place. I sat on the edge of his hammock—in the beginning it had been a trysting place for us when we were lovers; now I sat there out of habit.

It was dark there on the porch; even on moonlit nights the light bathed only the garden and yard. The Belgian lamp was left lit in the parlor by design so as not to attract the many bugs, beetles, and moths to the porch.

I don't remember how it came about, but one night the conversation centered on Delmiro. Laurindo, who was holding my right hand and nibbling at my fingers, suddenly interrupted the caress to point out:

"Aside from being Dorinha's bodyguard, where is he from and who is he?"

I withdrew my hand angrily and then Senhora with a certain malevolence told the story about the rebels. Happily it was the only version she knew.

From the benches the men began to speculate and *compadre* Eliseu, who had a reputation for invention, found that this comrade was born in Canudos and was the son of a *jagunço*—one of the fanatic followers of Antônio Gonselheiro.

I retorted brusquely: "Who told you that?"

Compadre Eliseu was a little frightened by my asperity—there were stories that he had been told in the street.

"Mr. Jeronimo of the bakery shop was saying the other day that many a son of a *jagunço* was astray in this *sertão* after the war. There were rumors that they killed everybody; and during the day when the soldiers entered Monte Santo, there wasn't a living soul there. The truth is that at night-fall, many a woman and child escaped when the men made them flee into the darkness on hidden paths."

I wasn't enjoying the conversation and was almost tempted to shock all those people and Laurindo, too, with the true story of New Moon, the bandit with the swarthy face. I could just imagine Senhora's rage, but I think the hired hands would have ended up forgiving him.

Instead I spoke as I thought I should, piling up tiny explanations.

"There's no mystery about Delmiro: He's a native of Riacho do Sangue, he always lived there until he made that trip to Piaui where he ran into the rebels and joined Prestes. He must still be known in his home, it wasn't long afterwards that his father died. According to what he told me, it was the old man whose name was Delmiro; he was baptized Raimundo; Delmiro then isn't his first name but his father's name."

"Good, perhaps he isn't a bandit," Laurindo concluded, "but he is a crazy old man who throws rocks and no one can deny that. Not even you."

I sighed.

Five days after that Laurindo killed the wild duck that Delmiro was nursing. He came home with his rifle slung over his shoulder, walked around the house, sauntered through the kitchen nonchalantly, threw the saddlebag on top of the table, and gave orders.

"Prepare this duck for my lunch."

After he left one of Senhora's servants, taking the dead bird from the bag, looked at it closely and screamed:

"May God forgive me if it isn't old Delmiro's wild duck!"

I was coming along the corridor and overheard. Angrily I entered the kitchen, took the duck from Zeza's hands, for it was she who had screamed, and asked, "How do you know?"

The girl was stammering, guessing the excitement that would follow, but she answered boldly, "Look here, Godmother Dôra, the little broken membrane that Delmiro fixed—see it here and not the bone—poor little thing. . . . She was such a gentle little thing!"

Like a snake I turned on Laurindo who was still leaning on the door with a smirk on his face, and he excused himself.

"How was I to know? If a duck is on the lake I shoot, and if I am accurate, I kill. Hunting is hunting. . . ."

My lips white, I answered, "Laurindo, this duck wasn't killed on the lake. You didn't come by the far side of the lake—you came from this side, from Delmiro's side."

"And perhaps you know the meanderings I took? I only passed by there on the way back."

The women in the kitchen were now all silent, stealing glances at us, but they didn't want to miss any of the argument. One of the girls sneaked out to call Senhora, who ap-

43

peared at the corridor door and saw me with the duck in my hands at the very moment when Laurindo was saying:

"If the duck was his why didn't that stupid old fool put a mark on it? I'm not to blame—he might have tied a string on the duck's foot, or put a band or ribbon on its neck, or even a metal marker!"

Then Senhora got excited and put in her two cents' worth; she couldn't wait.

"Here, nobody owns a duck, any animal of the fazenda belongs to the fazenda, especially an animal from the *mata*. Since when did Mr. Delmiro receive orders to make a pet of a duck that nobody can touch?"

She stared at me with her eyebrows wrinkled as she did in my childhood in order to frighten me.

"Don't be silly, Maria das Dores. Luzia, clean that duck and roast it for lunch."

Luzia was already taking the little wild duck from my hands; I gave her a slap and snatched back the little creature which was still warm with its neck almost severed by the shot, its beak open, and its dark, multicolored plumage all velvety in my hands.

I ran outside, crying as much from rage as from hurt. How many times had I played with that little duck, given it kernels of corn and cooked beans under Delmiro's guidance in his yard?

I took the path which led to his house and raced there at top speed. Running all the way, I could hardly breathe. I finally arrived; weary and out of breath I leaned on the fence.

"Delmiro! Delmiro!"

He must have been close by because he appeared at once and took off his tattered straw hat. I put the little duck in his hands and sobbed.

"Pardon . . . Mr. Laurindo killed the little thing by mistake . . . I'm so sorry . . . he didn't know!"

Delmiro, his head lowered and without looking at me, began to smooth the feathers of the little duck.

"He has already killed one of my songbirds, three *juriti* and four *rolinha* birds. . . . All raised here. . . . The songbird he left outside—afterwards, I found it and buried it. The others he carried off in his saddlebag. I saw it all. When he appeared here, I was working outside the fence in the pasture. One time he even wanted to jump the enclosure of branches and looked from side to side, but he changed his mind and went on his way."

I listened in utter astonishment. And if I were astonished could it have been that I wouldn't have expected such behavior from Laurindo? Delmiro himself was very much upset.

"Today he took advantage of my absence, for I had gone some distance to gather firewood. . . ."

I turned away and started walking gently along the path, calming myself and thinking. I entered the house and went directly to the *alcova*, slammed the door, and threw myself face down on the bed.

On the porch from the other side of the wall, Senhora and Laurindo were talking casually. I heard Senhora reading out loud a letter she had received from Dr. Fenelon. As if nothing had happened!

Young people don't guess certain things, nor do they wish to guess others. It's the same as when one receives a warning, ten warnings: One simply doesn't heed. I confess that it was thus with me then—a sort of arrogance. I found that I could pretend that all was well even while Xavinha told me her stories; and in vain I sensed Laurindo slipping me through his fingers as though I were a captured animal.

Yet what more serious sign, for example, than the malicious rumors Xavinha said were circulating in Aroeiras?

Worse than all, my coldness toward Laurindo—and his toward me.

I had thought that marriage wasn't a game but that once married, people were partners until death. I had thought that marriage was a blood union like that of father and son—people might fight and hate, but for all that they were united; and as terrible as it might be within the framework, it was worse outside of it. Blood is thicker than water in those things. With the knot tied by the priest and judge I had thought that I had won the victory forever and that now he was mine, confirmed by writ.

So I was observing, but I didn't become alarmed—or not *very much* alarmed. How was I to know what a man was like, a man's different aspects, a man's habits. In that house, as anyone who was mad at her complained behind her back, "there was only one man in that house, and that was Senhora."

As for the barriers that Laurindo was putting between

him and me, I, innocent as I was, thought that this must be "a man's way," as Xavinha would say.

The same might be said for the drinking. There were the times when he came home so drunk that he almost fell off the horse; in my mind that was natural in a man. I would try to lay him in the hammock, pull off his boots, unbutton his clothing, and bathe his face with a wet towel; for me these were the duties of a good wife. Meanwhile, I still tried to hide all of this from Senhora, but to no avail because she always found out and cast her green eyes on me with a smile of contempt.

When I couldn't cope with him alone, Xavinha would help me; seeing my face flushed and my eyes burning, she would try to console me.

"Oh, thank God he drinks and goes to sleep. Some men beat up their women and break up everything in the house."

Early the next morning, I myself would take him his tea (having a hangover he would refuse coffee), greet him good morning as if nothing had happened, and put the steaming pitcher on the table at the foot of the hammock.

He always slept now in a hammock in the room which adjoined the *alcova*. With so much furniture inside the *alcova*, especially the big four-poster bed covered with lace pillows and with the canopy of embroidered lace net billowing onto the floor, our *alcova* had no room for a hammock.

Laurindo didn't really like a bed. He had a saying that a bed was good only "to make love, give birth, and die"; so even in the early weeks of the marriage he took to a hammock. Since the hammock didn't fit into the *alcova*, I fixed it up in the room which was next to ours. Since that room wasn't occupied, we used it.

Senhora approved of the change and "in order to complete the furnishings" brought Laurindo a lowboy which had been my father's. She told about how my father was thus and so in this respect and how he never put aside the hammock and accepted the bed only when he was near his end.

(What pained me most was that I could pick up these incidents and memories of my father only when they were flung out in random bits. I tried to piece them together, one with the other, but they never quite fit. However much I pleaded and questioned when I was small, seated on the floor at her feet, imploring her to "tell me things about my father," Senhora would refuse; and the most she would concede was: "Your father was a very good man, but he died young and left me with too heavy a burden to shoulder. I have nothing to tell you; everybody's life is more or less the same." As I grew up I learned to keep my ears cocked to pick up and conceal, like someone stealing, any little happening or remembrance about him—a word of his, the color of his eyes, his way of laughing, his shoe size . . .)

Laurindo, listening to Senhora, winked at me and said that he was a little different from my father. He liked the bed at the beginning of the night: "But afterwards what I really want is my hammock."

I blushed and Senhora showed her disapproval also. She looked at him severely as if she didn't understand.

It was three years, two months, and seventeen days that I had been married to Laurindo. Counting them one by one there were one thousand, one hundred and seventy-two days: 1,172. One thousand, one hundred and seventy-two nights also.

He installed himself at Soledade as the son of the house—naturally wasn't he the son-in-law and the husband? Neither Senhora nor I thought any differently: The man of the house had the right to everything.

He worked when work presented itself, but he didn't run after it. He would set out on his horse, which was the only thing of his he brought plus his clothing and the surveyor's equipment. It was a tall, handsome gray horse named Violeiro, which the former owner said was pure-blooded descended from a thoroughbred race horse, hence it traveled only at a trot.

Xavinha liked to say, "My Lord, Jesus Christ, Mr. Laurindo can say that is an 'English trot,' but for all my life in my home that was called a *chouto*—that is, a tiny uncomfortable trot. *Chouto-pé-duro*—just look at that!"

But I adored seeing Laurindo in the stirrups, getting in and out of the English saddle (that was another of his luxuries, he hated a cowboy's saddle), in his high boots, jodhpurs, Hollywood-style cowboy shirt, and a slender whip in his hand. He looked like a movie star to me!

Laurindo's dream was to buy a car even though the car

47

would serve only to get him from Soledade to Aroeiras and even then with many a bump. For his profession only a jeep would have sufficed, but the jeep wasn't invented until the war. In that time no car, Overland or Model T Ford, was capable of getting across the narrow trails opened up with hatchet and scythe, where even the animals risked being wounded by the stubble and were certain to be crippled if they walked among the tree stumps and large rocks.

Behind the horse, Violeiro, followed the cargo donkey, urged on by Laurindo's "secretary," whom Senhora had provided for him; the secretary's name was Luis Namorado, a label put on him in his childhood because of his custom of going about with his beribboned hat cocked on the side of his head like a cow's deformed horn fallen to one side. The burro also had been a present from Senhora because Laurindo had found it necessary to sell the one he previously had owned to pay for his wedding outfit—Laurindo laughingly confessed this. The donkey's harness was a type of quilted framework box that was secured somewhat like a saddle. In the box went the tripod, stakes, and a green painted case where he kept the big two-hundred-and-fifty-meter measuring instrument, notebooks, maps, and the rest of the surveyor's equipment.

Then for fifteen or twenty days we hardly saw the man at home except occasionally when he came to take his bath, change clothing, and polish his boots. Then he would set out again at dawn.

With his absence Soledade seemed to return to what it had been before, I mean what it was before the marriage. I occupied myself with my plants, which had grown a lot, and I cultivated a section of grafted orange trees; I kept busy pruning, watering, and fertilizing. I also took care of my rather large brood of ducks. Or I locked myself up in my room when I managed to get hold of a new novel; or as a final resort I sat in the rope hammock on the porch with a piece of embroidery.

Senhora kept at her tasks, figuring out the men's work with Antônio Amador; or she was in the cheese room putting the culture into the milk, a task she didn't entrust to anyone else. Or she was screaming at the help.

"Girl, sweep this yard right; girl, have Xavinha let down the hem of your skirt, because you're going about with your cunt exposed! Zeza, go change the water on the flowers in the saint's vase there in the parlor. Luzia, give me broth. Luzia, make me coffee."

But she didn't pick many quarrels with Maria Milagre, the old black who was an independent soul. From time to time they might tangle. In general this was because of me, Senhora complaining that Maria Milagre had spoiled me.

On Saturday afternoons Senhora spent hours and hours in the little counting room, preparing the men's weekly pay, noting in the ledger the days worked, discounting the advances and purchases of supplies, and deciphering the illegible scribbling of Antônio Amador.

Days and days went by without her remembering I was alive; but if she turned her attention to me, it would be to criticize.

"Your days as a princess are over. You're now mistress of a house!"

(Imagine my being mistress of a house, in her house!)

"Pardon me for interrupting you, but your husband's shirt is torn in the back; and Xavinha no longer has the eyes for mending with fine stitches."

Xavinha with her eyeglasses for close work or even without the glasses continued to have the eyes of a lynx. But Senhora's aim was to annoy and hurt me.

It was at that time that on Sundays she returned to the old custom of reading from the *Flos Sanctorum*, which dated from my childhood days. Since Soledade was more than a league from the main road, the vicar had excused Senhora and her household from the obligation of Sunday mass; but he decreed that lacking the mass, the people should join together, read some pious selections, and pray a part of the Rosary.

As for the pious reading, there was at Soledade only the old *Flos Sanctorum* which had belonged to my great grandmother Olivinha, and it was kept wrapped up in newspaper and tied with twine in the table drawer of the oratory next to Senhora's rosary, some branches blessed on Palm Sunday, and a package of wax candles for departed souls.

Even though it had *Flos Sanctorum* printed on the binding there was another name: "Sanctuario Doutrinal," the Doctrinal Sanctuary. It contained (no, contains, because I still own it) an account of all the saints' lives, each one identified by his own day of the year. At that time we read the saint's life for that particular Sunday, and in addition one other if perchance some important saint's day fell during the week.

Ever since I learned to read, the reading of a saint's life had become my responsibility. I would sit down, that huge book opened on the table, with the women folk, and sometimes even a man or two around me listening. After the story of the saint, told from his birth to death and highlighted with plenty of adventures, some selections were read from "Conclusions and Morality." Then I would close the book, which was once more wrapped up and tied, and we would move to the prayer rail where we prayed on our knees the entire third decade of the Rosary, with its mysteries and singsong litany to the Virgin and saints, which Xavinha would lead, with the others responding.

This *Flos Sanctorum* was the first book I ever read in my life—and with what passion! Senhora wouldn't let me have it during the week; but on Sunday nights, if she were in a good mood, she would let me take it out of the drawer—the two volumes bound in embroidered paper, leather ribbed, and engraved in gold letters: "Sanctuario Doutrinal— O.M.P." That O.M.P. fooled me for a long time, I thought it was some religious code; but after I was grown up I learned that they were the initials of my great-grandmother: Olivia Miranda Pimentel.

With Laurindo away even the meals became simpler because I only liked to pick at tidbits. Senhora, whose diet was based on milk, had clabber, pumpkin, cuscus with milk, *mugunza*, cheese with coffee, and if it were the season of fresh corn, *canjica* and *pamonha*.

When Laurindo was at the table, fish came from the oven, together with chicken stews and the game which he killed— and those quantities of offal or organ meats which I detested.

There was also the beer, sweating as it cooled on the window sill, and a carafe of wine left open from one day to the next, souring on the buffet.

Since Laurindo's coming there was a new undercurrent in our daily routine. He was the macho man in that house of women and it seemed that even the air had changed. Despite the fact that he wasn't the owner—he gave no orders and asked for everything with an "if you please" (since even he didn't dare to challenge Senhora's position)—he was the beloved man, the dear master for whom all the women ran back and forth to cater to his tastes.

Perhaps I was the only one who didn't run. Sometimes I even became annoyed with those women pampering Laurindo as if each one of them owned a piece of him.

I would sometimes pretend that I didn't hear him when he yelled from the house, and I would take my time about answering—let him see that I, at least, was nobody's slave.

Truthfully our life was never like the life of any other married couple who lived in their own house. It began with the simple fact that it wasn't our house, and it could be said that we were more like a couple of married children playing at being husband and wife.

For example, Laurindo never gave me any money. He would bring me gifts, swatches of material, a pair of shoes, a tin of English biscuits, Colombo marmalade, or Cologne water. But as far as the household expenses were concerned, he contributed nothing—but at the same time was scrupulous about thanking Senhora. He always brought us gifts together, for her and for me; the packages of colored paper tied with ribbon (this was when I first learned what gift wrapping was) were always identical.

If he had money in his pockets, he was openhanded with everybody and scattered tips everywhere. But he didn't always have much to spend because a surveyor's income is uncertain since one earns only when called to a job. Laurindo complained that those old lands of the county were already all measured, and only in the event of a new inheritance, an old question reopened, or a sale to some outside person, was the surveyor called and could present a bill. If he had been ambitious, it certainly wouldn't have been impossible for him to secure work at a distance; but he rather preferred to remain in his office and let whoever wished beat on his door—this was what he said.

If I wanted to make some big outlay, I long since knew not to ask Laurindo for any money. Sometimes I wanted to spend money on him—as on one anniversary when I gave him a wristwatch—or to spend on myself, as that time in Fortaleza when it was a question of my teeth. On these occasions I had Antônio sell some cattle from my herd—one or two, as was necessary.

In the crisis of my stillbirth, the expenses of the doctor,

operating room, hospital stay, and car trips were horrendous. Laurindo had been without work for two months; I only know that after all of this, I was at home, sallow and weepy, waiting for the return of my health. I hardly ever got out of the hammock on the porch, having no heart to read, embroider, or to do anything at all. One evening Senhora came to see me with her ledger book and gave me an accounting of the situation.

"I've sold some bulls to pay for your medical expenses. Laurindo didn't wish this and spoke about getting a loan. However, I wouldn't allow him to do this: He who has cattle in the field has money in the bank. All in all, four head of cattle were sold."

She didn't identify which cattle had been sold nor did I ask. I only said: "That's well. You did well."

But I knew my cattle and could have identified what was sold. She, even better than I, knew all of the cattle, mine and hers. She could easily have told me I sold that ox, that calf, I sold so-and-so. But I didn't ask her: I didn't wish to give her the pleasure of answering my questions. I found out the details later from Antônio Amador. She had sold three calves, yes, but the fourth was my best milk cow which had recently calved, Garapu, bred from a red Holstein.

The joke was that the buyer of the entire lot—just guess who! None other than Senhora herself. The animals destined for meat were resold to the butcher of the slaughterhouse, but Garapu, still on the premises, remained in the fazenda corral. What she couldn't do was erase my brand which was the S for Soledade, placed horizontally with an *open flower* on each point. But I could swear that she tried to do it.

I was both sad and angry about losing Garapu. I suffered. When I was in the corral and saw Senhora nearby, I would call to the little Garapu who would come to nudge her head against the gateway and brought her head close to me so I could tickle her under her withers. Senhora would leave at once, pretending not to notice.

Summer was coming to an end. Not a leaf was left in the scrub land, the corn had been pulled up, the beans harvested, and the major part of the cotton already gathered.

Cheese wasn't being made now. The bullock yearlings

wandered at will, and the heifers pregnant with their new calves were let loose. The men were rebuilding the fences in the clearing and burning over the brush.

One night Senhora had bid good night to the men on the porch about nine o'clock as usual, and we went to the supper table.

At that time I was suffering from a stabbing pain in the side which seemed like the liver, or—who knows?—appendicitis. I was always terrified of appendicitis. I ate hardly anything and asked for a tisane of lemon mint tea which was soothing and induced sleep.

Later Laurindo sought me in bed, but annoyed and drowsy I turned my back to him. He didn't insist, went to his hammock. As he did at times, he closed the connecting door, not wishing to annoy me with the candlelight while he tried to put himself to sleep with a book.

I woke up in the middle of the night. The clock in the parlor had just struck twelve; it struck again on the half hour. A little time passed and then I heard in the nearby room a slight scraping of a slipper as if Laurindo were getting up. I waited. It seemed hours that I waited, and he didn't return. I was uneasy, who knows but that he was having some kind of trouble in the bathroom? I got up and reached the door—he was just returning. I didn't see him in the darkness; I only heard his steps. Strange, I had the impression that he came from the opposite side, from the front of the house and not from the rear where the bath was. I felt a shattering chill—what was Laurindo doing anyway running about the house at night in the dark? I ran to bed so he couldn't see me.

I heard him when he entered and later when as usual he half-opened the connecting door which creaked slightly. I tried to breathe naturally and he surely thought I was asleep. I even heard when he lay down in the hammock, and when the hooks holding the hammock groaned as he stretched out with a sigh.

A few days later my illness returned, again with fever and vomiting. I went to the doctor in Aroeiras—not to Dr. Fenelon, for I had no faith in him and people said he was little more than a horse doctor—to a new doctor who operated in the hospital. He said my illness was due to the gallbladder, some carry-over from the past year's infection. He gave me some drops, and terrified, I asked him if he would have to operate. (That stay in the hospital for the lost child remained indelibly on my memory like an unforgettable horror.) The doctor laughed and said it wouldn't be necessary to operate until I became an old lady and the gallbladder filled with stones. Just now it was only a minor irritation.

From then on, I had only to eat anything heavy and the illness would return with a vengeance. One Friday, for example, dinner consisted of baked *curimata*—everybody knows that *curimata* is the most difficult fish in the world to digest, and Xavinha warned me to remember this. But I was stubborn and ate it, and by night I was deathly ill. I didn't go to the table again; and when the others ate their supper clabber, I went to look for the medicine—Atroveran—which was new then and came in a little red box. I dripped the thirty drops into the glass and had trouble putting the bottle and dropper back into the box because the badly folded directions were too bulky. I pulled out the instructions and threw them on the table.

Laurindo picked up the paper, opened it, and reproached me.

"A medication without directions is dangerous. It's stupid to throw them away. Later you'll want to verify the dosage and you won't know how much to take."

I explained that I had another set in the drawer—from the first bottle; this was the third.

As Laurindo smoothed out the paper he said: "The third bottle? In that case you're already addicted!"—and after reading—"This medicine contains papaverine and as far as I know papaverine is poppy . . . and isn't poppy opium?"

"At least the illness goes away and it makes me sleep," I protested. He laughed.

"Do you mean to say that you are an opium addict?"

I didn't find this amusing and swallowed the thirty drops of medicine with two fingers of water, stretched out and waited, but I didn't get the relief that I had hoped for, much less the quick sleep of previous times. I rolled around in the bed with that sharp pain in the side, wondering if Laurindo mightn't be right, that I was already addicted and that the remedy was losing its effect.

I finally went to sleep; as on that other night, I woke up with the clock striking, but I couldn't manage to count the strikes.

Was it two, three? Drowsy, I lay there without going to look at the clock and wait for the other stroke, but the first to come in any event would be the half-hour, a single stroke, and that would tell me nothing. I luxuriated in that lassitude free of pain. Then I heard the light tread of an animal, a donkey perhaps, in the yard between the big house and the storage rooms. The clearing with my orange trees from Bahia was close by, and the noise there made me jump out of bed to see if the animal were doing any damage.

I crossed the corridor barefoot and peeped through the guillotine windowpane in the parlor; the moonlit night was very clear and everything out there could be seen distinctly.

Yes, it was a donkey I saw. But it carried a load and by its side was Delmiro taking down the cargo—an almost full sack that had been on the top of the cargo holder.

I laughed to myself about Delmiro and his scares, and I was afraid Laurindo and Senhora might wake up. Gently I opened the parlor door's iron lock so as not to disturb the household.

Delmiro as usual put the bag on the foundation under the porch, which went along the storage house, and he placed on top of the bag a long fruit—a melon, a watermelon perhaps? In the little over-half-filled bag, as I later saw, came beans and they were for barter. The melon was a present for me.

The old man was frightened when he saw the door being opened. He turned around quickly, but a smile spread over his face when he saw that it was I. He took off his straw hat and began to mutter something, but I was afraid someone would hear his heavy nasal voice—almost a deaf-mute's voice, the voice of one who uses it seldom and loses control of the tone—and I laid a finger on my lips. I already had enough trouble with Senhora on account of my crazy old man.

He then put another little package beside the sack, and I went to see what it was. It was a handful of *jeriquiti* seeds in a little cloth bag; and filling my cupped hand with its red contents, I laughingly said, almost in Delmiro's ears: "Oh, what you won't think up next!"

And he also began laughing, very pleased, and I began to pour the lustrous seeds from one hand to another. Suddenly a muffled sound was heard, the sound of a voice,

55

from the front room, Senhora's room, next to the parlor.

I heard her voice (never in her life was she able to talk in a low voice), yes, it was her voice: "Go now!"

Then Laurindo's voice, protesting: "She took the medicine. There's no chance of her waking up."

I don't know if Delmiro heard as well as I, but I saw that he understood. I went running across the yard, barefoot and in pajamas, for fear that the two might discover me. I sat down on a pile of bricks beside the storage house and broke into tears; it was more like a deep sob—my body was trembling all over and a violent gulp overtook me—oh, those two! Those dirty two!

The old man followed me slowly. He stood there, perhaps hoping that he might temper the force of the shock; he looked at me without saying anything. The clear moon was like a streetlight.

Finally, I calmed down and said to him the same words that I had just heard from the other one: "Go now!"

Delmiro turned to get the donkey who obeyed the guiding of the halter, and it walked gently as if it also wished to respect the night's secret.

Coming close, the old man touched my shoulder lightly—I had doubled up again on my knees with my face in my hands—and he advised me in a muffled whisper: "Go in the house. Look, it's cold. Go now!"

He put pressure on the halter, took a step and turned around.

"May God give you a way out."

I lifted my face at those words and replied with my own:

"Death is the only way out."

The next day I spent the morning in bed. No one found that strange, thinking no doubt that it was the usual trouble. Bilious!

Laurindo went out early to see a man for whom he had undertaken a survey near Serra Azul.

About ten o'clock Senhora came to the door, clean and smelling sweet with a sprig of *bogari* shrub in her hair. She asked me how I was feeling, and I wouldn't answer anything. Instead, I covered my face with a corner of the sheet.

I stayed like this for two days without getting up or eating, taking tea in bed and responding to no one. Amador sent me a message that he had weighed the beans from Delmiro and asked what was to be given in exchange—I answered that he should give what he wished. He put tobacco and raw sugar in the branch of the mulungu tree; but Delmiro didn't come to get it, and the next day it was full of ants.

Laurindo didn't return until the third night and by then I was up and about the house; however, I still wasn't talking to anyone. He kissed me as if nothing had happened and for him there had been nothing to it, all was as usual; nor was it anything more for her. The world had split open only under my feet.

He said that he was exhausted and wanted a bath, food, and his hammock.

I let Senhora provide him with everything. He washed, ate and drank, and chatted that he didn't know how he was going to give an account of that survey, things didn't look good because the claims were exaggerated. The landowners would go out to open trails with revolvers in their belts, and each of their *cabras* in addition to carrying a scythe carried large knives for cutting and cleaning fish.

Xavinha saw fit to recall that Serra Azul was a violent place full of fights and deaths, and didn't one see that the deceased Antônio—but Senhora cut in.

"A survey has nothing to do with fights over the land. The fight comes first, the surveyor is called in only afterwards, when the agreement has been made."

Laurindo perked up and laughed.

"I'm only an apprentice tailor; they give me the pattern and I cut the cloth. . . ."

It seemed that everything was back to normal. There was only one thing: I still couldn't look Senhora in the face, or Laurindo. This didn't make any impression on either of them; glances between Senhora and me had always been scarce, and Laurindo left again at dawn, mounted Violeiro with Luis Namorado and the cargo donkey following. He warned that he didn't know when he would return.

He came back at the end of the week. That night I had gooseflesh when he approached me and I made an excuse that I was ill. He didn't insist, he had his pride, and went to his hammock. My heart beat wildly. I was thinking that he

57

would probably go to seek consolation elsewhere. But I covered up my head with the pillow so as not to hear anything.

Sunday dawned with a fierce sun and eight o'clock was like midday. At ten o'clock Laurindo set out with his rifle saying he was going to hunt something for lunch.

Xavinha teased: "For lunch, at this hour? It'll more likely be for supper!"

And he adjusted to the leather strap across his chest his knapsack with brown stripes on which I had embroidered in needlepoint his initials "L.L." He performed a sort of dressage, crossed the patio in his light and elegant step, and may God have mercy, at the end of the patio he took the path which led to Delmiro's house.

I thought about the old man's little animals and wanted to warn Laurindo, but I didn't have the will to begin everything all over again. As far as Laurindo was concerned, he felt he had done nothing at all when he killed Delmiro's pet duck: "Why didn't he put a bell on the duck?" Everybody laughed and the story was soon forgotten.

Oh, that Laurindo was made of glass through which nothing penetrated, neither tears, love, pleas, nor demands; nothing made any impression whatsoever. This I had understood. Smooth, hard, and transparent.

Luzia arrived in the meantime and shouted that she had seen some *nambus* birds flying over the lake road. But he didn't hear and I stayed in the hammock doing nothing.

At lunch time no Laurindo. Senhora ordered all to wait until twelve-thirty which for us was very late. Finally lunch was served without him and they kept the hen and macaroni for him on the buffet.

In that Sunday calm no one appeared who could be sent to search for him. All the men were in the street full of rum, said Senhora, who was already uneasy as she paced up and down the hall to the porch. I went to the parlor and sat down again with a magazine.

About one o'clock I was the first to catch sight of Delmiro, who rushed up, breathing heavily. But the old man didn't come to me, nor did he look at me. He took off his hat to Senhora who burst into the parlor.

"Dona, there has been an accident."

I jumped off the sofa and ran towards him. Senhora, her face drained of color, inquired: "Accident? How come an accident?"

Delmiro continued without looking at me: "It seems that the young man's rifle went off by itself. I don't know. He fell near the fence."

Senhora looked at the old man for a few seconds as if she didn't comprehend; she wiped her face with her hand and began to walk.

"Let's go see."

I followed after her, crossing the patio. I don't know how I ran so fast with my trembling legs, but I overtook Senhora.

We entered the narrow path and Delmiro stopped from time to time to rest.

Halfway there Senhora turned to him.

"Is he alive?"

And Delmiro—I had turned around at Senhora's question—shook his head without speaking.

In grim reality lay Laurindo, fallen at the foot of the fence, face down in the dirt. I had stopped some ten paces away; Senhora shot past me, reached him, knelt down, and turned him over.

Yes, he was dead, dead. No doubt about it. His eyes open, in his mouth a bit of pink foam.

Senhora felt his chest to see if his heart was still beating, but she quickly withdrew her hand, which was all covered with blood. On the left side of the shirt, well above the heart, was that round hole about the size of a coin with a black powder burn around it. It was from there the blood flowed.

I also fell on my knees on the other side of Laurindo but without daring to touch him. Senhora stretched out her hand and with a light gesture, almost a caress, closed his wide-open eyes. Then she turned to Delmiro and asked in a strange, weak, and forced voice:"Did you see how it happened?"

Delmiro came closer, looking neither at her nor me but at the corpse.

"No, Senhora"—his breathing had returned to normal—"I was there in the house and I only heard the shot. I ran out thinking that sir had again shot one of my little animals. But I saw no one and was about to leave when I saw the foot of the boot sticking out behind the fence. I jumped the fence and found him. But he was already like that—dead.''

Senhora, still kneeling, continued to ask: "And what about that bruise from some blow on his forehead? The shot was in the chest.''

I had seen the bruise also—it was a red contusion on the forehead about the size of a fist with the skin torn a little. Delmiro came nearer and bent over in order to look.

"As far as I can figure out he was going to jump the fence as he did at times. The fence is high, he must have misjudged—who knows—and fell on the rifle and the shot went off. The bruise—he must have hit his head on that rock over there when he fell down on his face.''

I turned my eyes slowly to the rock. Yes, it was there, that must have been what happened. Delmiro picked up the rifle which we had hardly noticed and said angrily: "A gun with no safety pin, it's dangerous.''

Senhora now seemed as if she lived only to ask, discover, understand. She bit her lips; she dug into her memory and recalled: "Yes, once before, that rifle slipped from his hands and went off by itself. Don't you remember?''

I suddenly began to shriek: "Let's get him out of here! Let's call some people! Let's get him out of here!''

Then I touched the dead Laurindo for the first time; I put my hands under his shoulders, lifting up the damp body with the head on his chest and the body began to slide. It seemed a thousand times heavier than when he was alive.

Senhora continued to speak in that forced, calm voice, dragging out the words, one after another. That was worse than if she had screamed out.

"No, a little bit farther. No, we can't do it. Neither can the old man with his maimed shoulder.''

Delmiro offered: "I can go get my little burro.''

He didn't wait for an answer but quickly jumped the fence and plowed through the field of dry corn.

The two of us remained on our knees, one on each side of the body. Neither she nor I was crying, but we were breathing heavily as if we both needed air, as though we had been playing and had stopped for a moment's rest. I took my hands off Laurindo and supported myself on the ground while my eyes were on Senhora's face. Senhora didn't take her eyes off him, but neither did she touch him—she held her own neck with both hands as though she were suppressing a scream.

Just then, a great commotion, running about and a loud cry were heard.

"Jesus! Have mercy!"

It was the women from the fazenda; from the porch a servant boy had witnessed Delmiro's arrival and went to give the alarm in the kitchen. They panicked and ran after us screaming.

"Holy mother, it's Mr. Laurindo on the ground. Jesus help us!"

I looked at them, stupefied. Senhora still on her knees turned around, infuriated.

"Shut your mouths! I don't want all that yelling."

It was as if the women had been quieted with a whip. In the silence Senhora breathed deeply and asked: "What about Amador?"

Luzia, sniffling and full of tears, answered: "A boy went to his house to call him."

Delmiro approached with the donkey from the other side of the fence; quickly he was pulling out the posts until he could make an opening through which the animal could pass. The donkey came bareback, with only a halter.

The four of us lifted Laurindo and tried to mount him on the donkey, but we couldn't do it. The big heavy body slid from one side to the other. It was horrible, and I felt I was going to scream.

Until then Delmiro did nothing more than hold the burro's halter. The animal was frightened and recoiled with fear from the ill-omened cargo. Seeing that the others hadn't achieved anything, the old man dropped the rope, eased the back of Laurindo on his bad shoulder and with his right hand pushed Laurindo's right leg that we had put on the other side and placed the body face down across the animal's back, the head hanging on one side and the feet on the other.

Senhora pushed Delmiro aside.

"Oh, no! Not that!" and she tried to lift the body, which slid from her hands and the feet touched the ground on the other side.

Delmiro replaced the body face down, saying with authority, "It's the only way to carry a body on an animal, dona. There's no other way."

More people arrived. Two men came running with a metal stretcher. One of them was Amador, who explained while panting: "I had to work hard to get this. The equipment room was locked."

They pulled Laurindo from that horrible position on top of the burro and laid him on the stretcher—a very short one—the head and the legs were both dangling. Amador picked up a slab of wood from the fence, and put it on the shafts of the stretcher under Laurindo's neck; thus the head was held up. They did the same thing with the legs, putting another slab under the knees.

They left slowly and softly. Senhora walked at their side. I returned to my kneeling position on the ground. I watched all without interfering. The cortege gone, I dropped my head to the ground at the foot of the fence and my face was scratched by the dry shrubs. A hoarse sob shook my body, but no cry whatever left my mouth. I felt as if I'd suffocate.

The girls lifted me up by force. On one side Xavinha tried to comfort me.

"My darling, be patient!"

And the others echoed: "Be patient!"

I went with them. In front of us the slow-moving cortege now climbed the path; we could still see the figures in the leafless *mato* brush. I quickened my steps until I overtook them. When the path opened up into the patio and the line of people broke up, I jerked myself away from the women's hands, passed by the stretcher, and ran to the fazenda, where I waited in the doorway for them to arrive.

They put Laurindo on top of the dining room table. Senhora took off one boot, Amador the other. Xavinha got the bedspread off my bed and covered the body with it.

Amador said to Senhora in a low voice but I heard: "Before leaving I sent for Dr. Fenelon. It's possible that he may still be alive."

We were all huddled there numbed. From the corridor came the sharp cry of a girl whom I commanded with an irritated gesture to shut up.

I let them seat me in a chair; but I pushed away the hands which tried to comfort me, to give me a cup of water, to lead me to the bedroom. Senhora also sat down wearily in a chair that they brought for her. She drank a cup of water with sugar that Xavinha had brought to help her overcome the shock. She stared at the people gathered around—not at me. If someone raised her voice in the easy crying of the women, she fixed on the creature her look of outrage—and silence returned.

Much time passed—I don't know how much. Night had already fallen when Dr. Fenelon's automobile appeared on the pavement; and he entered by way of the parlor without speaking to anyone: he lifted the bedspread, looked at Laurindo's face, opened up the clothing, felt the chest, pulled his glasses out of his pocket, and when he had them on, he examined closely the wound and brown powder on the cloth of the shirt.

Finally, he stood up, rearranged his glasses, looked around, and said to us: "I can do nothing more. Call the police."

Most of the things which happened during those hours of horror I remember as if they were occurring now, but other important things I can't remember for the life of me.

But I do remember Dr. Fenelon pronouncing that word police. Senhora got up.

"Police? Why the police? It was an accident."

Then he explained that even in case of accidental death one must still call the police.

"And the sooner, the better, because they have to bring their own doctors since only they can verify the death."

He came over to me and put his hand on my shoulder.

"Daughter, go lie down. I'll give you a sedative."

I didn't want to lie down or take a sedative; I wanted to stay there and see everything. I shook my head, my teeth clamped.

Dr. Fenelon insisted. "Come. You have suffered a great shock. Let your mother and me take care of everything."

I didn't go. I stayed there in my corner, head lowered, silent, without crying. If someone drew near to console me, I pushed the creature away with an impatient hand.

We waited more hours, hours and hours. The police finally arrived, and it was well into the night. The lieutenant in uniform entered and offered his condolences. He extended his hand to me.

"My sympathy."

This was the first time I heard that word, and I didn't understand it immediately. The lieutenant went to look under the bedspread on the table; the other doctor introduced himself to Dr. Fenelon and asked that everyone leave the room so that the coroner could examine the cadaver. Cadaver! This was Laurindo.

I got up. Senhora wished to remain; but I saw Dr. Fenelon whispering to her, and taking her elbow he went with her towards her room.

Senhora cried out in a clear voice as if she wanted everybody to hear: "I'm going to the oratory to pray."

I entered the *alcova*, closed the door and threw myself face down on the bed, mortally fatigued. But I didn't sleep, I didn't cry. It was as if I were suspended in air, with no support, just sinking, sinking.

The police car left. They carried Delmiro away with them to the station and tried to get a confession from him. But the old man had the same story to tell.

"It was just as I told Dona," and he repeated all without changing a word.

This I found out later from Antônio Amador, whom they also took to the station. They wanted to press the old man further. It was Amador who helped to free him, explaining that the poor old man was half-crazy but good natured and didn't bother anyone, not even a lizard. On the contrary, his house was a haven for wild animals. Moreover, he was maimed in the shoulder.

At first, the coroner was concerned about that bruise on the forehead which had been made *when Laurindo was still alive:* No one fools a doctor on this point. This being so, when did the shot occur? Could someone have given him the bruise and then fired the shot which burned the clothing? . . .

As for the officers it was beyond all doubt an accident, and they convinced the coroner. Couldn't the old man's version be possible—that the man had fallen on the rock and hit his forehead, with a bullet in him but still alive?

Finally the coroner had no counter-argument. If the officers found it so, why not agree?

"Yes, the bruise of the forehead could have been made when the victim fell, still alive, and hit that rock with his forehead."

As for the rifle—had it not already fired accidentally in a previous incident?

This was told me by that coroner in person the following

day when I left the burial. He wanted to explain why he had delayed in signing the death certificate.

In such cases prudence is necessary for the sake of the bereaved family, in order to allay any suspicions whatever.

Later someone told me—who, I don't remember, perhaps Dr. Fenelon—that the police dispensed with the autopsy in view of the fact that it was so evident that the shot was accidental.

For my part I believe it was their fear of irritating Senhora any more which influenced the decision. Senhora's aversion to any authority made it risky for those from Aroeiras; she hated their presence in her house. Police entered Soledade only with their hats in their hands, asking for favors.

Finally, who would want to kill Laurindo, a likable chap, with proper upbringing, from a good family, and with no enemy in the world?

But at night in the dark as I lay in bed there kept coming back to me the first idea of the coroner: Laurindo put his head on top of the fence and someone hidden behind the thick foliage knocked him down with a slab of wood; knocked him down with a blow on the forehead, a blow delivered with a powerful left hand . . .

In the *Flos Sanctorum* which the people read on Sundays, on the 29th of December fell the life of Saint Thomas of Canterbury, archbishop and martyr who was born in England. Oh, I read that life many times. The saint's day fell near the New Year, a fact which Senhora appreciated.

He was born in cold Britain, as his country was called then, of whose king he was the boon companion in youthful excesses, although he was but the son of a merchant. His political astuteness led the king to name Thomas Archbishop of Canterbury (The Primate of England), thus obliging him to take holy orders. The prince hoped in this way, through the intermediation of his friend, to govern the Church of England according to his own will. Thomas, however, sincere in his conversion and by virtue and grace of the order of priesthood, took his pastoral mission seriously. He set himself against the designs of the king, heroically resisting the royal power. All of the king's old friendship for Thomas turned to hatred, and he persecuted the Archbishop who twice had to seek exile in France.

One night the king, extremely irritated, took notice of what was called "a new provocation of the Archbishop" and uttered these bitter words: "A sad king am I who does not have a faithful vassal capable of freeing me from a vile traitor!"

Two cavaliers of the royal house heard the king's complaint and deduced that the sovereign was talking to them indirectly, ordering them to kill the prelate. So with an armed escort they invaded the Archbishop's palace. Being a saintly man, Thomas took refuge at the foot of the altar in his own Cathedral. The assassins hunted him down there, fell on him with their swords, and took his life.

The king regretted those imprudent words he had spoken in anger; and he ordered the criminal nobles to be seized and handed over to the executioner. He himself made a pilgrimage of penitence, going by foot, in a sackcloth shift through the snow, with his head bare and a rope around his neck, walking from his castle to the church where the saint was buried. At the side of the tomb he ordered that they should lash his bare back until blood flowed, and for three days he kneeled there and prayed, asking forgiveness for his great sin.

May God be my witness, on that night when I cried "death" to Delmiro, I wasn't asking for anyone's death. If I spoke the word, it was out of pain and not rage.

I never anticipated the end.

I decided to stay at the fazenda until after the funeral mass. A car came to get me; I wore black but I refused the mourning veil (hers, for my father's funeral) which Senhora tried to make me wear.

At home, I had open house for the visitors who came from everywhere to express their sympathy; some came from miles away out of curiosity because of the tragedy. Since I didn't cry they advised me to do so. They said that tears held back poisoned the blood—as if I didn't know this.

Xavinha commented that never in her life had she seen the likes of such people—all that tragedy and never an outcry, no one going to pieces with hysterics; and when they began to comment on the celebrated hysterical fits I could stand it no longer and locked myself in my room. Otherwise I would have broken down.

Yes, I was going to stay at the fazenda until after prayers at the cemetery because I had sworn to do so; but I couldn't. On the night of the sixth day when all the visitors had left, I went to Senhora, who was dressed in mourning as I was, and informed her I was leaving.

For the first time Senhora looked me in the face.

"When?"

I wanted to go the next day. But I was exhausted, there were the arrangements to be made—well, three days from then.

Senhora saw that it wouldn't help matters to object and in a forced naturalness she begged me: "Don't go alone. At least take Xavinha. Or people will wonder and talk."

I shrugged my shoulders. At that stage what did people's tongues matter to me? And as if I would have that idiot Xavinha go with me!

But I answered nothing and Senhora didn't press the matter.

I took off the mourning weeds for the trip. If I could have torn off my skin, pulled out my hair, I would have gone in my raw skin.

Senhora protested when she saw me in my light blue suit: "So, you insist on causing a scandal?"

By dint of force I clamped my mouth shut, but I didn't change my clothes. I went all over Aroeiras, bought my ticket, waited and caught the train. In my blue suit.

End of Senhora's Book

II
THE COMPANY'S BOOK

I WAS GOING ON TWENTY WHEN FOR THE FIRST
time I stayed all by myself in D. Loura's pension. The pretext for the trip was the dentist, but actually I was there for
something much more exciting.

From the time I became a teenager I had been preparing
myself, building up courage for that adventure. Senhora
held me a melancholy prisoner in the house: Month after
month I went out of the house only to make purchases, and
very occasionally, very occasionally, a sleepover in Aroeiras
in the house of Genu and Peti Miranda, two old-maid sisters who did machine embroidery, distant relatives who
called Senhora "aunt" and received the blessing from her.
Even then Xavinha accompanied me. The occasions were
Our Lady's Coronation at the end of May, our patron
saint's festival in August, and Christmas Eve mass. Only
then could I risk going to a movie—and only if Xavinha also
wished to go.

I never went to a dance. The club sent us invitations, but
just see if Senhora would let her daughter set foot at its
dances; after all, everybody went and any old salesclerk
could ask for a dance! It was all right to dance at a wedding
or silver anniversary in the home of one's relatives; and I
used to go and have fun, but those family festivities didn't
satisfy me. My heart yearned to know the world. Theater! I
mean *real theater*—not those little occasional *colégio* dramas,
not those love stories like Ancilla Domini's plays which the
priest had given in the parish house. I wanted comedy, bal-
let, and operetta with artists from Rio de Janeiro in the José
Alencar theater of Fortaleza.

In Soledade the only newspaper we subscribed to was the
Bishop's daily, *O Nordeste (The Northeast)*, but even in that
there were theater announcements. I would clip them like a
silly girl who cut out and saved love sonnets.

Then, as it happened, the season of the Vicente Celestino
Viennese Opera Company was announced in September—
with Laís Areda, my old acquaintance of many years of clip-

71

pings. The publicity in the priests' newspaper was scanty, and its commentaries censured the morality of the plays so severely that I then ordered other dailies to be taken off the train. Thus I secured clippings half a page long, explaining in detail the names of the artists, including even the characters on stage who had no speaking parts, the repertory in the order of the presentations, the price of the tickets, and the places they could be bought in advance.

Then I thought: It is now or never. I decided to use the plan I had been perfecting for years. First, I sent a letter to D. Loura asking her to reserve two seats for the Vicente Celestino season, for her and me. (One difficulty in my planning was, who would be my escort? I ran over one and another of my acquaintances, no one of whom was in on the secret. All at once it came to me: D. Loura herself, whom I had thought of previously only as providing hospitality; she ended up being the ideal companion and accomplice— she was crazy about music, was always complaining about not having anyone to go out with or money for amusement, and finally she had given some evidence of caring a great deal about me.)

And so, quickly, without allowing any time to change my mind, I sent the letter. I added a P.S. explaining that I would pay when I arrived; the ad stated it was sufficient to "reserve" seats in advance, that payment could be made up to the night before the opening. I let Xavinha in on the secret, not because I wanted to, but because I needed her help; and I asked D. Loura to send the reply addressed to her.

Then I progressed to the second part of the plan. With a large needle I pulled out the already loose filling in my last molar, and showed Senhora the need for going to the dentist; also that I had other cavities beside that one and felt twinges of pain from time to time.

Senhora fell for it and had Antônio Amador sell a one-year-old steer (mine to be sure) for the expenses, and I asked:

"Could you sell another yearling (also mine) because people complain that he is a thief—you know how expensive dentists are. . . ."

Senhora agreed and on market night, Saturday, Amador handed me the money. On the next day came the reply: D. Loura was enchanted to join the conspiracy. Xavinha, poor

72

dear, spent three days sewing, even until late at night, making me underwear and blouses. On Wednesday (the opening would be on Saturday) I took the train for the city.

As soon as I arrived there we attacked the problem of my clothes of which I had long been ashamed. D. Loura was an angel. In the three days before the opening she and I made two dresses for me, and then even a third, so I would have no repeats. Nothing was said about a dressmaker which would have cost more than I could afford. (She had no problem about what to wear—she had her little black silk with the velvet toque, kept for just such occasions. A widow has the advantage of not needing many changes.)

D. Loura and I worked until late at night like Xavinha, and even her daughter, Osvaldina, helped with the hems and basting. The styles then were simple; there was no waistline, a belt was fastened to the hips, the skirt in a straight line, sleeves from armholes, knees out, and presto—finished! We bought pink, lemon yellow, and light green crepe de chine and georgette; I was sweet twenty and, oh my! did I feel beautiful, on top of the world!

Everything came off as I had dreamed and even better, as much for me as for D. Loura, who was a debutante like myself. In her difficult life the poor thing had no time for pleasure. Work first, play later! The most she might go out was to attend a Sunday matinée movie so she could take the daughter; or she might be invited out some rare night (this probably happened only twice in her life) by some boarders, once as a social obligation while they were alive or later at a funeral for one of them. She had to make many a bed, serve a lot of soup, and wash many dishes to pay for Osvaldina's studies at the Colégio das Dorotéias. Tuition at the normal school was free, but D. Loura was prejudiced against normal school girls—to be eligible a girl had to attend a nuns' colégio.

"It is bad enough for the poor little thing to be the daughter of the operator of a boardinghouse."

We attended all but one of the plays in the repertory. We were delirious. *Princess of the Dollars, The Count of Luxembourg, The Merry Widow, The Blue Mazurka, The Duchess of Bal-Tabarin.* The one we missed was *Chaste Susana* because it was supposed to be risqué, and D. Loura thought it wouldn't look right for us to attend. We gave the tickets to two student lodgers, "two very serious lads who paid well and were from good families in Granja," for whom D. Loura enjoyed doing pleasant things.

Now, so many years after our fabulous theater adventure, I arrived again in Fortaleza. I telegraphed asking for a room; and D. Loura, who had read the news of Laurindo's death in the newspaper, came very solemnly to meet me at the station with her daughter and son-in-law, because Osvaldina was now married. She had improved little since her childhood: She was still a skinny, washed-out blonde, and sickly. She never studied hard enough to get ahead, and the nuns were grateful that she finished with her class at the end of the year. When she was seventeen, she fell in love with a boy off the street, a telegraph operator, low class, and sickly like herself; at nineteen she received the diploma and got married.

D. Loura at the time wrote us the news of the marriage and begged forgiveness for not sending an invitation; the ceremony was simple due to the groom's position.

Osvaldina continued to live in the pension since D. Loura didn't wish to be separated from her daughter. The mother never lost her fear that the daughter might become tubercular, she was so tiny and frail. The telegraph operator was happy to agree: With his salary he couldn't possibly provide a home for Osvaldina.

Now she was twenty-two and he not quite thirty, but they were already like an old couple set in their daily routines. Sunday they went to worship because the telegraph operator was a believer and had converted Osvaldina to Protestantism. Movies on Wednesdays, at the Majestic's colossal showing—two main features, a cowboy film, and five shorts. Ordinarily Osvaldina didn't do much of anything, just going from bedroom to parlor and back, dragging her house slippers, while he dispatched telegrams.

D. Loura must have had other dreams for her daughter; but now, if she was unhappy, she didn't say so. She didn't even lament the lack of a grandchild: The boardinghouse served as her family. The permanent guests gave her a guaranteed income and the transients provided activity and distraction.

After that theatrical season exploit of ours, D. Loura had taken a liking to theater. Osvaldina and I teased her that she was in love with Vicente Celestino: She almost fainted when she saw him in tails. Actually she managed to scrape together enough money to attend a show whenever there was a new company at the José de Alencar. At times she wrote me about what she had seen, and I would sigh with envy; but I had to console myself with just the sighs.

But for all that, D. Loura never thought she would accept comedians as guests in her house until one day she felt obliged to grant a colleague's request. That colleague was the widow of a judge, D. Silvina, the mother of two daughters who were music teachers, and who set up her boardinghouse in the big house with the garden and usable basement on the Coração de Jesus square. There she had lived with the judge, and it was her only inheritance from him.

D. Silvina telephoned.

"Lourinha, my dear, please help me out. I have a houseful, with people even in the hall. I wish you would take a very distinguished couple that I cannot accommodate. They are actors, but don't be afraid, they are very well brought up—and married! No one would guess they are theater people; you can give them hospitality without fear of gossip."

Then a little later a fat gaucho beat on the door, the soul of charm, dragging behind him his wife, a tall redhead, pretty but already past her prime. He called himself Brandini, he was the impresario—a director of the Brandini Filho Company of Comedies and Musical Farces; his wife was D. Estrela.

He was the one who entered first and turned the charm on; he won over everybody, and he captured D. Loura's heart. She no longer remembered her reservations about comedians. Later, it even got so she would be offended if there were a company in the city and some actors (the directors, and they had to be *married* of course) didn't take room and board in her well-known pension.

In the beginning the Protestant son-in-law didn't much like these new social patterns, but he was timid; and since he didn't pay for room or board, he kept his mouth shut.

75

The most he could do was to prevent Osvaldina from going to the theater with her mother when the guests gave her free tickets—which turned out to be always.

D. Loura reserved a good room for me in the front with a window on the street, a canopy bed and a wardrobe with a mirror on the door; and I had the place of honor at the table beside the lady of the house.

She unpacked my trunk while I sat on the bed. "Let me do it, dear, you are so depressed!" I had to tell her in detail about Laurindo's death. The telegram announcing my arrival took D. Loura by surprise, and she was astonished when I told her I had come to stay.

"I couldn't stand it any more. I couldn't stand it, D. Loura. If I had stayed there any longer, I would have died too."

She made no comment; she draped the dress she had in her hand on the clothes hanger, came close to me, put my head on her neck, and kissed me on the hair.

"I know, my dear. I have always sensed the darts flying between you and your mother."

Upon leaving I had ordered Antônio Amador to sell the rest of my cattle and my part of the sheep and goats. As on that occasion of my illness, Senhora herself bought all or nearly all. I still had left a planting of cotton, from the time when Laurindo became engrossed in plowing up a field, but not much work had gone into it and the crop was scant.

I deposited the money from the settlement in the bank, and all in all it was not very much and it would not last me very long to pay room and board, to dress myself, and to cover the other necessary expenses.

Then in the second month D. Loura, who looked ahead, made me an offer as mother to daughter: I could sleep with her in the big room, using the bed and wardrobe that Osvaldina had used before she married. I could help with all the pension's bookkeeping, keeping the guests' accounts, paying the taxes, light, storage and street expenses, noting down all extras, chiefly the drinks, her greatest headache; and also post the bills of the transient guests, which had to be presented daily to the police. Thus I would pay for my board and lodging, "and much more besides, and still you are doing me a favor."

And D. Loura put on the finishing touch.

"One of these days I'll be sending Osvaldina to spend some holidays at Soledade, to take milk and fatten herself up, and Cousin Senhora will be the one footing the bill."

Little did she realize that my departure from that house hadn't been due to one of those passing griefs. For I had cut the umbilical cord which held me tied to Soledade for ever and ever. I now wanted only distance from and few remembrances of Soledade and its mistress.

D. Loura found it strange that I didn't wear mourning.

"At the station I didn't say anything, but I was truly surprised. . . ."

I explained to her that I had a horror of mourning, that they told me my father was like this and that he didn't even put on mourning for his mother, even in those days! Isn't it enough to bear the pain that gnaws inside us—why must people suffocate in black? I could promise not to wear bright colors, I would stick to blue and white, but black—no, she shouldn't ask that of me! No!

D. Loura, who so many years after the death of her husband still didn't dare to wear more than a black and white print, then tried to make excuses for me.

"Yes, mourning is a part of religion, and you were never religious. Besides you don't have a child—it's a child who finds these things unacceptable."

I was very conscientious about paying for my keep in services. I helped with everything as if I were the daughter of the house, or even the "manager"—not to speak of taking charge of the chambermaid Socorro, a *cabocla* not yet broken in and with a wild eye. The students from Granja joked with Socorro and would cry out for her: "Help, Help!"; and when the girl ran to find out the reason for the call, they explained that it was nothing, that they only wanted a towel.

"Don't you know that *socorro* is *help* in English? You never heard it in the movies?"

Socorro got mad, and said her name was Maria de Perpetua Socorro, and they were just stupid boys.

I had already been living with D. Loura for months—I only heard news from Soledade when Xavinha sent some little note to which I didn't respond—when the Brandini Filho Company arrived in the city for its annual season.

Three members of the company came to our house: the Brandini couple, already old patrons, and in addition the ingenue of the troupe, a small pretty girl with the temperament of a wild beast, Cristina Le Blanc. She was very proud of her name, her own and not a stage name, inherited from her French father.

Seu Brandini's wife was D. Estrela. No one would say that she was the same Estrela Vésper, the leading lady of the company. She was thin, calm, not fussy about food, and gave no one any trouble. When Seu Brandini talked, his gaucho accent full of *rrr*'s trembled in the air. In two minutes he was a childhood friend, and with one hour's friendship he was already your brother. When he had money he paid, when he didn't he cheated, but Estrela said that he was quite capable of robbing from one to help another in a tight squeeze. He lived with his accounts all mixed up with those of the company's personnel. He had a devastating charm with the ladies, and even Cristina kidded with him; not that he took the advantages he could have: some caresses or kisses on the neck were enough for him.

He brought presents for D. Loura and gave her free tickets even for the actors' benefits, which was strictly forbidden.

It was apparent that D. Loura adored him; she told me herself that during the past year's season he had paid his accounts with a check: When she went to cash it there were no funds. D. Loura sent a telegram to Pará where the company was and received the answer that the check was dated before there was money to cover it; that she should keep it and that at the end of the month he would send her the amount due. He did in fact send it, not all, but nearly all. And as proof of the honest person he was he never reclaimed that first check; even more amazing, when D. Loura ordered me to return it at the first opportunity, Seu Brandini laughed.

"Keep the check, girl. If perchance the bank might have something to cover it, the cash is yours."

Seu Brandini was like that.

He also had problems with authors of the plays presented because of "arrangements by Brandini Filho" routinely printed on the programs. One day a policeman appeared to halt a production because the furious author got a lawyer alleging that there was no arrangement whatsoever: The play was all his and he was being robbed.

Seu Brandini produced the original manuscripts, convinced the investigator that only the ideas of the two coincided, even the names of the characters were different.

"In his play the girl is named Pureza, in mine she is called Dalila. There, the gentleman can see for himself!"

He took the man to the dressing room where the actresses in underwear were making themselves up. He even left him alone for a brief time with Estrela—"our great Estrela Vésper"—who, in a loosely closed gown, was arranging in front of a mirror a wig of curls over her short hair. Estrela smiled and entertained the policeman bravely until Seu Brandini appeared with a copy of the complete text of his play, "practically" approved by the censor.

When the performance began, the policeman was watching from the wings, which was more fun than stopping the performance; and afterwards he had supper with the actors in a seafood restaurant on Iracema beach. At this juncture clearly he was also a brother.

Later, whenever the company was due to arrive, Seu Brandini would send him a telegram; and when the boat anchored, Inspector Jones was the first one on the Metálica Bridge to help out with any debarkation problems.

Only three days had passed before I became in effect Seu Brandini's "assistant." I began by copying the roles of a new play that he was "adapting," and truthfully it was a Portuguese translation of a Spanish comedy, but Portuguese from Portugal, not Brazilian Portuguese.

Seu Brandini had "translated" the speeches, putting them all into the *carioca* jargon of Rio, changing a scene here and there but chiefly cutting out characters because his troupe was small.

He didn't use dirty words outright, but there were many bald risqué insinuations and sometimes I blushed at them. My work was long and tedious and demanded good handwriting and patience; for I had to copy each role in a different notebook and in each copy only the speech of that character with the last words of the previous speaker, the cues between the speeches. Today this is done on a typewriter, but in the Brandini Filho Company this was all scratched out by hand.

I found the work a pleasure—I have yet to meet a woman who is not interested in the inside secrets of the theater. One could say I practically came from a private prison in the middle of the woods and was anxious to know the world.

Later I began to assist in the rehearsals—Seu Brandini was also the director of rehearsals (he said *régisseur* or stage manager).

The billboard had to be changed every day—only the best plays were repeated. There didn't exist then the idea of a whole season consisting of only one play as today. The rehearsals were disorganized, with no discipline; if a character knew his role well, he didn't bother to come.

Cristina Le Blanc was the worst offender in this respect and didn't even go to the bother of making up excuses. Many times I spoke her speeches, reading from the notebook while Seu Brandini rehearsed with the other less finished actors. Especially the extras who were hired on the spot, like the civil guard who played the part of a civil guard, the students from the boardinghouse who figured as background characters in a cabaret scene, drinking champagne (it was *guaraná*, a stimulating and refreshing Brazilian drink) in old French champagne glasses; Seu Brandini wanted to use just plain water, but the young men insisted on *guaraná* at least!).

Even Socorro played a small part as a little maid, and Seu Brandini created a comic scene just for her: The little thing appeared in the play with even the name of Socorro, but he only called her SOS. He got angry because the audience didn't understand and failed to laugh.

Socorro appeared in black uniform with a dust mop in her hand, and her role was to usher the bill collectors in and out in a farce called *The Swindler King* (which Cristina said was a true portrait of Seu Brandini himself). Socorro adored the stage and hung around Seu Brandini, saying she wanted to play a part in satin tights; he asked her to show her legs—alas, they were not made for tights. Seu Brandini then shook his head and told her it was better for her to continue

in the apron, that it was a rare play that didn't have a part
for a waitress in an apron.

Clearly when the Brandini Filho Company stopped in our
city it was like a breath of fresh air which blew over the
boardinghouse giving new life to everybody.
Only the telegraph operator remained on the outside
with poor Osvaldina. As for her, she would have been
happy if she could have gone with us to the theater or when
we returned stayed up all hours in the parlor helping to im-
provise a supper when Seu Brandini was low on cash and
couldn't afford the restaurant: scrambled eggs, sardine om-
elet, leftovers from the luncheon soup, beer, and coffee.
Only the beer was put on the bill; the rest was on the house.
D. Loura was trying to repay Seu Brandini's kindnesses.
The telegraph operator told me once that thank God the
man was married (which by the way, he wasn't, at least to
Estrela, as I found out later), or his mother-in-law was capable of going off with the company as a comedienne.

From Fortaleza their itinerary took them from Pará to
Belém (Bethlehem), "to join the Candle Procession"—to
take advantage of the festival season, the season of Our
Lady of Nazareth. They already had a yearly contract with a
little theater right in the hamlet of Nazareth, in the basilica's
square. At least this is what Brandini said; and if they were
lucky, they could make up the worst of the year's financial
losses.

I was convinced that the troupe presented the succession
of low comedy shows, and gave performances from city to
city for the love of it: It certainly couldn't have been for the
money—Seu Brandini was always losing money. His pride
was that he never abandoned his actors during a tour because of the company's failure. In failure, he yet always
managed to get his people back to Rio, his base.

Then the day came when all was ready for the trip to
Pará. Each actor had made his benefit night—I don't know if
that is done today, I suppose not. At the end of the season
one night was reserved for each of the most important actors who, particularly interested in the box-office, did a special number at the end of the performance or between the

acts in order to get more money from the audience. The box-office receipts were his, less expenses, of course.

Well, every one except Estrela had had his benefit night; for her Seu Brandini had reserved the best play as a closing for the season. Between the acts Estrela came out in person to sell postcards with her picture, in the costume of the Queen of Hearts worn in the farce of that same name, a story of Carnival. Cristina jeered and said that the business of selling pictures on the theater's main floor was a circus custom; only in a vagabond milieu did one see this sort of thing. But on her benefit night she also sold cards with her picture—a picture with her shoulders exposed without any sign of a dress called for a discussion with Seu Brandini who complained that this was not an ingenue's picture but one of a leading lady. Cristina was furious and said if there were any justice in that company, she would be billed as the star. She was already fed up with the roles of young girls and their mawkish scenes. She knew how to sing and dance and had good legs; moreover she did sing and dance, and received no additional salary for anything she did over and above straight acting.

Estrela didn't like Cristina's tirade but she kept quiet. That night, when they were rehearsing their benefit play, a telegram from Rio arrived addressed to Cristina.

Seu Brandini wanted to open the envelope in order to find out the cat's little secrets; but Estrela, who was above meddling in anyone's secrets, wouldn't let him.

Cristina arrived late as usual, and was given the telegram. She let out a cry and put her hand on her heart: My God. It was a telegram from the secretary of the renowned Procópio, and he was inviting her to play a role in Jaracy Camargo's play slated to open at the Trianon, at that time the top theater. By then Seu Brandini had left; and when Cristina came petulantly to demand her salary because she had to buy passage to Rio, Estrela lost her cool and started a row.

Estrela began in her quiet voice, calling the other irresponsible, but Cristina in turn called her an ugly name; then Estrela slapped her, and the two grabbed each other.

I believe Estrela had wanted to slap her for months. Seu Brandini returned in the middle of the fight and tried to separate the two, saying to Estrela: "Little love, little love, what is this all about?"

And he held Cristina with the other arm: "You yellow cat, don't you meddle with my wife!"

When the two were separated, he asked me what had happened; and I told him about the invitation in the telegram. Seu Brandini, furious, said out loud to Estrela: "That's what comes from your scruples! If I had read the dirty telegram and torn it up, we would have been spared all this confusion."

Cristina, hearing this, began to bellow that the man was a low-down rascal without any morals, that to tamper with the mail was a crime calling for police action, and speaking of police: "Either you pay me my money, or I shall put the police on you!"

Seu Brandini didn't lose his composure and exclaimed: "Shut that big mouth, little beauty, or I shall shut it for you with a slap."

Everybody backed him up because the majority of the company detested Cristina. Then Seu Brandini said that she wouldn't gain anything by going to the police because the only money available was in Pará. The existing proceeds would hardly cover the theater's rent, fares, and freight for the scenery; and still one could thank God that they could travel.

"This time the season in Fortaleza was most disastrous as everybody in the company knows all too well."

Cristina left, slamming the door, almost without hearing the boos. A piece of good luck for her was that she had a protector, a rich gentleman who owned shares in a bank, who paid her passage. The next day, Wednesday, she left and took the Ita—the boat for the South.

So there was the problem of who would take the ingenue's place. The only two actresses who remained—Estrela Vésper and the impersonator, D. Pepa (a slovenly Spaniard who smoked cigars and was addicted to playing the numbers, and according to evil tongues, capable of wasting all the money she might lay her hands on giving presents to young men)—these two were out of the question. And it wasn't possible to cut out Cristina's roles in that repertory as nearly everything depended on the ingenue.

Perhaps in a pinch it might have been possible to substitute Estrela, who was now no longer a chick, also a little fat—but then who would play the part of the leading lady?

Suddenly, Seu Brandini turned to me and began his campaign.

"You could play her role very well—just for a few days."

"But Seu Brandini, me? Are you mad?"

"Only as a part-time job during the run in Pará."

"But Seu Brandini . . ."

"Only during the festival!"

I appealed to Estrela: "Estralinha, tell him that it's impossible!"

But Estrela remained silent, smiling, pleased with the idea. Seu Brandini continued: "If we miss out on the festival all will be lost. We won't even have anything to pay our debt to D. Loura."

"But you can get someone there, in Pará . . ."

"At the last minute, who? In this excitement with the festivities taking priority, they are even asking Indians from Amapá to dance in the chorus. . . . Don't be selfish, Dôra!"

I can't say that I wasn't tempted. Once, when I was a young girl in the *colégio,* I played the role of a witch in a drama at the end of the school year; after that I was so intrigued by the theater that I even told Senhora that my dream was to study to be an actress. You can well imagine Senhora's reply, which put me six feet under. (But from then on I began to collect the ads of troupes and photos of stars.)

Perhaps when I began to copy the roles for Seu Brandini I had told him, smiling, about those old dreams of mine—he was surprised that I knew how to put the cue within parentheses, between one speech and the next. So Seu Brandini in that hour of pressure no doubt remembered the confidences, and he declared that I had been born with talent and indeed had some experience! I didn't look my twenty-six years—no one would take me for more than eighteen—and when made up and with my hair styled, I would be a sensation.

Hearing that, Estrela continued to smile and approved with a shake of her head; and when Seu Brandini asked her to convince me, she said that she wouldn't put any pressure on me.

"If Dôra herself wishes to go into the theater, she will do so anyway."

In order to prove to me his good faith and the serious state in which the troupe found itself, he showed me copies of some of the telegrams ("Very expensive!") that he had sent to Rio; but among all the girls called, only two answered, asking for their passage and some money in advance for expenses and, of course, the problem was money.

"Those cows!"

We both laughed out loud. After all, how could the girls come without passage money? But he continued to nurse his anger.

"Girls nothing, they are nothing but tramps. I called on them as a last recourse—one sings a bolero in a circus of Niteroi, the other is free because she has just got out of the hospital. They ought to get down on their knees and thank me!"

And he turned to me again.

"Girl, you are certainly the one to do it. You are here and have the making of a great star. I have intuition, I know!"

He made me lift up my skirt and praised my legs as if he had never seen them before.

"Who would imagine such a skinny thing with those legs! It is all the better to be thin to play an ingenue. What do you think, Estrelita? Come woman, help!"

But as before, Estrela only shook her head.

This war lasted five days; at the end of the fourth day I had already more or less made up my mind, and on the fifth I lowered the flag.

Even D. Loura entered into the conspiracy and offered to make up a lie for Senhora telling her that I had landed a good job in Pará and had left by surprise—and then Seu Brandini interfered.

"Tell her that she is in Rio, the company's base. If she sends for her daughter, she will send to Rio; and when we leave Pará, the thing will already have cooled off."

I then announced disdainfully that I was a widow and independent. My mother didn't rule me, and I didn't have to tell lies to anyone. All the same I let D. Loura write the letter. Deep down I feared some interference from Senhora: The fact is that I still wasn't accustomed to my new widow's freedom. I still had a prisoner mentality.

* * *

85

Speaking of Senhora, it was at this very time, when I was studying Cristina's roles and getting ready to travel, that the letter from Laurindo's sister arrived.

The letter, which had been opened, was forwarded from Soledade, the answer to the telegram that Senhora had sent for me to São Luis de Maranhão. It had been composed by Dr. Fenelon:

"Desolate lament to inform you of the death of our dear Laurindo victim of accident by firearms." They had put my name at the bottom.

The sister, very sentimental and tearful, begged pardon for the delay of months in sending a reply; and further: "We ought to thank the good Lord that our little mother is in heaven and doesn't have to suffer this loss. . . ."

Actually Cousin Leonila had died more than a year before, there in São Luis, without ever having met me. Senhora believed that the cousin had died of cancer, but her family hid the news. In the last week they called Laurindo, who went by plane to be with his dying mother. He spent ten days there, traveled back after the burial, and arrived worn out and downcast. He had really adored his mother. He brought back as a remembrance a little gold watch, one of those antique ones in the form of a pendant on the chest in a brooch or in a *sautoir* or watch guard.

Senhora paid for his trip, and at Soledade nothing more was said about his sister, Carmita. Laurindo couldn't stand her husband.

Carmita ended the letter by saying I might not know it but she was poor and "had the right to inherit—into my unhappy hands—my father's estate through Laurindo!"

Senhora had written in big letters and underlined them in the margin of the letter:

"She has no rights whatsoever!"

All the same I consulted D. Loura's lawyer, and he said that Senhora was right. "A sister doesn't arbitrarily inherit, only the mother inherits his half if she survives him. But the mother having died before Laurindo, his wife comes first, ahead of brothers and sisters." Therefore I was Laurindo's heir.

Hence I kept the little watch that I had been disposed to return to São Luis, and I didn't answer Carmita's "missive." Let her be damned with that husband of hers. Laurindo often told stories about him, the wretch.

86

* * *

Once again I plunged into learning the roles by heart and taking part in rehearsals. On board the boat we were shut up nights in the bar rehearsing, when it wasn't open for the passengers; Seu Brandini tipped the steward, and we practically became owners of the salon. Although I was a little seasick during the entire trip, it was worth the sacrifice to begin being an actress.

I still had the problem of a wardrobe, the dresses had been made for Cristina, who moreover had taken along two which weren't hers, a yellow evening dress and a pink *charmeuse* with the skirt falling in petals, the one for the Melindrosa number; D. Pepa didn't remember to check the clothes until after Le Blanc had embarked for Rio. Seu Brandini, upon discovering the theft, bellowed again: "What a whore! what a thief!" He swore he'd deduct the cost from her pay: as if he had any intention of paying the creature— this I had already understood.

In Pará they remembered a seamstress known of old to the troupe who perhaps might do work on credit; Seu Brandini bargained with her, bought two cuts of cloth and gave her some of Estrela's old dresses too torn for her to use, which could be cut down for me.

The opening day finally came. My knees trembled and no word left my throat—Estrela understood. Seu Brandini gave me the cue thinking I needed the last word; but I needed no prompting because I remembered everything very well. It was just that my voice didn't respond.

After the last act they brought me a bunch of assorted flowers from an admirer. At the time I almost cried, but the next day a little Portuguese boy came to collect the bill for the flowers; and I understood that it had been the doing of Seu Brandini to encourage me. When I thanked him he blushed: Seu Brandini was like that.

In the country festivity campground of Nazare the demand on me wasn't so great, as it would be with the audience in the Teatro da Paz, which was accustomed to troupes even from Europe. The people in Nazare were country hicks; they wanted to hear wisecracks, sentimental or spicy ditties, and comedies with happy endings. Seu Brandini piled on the wit, even Estrela made an effort but she lacked humor. D. Pepa let herself go and often upstaged everybody.

I performed my part well enough and that was all they demanded of me.

I now even sang a little, in a play in which I portrayed the role of Maria, an innocent girl who runs away from her cruel father with a traveling salesman. The father sets out after her. Maria is working in a cabaret whose owner is Estrela Vésper. But in the sinful atmosphere Maria maintains her purity and hardly dances with the clients; Estrela Vésper (called Lola, the She Wolf, in the play)—she who never knew what it was to be pure!—is concerned about Maria's innocence. The salesman constantly makes a play for Maria; she, however, declares that she will leave with him only as his wife. The old man wanders everywhere searching for his daughter, and finally by chance comes upon the cabaret, arriving at exactly the moment when Maria is singing a childhood song: ''Open the window, Maria, for it is day.'' Lola, the She Wolf, (in a clinging black dress slit at one side to the hip revealing a red garter, in her wig of golden curls and with a long cigarette holder), sits down at his table. She is drunk. (Estrela thrilled the audience with this drunken scene.) She tells the old man, between bursts of cynical laughter, that the attractive young girl, just imagine, is still pure and a virgin: ''I take care of her—I want her to be what I never was!'' The old man begs Lola to introduce him to Maria: ''She reminds me of a young girl I knew long ago.'' With a gesture Lola calls Maria who, upon seeing the old man at the table, cries out: ''Jesus, it's my father!'' The old man, who now knows everything and can forgive, opens his arms to Maria: ''My daughter!'' Then the traveling salesman arrives, sees the embrace, joins them and says: ''My betrothed!'' The orchestra plays, Lola goes to the stage and, since the play has to continue, she sings her snappy Argentine tango: ''Tonight I get drunk.''

It was my first play, and even today I can still recite it all, word for word. In the first act some peasant women came to wake me up with the song, the theme song of Maria. I appeared sitting in the window and then I sang alone; afterwards we sang in chorus and then, in the finale, a panel on which the words were written was dropped from the ceiling so that the audience could join in:

Open the window, Maria, for it is day
It is eight o'clock, the sun is shining
The birds have made their nests
In the window of your bungalow!

I was supposed to direct the singing, opening my arms
and crying "Everybody!" but I was very shy and never succeeded in crying out loud enough or making the movements with self-assurance; then, D. Pepa, who directed the
chorus disguised as a peasant, with a colored handkerchief
tied under the chin, would take the initiative and shout
"Everybody!" so boisterously as to shake the wings.

Seu Brandini wanted to protect me as if I were his daughter, fulfilling the promise he made to D. Loura. So he
wasn't pleased when I accepted a car ride with an admirer,
a lad from the Bank of Brazil who never missed a show.
Later I had supper with him; but he was one of these men
who fell on women with a fury, and once he even stopped
the car. I said that if he didn't start the car again at once, I
would scream; and we returned to the hotel without any
further to-do.
    I had another admirer, a Portuguese with a gold tooth,
very young and shy; he would bring flowers to the dressing
room, little mixed bouquets, but I never went out with him.
The banker had left me wary; as a matter of fact I still feared
being seduced.
    Estrela also warned me to be cautious; she said she was
going to give me Lola the She Wolf's advice, that life could
be very deceptive and that a good companion was worth
more than a thousand lovers, but people learn only by
paying through the nose. Estrela admired the calm with
which I faced each new situation; and I replied that I had
had a long time to imagine any situation whatsoever, for I
had just left behind me twenty-six years of prison and a
jailer.
    But I talked just to be talking, perhaps to have the last
word, because it is always half humiliating when advice is
offered—even when one accepts it. The truth is that those
twenty-six years served no purpose for me, and I only
wanted to forget them.
    In the *colégio* I had a nun professor of "Lessons about

Things" who liked to tell about horrible happenings which had taken place in all parts of the world; I don't know where she got them: the fire in a New York retreat where eighty-six old people had burned up; the killing of seals with clubs on the frigid islands of Canada; the mummified heads the size of an orange of Bolivian Indians which they prepared by taking out the bones of the cranium and leaving only the scalp which shrunk. But for me the worst example was the case of the fox on a sierra in Spain, who was caught in a steel trap; as it couldn't get free, it gnawed the joint of its bone, tore open the skin and flesh until it separated them, and finally was free—maimed but free, leaving the paw in the trap. The next day the hunter found only that bloody paw, caught in the steel teeth.

At that time I considered myself to be like the fox: I left my bleeding flesh at Soledade but I had freed myself. I didn't ever again wish to think about anything of that past. I was still in pain, and how I suffered at night! I almost reached the point of getting out of the bed and screaming—oh yes, I suffered, but I had to get better. I kept on getting better little by little, and sometimes I even went an entire day without remembering anything.

In all of this I was helped a lot by the half-mad life in the theater, where everything was uncertain and different, and by the people in the troupe, and by the affection of Seu Brandini which had in it much of the paternal, and by Estrela's quiet, altogether authentic friendship.

With my feeble resources I had more or less solved the problem of the company's ingenue, but up until then no one had solved the problem of the leading man.

Seu Brandini took the roles himself, and I was not convinced by his argument that a big belly and age were of no importance in making love to a woman. If this were so Chaby Pinheiro couldn't put his feet on the stage. But it made a difference, yes. I was one who couldn't take Seu Brandini seriously: To say that I was crazy about him and would commit suicide rather than live without him was merely funny for me. But he didn't take himself seriously either, because in the most dramatic moments he would roll his eyes and the audience could hardly keep from laughing.

He took advantage of the kissing scenes and was furious

when his partner kissed with her mouth closed, only brushing the lips as it is done on the stage in order not to smear the makeup. He hardly got backstage before bellowing: "Learn to kiss, girl! Kiss your leading man right! How can I express realism next to a partner like you with a wooden mouth."

Estrela would laugh.

"Poor little Carleto, at least he deserves that reward for the effort he makes to hold in his stomach!" and she would give him a loving little tap on his stomach.

In the play of *Maria* Seu Brandini had to play the part of the father, the most important part; he considered putting the maestro in the role of the traveling salesman, but then he would have no one to direct the orchestra or play the piano. He ended up getting the secretary of the company, Seu Ladislau, a skinny old man, graying, with a very hoarse voice, who almost never lived with us because he was always traveling ahead to arrange the bookings.

As this run in Belém was longer, he was able to stay, saving the situation; moreover, the salesman's part was small, and he didn't sing. Made up well, Seu Ladislau lost twenty years, he was slender, and on the whole he didn't do badly.

The second play of the repertory, *Darling of My Love*, was Seu Brandini's favorite. It took place on the pampas. Seu Brandini said he wrote it; at least he signed it. The authorship notwithstanding, it seemed tailored for him; he adored the role, especially the number, "The Andorinha," which he sang. He would then open up his thundering voice (he explained that he was a baritone), and I can only say that the audience went wild and asked for encore after encore. The costume which Seu Brandini wore in that number was the most elegant in our wardrobe—blue velvet gaucho trousers, boots which came halfway up his calves, and a big authentic poncho of striped silk with tassels, bought in Uruguay.

He carried a whip which he cracked at the chorus, dragging the enormous spurs which he jangled.

He would begin the Andorinha number very softly, almost inaudible, and at the rehearsals he almost always had a fight with the maestro because of the stridency of the brass instruments.

"This is a romantic song, Mr. Jota! How stupid can you be?" But in the end the orchestra gave its all and he sang as loud as he could:

Return, return then if by chance
you have not made a nest on another's chest!
Return for it is time, it is already late,
I am already tired of living alone!

And when he caught his breath after a pause the gaucho would crack his whip and jangle his spurs; and the audience would join in the chorus. It was a madhouse. Just because of this one role and the Andorinha song, I don't think Seu Brandini exerted much effort to find another leading man.

The former leading man had gone when the company was still in Paraíba, before the Christmas season in Natal. He was a cariocan youth, one of those happy-go-lucky people who doesn't stick to anything, who had a certain charm although he was short; and in order to act the love scenes with Cristina Le Blanc, he had to climb up on something, a packing box or a bench, or she was seated and he standing. Because of this factor, the two were always fighting, he claiming that she wore twelve-centimeter high-heeled shoes on purpose, that if she would just wear two-centimeter low-heel shoes all would be well. Cristina would smile in her cynical way.

"My God, he doesn't want much, just that I should sacrifice my elegance as an actress!"

She herself told me about the fights, repeating the retorts and rejoinders. Another reason for the quarrels between the two was that the young man spoke with a lot of chirping, drawing out the s's; and Cristina, who was born in Botafogo and raised in Copacabana teased that his manner of speaking with a chirp could not be right for the suburbs of Cascadura and thereabouts; the southern zone of Rio had soft s's, almost without a hiss.

In a performance at Paraíba—Estrela told me about it —it seems that on one occasion the leading man gathered up his courage vis-à-vis the ingenue, and in fun or perhaps out of boredom, put his hand where he shouldn't have; Cristina slapped him right in the middle of the scene. It created a terrible scene although some of the audience thought that it was part of the play, and there was much laughter and even applause.

But the cariocan left the stage and never returned for the final act and Seu Brandini ordered that the play be ended with the slap. The performance closed with a little variety act improvised on the spot.

Seu Brandini was wild with rage: That idiot had shown the maximum lack of professional spirit! Come what may, the show must go on! And he pointed with his trembling finger to the signs that he had pasted on the sides of the scenery, on the trunks, and on the mirrors in the dressing rooms: THE SHOW MUST GO ON. He had stacks and stacks of those printed signs, and I believe it was the only English phrase that Seu Brandini knew. It was his battle cry—he considered it the very essence, the summing up of the profession: "The show must go on!"

And for the thousandth time he told about the incident one night when on the circuit in Minas, he was playing a batty comedy and they handed him a telegram telling him of his father's death, the old Brandini, in Rio Grande do Sul. Brandini Filho read the terrible news during the intermission, but he returned to the stage and continued to say his inanities and made the audience laugh until the curtain fell, and only then did he lock himself up in the dressing room and weep, for he adored the old man.

One time when he repeated this story while I was present, I head Cristina comment with a superior smile: "I have heard that anecdote with at least ten different actors as protagonists, beginning with Talma and João Caetano . . ."

But Seu Brandini wasn't upset: First of all, it wasn't an anecdote, it was a true dramatic story; and secondly, if it had happened with others, this was just proof that all great actors—and the very ones she cited, Talma, João Caetano—shared the same high professional standard.

No one could get the best of Seu Brandini, not even Cristina. That snake.

On the day following the slap, when the city newspapers commented on the incident, and a critic characterized the episode as a lack of consideration for the public of Paraíba and its civilized rights, Seu Brandini fired the cariocan; and without paying him a cent—let him go to the police if he dared.

Cristina was triumphant, but then she began to have trouble with her new leading man who was none other than Brandini Filho himself as there wasn't anybody else; and later she herself left in a betrayal as I described above. They put me in her place and never was there on any stage in the world a pair more badly put together than Seu Brandini and I.

"They seem more like father and daughter," commented Estrela in that quiet way of hers.

There still remained also the problem of accent because, as I said, Seu Brandini spoke pure gaucho, which to our ears sounded almost like Spanish; and I had my drawling speech of the northeasterner with the open vowels—there was indeed some confusion.

As a solution everyone demanded that I practice a new accent; and I chose the cariocan one because all my life I had found it pretty and still do.

In those days what was most heard on the Brazilian stage was a Portuguese accent, or at least an accent influenced by Portuguese which was used by nearly everybody in the theater. The Brazilian theater in those days followed the Portuguese school, and many a Brazilian actor spoke his part as if he had just gotten off the boat from Lisbon that day.

Estrela, who was from Minas and had been brought up in Rio, gave a Portuguese intonation to her speech; and Seu Brandini when he was young had made a great effort to follow the general usage—but there was no Portuguese that could do much for that gaucho speech!

Or maybe it was just his personality, as Seu Brandini liked to say. As for me my tongue couldn't adapt itself to speak Portuguese; I then tried to imitate the cariocans as best I could and I took Cristina's chatter as a model. The result was hardly splendid, but at least I no longer spoke so markedly in a singsong manner, nor did I open the *e*'s and *o*'s. The speech that was left was a mixture, but in the end it wasn't as bad as it had been at the beginning. And in Pará I always tried a little Paranese accent which I also found very pleasant. Even today I still meet people who ask me if I am from Pará. Oh, I like that.

A note appeared in the Belém press complaining about the lack of a proper leading man in the Brandini Filho Company. It was a sign that the public was resentful, however strenuous Seu Brandini's efforts. And the worst was that the lack of a leading man influenced above all the choice of plays we could use since only comic plays could be presented; and of course our repertoire included many plays that weren't comedies. Estrela's roles almost all belonged to romantic plays, and she was unhappy not to have more occasions to play *la femme fatale*, the vamp.

Then one afternoon during rehearsal a candidate for the leading man, a lad of presence, fell to us from heaven. Seu Brandini tested him: The boy knew how to say his lines, he had self-assurance on the stage, and the best thing was that he even owned a dress suit in addition to several three-piece suits. Hence there would be a wardrobe problem only with character plays, but for those parts the other leading man's clothes in the trunks could be touched up.

The lad's name was Odair—Odair Esmeraldo. He didn't come from the legitimate theater; he wasn't a comedian, as D. Pepa had thought. Up until then he had been a magician; for this reason he owned the dinner jacket, tails, and even a top hat and used the stage name of Professor Everest. But he had been slapped with an attachment and ended up losing all of his equipment to his creditors.

Seu Brandini didn't believe that story: The law never attached working tools; otherwise, how would the attaché be able to earn a living and pay off the creditors?

"I am a specialist on this subject of creditors!" he said with a shameless smile. And he continued: "A magician's equipment makes up his working tools, like a sewing machine for the dressmaker."

But no one bothered about that detail; one doesn't look a gift horse in the mouth. Let Odair tell his story as he wished. It was his life, each one is allowed to have his own version of his particular story, nothing was gained by speculating on another's past intrigues.

We opened with a play in which I was in a window while Odair sang serenades and Seu Brandini, my father, threw a vase of flowers (a cardboard vase with paper roses) at the leading man's head. This play, although it was one of the most applauded, had been filed away because the two men were on the stage together at every moment and only if Seu Brandini had been a quick-change artist like the celebrated

Fátima Miris would he have been able to play the noble father and the young boy at the same time.

Finally we found out—he himself told us—Odair's story hadn't been a happy one. He came from Manaus, and there he had fallen in love with a young girl, a minor; she fell in love with him, and they ran away together.

The family didn't accept what it called the kidnapping, and the police impounded all of the magician's equipment left behind in the hotel while Romeo and Juliet escaped down the river. They stayed a week in Santarém and finally arrived at Belém.

Odair was frightened, but he hoped that the family would give up the chase as a lost cause since in the end the girl could no longer go back and start her life anew. After all, who, from the good families of Manaus, would want to marry a girl led astray by a magician—and a married one at that!

Yes, the worst thing was that Odair was married; however, he always excused himself saying he might be married but had no children. Now really!

Also, as Estrela used to say, it was possible that most of his stories of mystery and persecution were invented to make drama. Oh, how actors liked to dramatize themselves!

At times Odair would say furiously that the parents kept on begging the girl to return so they could put her in the convent of Bom Pastor; but I, for one, never believed that. Just see if there is any girl today who would subject herself to Bom Pastor. Perhaps some illiterate from the hinterland might, but this girl was knowledgeable and had attended the normal school. Finally we discovered that there was no Bom Pastor convent in Manaus.

It wasn't only in this story of the kidnapped girl—Odair liked to be mysterious about everything; for example, he let it be understood that he had another name which he hid because he was from a traditional family with heroes from the war with Paraguay.

It could be—heroes from Paraguay could have had sons and grandsons, and I, wasn't I now calling myself *Nely Sorel*? Oh, it was a war, that choice of my stage name. Estrela said: "Why don't you use Dorita? In this way you can keep something of your own name." But then I remembered Senhora's lap dog when Xavinha spoke precisely of this name of Dorita. Besides, I detested it.

Then each person had suggested a different name— someone spoke of Priscilla; I was thinking, but Priscilla what? I had to have a French or English surname to complete it, one could say that such a name was de rigueur at that time. What gave charm to an actress was a Hollywood name.

It was Osvaldina (because during all of this discussion the company was still in Ceará), who was a fanatical movie fan and had a collection of *Silent Movie*, who came across that name of *Nely Sorel*, composed of two actors and didn't it seem to be the name of a movie itself?

Everybody liked it. Seu Brandini kept rolling the name over on his tongue: *Nely Sorel*. D. Pepa counted the letters, nine, a multiple of three, it was lucky.

A pitcher of beer was opened and D. Loura baptized me as Nely Sorel; after supper she brought out a cake to celebrate the baptism. (And all the time I was thinking about what Senhora would say when she found out.)

Odair Esmeraldo's stolen girl traveled with him, but she didn't mix much with us. She was shy, more so than I, and silent; and on the rare occasions when she appeared during the rehearsals, she remained quietly in a chair, with a little bashful smile. Poor little thing, she still hadn't regained her composure since the turmoil and scandal of the flight from Manaus.

Odair told us that he practiced magic tricks with her every day in the room of the boardinghouse. He considered his time in the theater as only temporary; and as he didn't have the courage to return to Manaus to face his angry father-in-law and recover his equipment, he was gathering new props bit by bit; some he was making himself, sending the pieces to cabinet makers and tinsmiths and ordering his wife to sew the stuffings and make silk fringes. Araci—his wife's name—proved to be very clever with the needle and spent her time shut up in the room fastening the stuffings and false bottoms while her husband slept.

In Maranhão he performed small tricks of magic between acts; he was assisted by Estrela who wore her red evening dress and seconded very well his prestidigitation. From then on there was always a magician's act in our variety show; only now Odair appeared made up with a small pointed beard and a turban and insisted on being introduced as "Professor Everest." Seu Brandini made fun of him behind his back, saying that Everest is the name of a mountain in India; so one could see what a cretin Odair was.

I speak of Maranhão, Belém, Manaus, Natal as being the same, perhaps even mixing them up, because in theater life—*mambembe* or traveling theater life as they said then—people even lose the sense of place.

Even so each audience is different. Each audience reacts in its own manner and shows its preferences. (Is there an actor or actress on the circuit who isn't capable of identifying the audience with his eyes closed only by virtue of its reaction?) But with places—squares, streets, and hotels—traveling actors can get confused.

I remember places in this manner, for example: São Luis was the place where that fat businessman sent me a card with a bracelet; then he sent me another card inviting me to a boat outing. I didn't go and he wanted me to return the bracelet. But Estrela said that I was entitled to keep it; I had in my possession the written proposition which accompanied it so that was that.

In Natal, there was the problem with the owner of the hotel, and also the wrenched ligament of D. Pepa, who couldn't walk; but as she would say, as a disciplined old war-horse, she didn't need to read Seu Brandini's notices of "The Show Must Go On," she would play her roles. Leaning on her cane and hobbling about she was funnier than ever.

As for D. Pepa, I don't know, I don't know. She adored the laughter of the audience, she got drunk on the guffaws, she kept on making jokes and stretching out her speeches until Seu Brandini intervened; yet at the same time she resented the laughter, the buffoonery and the role of impersonator.

When she was in her cups she liked to talk about past glories.

"Ah, this ugly old woman with a mustache—God—when I think about what I gave: The audience called me for a number and I let myself go with monkeyshines—but do they think I fool myself? Do they really think so? I know very well that I am a ridiculous old woman, sloppy, fat, and a clown! Impersonation is clowning, so I am a mimic by profession and proud of it!''

And then she was crying and forgot what she had begun to say.

''Don't be fooled, the comedian is the main prop of a revue; do you know, even Getulio—yes, sir, Getulio laughed until he cried when he saw that number I played as a pregnant bride— don't you remember, Estrela? He had to dry his eyes with a handkerchief, he laughed so much—Getulio (Tr. note: Getulio Vargas, Dictator of Brazil during the years before and after World War II.) in person, with his guards in the box and Beijo, and from the stage I could hear their roars of laughter.''

She drank another swallow of beer.

''Well, that's impersonation. But there was a time when I was beautiful. I wasn't always like this, nor this''—and she passed her hands over her double chin, her belly, and her enormous thighs—''there was a time when I was very thin, slim as the stem of a flower! And if I were to tell you of the bachelor quarters I visited, the rich boys' rooms, oh, in my time! The nights of champagne, then it was only French champagne, Veuve Cliquot! Oh, the life of an actress was something! The life of an actress today, pardon me, but it is as they say in my country—it is a *porqueria*—something for the birds.

Estrela listened and shook her head.

''You know, Pepa, I had my times, too, before Carleto. And I can tell you something, what I know from all of that big talk with the boys is: Get a man, one from your own people. I don't wish to be more proper than anybody else. I did some foolish things, the bachelor rooms and the champagne; but when the time comes to grab someone and go to bed, the best thing is to find a man from your own people.''

D. Pepa gestured with the glass in her hand.

''Such as who? A rich man in a silk shirt and perfumed? Go on, girl . . .''

''And drunk,'' ventured Estrela. ''Drunk, they were always drunk then; it always happens when people have too much to drink. For me, cold-bloodedly, it was like going to the doctor.''

D. Pepa, who got angry easily, was irritated.

''Don't make yourself out to be a saint, Estrela! I remember you with that gang from Recreio—was it in 1925? People said that the real show began after the curtain fell, do you remember? And it wasn't couples, it was gangs! Hmm, you remember, don't you?''

But Estrela wasn't offended.

"But isn't that just what I am saying? I speak because I know. And I can say further, Pepa, that it was with that gang that I got fed up and was through. To drink and frolic with all those men with nothing of love . . . One day a teenage girl happened to stay overnight with me, I don't know why, and said something I have never forgotten: 'I feel like that day when I went to the clinic to have a curettage without anesthesia . . .' I never forgot.''

D. Pepa let out her coarse stage laugh.

"Abortion—that's a good one. Boy, I'm going to put that in the scene of the impassioned Portuguese to get belly laughs: 'Do you want a sexy curettage, my pretty little one?' Good, good.''

Estrela shut up and turned away. Afterwards, she said in a low voice, but I heard her: "Old cow!''—Seu Brandini's favorite phrase when he tired of D. Pepa's obscenities.

Our arrival in Fortaleza was a festive occasion. D. Loura, Osvaldina and even the telegraph operator had come to the Metálica bridge to meet us, not to speak of Inspector Jones who never failed. There was a special lunch to which everybody was invited for free.

What I found most touching was that my bed was made up as always in D. Loura's room: My new position as a comedienne didn't lower me in her esteem. My big actress trunk which Seu Brandini had decorated with hotel stickers from nearly everywhere in the world to give the troupe an international touch—he bought them from a character on Alfandega Street in Rio—that steamer trunk was swimming in the middle of the room like Noah's Ark.

Osvaldina made a point of tidying up all of my things, mending, ironing, shining my shoes. What interested her most was my cosmetic box—not that it was a proper leather kit like Cristina Le Blanc's, or even Estrela's threadbare, well-stocked kit; it was only a box full of rouge, tubes, flasks, little pots of cream, pencils, brushes and lipsticks; but Osvaldina could never imagine herself bold enough to use such things. One day I decided to make her up for the stage and what a surprise! As Seu Brandini said, that girl had a special contour of face made for stage lights; and it was so, the eyes seemed enormous under the lights and from a distance one could say that she was a beauty.

As for herself and also for D. Loura, Osvaldina could have kept on the makeup for the rest of the night; but, looking at the clock, she ran to wash her face: it was time for the telegraph operator to arrive.

And D. Loura, seeing the daughter leave so quickly, sighed.

"My poor little daughter. Is it for this that I brought her into the world and sacrificed so much to raise her?"

Then Osvaldina returned with her face washed, and very sad; I believe that she recalled the triumph of her beautiful made-up face for the rest of her life and consoled herself with that remembrance when life was difficult. She must have thought: "If I had wished, I could have . . ." I know how it is.

In Fortaleza, I found a letter from Xavinha. Everything was the same at Soledade; a mild winter that meant abundant crops. Senhora seemed to be suffering from high blood pressure. Dr. Fenelon gave her some medicine and prescribed a diet so she could lose weight. I doubt that she submitted herself to the diet; she always used to say that she ate almost nothing, that she was fat from birth, by nature.

Old Delmiro, queerer than ever, now "negotiated" with Antônio Amador in my stead and was very thin and withdrawn and didn't even say good morning to anyone. He hid himself more and more from Senhora.

Poor Xavinha. I felt sorry for her and wrote her a few lines; but I didn't give her the big news of my life. I only said I was in good health, I had been traveling, and very soon I would return home. When I had a definite address I would send it to her, but for the time being she should continue sending her letters in care of D. Loura who would see that they reached me.

A disagreeable incident took place in Fortaleza: A rumor broke out that I was a rich heiress from the interior—just imagine—who had broken with my family and for that reason had entered the theater. They placed me as belonging to the Fulano do Crato or the Beltrano de Sobral families, and the parish newspaper published an article lamenting the terrible influence of modern customs on the Ceará families, if perhaps it was true that a senhorita of a traditional Ceará family had exchanged her Catholic hearth for the glamor of "light theater"—to use a charitable figure of speech. If I had chosen a singing career like Bidu Sayão, the niece of a Brazilian president, it might have been different. But those comic, spicy and lewd sketches, etc., etc. . . .

But I was no senhorita. I was a widow and of age, and I didn't come from the Crato or from the Sobral families. My family wasn't of such high position, however much Senhora bragged about her grandeur.

There was much curiosity and gossip in connection with the article. The box office benefited. Seu Brandini was delighted and wanted to expand the story even further; but he got frightened when I burst into tears and said I was going to leave the company.

The fact is I was horrified to see myself suddenly the center of gossip, and D. Loura even hid from me half of the malicious gossip.

The telegraph operator forbade Osvaldina from going out with me "so she wouldn't get involved in the scandal." Then Seu Brandini decided to act.

He made friends with a reporter of Fortaleza's other newspaper and "obtained" for him an "exclusive interview" with me. My good luck was that nobody knew me in that city. I hadn't even attended a *colégio* in Fortaleza and so there was no risk of a classmate or teacher identifying me. Aroeiras was a long way off, and the people from there were modest and played no great role in the capital.

In view of the fact that I was much better with an accent unfamiliar to the Northeast, Seu Brandini presented me as a girl from Minas who had gone to live in Rio as a child (as was the case with Estrela). I was supposed to be the daughter of a high functionary, but I had the theater in my blood: As a girl I put on plays with my brothers and sisters, making a stage of the dining room table. As a young girl I fought hard to convince my parents to let me follow my destined career. Today, reconciled, my family was very proud of my successes.

That Seu Brandini! I had the theater in my blood! But in fact the lie stuck, and on the day following the publication of the interview the public's reaction was very curious: They came to hiss me and stamp their feet when I came on the stage because of my pretension to pass for a girl from a Ceará family!

Our stay in Fortaleza was short. We hadn't obtained a good theater but were in an old movie house with extremely poor acoustics, built for silent movies. The actors had to strain their voices when singing or speaking, to make themselves heard even in the middle of the orchestra. There was also the high rent and Seu Brandini complaining of the financial difficulties.

Then we left for Recife, and I cried in D. Loura's arms on the day we left. Hers was the only place in the world that from day to day I could call "home." At least that was what D. Loura told me, urging that I use judgment and care in the theater life, a life so different from that in which I had been raised.

"And don't forget, child: As long as I am alive, you have a home!"

From the very beginning all went well in Recife; for me theater life was already a routine. Whoever doesn't know thinks that an actress's life is all fun, pleasure, handsome youths, and rich old men, as in the remembrances of D. Pepa. For me, at least, it wasn't like that.

Perhaps I wasn't pretty; I was merely cute, and even then only on the stage with the proper makeup. Or perhaps I didn't have the art, or maybe stories like Pepa's were a long way from the truth.

As I have already explained, I received proposals; and lovers even presented themselves. But no man came along who captured my enthusiasm; one might be rich like the bracelet man, but mean and one who would take advantage of a girl. In view of the reputation that an actress had, the men who are worth anything, chiefly those who are worth anything in terms of money, are warned against them and are afraid of being dragged into some dangerous adventure. Moreover, with our short stays in each city, I couldn't get to know anyone very well. A small affair might begin in Natal, but the next day one was already in Paraíba; and only a gypsy would go traveling after a company. Those mad passions, alas, happened only in *Camille*; and today counts and bankers who can cover a woman with diamonds and provide her with a carriage no longer exist. Perhaps it was so at one time, as old Pepa bragged. Her senators, million-aires, and Portuguese commendatores now were as dead as doornails.

But as I said, we had a marvelous time in Recife.

Odair worked very well in the group, and now even Araci came more often and tried out for parts in some numbers under Estrela's patient eye.

But suddenly—it always happens so—the sky collapsed on us. One afternoon we were rehearsing, more for the company's honor than because we needed practice inas-much as the play was learned and overlearned, when Seu Brandini burst into the theater and exploded a bomb: "The boat on which the company was going to embark had been sunk!"

That was during wartime. Until then, in every part of Bra-zil we touched, no one was unaware of the war in Europe, for the radios and newspapers talked of nothing else; but it was distant news, from the other side of the world. But now, suddenly like a bolt of lightning, the war hit us; and I can never forget the shock of those sinkings.

Now the war meant the dead, the Nazis, the airplanes, and the submarines; it wasn't something far away in Eu-rope like snow or Maurice Chevalier.

For me it was a blow in the solar plexus, and I thought about the drowned people on board whom I knew, because we had already traveled on that boat.

Seu Brandini, who was very patriotic, reached a pinnacle of indignation, and that night he paid homage with a grand finale, an open invitation for dinner.

The entire company and ten extras on the stage were put into soldiers' uniforms (Seu Brandini had arranged for the uniforms with a good friend of ours who never missed a show). Seu Brandini played the part of General Osório, Odair the role of Floriano Peixoto, the Iron Marshall. Estrela in a white tunic, playing the role of Pátria, recited some verses about the national flag by Petion de Vilar which she already knew from an earlier celebration, occurring on the seventh of September. Following the verses, Osório and Floriano were crowned with laurel wreaths. Seu Brandini demanded that the wreaths be real laurel: He wanted the "authentic touch." We got the laurel branches at the market, and I myself made the crowns, intertwining the gold silken cord with the leaves. At the time the stage smelled so much of laurel that D. Pepa said that it was reminiscent of a good *feijoada,* and Seu Brandini screamed at her: "Shut up, old Spanish cow, Franco fascist!"

D. Pepa was offended also because being fat they didn't let her take part in the parade (not even with a cane).

The soldiers paraded to military music at the beat of the drum, with me in uniform also in front as the flag carrier, holding high the green and yellow flag, and everybody was singing the Soldier's Song. The entire audience stood up and sang with us. A high-placed man made a speech, and Seu Brandini was so overcome that he cried right there on the stage.

Much later, after the expeditionary corps had left for Italy, Seu Brandini liked to boast that it was the Brandini Filho Company which was the first to pay tribute to our brave "Brazilian GI's."

From then on all of our shows had a patriotic number; and if we didn't have the parade every day, it was only because we had to return the uniforms. Given the change of our circumstances, to make our own uniforms was unthinkable, not to speak of the cost of hiring extras.

But Seu Brandini dug up an old play from the First World War and updated it. Estrela played a nurse who was shot by the Nazis (in the old play, "The Huns"), with a large cross serving as a target on her breast. And when Estrela fell she would cry, "Long live Brazil" and the audience applauded wildly.

Estrela herself would protest: "But, Carleto, am I not a Belgian? And shouldn't I then say 'Long live Belgium'?— that would be logical."

But Seu Brandini insisted on the "Long live Brazil." We didn't understand the psychology of the crowds: Passion has no logic. The public then wanted to give the "long live" to Brazil. And Seu Brandini must have been right because no one ever really objected.

It may be that in Seu Brandini's patriotism there was a little commercial exploitation in order to help the box office. But the truth is that we, the actors, were always moved

105

chiefly by the public's reaction and by the speeches that were made almost every night. When the parade with the flag came on stage, it was surefire theater.

There was a mayor of the interior who wanted to make a speech in an open scene during one performance, and he brought his band to the theater door. The band members didn't come inside next to our orchestra only because they were not musically trained and our orchestra couldn't have played with them. The people cheered these little bands wildly, but they were really country bumpkins.

Well, I am talking about shows in the hinterland cities, because in light of the general difficulty of transportation, and the fear of ships being torpedoed when transportation by boat was possible, our solution was to play them. Seu Brandini was the only one of us who swore he had no fear of going to the bottom of the sea. Estrela didn't hide the fact that she preferred a thousand times to leave the company and go by land to wait for Carleto in Rio when he arrived there.

"If he arrived there. . . ."

I was also fearful, and old Pepa was much worse; even Araci, Odair's wife, was afraid; she was already acting in the bit parts, thus representing a means of economizing on extras.

The solution for Seu Brandini was to make short trips to the cities that were closest, Vitória de Santo Antão, Jaboatão, Gravatá, Goiana. We even went to the famous Caruaru.

We went by train, used the local theater, carried only a minimum of scenery—a curtain which served as a backdrop for nearly everything. We carried by hand the props for the varieties, little songs, monologues, and sketches which the public liked so much.

Seu Brandini never failed to perform the song of the Andorinha from which he took "My Native Land" as if it were an independent number. It was always a big hit. That crack of the whip and the jangle of the spurs!

I had already worked up an Argentine tango. Old Pepa commented that the company gave nothing more than old-fashioned traveling shows.

None of us complained very much, and we even discovered that those hinterland cities were much more important than we had originally thought; they had a newspaper and fine people who were knowledgeable about the theater. The sugar cane mill owner families didn't attend our shows; they were accustomed to European theater and Rio's Municipal theater. I say families because the young macho sons came to our shows and were thrilled.

At least that was what a journalist wrote, I don't know where, complaining that the local elite didn't support Brazilian art and preferred foreign art. Seu Brandini nailed the clipping to the bulletin board and later pasted it in our publicity album. If there was one thing that made him raving mad it was the elite.

"Just let any potbellied dago bellow an opera dressed up like a clown and the elite dies of ecstasy. But if a Brazilian clown asks for the stage of the Municipal theater, he will spend thirty years in jail for his effrontery!"

Seu Brandini even wrote a letter to *The Morning Post* when Dudu the clown died, urging a national homage be paid to the artist; he also noted that some contemporaries had given much attention to Piolim—but they were avantgarde. In general the establishment supported only foreign artists, and for them that was all that counted; but the legitimate heroes of our Brazilian theater found only rejection and insurmountable obstacles.

Seu Brandini used to write letters that he didn't sign because he didn't want to risk reprisals. He wrote to newspapers and to individuals as well. He pointed out to the company that they couldn't be called anonymous letters because anonymity implied a slanderous intent which he didn't have. He certainly didn't intend to slander. For example, if an actor whom he was enjoying was destroying something of the play's total effect by some mannerisms on the stage, Seu Brandini would write him an *unsigned* letter, pointing out the fault. And he explained: If he were to speak personally to the actor, he could get very angry and certainly wouldn't listen; but receiving the correction in a letter without any witnesses, the actor could heed the counsel gracefully.

He wrote to mayors, to captains of ships complaining about the service on board and at the same time included praise because he didn't like to be unjust; moreover, praise helped the complaint to be well received. Never in my whole life have I met another person like Seu Brandini.

* * *

Such one-night stands aided but didn't resolve our difficulties. Finally, we didn't have a theater to use anymore in Recife. We had to pay for the pension the entire time, even when on the road for four or five days, because it didn't pay to move every time.

Estrela thought about renting a house, but this wasn't practical; it was impossible to bring together such different people, as for example D. Pepa with her boys, Seu Jota do Piano, who had a bad reputation and drank a lot.

Then there was the prompter, of whom one never spoke except saying that "the prompter was heard" or "the prompter wasn't heard"; in the meantime he existed, a silent fat man, whose physique was entirely inappropriate for his work; for he could hardly squeeze himself into the prompter's box in some theaters; in others—in the movie houses, for example—there wasn't even a prompter's box and the poor Antenor, for this was his name, had to do his prompting from the wings.

Nowadays a prompter isn't used anymore. I am no longer in the theater, but I think I would die of fright if I had to depend on memory alone. In our time it was a new play every night and not even a Sarah Bernhardt with an elephant's memory would be able to remember all that dialogue.

Antenor wasn't bad looking; he wore a mustache; he knew the plays in rehearsal by heart, but he said everything mechanically. At times the cast didn't understand him because intonation is what makes speech, as Seu Brandini explained to us millions of times: Even if you say *pass the salt* you ought to use the correct intonation.

When the maestro argued with the property man, Euclides, which was most of the time, Antenor would break the impasse. But in each place where we arrived, Antenor was hardly ever with the company; we didn't even know his whereabouts from the end of one performance to the beginning of the next rehearsal. Some said that he liked to live only in the red-light districts; he would rent a room in a boardinghouse for whores, and he would live there like a member of the family.

Who could have thrown together such individualistic people in the same house, as Estrela wanted to do? For the sake of argument, Seu Brandini objected: To rent a house demanded credit, and Recife was no little city in which everyone knew everyone else. So where in the devil could we dig up a creditor? If we could arrange a little credit, it would only be by the grace of God!

The calls for payment of our debts began to be annoying. There was the lady who ran the boardinghouse, for example, a low-class Portuguese, who made us long for the affection and confidence, chiefly confidence, of D. Loura.

Seu Brandini began then to hatch up projects (those were Estrela's words).

One of these projects was to offer free performances for our armed forces, as is the custom in nations at war. The Air Force could give us transportation and hospitality as long as the engagements lasted in the garrisons, and at the end they could leave us at our base in Rio.

It was a beautiful project that did honor to the sentiments of the Brandini Filho Company; but, according to the colonel commander with whom Seu Brandini spoke—he had taken Estrela and me along to sweeten the offer—it was necessary to remember that Brazil wasn't at war and therefore wasn't fighting. . . .

Seu Brandini interrupted.

"But Colonel, don't you find this a mere technicality?"

". . . and then that custom of sending troupes to give shows for the soldiers is usually observed only in established theaters of war. But, even if our declaration of war were official (hopefully in a short time it will be, I tell you this confidentially), it will still be a long time before Brazil finds itself on the battlefield. Most probably Hitler will be defeated before then. Isn't Russia launching the winter invasion?"

The colonel said many more things; he chatted with Seu Brandini as with an equal. After all, we are all Brazilians, and we love our country.

Seu Brandini was ecstatic about the conversation; but unfortunately it produced nothing that would resolve our difficulties.

A while back, I spoke of Antenor, the prompter, the secretive one; and now I see that I haven't mentioned any details about Seu Ladislau, the secretary. As I said before, he was rarely with us. When we began our tour in a city he had already left for the next place, to prepare everything, to deal

with publicity, to rent the theater, reserve accommodations
—all, to pave the way for the company.

I have already mentioned that he was a little, dried-up old
man. Formerly he had been an actor; but he had to end his
career because of trouble in his vocal cords, and he almost
lost his voice.

In love with the theater as he was, he had tried first to be
an impresario, and in this adventure he lost everything he
owned, a little house in the Novo Engenho neighborhood in
Rio, an inheritance from his Portuguese father. In this same
house Ladislau had been born and brought up—in the back
part, because the front was his father's fruit shop. After his
mother's death he tried to turn over the little he inherited to
finance his theater company. But the company failed with a
big bang; the cause, some said, was that Seu Ladislau fell in
love with the leading lady, an Argentine tramp. (Some time
later I met her. She was already fat and old and was no leading lady but was the wardrobe mistress. She also sewed for
a very shady company which sometimes played in the
Tiradentes Plaza.) Finally, Seu Ladislau ended up joining
Seu Brandini, and the two made a marvelous team. I believe
our company was already the third with which they had
been associated.

But Seu Brandini objected to this kind of talk. It wasn't
the third company; it was the *third phase* of the Brandini
Filho Company of Comedies and Musical Farces. The legal
status might be different, at times because of financial circumstances, but the company was the same—in essence.

Seu Ladislau had shared in the company; he put up a
little capital, and I believe if it hadn't been for him, things
would have gone much worse for us. Seu Brandini had a
good head but, as Estrela complained, this led to few con-
crete results. He racked his brains and started projects, but
someone else had to carry them through and keep them in
order.

In Recife the troupe got along better with Seu Ladislau's
help, and he accompanied us on those one-night stands
into the interior. It was he who began the project of getting
us back to Rio by land—no easy feat then because only
much later did they tear up the countryside to make roads
like the Rio-Bahia highway. At the beginning of the war this
highway was only big talk, but actually to cut across the
sertão took a long time. Seu Brandini and Seu Ladislau got

some maps and began to make plans. The idea was to go by train to the end of the line at Rio Branco, and from there to take a car to Petrolina.

At Petrolina, which faced Juazeiro da Bahia, on the other side of the São Francisco River we would take a ship of the Bahian Navigation Company on the São Francisco, and would climb to Pirapora, in Minas. Pirapora was another railroad terminal, and from there we would take the train for Belo Horizonte.

Belo Horizonte to Rio, that had already long been our circuit, I might add, a circuit of many seasons: Ouro Preto, São Joao del Rei, Barbacena, Juiz de Fora.

Seu Brandini became enthusiastic at once and imbued us all with his enthusiasm. He wasn't a man to drink his tea alone, others had to join him.

D. Pepa was difficult; she certainly wasn't going to embark on any boat, not even a riverboat.

"A submarine can also enter the São Francisco River. You think I don't know that river? When you come by the coast and enter its mouth you can see the yellow streak of the river cutting the sea water. A pilot showed me one time: 'See the São Francisco River!' The damned thing runs into the sea! A submarine can enter it quite easily."

Seu Brandini went to look for the map.

"Look, Pepa, even if a submarine can enter the river, which I don't believe, it would have to climb the waterfall of Paulo Afonso to reach our boat. The navigation line begins only above the waterfall; see, here it is on the map. Can you read? '—Paulo Afonso Waterfall.' The boat departs much higher up, here, look, in Juazeiro."

In the end, the other alternative was to go by plane. And even if old Pepa had saved enough money for air passage, she was more afraid of an airplane than of any old German submarine. Moreover, it was well nigh impossible to arrange air passage as there were priorities, and one had to wait in line for months.

The question was put to a vote, and we decided to make the trip by land: the "Recife–Belo Horizonte excursion," as Odair would say in mockery. Even D. Pepa ended up agreeing. Since nobody had any money and even less credit, it was agreed to give impromptu shows en route wherever there might be a chance. Something light that wouldn't require the large pieces of scenery; the maestro thought he could assemble a stray orchestra by appealing, perhaps, to one or two local talents in the larger places. If there were a piano, he would play it himself; and when there was no piano, he would use his accordion. Besides, a piano was an instrument that the Brandini Filho Company never owned because, as he rightly said, any theater worth its salt had its own piano. However, it couldn't be said that *every* theater where we stopped was strictly speaking a theater that was worth its salt.

As usual Seu Ladislau went ahead of us to lay the groundwork for the first show that would be given in Rio Branco, at the end of the railroad.

Our departure from Recife had to be more or less on the q.t., since Seu Brandini feared some nasty creditors.

It is incredible how a theater company can pile up such large debts: There is the lighting, electricity, local personnel, billboard painters, printing of programs, bar account for snacks, light lunches and suppers (miserable sandwiches and worse coffee). That creature at the bar demanded cash payment then and there. It was difficult to arrange credit, and if one arranged it how could one pay on demand; if a person asks for credit, it is because he has no money—that's obvious, isn't it?

Seu Brandini explained all this to us, demanding the greatest secrecy as to the hour and place of our departure.

It was rumored throughout the city that we would hardly leave until after doing a weekend show, a lie for we would then be in Pesqueira—thus avoiding the creditors. Ah, life was hard.

So we set out on the adventure by land without big complaints. D. Pepa fussed a little, but deep down the old warhorse was proud to be in on such exploits at her age—even with all her weight.

As for me, everything was new. Estrela didn't lose her cool while Seu Brandini ate and slept badly—that is to say, he ate an immense amount, but standing up and at odd hours: an enormous sandwich, a platter of some kind of macaroni casserole, or six fried eggs that Estrela prepared herself in the room on the little alcohol stove which she always carried.

Seu Brandini lived with a pencil in his hand, making calculations, figuring the necessary expenses of freight, moving vans, passage and baggage on the ships and train fare from Pitapora to Belo Horizonte.

As for the boardinghouse in Recife, the total payment was postponed until later; however, it was necessary to give some little something now on account, or the Portuguese operator was capable of putting the police on our trail. Each one was to take care of his own bills at the bars and coffee shops. Still to be paid were the orchestra extras, but Seu Brandini had a confidential talk with them. In the end they were practically colleagues; artists and colleagues don't cheat one another. Estrela, half frightened, asked: "But you aren't going to give them a check, are you?"

"What? Just imagine! A check to a musician! I am going to give them some IOUs. An IOU is the same as money. In the companies in which I first worked I never received any salary, I only got IOUs."

Estrela smiled sadly.

"Poor musicians!"

Then Seu Brandini, who was already as nervous as a cat in a thunderstorm, got wild.

"Why, poor? Poor only if I gave them nothing, and left without doing anything about it! I gave IOUs—to prove my good faith! When I have the money I pay. And that's a lot more than many people do!"

He went out the door, grousing that his wife didn't understand anything about accounts or administration.

We had thought that the greatest problem would be to get the packing boxes with the scenery out of the theater without alerting anyone. But as we were ending our contract it was the owners of the house themselves who asked us to remove the scenery; and even then Seu Brandini delayed the matter for some days (while they objected) so it could be sent directly to the train station, and he wouldn't have to pay storage in a warehouse.

Seu Brandini spoke high-handedly to the director (to whom he owed money) saying that he was negotiating with another movie house—and he even mentioned the name of one, I forget which—and the man was offended: If Seu Brandini wished he could extend the contract; it wouldn't be necessary to go to a competitor.

At that suggestion Seu Brandini's face revealed his craftiness, he winked (I saw him, I was there with Estrela and Odair) and said no, that these pastures were already exhausted, that he was going to experiment in a new area with new customers. Recife still had many publics to be exploited, and he calmly offered to sign a promissory note for the rest of the debt.

But the man didn't want that—the business of a promissory note with an impresario was always a headache.

"I shall be expecting you to pay me with the box office receipts from your new audiences."

As he left, Odair commented that it was difficult to say if the man had any sense at all or if he was a scoundrel. Seu Brandini, who walked in front of us on the sidewalk, decided:"A scoundrel! Does he think he can pull my leg?"

Poor man. But that was the normal way Seu Brandini functioned in time of crisis. When he was preparing to cheat someone he had to be very mad with the person in order to get tough. If he cooled down he became remorseful and would bungle everything up. But to pull the rug from under the feet of a shameless person gave him no remorse at all. "Better he than I. Charity begins at home. If I give him an inch, he'll take a mile. If I don't eat breakfast off him, he'll eat lunch off me." He had millions of proverbs for every occasion.

We left Recife on a rainy morning. Morning? No, dawn. And with that wartime activity on all the trains, the trick was to go to the station in the middle of the night or ride standing up.

It was a very tiny train with cars like that little one we traveled on at home in Aroeiras. The conductor reminded me very much of a cross-eyed acquaintance but he was someone else. He was so similar that he might have been a relative.

What sadness, longing, and unhappiness I had experienced there: My eyes filled with water. Estrela laughed softly.

"You are leaving memories of someone in Recife?"

No, the nostalgia was for something else, but I didn't wish to explain.

I had no yearning for Recife. That experience in the bachelor's quarters—what can't happen, oh God!

I had heard of bachelor quarters, the love nests of single men: they were beautiful in novels; it was natural that I was filled with curiosity.

There was that mill owner's son who didn't miss a single one of our shows, in the front row, eyes glued on the cast. At intervals he would appear in the dressing rooms carrying a glass of beer or port wine. Seu Brandini ordered him outside at once—the gentleman surely knew that the artists were prohibited from drinking in the dressing rooms. (However, Seu Brandini always had a boy bring him a cold beer from the nearby bar.) The friend should understand; after the show there was no objection—outside of the theater, of course!

It wasn't easy to handle him because he was of an important family; and in Pernambuco it is folly to tangle with an important family, or so it was said there.

At first the lad, named José Aldenor, was attracted to Araci, who, as I have already said, was regularly playing her own role in the variety act; and she also took over the small parts that heretofore the extras were paid for. He attached himself to Araci; and such was his bad luck, that the first time he put his foot into our dressing room alone and was sliding his hand over Araci's shoulder as she was making up, Odair walked in asking for his white tie.

(There were only two large dressing rooms, one for the women and the other for the men.) Seeing the character so daring, Odair gave him a couple of punches, and the lad, poor thing, was trembling; and when he found the exit, he pretended he was more drunk than he really was, as if he had put his hand on the girl's shoulder for support, nothing more.

Seu Brandini, I don't know how he got wind of the thing, showed up at once, and grabbed the lad by the scruff of the neck, almost dragging him to put him out. The boy let his legs go rubbery on purpose to impress Odair with his drunkenness.

He was a chap with a small face who always wore a dark three-piece suit; and he had enormous ears, like two wings decorating his head. D. Pepa liked him, but gave him the nickname of Cute Bat—it suited him to a T and it stuck.

On the day after the incident with Araci, Cute Bat missed the performance for the first time; but the next night, Saturday, there he was, with such a big bouquet of carnations and roses that it looked like a funeral wreath.

This time it was for me. When I finished my number, he threw the bouquet at my feet and almost knocked me down, bawling: "Bis! Bis! Long live!"

The theater public is funny. They hadn't applauded me—the number was weak, but seeing that crackpot with such enthusiasm, everybody caught the spirit and began calling Bis! Bis! I almost had a triumph: three curtain calls at the end of the act with Cute Bat heading the claque.

Even so when he came backstage to talk I withdrew from him—tactfully, but I withdrew.

He kept on insisting and I ended up saying emphatically: In our milieu his type, who secretly wanted to make a conquest of all the actresses in a company only for the glory of adding to his collection, was well known. Did he think I hadn't seen his passes at Araci?

But the guy had a gift of gab with his smooth talk, filled with s's. He swore that he threw himself at Araci only to impress me. Since I was conceited, normally I wouldn't have thought twice about him—his trick was to catch me on his rebound.

I accepted a box of chocolates tied with ribbons, a flask of Argentine perfume, and some writing paper with the name "Seduction" painted on the kind of box I thought no longer existed. It was almost like one Laurindo had brought me, years and years before; after the paper was used up I gave the box to Xavinha, who wanted it.

And flowers. And an invitation for sherbet in the Gemba. And an invitation for a spin in his car along the Boa Viagem: ("Accompanied, if you don't trust me.") And a swath of printed silk. And an invitation for lunch in the Floresta dos Leões.

Except for his bat ears, he was pleasant, well-dressed, perfumed, and wore a university ring on his finger. He even had his own car. I went on the drive. I had sherbet. I dined with him. I ended up going to his bachelor's quarters, may God forgive me.

I don't know what I expected, but I didn't expect what I found. In speaking of love nests, I imagined perhaps a house, a little cottage in the middle of a garden, all modern, rich, and elegant.

This was a second-floor room in the new part of a mid-town housing complex, reached by going up a dark cement staircase. Perhaps it was adapted from an office—or an office that doubled for two uses, one by day and the other by night—because one entered through a room with a desk, telephone, and a connecting door with the "nest" or room or *alcova* or whatever it might be.

It had a student bed or cot with a green coverlet and a table with a mirror but not a bevel-edged mirror, just an ordinary mirror hung on the wall. On top of the table a box of the cheapest rice powder said everything; and a black comb.

On the other side of the room was a calendar with the picture of a naked woman. If I live one hundred years, I shall never forget that bachelor's quarters. It was worse than some of those boardinghouse rooms where the cast sometimes stayed. A hundred years? If I live a thousand years, I shall never forget.

I was lucky that he was drunk; he couldn't even park the car straight and left it on the sidewalk.

He went up the staircase, tripping as he went, and he gave me the key to open the door. Entering, I crossed the foyer and went directly to the room. He grabbed me, dragged me to the bed and threw me down on it with him. All dressed and even with his shoes on.

I felt all of my joints stiffen as if they were glass or ice. I didn't resist because I was so ashamed; after all I had come there of my own free will.

But when he fell on the bed and his head hit the pillow, he put his hands around my neck and tried to kiss me, whispering in his smooth talk: "Darling, let's sleep a little while. I am so tired, so tired!"

And he fell asleep holding me. I was sweating, red-faced and furious. I let him get into a deep sleep and then I slowly freed myself. He opened his eyes halfway but fell asleep again.

I slipped out of the bed, went to the mirror, ran a comb through my hair, and escaped by the staircase.

The street below was deserted, happily. On the corner I

117

met a policeman, and I tried to sneak past him; but I didn't succeed.

"Where are you going in such a hurry, beautiful?"

I pretended that I didn't hear and tried to keep going, but he caught my wrist.

"A woman alone in the street, late at night, orders are to take her to jail."

I looked at him, offended.

"Mr. Policeman, I am a girl from a good family. I am passing through Recife, and I came out to buy some medicine for my mother who has a headache. But I don't know my way around the streets and became confused as I looked for a pharmacy. . . ."

I was so nervous I began to cry.

"Now I am lost, and you wish to lock me up!"

The policeman let me go.

"Where do you live?"

He was a new policeman without much experience. I said: "In the Oriente Boardinghouse"—which fortunately was nearby, and the policeman believed me.

He took me to a pharmacy in the next block which was open at night. I bought a bottle of Atroveran—it was the only medicine I could think of. The policeman accompanied me to the corner, to a block of boardinghouses.

"I can't walk with you to the door because I can't leave my beat. Take my advice: When in Recife, if you have to go out at night, arrange to have company. If you go out alone, you can be taken for a streetwalker."

I shook the policeman's hand and thanked him. As I said, he was new, perhaps a recruit, so he didn't expect this and was embarrassed. In farewell he said: "An innocent girl like you doesn't know the risks you run in these streets at night!"

The next day Cute Bat appeared. Fortunately he was ashamed and supposed that I was angry because he fell asleep! I took advantage of his cue and refused to listen to his explanations. When the creature accosted me in the hall, after waiting there I don't know for how long, I withdrew saying simply: "Don't insist. What has happened has happened."

He still caught me by the arm.

"But I can't endure the thought that you are peeved!"

Odair and Araci came by and I left with them. Seu Brandini, who came along afterwards and had been spying on me since I went out the night before and had said nothing as yet to me during the day, pushed me aside when we reached the sidewalk.

"What did you do with Cute Bat? Didn't you go to his slaughterhouse yesterday?"

Ah, so that's what it's called—the slaughterhouse. The name pleased me for it was apt. I talked with Seu Brandini over my shoulder.

"I went, but I returned without a scratch. He was drunk and I escaped. I don't go for this—one time has convinced me."

Seu Brandini gave a satisfied laugh and put his arm around my waist.

"The matador was drunk! It isn't worth it. Leave it alone, girl. You haven't met a real man yet. Those little shits are good for nothing; they aren't worth a damn."

If I remember correctly, Rio Branco was the name of the city where we gave our final impromptu show before abandoning the train. "Blitzkrieg season" Seu Brandini put on the billboards, taking advantage of the word then in vogue because of the war.

Everything was going along well until the night before when I had begun to feel bad because of the arrival of a letter from Xavinha which D. Loura had forwarded to me in Recife.

She said that all was well, even if Senhora continued to have her chronic health problems and stubbornly refused to follow the doctor's orders. She, Xavinha, was sorry to have to tell me some fairly unpleasant news which was going around Aroeiras:

Just imagine, a woman who lives on the heights of Santo Antonio went to carry a little cross for the grave of her angel son who had been buried the night before in the cemetery, and when she was returning at twilight, and passed near the late Laurindo's tomb, she heard some sighs coming from there. Frightened, she ran and spoke to everyone she met, and the people took it upon themselves to go to the cemetery to verify her tale. You know how it is with superstition; many people claimed that they, too, had heard the sighs.

"My savior Jesus, what can that mean?" asked Xavinha, and I asked myself the same question, more worried than she.

She ended the letter by saying that when the buzzing reached Senhora's ears, she sent Antônio Amador to the woman's house with the threat: Either she would cease her charades or she, Senhora, would have to report the matter to the police. Xavinha, for her part, had a mass said, and every night with the girls she recited the litanies for a blessing on Laurindo's soul—may he rest in peace!

As for myself, I confess that I got goose pimples. Who could that creature be, and why did such an awful person come to dig around in the grave of the dead?

However, in certain respects I had confidence in Senhora's interference. She was woman enough to make the officer of the law apply a dozen blows to the scandalmonger, in spite of the fact that today it isn't as it was in the old days, when she made them give a thrashing to a former servant girl who had fled Soledade and went around speaking ill of the house. But even today the law officer was a friend of hers and came to the fazenda on Sundays, bringing traps under his arms to catch canaries for his cages. People said that the devil loved jails so much that he wasn't content to imprison Christians; he even had to put wild creatures behind bars.

But he—what was his name, Dôra? Braulino, yes, I remember that it was Braulino—used to say he only caught the canaries because he was crazy about their singing, and he would put red pepper in their food so they could trill better. But one of our half-breed peasants was put in jail one day, and he discovered that Braulino liked the canaries, all right; but it was to sell them in Fortaleza as "fighter canaries," much sought after birds in the city.

What if Delmiro heard about the story of the sighs, even though it might be a lie, and also got frightened? Might he not beat on his chest and confess his sins? And the whole point was that his judgment was already shaken. Could I

120

ever forget the day when he made his confession to me? There are always people like him who have a mania for confession.

I recalled the pleasure with which he beat his chest that morning when he confessed to me and said, "I am at your feet, amen, amen." And he cried and cursed himself: "Savior Jesus, have pity on this miserable sinner." Poor Delmiro, as if we all aren't sinners, amen, amen.

The following night's performance, the first that we gave there in Rio Branco, was only a variety act—I sang a very sad tango that went like this: "Where are you, my heart, I don't hear you beating . . ." and I left the stage crying. It is understandable that I was nervous, with so much remembrance, unease, and unhappy presentiments.

The railroad line ended there and we began the long overland trip by truck.

Seu Ladislau was waiting for us with two freight trucks, the larger still in good shape; but the smaller, an old all-purpose truck, was falling to pieces.

Neither of the two had a steel cabin, as they usually came from the factory closed up and hot as ovens; the truck owners were ingenious about changing the steel cabins to wood. They were spacious: Three passengers could fit in alongside the driver.

The four women of the company were divided—two in each truck. There being but one other place on the driver's seat for the men, all of them took turns, except Seu Brandini, of course, who being the impresario naturally had his place reserved with Estrela and me in the first truck. The others, when it was not their turn in the driver's seat, rode on top of our sizable load of baggage and scenery.

We left early in the morning, almost at daybreak, most of us fuming because there had been a performance the evening before and afterwards we had to pack the curtains, costumes, and props. Some didn't even have time to go to bed. Estrela wanted to bring some provisions for the journey, but Seu Brandini wouldn't let her—hear, hear, there were plenty of eating places along the road. Fortunately, she insisted on taking along some packages of biscuits and bananas that she had kept in her room. I brought two cans of condensed milk and an apple.

Around eight o'clock in the morning we passed a little

121

place where everybody got coffee with millet bread for breakfast. At least we weren't famished.

But by midday the smaller truck had the first of its breakdowns—I never forgot the cause of those breakdowns; however, even today I don't know precisely what is meant by a broken piston rod.

We stopped at the cries and honks of the others, who were fairly far behind to avoid the dust we kicked up. That piston rod couldn't be repaired quickly—twelve-thirty passed, then one o'clock, then two o'clock. We got hungry.

We didn't suffer from thirst as each truck carried its own leather bag full of water, hung on the outside of the body; to our amazement the water was quite cold as if it hadn't been in the sun.

This place was far away from everything, and even seemed to be the "heel of the world," with no trees whatever, only the sparse leafless vegetation—it was mid-November. Even I was astonished, used as I was to the rigors of a northeastern summer; but our tablelands weren't so bare—May God spare you those forlorn dry lands.

The drivers worked on the truck while the other men kibitzed; the women sat on the rocky ground in the shade of the larger truck—there was no other shade. D. Pepa put her hand in her sack and pulled out a can of sardines. Nobody had a can opener so she went to beg the men for a knife. Seu Brandini, hearing sardines mentioned, realized he was hungry; he called the cast together and appealed for the spirit of solidarity: "Whoever has food should share it among all in a brotherly way. As in war, as in war!"

A newspaper was spread on the ground; all in all we gathered together two cans of sardines (the other came from the maestro), bananas, crackers, a can of corned beef (from Odair), and a can of sausages—I don't know from whom.

To our amazement, one driver came out from under the car and put a sack of manioc meal and brown sugar on the seat. I gave up only one of my cans of condensed milk. Estrela told me to keep the other for later—we didn't know yet what was ahead, and she held back the biscuits.

The meal finished, Seu Brandini made a hole in my can of condensed milk and gave each person a sip—it was dessert. And Seu Ladislau gave his little speech: Everybody was behaving in the spirit of a picnic.

122

* * *

Although I feigned relaxation, I was deep in thought, anxious as I was about that cursed letter from Xavinha. Fortunately I didn't believe the story of the sighs—but fear doesn't depend on belief or disbelief: Fear enters through the heart; believe me, it seeps into the pores.

You may not have religion, go to mass or confession, or pay attention to the father's sermon: but when you find yourself on a dark night in some terrifying place, you might say out of bravado that you aren't afraid; but you are afraid, yes, and if no one is looking you cross yourself just in case.

At Soledade for years I was afraid of a certain ghost which an old neighbor told Senhora about:

A man from Areias Pretas, well known at our home, went out of his house in the middle of a clear moonlit night to defecate on the ground; suddenly he saw in front of him an enormous figure, some three spans tall, who had a big head without a neck and a very red tongue hanging out. Our poor man was scared stiff and turned to go back into the house, all the time pulling up his trousers. Then the figure gave a sort of laugh, shot out a long arm and gave a little slap on the man's behind, as if he were joking.

Hours later his wife, missing him, went in search and found the poor man incoherent, lying in the entryway; and on his exposed buttock was a burn on the naked skin in the form of a big hand.

The unhappy man regained his senses only three days later and told his story. From then on he died bit by bit, and within a few months he had departed this world.

I knew this man very well, and for years I had a deadly fear of such a ghost. If I was outside at night by myself, I made the sign of the cross time after time until I was safely inside. Yes, they said that when the man died, the burn that had almost healed turned red and was irritated again as it was on the first day after he met the ghost.

Now there were those rumors of the sighs from Laurindo's tomb and the people's evil sayings which came to burn me like the mark of the devil's hand on the body of the man from Areias Pretas. I thought most about Delmiro—oh God, it even seemed that I was seeing him in the flesh. If the old man's crazy notion was to seek someone to whom he could confess, perhaps Senhora, whom he feared and hated, he

123

would kneel on the ground, tear open his shirt and pour out his sins. Senhora, I knew, would wish only to cover up everything. But she couldn't tie people's tongues. And what then? What then?

I vowed that at the first city I reached, I would telegraph Xavinha asking for news. But when I took the pencil and began to write a telegram on a piece of wrapping paper (the repair of the piston rod continued), I discovered that a telegram was impossible.

What would I ask? "Beg news sighs Laurindo's grave"? Or: "Report if Delmiro confessed"?

Senhora would still be able to understand my coded words—I was certain that she was no fool about what had happened: She knew as much as I. But how could I guess what was going on in that hard heart that never held any love for me?

The look in those cat eyes which she fixed on me that day when we were on opposite sides of Laurindo's coffin, Senhora white as the whitewashed wall behind her; and her mouth tightly shut in a line which hid her lips and appeared to be a scar—ah, no, not she! She wouldn't reveal anything.

Besides, I didn't dare. I didn't dare appeal to her. However, most probably she would be on my side, for fear of a scandal. But I couldn't be sure, I couldn't swear that Senhora, furious because of my independence and the new kind of life I was leading, might not suddenly and openly take the side of the dead one.

What would she gain by openly declaring her love for him?—and only God and I could imagine what that love could be, for she understood neither pain nor sin and crushed me under her feet. If it were not for that fatal "accidental" shot, how would all of this have ended? When the sign of the devil's hand pained and burned her what would she do?

No, Senhora, no. You can't let this all be brought into the open.

In another letter which came earlier—didn't I mention it?—Xavinha wrote about Delmiro, ever more loony and withdrawn. And he seemed to be sick and thin, and had swollen feet. People said that he would end up mute because he talked so little with anyone.

124

At one time his muteness had left me free of anxiety. I could see the old man again, on his slanted tile roof, putting cracked corn out for the birds. Also that quick smile when he saw me, and the presents he gave me. And the dead wild duck, still warm in my hands.

What hell, what torment! They finally fixed the piston rod and the trucks left, only now the small truck went ahead of us so that in case of another breakdown the people in it wouldn't lose sight of us, and we wouldn't have to turn back.

Estrela began to sing a sad folksong. Seu Brandini crossed his arms and buried his head on his chest, no doubt thinking about his weighty problems.

I wanted to get away from that piston rod and walk to Soledade to see for myself what was going on there. Well, if I wished to go, I could, for I only had to find transportation to Crato and from there take the train.

Perhaps everything at home had already exploded: the secret of that cursed moonlit night, the two voices, the little donkey below, and Delmiro overhearing everything and consoling me in my desolate weeping.

Yes, and what if Delmiro, crazier now than ever and fearing the deceased's sighs, should suddenly expose us, Senhora and me, for all the world to see the marks of the devil's hand on our bodies?

We traveled all afternoon and part of the night. Close to one A.M. we arrived at a poor hamlet that was asleep; it was hardly more than a street of houses on the highway's edge.

The truck's headlights lit up a beer ad and the sign "Tourist Home" above the door.

Seu Brandini knocked on the closed door with authority. Some time passed. He knocked again and then a woman wrapped up in a sheet appeared.

Scowling, she opened the door, lit a candle, and asked how many of us there were.

We were counted: twelve, including the drivers. Seu Brandini asked: "Do you have room for all of us?"

Yes, she had room; and then Seu Brandini asked her to arrange the twelve beds for a dozen travelers who were worn out.

Ah, she had no beds, only hammocks. And she didn't have twelve of these, only eight at most.

One of the drivers said that they didn't need hammocks; they had brought their own. They weren't going to sleep in the pension; they would sleep between the trucks and guard the luggage.

Seu Brandini pushed his way into the house and we followed; he swept the woman aside, entered, went through several rooms and finally discovered in an alcove a plain bed with a straw mattress.

"I will stay in this room with my wife!"

But the lady of the pension protested that the bed was reserved for a traveling salesman client who was due to arrive early in the morning, and he didn't fare well in a hammock. Seu Brandini cut in.

"Worse than I? I doubt it!"

Estrela explained it was only for the rest of the night; early in the morning we would be going. The woman still muttered but Seu Brandini cut her short.

"And now, big flower, go get the hammocks; the problem is solved. Not counting the drivers, and with my wife and me in the bed, we need exactly eight hammocks."

Then it was D. Pepa's turn to object; never in her life had she slept in a hammock and she had no intention of beginning at her age. Seu Brandini gallantly offered to sleep with her in the plain bed.

D. Pepa shook her cane in his face: "You think I am afraid? I shall sleep with my cane between us like the sword between Tristan and Isolde!"

Seu Brandini began shouting: "Do you think, Pepa, that you could tempt me?"

D. Pepa retorted that in Spain there is the saying: "In the dark a scullery maid is like a queen!"

At that point Estrela threw water on the blaze by saying that D. Pepa would sleep in the bed, but with her, Estrela. Let Carleto settle himself in a hammock. Seu Brandini protested no more. The woman came with hammocks, and he reached out for the one on top.

When I went to arrange my hammock in their room, I could see that the bed filled it (I recalled our alcove at Soledade where the hammock also couldn't fit). I ended up being in a little side room with the connecting door open. Just like that other one, a thousand years ago.

126

While we were putting up the hammocks, a boy announced that supper was ready; but we would have to eat in the kitchen because people were sleeping in the dining room. The owner of the house had put her son there to make more room available for us.

The table was leaning against a dingy wall, and on this wall a hanging lamp provided light, making a big black funnel of soot. There was a porringer of clabber, some fried eggs mixed with flour, a plate with some slices of roasted goat meat. Never had we eaten anything so good; it dissolved in the mouth like a biscuit—and a pot filled with coffee that was very hot, very black, and very sweet.

If the troupe hadn't been on guard, Seu Brandini would have eaten up all the meat; he found it a delicacy, but then he went on to the eggs. At such times Seu Brandini was a glutton, but he excused himself, saying that he suffered from diabetes.

Finally, our hunger satisfied, each one of us fell into his hammock as he could and Seu Brandini, from the room in front of ours, sighed in his stage voice: "Pepa, cruel Pepa!"

Estrela shushed him while D. Pepa replied with her gross laugh; but the joke didn't come off, everybody was so overcome from the terrible trip: the highway, dust, and fatigue. All of us put out our lights.

My body ached all over. My head, too—I had a stabbing pain above the eye; and the crushed letter was smoldering in my blouse pocket. It seemed that it was even burning my breast. It had only to talk. I couldn't even cry: Crying can help a lot; it is the consolation of the afflicted, but I only had a choking in my throat and the agony of insomnia.

About then one of the men in the next room got up. I heard him open the door and go out; after a little time he returned, walking softly on the brick floor of the hall.

My door, closed but unlocked because I hadn't found the key in it, opened slowly, creaking; and for a moment I remembered how in that other house, at another time, Laurindo would open the door connecting his room with the *alcova* and came to seek me.

I breathed deeply as I heard the man's short breaths; one hand grasped the cords of my hammock, the other groped for my body.

I could have cried out—I almost did, but I kept quiet. There would be a big uproar, everybody getting up, the

127

man running—what good would that do? And then I got another impulse.

I took the hand that was groping for my breast; when he felt my fingers he opened them and let his hand be guided, and I put that hand to my mouth as if to kiss it. The man was already taking the other hand from the hammock's cord and was grabbing my knee. I opened my mouth on that hairy hand smelling of smoke and sank my teeth into it with all the force I had.

At the same time I freed my knee, which he had covered with his other hand and with it pushed his body that was bent over the hammock with every ounce of my strength. I don't know where I planted my knee, perhaps in his groin; I felt blood in my mouth, and the man pulled his wounded hand from my mouth with such force that my lips were bruised.

But he didn't utter a word; he only groaned like a wounded animal. I hissed between my teeth like a snake: ''Get out at once, or I shall scream!''

He went running in his bare feet to reach the hall without even bothering to close the door.

When I had stretched out in the hammock earlier, I had put a box of matches on the little table at my bedside as I was accustomed to do ever since I joined the company. (Later the Captain gave me a tiny flashlight which I still have today.) I groped in the dark, found the matches, lit one, covering the flame with my hand so as not to awaken Estrela or D. Pepa in the next room with the door open to mine.

I spit that blood in my mouth on the floor with disgust. On the little table at the side of their bed I had seen a small jug of water and I had an urge to get a little water to wash my mouth out, otherwise I was going to vomit.

Fortunately the little table was on the side next to the connecting door to my room and I only needed to light one more match; even so, when I, while controlling my queasiness, carried the big cup to my mouth, Estrela sat up in the bed, frightened.

''What's wrong, who is it?''

''It is I, I came to get some water, I was dying of thirst, excuse me.''

Estrela still said: ''I had a scare!'' and she lay down again.

I took advantage of this, filled the cup again, and drank

like a fool; now that all was over, my heart beat as if it would leap out of my mouth.

Who was that dirty man? I didn't recognize the hand, I only caught the smell of smoke—but, well, everybody smoked. I lit another match, closed my door to the hall, and put the little table against it—at least it would make a noise if anyone pushed it open.

I lay down again, my headache was worse than ever and I expected to spend the entire night awake. In spite of all the water, I spit on the floor again with disgust.

Then I fell asleep so quickly that I didn't know how it happened. The next thing I knew it was early morning. Estrela shook my shoulders, saying it was time to get up.

Again, trouble with the piston rod of the little truck held us up still another day and night.

The second day was better than the previous one only because we at least had lunch—a roasted hen, rice, and bananas at the highway's edge in a thatched country store. The cooking was done outdoors with a clay pot on top of a triangle of stones. There was also fried fish and sweet potatoes. Fresh-water fish! What a banquet!

I looked at the men's hands to see if I could discover my teeth marks on any one of them. But the people around the counter of the store were eating standing up, hence no one showed his hands as at a table.

Antenor, the prompter, installed himself and D. Pepa on a little pile of bricks which the woman of the store had on hand to build "a good oven, with an iron grill instead of that crazy pile of stones."

"Cooking while squatting destroys people's spines!"

D. Pepa pushed Antenor away.

"Go on, fatty!"

Antenor waved his plump hands in the air. They were fat and covered with dirt but free of any wounds. It wasn't he!

"Fatty! Look who's talking! I only have fat hands and legs. You, Pepa, are the opposite: You are fat from stern to prow—all of the weight is in the middle of the boat."

D. Pepa hesitated as she toyed with a bone and then took another chicken thigh.

"That's true but I detest fat people! If I could I would

129

scrape off this fat of mine with a knife and be as thin as a string. I am a fat cat, but I have the soul of a swallow!"

I was looking at right hands only, but then I remembered: What if the person were left-handed? Just when I got that idea lunch was over and the entire company returned to the trucks, and I couldn't discover anything more at that time.

This time it was I who was silent with my chin on my chest. I didn't want Seu Brandini to joke with me. Estrela pleaded: "Carleto, leave the girl alone. Do you think everybody is a nut and laughs all the time, like you?"

If it had occurred months before, that night attack would certainly have frightened me, insulted me, and perhaps made me run far away. Just imagine, a man whom I didn't know, in the dark—in my room!—putting his hands on me.

If Senhora knew this, what would she say? At that point I laughed. "Whore!" at the least. A whore is one in whose room a man enters at night.

A new way of life teaches quickly, and I had learned a lot in the company. A man is not a beast; he is a human being, a person like me; his law is to attack. A woman who doesn't want to defend herself as a man surrenders. Seu Brandini had his saying in this respect: "You ask all, one in a hundred gives, you give if you wish to do so. The asking is no affront." "Two can't fight—or frolic—unless both want to": also an adage of Seu Brandini. Ah, he was an expert in this respect. "If you don't wish, you don't wish; no evil intended, my dear; the thing is to try another, there's no offense."

Avoid making a scene, calling people, scattering blood because a man pats you lightly with his hand or looks at you on the sly.

The old Maria Milagre used to tell the story of a young girl who went to the king's palace to complain: The prince had wronged her against her will, and she came to demand redress.

Then the king sent for a needle and a piece of thread and said he would hold the needle and the girl should try to thread it. The girl took the thread, twisted it, wet it lightly, and made it thin; but every time she tried to put the end of the thread into the needle's eye, the king would move his hand and the thread didn't go in. Finally the girl lost her patience.

"King, my sir, if you play the game this way, there is no seamstress who can thread that needle!"

Then the king said: "So it is when my son, the prince, wishes to sew with you; if you had withdrawn the needle, he could not have made the connection. Go away, woman, for you weren't born for a king's son!"

It does no good to be offended because there is the type of man who asks as if he were making a pleasantry, as if he might be saying good morning, good night, it's a nice day, isn't it? She who wishes to, accepts; she who doesn't goes her way.

D. Pepa also had her proverb: "It's a game which takes two to play."

Well, all I wish to say is that before I joined the company, I held my body as if it were something detached that I kept in reserve, that I could give only to the legitimate owner; and after giving it to this owner, it was solely his. It didn't matter whether I wished to govern my own body or not, because I didn't have that right; I lived within it, but the body wasn't mine.

Now my body was mine, to keep or to give, as I wished. I would give if I wished; if I didn't I wouldn't give; that was all there was to it. This change made a tremendous difference to me, a tremendous difference.

It isn't that I wished to give to this one or that one. Most of the time I didn't wish to give to anyone; actually I thought very little about it. What I had already suffered was enough. But the important thing was to know that what happened depended solely on me, without the threat of a shot or a knife, without death for the man or dishonor for anyone.

If what happened the night before had occurred in former times, most likely I would have run to Seu Brandini to tattle and ask his protection; I would have the attacker declared mentally deranged, demand the police, jail. Now, no; it was my own private business only.

I couldn't have any peace of mind, however, as long as I didn't discover the culprit; it was necessary to know for my own protection. Who knows, I might innocently treat the man decently—after all, we were all companions. The cast formed a sort of brotherhood, half disunited and different each from the other, but a brotherhood all the same. Above all, after we made that overland trip—Seu Ladislau wasn't joking when he said that now we were a band of Captain Carleto's gypsies, and he called Brandini *gangão*—"gypsy king"—which Seu Brandini loved as it was a term of honor.

After nearly three days of dust, a broken piston rod, aching bodies on those impossible seats (I covered a broken spring under mine with a piece of cloth to keep the wire from jabbing me), hunger, abundance and protests, we finally made it to Petrolina.

A city I shall never forget. At that time it was a tiny place with an imposing cathedral rising up in the midst of wretched houses; it looked like a big house surrounded by a herd of sheep. We found the town strange and beautiful.

Our caravan went directly to the boardinghouse, one that was very much like the others on the road. Even the owners seemed the same: However, this one in Petrolina, who was full of smiles and agreeable, offered hammocks for the women—even a bath in the garden shower house—and afterwards an excellent lunch.

But Seu Ladislau wouldn't allow us to touch the large baggage because our destination was Juazeiro da Bahia, on the other side of the São Francisco River; and the trucks still had to cross by ferry to reach it.

At that time Juazeiro was more important than Petrolina. I don't know if it still is today; but in Juazeiro our show had a contract arranged by telegram, and hotel rooms awaited us.

While we were still in Petrolina, and sat at the table for lunch, the pianist, who was in front of me, calmly put his hand on top of the table cloth. There for everybody to see, on the back of his right hand, at the base of his little finger, was the mark of my teeth in the form of a half-moon.

It was natural that I should taste his blood again: My

132

teeth had sunk deep, and the bite was now inflamed and red.

I also blushed upon making the discovery, as if perhaps I were the guilty one. So, I lifted my eyes slowly from his hand to the man's face, and that shameless bastard was smiling at me as if he were showing me something beautiful!

I believe that I have spoken of how irritating this pianist was only in passing—we called him Seu Jota do Piano. In our daily life he was hardly of any importance; but at showtime he took his revenge—then he was a tyrant. Even Seu Brandini obeyed him; he wanted to be the maestro with a baton in his hand, and for this it was enough to gather together two musicians, three with himself. He played any instrument whatsoever; he was master of the guitar, but wouldn't put his hand to it except only when the plot of the play demanded it or when some other instrument was lacking. He said the guitar wasn't an instrument for musical comedy. He preferred the piano, flute, and concertina which he simply called accordion.

He said he was a true cariocan, "of the yolk born in Praça Onze"; he was tall and scrawny, with a little mustache and thin, long hair, parted on the side; his color if not altogether white, was pale, I don't know if from birth or from the lack of sun. He thought he was tops in music and didn't take his hat off to Noel Rosa, whom he knew when Rosa was alive, or to Ari Barroso, the king. Whenever he could he would put into our repertory a samba of his own composition, although I fear that in this matter of authorship, Seu Jota followed Seu Brandini's example, and passed off as his own much work that was taken from someone else. Who could question him?

In general nobody in the company liked this Jota do Piano very much; at rehearsal times he would scream at the actors; offend them, and say mean things; even Estrela lost her patience at times.

"Enough! Toscanini!"

D. Pepa gave him tit for tat. He respected the Spaniard, perhaps because she never sang anything and only entered the fun choruses, got off key, and said she was out of breath.

Yes, Seu Jota do Piano's name, as it was printed on his compositions (I only saw one such composition; but he said

133

that he had many, many more, published by the Vitale Brothers) was J. Narciso. But the members of our company always called him Jota do Piano.

He had been most demanding of me; at times I hated him so much that I cried; he would give me the pitch before the overture and then at the beginning of the number stop everything because I was off key.

"Girl, do you think you are singing in a church choir?"

Or then: "Stop, stop, dearie, that's the beat of a litany!"

And if I hurried up he also stopped me.

"This isn't the beat of a voodoo dance; this is a samba, child, a samba of Rio. Listen to the beat! Follow the beat of the *cuica*. What the hell!"

And I would stop, sulk, sit down, and swear I wouldn't rehearse anymore. Seu Brandini would comfort me, saying it was all nonsense, it wasn't important, it was only the maestro's fiddle-faddle.

"After all, you didn't sign a contract as a soprano. You are an actress of legitimate theater!"

Well, I don't know if I was that kind of an actress, but a singer I certainly was not. I only sang a little to fill in, and no one could expect me to be a Carmen Miranda.

The pianist would look at me and Seu Brandini with a sneering smile. I would get up, return to the stage and the rehearsal would begin all over again. He would continue with the same bad temper. We all hated him. Odair, who at that time wasn't a singer by any means, had a fight with him once; we were still in Fortaleza and the two went rolling in the middle of the aisle. Seu Brandini even reprimanded both on the bulletin board.

From that incident came malicious gossip. Seu Jota began to spread the rumor among us that Odair was letting his wife go out with a rich old man. "He is in the habit of 'taking the siesta' all alone locked up in his room, and sends Araci out, to go to the movies; whoever wishes can see the little doll getting into the old man's automobile. Meanwhile the husband is taking his siesta."

I don't know if Odair got wind of the rumors, or if they were true or not; D. Pepa said that "the magician's girl had hot pants." But there was no new fight. Perhaps after the censure on the bulletin board Odair was afraid of being fired, knowing that he was in the weaker position of the two. The other was more important because of his ability to create "arrangements." Even a maestro as insignificant as Seu Jota do Piano would be more difficult to replace.

Aware of the general antipathy against him, Seu Jota never joined the rest of us when we were relaxing. He spent his time with Antenor do Ponto and the *contra-regra* or property man. To economize they would take a room together in a boardinghouse in a red-light district—he called it "a Bohemian section."

It was also said there was a special friendship between Antenor and the *contra-regra*—what was his name? I think it was Euclides, but nobody ever called him that—it was only "*Contra-Regra* this," and "*Contra-Regra* that," as if *contra-regra* were his name.

People said that Antenor, with his roly-poly body, and *Contra-Regra*, a big strong mulatto, formed a couple; if they were ill matched in appearance, they were well matched in the heart.

For a long time Seu Jota do Piano made no mystery about the fact that he was a fool about women; he even boasted about it. Happily, he didn't bother the actresses; they weren't there for his enjoyment. Seu Brandini had already roared this more than a thousand times whenever he made passes at the girls.

But that miserable bastard dared to take advantage of the trip to try me out—and he was insolent enough to show off the bruised hand as if it were a proof of intimacy, a secret between the two of us!

I was purple with rage, I looked him straight in the eye, challenging anything he might say. The shameless one met my eyes, didn't hold them very long, and then turned to Seu Brandini, asking if he should round up some singers in Juazeiro.

Seu Jota was also in charge of locating the extras for Seu Brandini to hire for the troupe's stay in some local place; and in general, he kept on hand many no-good women who took advantage of the occasion to be on the stage, and afterwards they claimed that they were actresses.

At times some little girl would appear who was already off on the wrong foot, a widow's daughter, a waitress, or an apprentice in a factory who dreamed of running off with us and making a career in the theater. But only rarely did Seu Brandini accept these types because in the end it always ended up in fights with the family or with some judge for the protection of minors.

"Work on the stage is for professionals!" he would cry. "An amateur girl is a key to jail."

In Juazeiro, the next day, Seu Brandini wanted to have a beer and we entered a bar. It was between lunch and rehearsal; inside only one other table was occupied besides ours. Three men were there, two short ones and a tall one. The tall one was pouring beer for the other two.

I fell for the tall one. At long last the one I had been waiting for. Tall, handsome, and he appeared not to be *simpatico*. He spoke in an imperial manner, as if he gave orders to the other two. Dark, very dark, black hair, straight like an Indian's. He had a fine head and a muscular neck which emerged from the open collar of his yellow shirt, and his large shoulders matched the neck.

I thought, what a handsome man. And it seemed that he also perceived himself handsome, because he looked around as if he owned the world. The corners of his mouth were turned down a little; his glance rested on Estrela and me—more on Estrela than on me. She sensed the preference because she smiled a little and spoke with me out of the corner of her mouth, putting her head close to mine.

"Did you see the handsome man looking at us?"

Seu Brandini, who had his back to us staring at the other table, wanted to know what we were whispering about; he couldn't tolerate whispering without being in on it, saying that it showed lack of breeding.

Estrela explained. Seu Brandini turned to look. Like a rude child he always did this when someone nearby was referred to; at times his stare embarrassed us.

Then he said that he saw nothing handsome about that face: "Rudolph Valentino was a handsome man and he died of colic!"

Estrela and I looked at each other with understanding. Seu Brandini was offended and began explaining one of his theories—that the world belonged to the ugly people: One never saw a president or a dictator or even an important artist who wasn't ugly. The handsome ones thought they had a right to everything just because they were handsome. They didn't have to fight for anything and expected everything to fall into their laps. A handsome actor might well succeed in the movies; everybody knows that in the movies an actor is but a puppet in the hands of the director. He sits, stands, grabs the attractive young women, kisses, no, he is weak, and presto, he is cut. He had watched filming, he knew.

"But in the theater when the curtain went up, the hour of truth between the actor and the public has arrived, and he who doesn't have guts can't deliver the goods."

Just see if Chaby Pinheiro (he was his idol), or Leopold Fróis, or Brandão Sobrinho, or Procópio had pretty faces for Mamma to kiss! No, it was all talent, that was the essential thing.

But just put on the stage one of these not-too-bright youths from among those who can only make an impression: They can't deliver at their exit any more than at their entrance!

"If perchance I were handsome, would I have been able to accomplish what I have? I got where I am because I am ugly, with a big stomach, almost big-toothed, and with a tendency to baldness!"

Estrela and I were laughing at so much modesty, and Seu Brandini was peeved because we didn't accept his reasoning.

"Now, take Napoleon, you know who the Emperor Napoleon was, don't you? Wasn't he ugly? He was short, more pot-bellied than I, and bald-headed to boot. He was master of the world! He had all the women he wanted because women might like the handsome ones but prefer the ugly ones. Hitler is ridiculous and Mussolini even worse, with that big bull head and neck, like a huge fantoche on a Carnival float. Handsome, bah! I wipe my hands of them! Boy, another beer!"

As for the handsome man, he was still looking at us, perhaps half-intrigued with Seu Brandini's loud-mouthed argument; however, the bar was big and the man wouldn't be able to hear very well from where he sat. Then one of his companions looked at his watch; they called the waiter, paid, and got up to leave.

As I had guessed when I saw him seated, he was indeed tall and towered over the other two almost by a head. Before leaving he stood for an instant, looking at the two of us—more at me or more at Estrela?—behind Seu Brandini's back who, still muttering, just then knocked over the glass of beer.

They left.

I don't say that I had then discovered the man of my life. But I wanted him to be so, how I desired him. A handsome man like that, even if not *simpatico*—I don't know, I always went for handsome men.

Estrela commented to her husband: "You spoke so much about ugliness that you made our handsome man leave."

Seu Brandini, who had now finished off his second beer, less the half glass with which Estrela had wet her lips, was still angry and beat on the table with the glass holder.

"Long live the ugly people! Yes, ma'am, long live the ugly ones! I'm going to order another beer, do you want one, girl?"

I didn't wish anything. I felt queasy. Still that devilish letter. Worn at the corners and crushed in my blouse pocket, it was still troubling me.

At the rehearsal Jota do Piano was already there on his high horse ready to strike like a snake at whomever passed. He began to beat on the music stand with the baton, fussing about our late arrival—including Seu Brandini, can you beat that! Two local musicians were already there; one of them was playing the clarinet and suddenly raised to his mouth a type of cornet and played a solo, and nothing was ever more beautiful. Seu Brandini was enthusiastic.

"You have a contract! What are you doing in this end of the world, boy, come to Rio with us!"

But the boy explained that he suffered from weak lungs; he could only play there once in a while, and if he left Juazeiro he would have a relapse. For that reason he even had to leave the marine band; he couldn't tolerate the seacoast climate.

The other musician had an accordion, but he could play only a backwoods song and that too loud, he pushed the bellows with force; it was good for a shindig, but it wasn't a suitable accompaniment for us.

The boy with the clarinet knew someone who could play the guitar in an acceptable way, but by ear. The man with the accordion, mad because he had been thrust aside, worked the bellows and began a devilish schottische that made everybody laugh.

Then Seu Jota do Piano called the girls, candidates for the chorus, who were waiting, all of them laughing, seated in the back rows; and they presented themselves, one by one.

Seu Brandini, enthroned on the stage with his legs crossed, made the important decisions; he had each girl go up and began the questions.

"Any experience?"

Of the nine none had had any experience, except a little roly-poly one with short hair who had worked a few days as a mime in a circus pantomime.

And Seu Brandini asked: "Why did you leave the circus?"

"The man didn't pay us and besides he wanted to sleep with us for free."

"Lift up your skirt. Show your legs. Higher. Have you ever worn a bathing suit?"

"Here, no. People are afraid to bathe in the river because of the piranhas."

"Play something, maestro. Let's see who can dance."

But before Seu Jota do Piano could sit down at the piano, the man with the accordion played a leaping step and the girls began to whirl. With time and work four were chosen. Of those rejected, one had varicose veins, another had a front tooth missing; the peroxide blonde with the pretty little face was six months pregnant; the second blonde, a peroxide blonde also, was ill shaped, with joints like a fried chicken.

"Beat those bones against one another and you get sparks!" jeered Seu Brandini.

The four who were selected—a little mulatto with green eyes, "a darling" in Seu Jota's opinion, one with a gold tooth, and the two others just so-so—were sent off to D. Pepa, now in charge of the costumes.

"Go try on the costumes; D. Pepa will make the necessary adjustments. Return in fifteen minutes for the rehearsal. Yes, I pay five milreis per night. Each must bring her own black shoes—stockings aren't necessary."

Then with the same stern face Seu Brandini instructed the maestro about the choreography for the chorus girls (and

because of this Seu Jota bragged that he was also a "chore-
ographer").

Seu Brandini had a soft heart, and so before beginning
the rehearsal of the farce with us, he made a deal with the
accordion player to include an extra musical number in the
variety act—a dance from Algoas to be performed by the
girls: It depended on whether the maestro could work in a
rehearsal. The maestro who was waiting anyway while the
clarinet player went to look for the guitar player, promised
that he would rehearse the act. In the interim he went to the
door with the rejected girls and whispered his thanks to
each one and ended up sliding his hand over the behind of
the skinny one.

He tapped the girl and then snatched back his hand as if it
had been bruised. When he passed me, I saw him patting
the wounded hand.

"Ay, it hurts! Will I need to get a shot for the wild cat's
bite?"

I wanted to scratch his eyes out right then and there. But
finally I thought—sufficient unto the day is the evil thereof.
We have to bear everything, the good and the bad.

He hadn't looked at Estrela; he had looked at me.

That night, the handsome man was there in the theater
(even though it was a movie house), seated in the second
row, this time with four companions. They shouted *"vivas"*
and clapped, and at the end of my tango they stood up and
applauded. Since they were shouting "bis," the entire
house joined the "Bis! Bis!" I gave the encore. What a triumph for me!

Seu Brandini said they were full of beer and that the audience had stood up because they followed the bis and
thought it was the end of the show.

Estrela smiled at me.

"Carleto is jealous."

The ship was a beauty; its big wheel in the stern reminded me of the waterwheel of the mills in the *serra*. It appeared light, as if floating on top of the river, with its upper
deck like the *gaiolas*, the Amazon paddleboats.

On the fourth day after the opening, with only three performances in Juazeiro, we boarded the ship.

Some men from the hold, in a line like umbrella ants, were balanced on the gangplank, each with a bundle of wood for the boiler. Passengers climbed up another gangplank that reached the upper deck, carrying their hand luggage and last-minute bundles. The big baggage was already on board.

The gangplank was narrow, little more than the width of a plank, and I was about in the middle, with Estrela behind me so scared she was stepping on my heels, when I suddenly looked up. I don't know how I managed to keep from fainting.

Leaning on the rail and looking at us, in white uniform and his kepi decorated with gold, was the boat's captain. It was he, the handsome man. Yes, I don't know how I managed not to fall.

He took two steps forward, offered me his right hand, gave the left to Estrela, and helped us jump from the gangplank to the deck's wooden floor. Then he said: "Good morning, I hope you will enjoy the *J. J. Seabra.*"

At first I was confused, thinking that to be his name; but then I remembered the ship's name was *J. J. Seabra*. I broke into a big smile which no one understood; they probably thought I was nervous.

I had supposed that such a riverboat would be a type of launch with the passengers scattered along some benches, nothing more. Oh no, this boat propelled by the big waterwheel was like an ocean liner inside—hardly smaller and more open to the breezes. The salon was on the upper deck protected from rail to rail by large green canvas curtains faded by the sun. Also there were some little staterooms. Later, in the darkness of Minas Gerais, I would come to know a similar one. You could hardly fit into it and you felt as if you had entered a dollhouse. In each stateroom were two bunk beds, one on top of the other. D. Pepa, assigned to be my roommate—we were the two single women—took over the lower bunk; and I roosted on the top.

When the luncheon bell sounded, the boat had already gone a long way up the river. I soon found the São Francisco to be more beautiful than the Amazon, which I knew from Pará, because the Amazon, different from the ocean only in its water being yellow, and having no waves, is in its width and boundless horizon more or less like the ocean—a muddy and smooth ocean.

From this river the people could see land on both sides; and when the ship weighed anchor, the church of Petrolina seemed to be floating on top of the river. One always saw birds in flight, and didn't smell that strong, acrid sea odor when the tide was out; and it didn't toss as on the sea.

For us who came from the hungers of the desert roads and the uncertainties of the piston rod breakdowns, the food was more than excellent; fish from the river, chicken and fried eggs if you wished, and meat.

The core of the company: Seu Brandini, Estrela, D. Pepa, Odair, Araci, Seu Ladislau, and I—we were invited to the Captain's table. Seu Brandini preened with pride and acted as naturally as if he were the captain or as if he were accustomed to eat only at captain's tables.

He ordered beer, and the Captain asked me what the ladies drank. I said I didn't wish anything, only water—water from the São Francisco River! Everybody laughed. I didn't know if it was the custom to drink water from the river or if it was necessary to bring water from the ports. Then the Captain asked if I wouldn't like at least a *guaraná*. At that moment a steward brought a platter, and the Captain said that he supposed I wasn't acquainted with that fish, that, yes, it was from the river and was called *surubim*.

Seu Brandini interrupted before I could answer: "She hated *pirarucu* in Pará."

Somewhat annoyed I cut in: "But that *pirarucu* was salted. I don't like dried fish; *pirarucu* reminded me of the *seca*. You didn't know that during the drought the government sent us bundles and bundles of salted *pirarucu*? To me, it has a rancid taste. It's horrible."

Meanwhile that *surubim* was fresh, each slice enormous, in a coconut sauce, delicious. For the rest of my life I always ate *surubim* when I could get it; unfortunately it is rare.

Sometimes the Captain would get some for me in Rio de Janeiro, but that was much later.

Hardly had the lunch ended when the Captain got up, put on his beret, made a military salute as a sort of joke, and begged to be excused: He was going to the bridge, which is what they called the place where the pilot wheel was. The boat had to cross a channel which was dangerous.

Then everybody began to kid me, even Estrela: that I had made a conquest, that the Captain didn't take his eyes off me, that he was "drooling over me"—this D. Pepa said.

I managed to laugh, embarrassed, saying that I didn't mind their teasing, and deep down I was praying to God that it was all true, that he was drooling over me. I had perceived that this man, if he only wished, could have me in the palm of his hand.

At night after dinner, the sound of a concertina came from second class, from the lower deck. The Captain sent for the player to come up, and it turned out that he was ours, the one from the variety act, who had come along to try his luck upriver on the heels of the company, I suppose.

A dance was improvised and Seu Brandini hurriedly grabbed me to dance. When the music changed the Captain was already standing, waiting for me, and he took me in his arms; and we danced and danced and danced.

In this state of elation nobody's kidding bothered me. I let myself rest against him, and it wasn't cheek-to-cheek dancing only because my chin just reached his chest; but I felt his face in my hair.

The accordion player, a good-for-nothing yet astute person, sensed what was going on and began to play slow love music.

By ten o'clock the bell sounded again, and a sailor came to give a message to the Captain. He let me go and looked at his watch; the accordion player stopped the music.

Then the Captain went to the middle of the salon and explained to the passengers that our little party for today was ended. As always he had to go up to the bridge. He wished all a hearty good night.

While the people were dispersing, he caught my wrist as I was leaving with the others.

"Would you like to go with me and watch the boat going upstream at night?"

He looked at his watch again.

"It is ten fifteen, we ought to have a little moonlight about now. . . ."

It was indeed beautiful from up there, the long river, a bit of moonlight shining on the waters, in the distance the black *mato* forest closing in. From time to time a fish would

143

jump up, the ship was advancing slowly, and from behind came the sound of the turning wheel, going chop, chop, in its own rhythm.

Then the Captain came close to me at the rail, put his hand on my shoulder; we were silent a long time, just looking at the river.

It wasn't he who piloted the ship as I had thought. It was another man handling the big wheel—the Captain called him Zequinha and the others Seu Zeca Piloto. I asked the Captain if he shouldn't be steering the ship, and he laughed, saying that Zequinha knew the channels of the river much better than any captain.

We looked at the river again. I sighed, he sighed, as if in one breath, and we both laughed. We were silent again, and I said something about the river being so long and serene; and he said that up above Pirapora the river was different.

"Pirapora is still in Minas, isn't it?" I asked.

"Yes, it's in Minas. I was born there."

I had never known anyone born in Pirapora, and suddenly that seemed to me a marvelous circumstance.

"Well, yes, I was born in a little hamlet some distance from the river when my father was trying to be a farmer. By the time I began to creep he was already convinced that he wasn't made for agriculture; and he moved to town, opened a farm store, and failed. Afterwards he went to Juiz de Fora to work in a factory, but that didn't pan out either; he then began to travel for an agriculture firm—he considered himself knowledgeable in that line due to his experience in the Pirapora store—which failed—while the family continued to live in Juiz de Fora."

As a youth the Captain went to school for a while. Later, following his father's example, he beat around here and there, Belo Horizonte, Rio de Janeiro, especially Rio, until he settled on the river. Then he fell in love with Velho Chico, "Old Frank," the São Francisco River. He apprenticed for some time on board the riverboats and then took a simplified course in piloting—at that time it wasn't so difficult to get a pilot's license—no stiff requirements as nowadays.

"Now, it's almost necessary to take a course in Naval School to pilot a boat on the São Francisco."

He also told me that he was all alone; he had had a wife

some time ago—he wasn't certain exactly how long ago, but he thought they had been separated for about eight years.

"I never had any more attachments. The old people died. I have a married sister in Minas; she lives there in Uberaba. I almost never see her."

Then I dared: "And girl friends?"

He spoke with indifference.

"Oh, some, here and there. But nothing serious. Nothing important. I am still waiting to meet someone I like and who likes me. This life on the river isn't satisfactory, here today, there tomorrow. And I don't want to leave a wife on shore."

There was still another question that was important to me: Did he have any children with the wife?

"We had a little girl; she died when she was two years old."

I don't know how, I who never talked about intimate things—how his confidences invited mine, and I let slip: "I also had a child, only one. But it was born dead."

The Captain, who was leaning on the rail, with his eyes on the night and the river, turned quickly and inquired with a different voice: "Ah, you are married? I would never have thought so."

"I'm not married, I am a widow. For three years now."

He turned to his previous position, was silent for a moment, and then said: "Widow, huh? I didn't think that. So much the better."

"Why? Why so much the better?"

He laughed, turned to me again, raised his hand and smoothed my hair that the wind from the river had whipped up over my head.

"Because this way I'm not going to have to exchange shots with some character on your account."

And he continued to draw me out: birth, girlhood, name.

"So your name is Dôra or Dóra? I know a Dóra; I never met a Dôra."

I confessed that my name was Maria das Dores—"a promise made by Senhora . . ."

"Who is Senhora?"

"My mother, but I only call her Senhora, ever since I was little. We never got along well."

I spoke of my father, who died when I was little. Of

145

Soledade, of the cattle, of Amador, of Delmiro, and of Xavinha. Of my orange grove from Bahia, of my little garden, and of the clump of carnations and the odors of the white flowers surrounded by rose bushes under my window. In that hour it seemed important to me to recall those carnations and the odor of the white flowers surrounded by rose bushes which wafted through the closed window at night.

And finally I spoke of Laurindo: rapidly, so as not to suggest he had a big place in my life. Married for such a short time. He was a surveyor; he lived almost always away from home, at his work.

Later, after Laurindo died in the hunting accident—nobody knows yet how that gun went off—I decided to live in the city.

This brought me up to the time of my relationship with D. Loura, our relative, and her family boardinghouse on the Tristão Gonçalves Street. In the beginning I had tried to earn my living by helping D. Loura to run it: a boardinghouse which demanded a lot of work with many rooms, a big turnover, and bookkeeping she didn't know how to do and had formerly paid an outsider to do.

I rattled on about her acquaintance with the Brandinis, the help that I gave the company in my free time, the kindness of D. Estrela, the couple's friendship with D. Loura—a friendship that dated long before my time.

Later I told about the fight with that Cristina Le Blanc, and how all had joined to practically force me to accept the ingenue's role.

"I don't know how I found the courage to walk on the stage. I was always shy; but Seu Brandini inspires confidence, and when he really wants something there is no one who can resist."

"And your mother, she agreed to your joining the company?"

"I didn't ask her; I didn't consult her or anyone else. After all, I am a widow, I am close to thirty years old and I do not have to obey or please anybody."

I was excited. I paused briefly but then went on.

"You can't imagine how good these people have been for me; they are almost like my family. Seu Brandini watches over me and helps me as a father. Estrela—I don't know if you have already noticed it; she, too, builds up confidence.

146

People speak badly of theater folk, but they are human beings like everybody else. I have known much worse people. . . ."

I was already becoming defensive—and he was listening silently. Listening.

The story of my life finished, the Captain began to speak about himself. He wanted to leave the river—navigating a ship ended up with the ship becoming a prison. He was thinking of going into the business of selling semiprecious stones and commercial diamonds—maybe even precious stones. In the region of Minas it was the only thing one could do. And now, in war time, it had a great future.

He took me inside where it was light, and there he showed me a little chamois sack which he carried in his pants pocket; he made me hold my hands open like a shell and poured into them all the contents of the little sack. My hands were full of varicolored stones, some very small, the size of a grain of corn or even smaller, so tiny that they were a mere bit of light; and the largest of all was a purple one, an amethyst, big as an olive.

He looked pleased as I played with the light on the stones in my hands; and finally, when I was putting the fistful of stones back into his sack, taking the utmost care lest I drop some on the floor, at times holding one up between my fingers in order to see it better—they were so beautiful—he picked up the magnificent amethyst and said I was to keep it as a remembrance.

Not for once did I think of refusing it (later he said that he always loved me because of this); and I accepted it with the greatest naturalness, lifting the stone up against the light, drawing flashes, enchanted with it.

At this time, because of the war, we wore clothes influenced by military style; the blouse I wore that night had on top of the left breast a little pocket with a flap as on a soldier's tunic, closed with a button. Then the Captain unbuttoned my pocket, took the stone from between my fingers and put it in the little pocket. Then he slowly closed the button.

Neither he nor I said anything. We scarcely smiled.

It was then almost five o'clock—five o'clock in the morning! Day was breaking, and he escorted me down the ladder and along the corridor to my stateroom door. There he made his little salute, smiled again, and left.

147

I lifted the latch as lightly as I could, and gently pushed open the door, but even so it creaked. Some light entered from the corridor through the transom, and I saw that D. Pepa was raising her head, half frightened.

"Who is it?"

But seeing that it was I the old lady muffled a laugh.

"I thought you were in the Captain's stateroom."

"No, Senhora D. Pepa. I was with the Captain but on the bridge watching the ship go up the São Francisco."

She only clacked her tongue and I, always so easily impressed with what others might think, suddenly didn't give a damn. I would make no excuses to anyone; let the old bitch think what she wished.

I undressed and climbed up the little ladder into my bunk, but before doing so I exchanged smiles with the old lady, who still had her eyes open. I understood very well what she was thinking, and I was saying to myself that I wished to God it had been true.

In that long conversation, which had lasted all night, I understood that his name was Amadeu, and so I said this the next morning to D. Pepa who had a mania for inquiring about everyone's name, surname, age, place of birth, and civil status. Amadeu Lucas, without father or mother, from Pirapora, Minas, forty-two years old; and this was all that I knew. Yes, single.

At the lunch table D. Pepa saw a little hamlet that loomed white along the bank of the river and wanted to know what that place was.

"Captain Amadeu—"

He interrupted almost harshly. "My name is not Amadeu. It is *Asmodeu*."

D. Pepa turned to reprimand me.

"It was Dôra who told me Amadeu."

And he also turned to me; everyone's eyes were on me.

"Dôra misunderstood: I told her Asmodeu."

I could see at once that the change in the letters of his name was very important for him. Well, if someone is called Amadeu it isn't an offense, and it's even pretty; and Asmodeu—I had never met anyone with that name.

Seu Brandini, the only one of us who read to any extent, pressed the subject.

"Pardon me, Captain, perhaps I'm mistaken, but isn't Asmodeu the name of a demon? I read a play . . ."

He stopped in the middle of what he was saying and there was an uncomfortable feeling at the entire table. Seu Brandini was a bomber with his boners. Estrela looked at me from her place, and I knew what she was saying to herself: *Carleto will never learn.* The man was in charge of the ship and that fool was saying that his name was the name of a demon. . . .

Finally I gathered up my courage and looked at the Captain only to discover that he was smiling with self-satisfaction, facing Seu Brandini.

"Right, he is a demon."

And he recited: "ASMODEU, a diabolical entity who figures in the book of Tobias as the demon of impure pleasures. He also has been called 'the lame devil.' He raises the roofs of houses and exposes the intimate secrets of the inhabitants."

He smiled again, as if he had told everybody an important secret.

"It's in the dictionary. I memorized it when I was a child. No one else in the world has that name"—and then he laughed heartily—"only the original Asmodeu, Asmodeu the First. I am Asmodeu the Second."

An embarrassed silence fell over everybody; it was natural, no one knew what to say. It was D. Pepa who continued: "But the holy father baptized you, sir, with that name?"

"The priest? Of course he refused. My father was always at cross-swords with him; my father was a mason, anticlerical, and always inventing something to bait the vicar. He even founded a little journal called *O Triângulo* which lasted for a time. The people of that place wondered about the triangle; they only knew about the Triangle of Minas which was far away. My father was irritated with so much ignorance: The triangle, of course, is the symbol of the Masons.

"He chose names for his children in order to shock people. He named my oldest sister Lilith—Lilith was Eve's rival, Adam's second wife. It is pronounced Lilite, and he was so mad when people called the girl Lili. (Moreover, by then, that sister had already died.) He named the other girl Zolita, in honor of Émile Zola, the novelist who created such a big scandal during that time, the author of some books which told about the swindles of Rome and the phony Lourdes. My father was a fanatical disciple of his."

Seu Brandini knew Émile Zola well.

"A naturalist. I read everything of his when I was still a boy in Porto Alegre. I had to hide his books. To the asses he was immoral. He had every case that I could tell you about. Including the case of the priest—the Abbé Mouret . . ."

D. Pepa persisted in asking about the baptisms.

"But the curate—the priest—in the end he baptized you?"

The Captain smiled again, with that old memory.

"He didn't wish to baptize me, and there was the biggest fight. Ah, he wouldn't baptize a puppy with that name. My mother and my aunts cried for fear that I would remain a pagan—and certainly with that name, which the priest clearly explained to them. The priest finally gave the impression that he would agree to the baptism, but at the appointed time he made the same mistake as Dôra: Instead of 'Asmodeu' he said: 'Amadeu, I baptize you . . .'

"My father interrupted the baptism, said he was going to get a gun, but the priest crossed his arms and declared that the baptism was now done:

" 'The water has been poured, the Latin words have been spoken, the sacrament is irreversible.' That priest was brave. And he wrote in the baptistry book: 'The innocent Amadeu.' "

Then the Captain looked at me, somewhat irritated.

"And even today that name of Amadeu pursues me."

"And in the civil registry?" questioned Estrela.

"In the civil registry it is *Asmodeu* as it should be, with all the letters. It was my father's victory over the priest: According to law I am Asmodeu; a baptism has no weight in law."

"But your sisters, were they baptized?" D. Pepa wouldn't give up easily.

"My mother, already infuriated by then, took the girls to have them baptized in a nearby city that had a very old deaf vicar; he noted the names of the girls as Lilita and Rosita —my father never found out."

I wasn't enjoying this subject. I didn't know if the others took these explanations as a joke, but I saw that the Captain was very serious about the eccentricity of these names; I had the hunch that the man when provoked was capable of exploding (from that day long ago I learned to be afraid of his outbursts) and to change the subject I asked: "And the little journal, *O Triângulo?*"

"Oh, it folded up. I don't think it even had ten numbers. Nothing in which the old man got involved had a long life. He was always changing land and profession."

Seu Brandini was thoughtful.

"You know, Captain, I am not religious, but I don't know. If I were in your place, I would feel a certain fear . . . if it were only I and the other . . . that one . . . you were never afraid?"

The Captain laughed again and with a certain pride.

"Of whom? Of Asmodeu the First? No, he never bothered me."

I believe that he was sincerely proud of that horrible name. It seems that he liked to be different, to provoke; he must have taken after his father.

From the very first day I detested his name. During our life together, I never used that name, except for once, and I never put it on paper. I addressed his letters to "Captain A. Lucas." When I spoke of him to others I would say "The Captain." And between the two of us, I never called him by name; I called him: *"dear, my love, dearest one, creature, man*—and *devil, Mr. Devil"* in times of rage and passion.

Many times in the dark, when he, Asmodeu the Second, was sleeping and I had insomnia, I would suddenly have a cold fear that the other, Asmodeu the First, would raise the roof in search of company.

During the voyage he had to work during the day because it required much work to run the ship. He had to land on banks to take on wood; the wood stops were almost never in a city or a port, but on the red banks where the land was brutally cut by the waters. There on the bank was that pile of wood, waiting. The crew from the hold quickly organized themselves to load the mountain of logs. Then the whistle roared like a bull, the wheel started to churn the water again, the ship took a long curve and sought the deep channel which was its road.

The Captain had to deal with the practical things and Zeca Piloto with the new sandbanks, rocks uncovered in the night by the current, and the anchored rafts that were not there during the descent voyage, days before.

The Captain had to take care of the provisions, along with the dispensary. At that time there was still no refrigeration, and the icebox of the ship was hardly sufficient for the drinks.

He had to manage the sailors—half-breeds from the banks, almost all fishermen and canoe drivers who knew nothing about the new work laws. He had to prevent the engineer from getting drunk; he was a very good mechanic, but if you left him to his own devices he began drinking. This was the job of the next in command (the first mate), but you couldn't count on him either: He was also just another drunk. An old friend who expected lenience.

A routine had been established between the Captain and me; after dinner, when he was free, the accordion player would come up, and we danced a little. By ten thirty the music ended; the Captain would press my arm, say good night to all, go up to the bridge and wait for me.

I stayed below a little longer, with Estrela, Araci, and D. Pepa, while Seu Brandini and Odair arranged partners and organized their poker game. Gambling for money was forbidden on board, but they locked themselves in Odair's stateroom and sent Araci to keep Estrela company while the game lasted. I took advantage of the poker game and went up to the bridge; and D. Pepa, not to be fooled, winked her eye, indicating that she knew it was time for me to leave.

Yes, a Captain, even on a riverboat like that one, worked a lot, he explained to me in our nightly conversations—the two of us alone up there, seated together at a little table, he drinking a beer slowly, smoking and talking, I listening, speaking little. We were silent, his hand on top of mine, the night air bathing us—then there was no more moon—and he kept returning to what was on both of our minds, how were we going to solve our problem?

I didn't wish to go to his stateroom. At every hour someone was beating on his door; even he complained: On that river no one respected night or rest for the captain; at every instant some practical matter was brought to his attention—we are going to enter a channel; "Captain, the mechanic is drunk and is threatening the others with a piece of broken glass in his hand"; "If you please, Captain, a telegram from Belo Horizonte—you have to stop in Januaria—it is from a deputy who is coming from his fazenda with a sick wife, he begs to reserve a special stateroom; we can put those rich gold prospectors in the salon to sleep, but you, sir, have to speak with them. . . ."

I trembled at the idea of those men knocking on his stateroom door at all hours; it was a little door, more like a venetian blind which gave no protection whatever. Perhaps they could even spy.

We obviously couldn't consider my stateroom which I shared with D. Pepa. The boat was full; no other stateroom was available, not even to take on that big shot in Januaria; it was necessary to make the prospectors sleep in the salon. . . .

Until one night a storm blew up. It began early, before dinner was finished; everything was so dark that it seemed like a black wall enveloped us. The wind whistled wildly and seemed to blow from all sides.

They had to unroll and tie down the canvas curtains of the salon and even so the water came thrashing inside, as if the wind itself were breaking up into rain.

The Captain cleared the table, excused himself, and stood up. He spent some time above, all of us waiting, while the wind continued to lash the curtains; and the water threw sheets of rain like big gobs of sand on top of the canvas; from one instant to another one could perceive that thunderbolt or flash of lightning; and the clap of thunder would break above us, jolting the boat.

I don't know how the pilot managed to keep to the channel in the midst of that rain, wind, and pitch-black night. Finally the pilot became frightened, and in a short time we understood that he was leaving the middle of the river and was heading toward shore.

Then suddenly there was a sound of splintering branches as if the boat were scraping the ground, opening up a road through the forest. Some women who were frightened screamed. I caught Estrela's arm; Estrela clung to Seu Brandini, who with white lips said: "Be careful, partner, by land no!"

Then the Captain's white shoes appeared at the top of the

ladder, and he descended rapidly to calm the anxious passengers.

"Don't be afraid, it's nothing. It's only the wheel breaking the branches on the bank."

And as we didn't understand and the explanation seemed to heighten the fears, he continued speaking with his calm smile as complete master of the situation.

"You see this storm? Velho Chico is angry. To be safe I have moored the ship on the bank; I have tied her up, and we are going to sleep while we are anchored."

Then the electric lights went out and some kerosene lamps were brought out so we could finish dinner.

After-dinner coffee came; the Captain got up and advised the people to relax.

"Nobody should be afraid, the ship is safe, safely tied. The worst of the storm has already passed. Good night!"

The passengers began to leave, half tripping in the dim lamplight. The Captain took my arm and pushed me quietly to the corridor.

"Today is the day. Today you can go up there. I gave orders that no one should bother me, come what may. And there isn't going to be anything."

He lit a flashlight to guide me along the dark corridor which led to his stateroom; and when he opened the door, he said to me in a low voice with a smile: "It was I who ordered the lights out!"

He pushed me inside, and once inside, he turned the key and bolted the door.

"All locked up, did you see? In the greatest security. You can relax."

Relax? My heart was pounding like mad, my face was on fire while he embraced me and then began to undo the buttons of my military blouse, the same one I was wearing that first day.

The amethyst was still in the little pocket—I hadn't wished to move it from my person, and I felt the stone pushing into my breast as he pressed me against himself.

Seu Brandini loved fishing, he loved to tell how when in Rio he always found time to go out with fishing pole and basket and on the rocks of Botafogo to kill his *cocorocas*; or

154

make an expedition to Barra da Tijuca, carrying net and bait for crabs; Estrela even got mad not knowing what to do with so many crabs!

On the first stop of the voyage, Seu Brandini went on shore and bought rod and fish hooks and spent hours trying to fish with little results. The Captain saw those attempts and promised: "One of these days we shall pass by a good fishing place; I will have the boat anchored, and you can see what fishing with a hook is like in Velho Chico."

Seu Brandini didn't forget the promise; he was impatient and wanted to buy more fishing gear, a long line, with gauge and bait! The Captain wouldn't let him.

"Be patient. We already have everything you need on board."

Two days later, it must have been about ten o'clock in the morning for the sun was already strong, the Captain sent for Seu Brandini; the wheel at the stern which propelled the boat was stopped, and we anchored in the middle of the river with the current lightly dividing the waters at the prow, as if the boat were an iron island.

Alarmed passengers came to find out the reason for the halt, and the Captain explained very seriously: "Be calm. There is nothing wrong with the machinery. We stopped on purpose. The fish supply is down and we are going to replenish it."

He leaned on the rail, at starboard (I had learned all of these terms from him).

"Stay there. In a little while you will see the sailors throwing out the nets. And the fish!"

People ran to lean over the rail; the Captain signaled to Seu Brandini and me to climb up to the bridge. Up there they were operating the fishing lines, poles, and bait.

Most of what they caught was piranha. I knew piranha very well; in the *sertão* that was what we had mostly. The Sitia stream, a tributary of the Salgado, in turn a tributary of the Jaguaribe, was where all the *sertão* piranhas came from. But ours was a little fish that got no larger than the palm of one's hand at most; and there were two kinds of them, the white and the black, the black being the more ferocious. When I was a small girl, Senhora sometimes called me a *black piranha* because of what she called my evil nature.

But those piranhas of the São Francisco were enormous,

the likes of which I had never seen, and with that beautiful flashing red changeable color. One might say that those fish of the old river had been artificially colored. More lustrous beauty couldn't be imagined.

Seu Brandini caught the largest fish of all; the creature writhed on the deck, leaped half a meter in the air and glittered in the sun. Seu Brandini threw himself on top of the fish and held the gills in order not to be bitten (in the *sertão* there is the saying that the piranha bites even after it is dead), and he let out that yell of happiness that was like Tarzan's roar: "My God, but this is the life!"

He cried out to Estrela whose head just then appeared above the first step of the ladder, like the head of St. John the Baptist on the tray: "Woman, woman, come look at the miraculous fish!"

Estrela finished climbing, went to admire the heap of fish which already filled a hamper; but for her the best thing was to bask in the joy of Seu Brandini, who continued shouting like a bewitched child every time he hooked a fish. She smiled at him and scolded: "Not so loud, Carleto, you'll frighten the fish!"

I approached the Captain, who a short distance away silently threw out his line, concentrating.

"Are you crazy about fishing too, like Seu Brandini?"

He drew in the clean hook and put on new bait.

"In the past I liked it very much. Now, frankly speaking, I feel myself a prisoner of this life."

"What holds you? The boat or the river?"

"It's all: the ship, the river, this way of life."

"Then you are tired of life?"

The people around us were conversing in a low voice while the two of us leaned over the water, seeing if the fish were biting. But at my question—tired of life?—he turned around, with the sun in his face and his eyes sparkling.

"Tired of life, no! Tired of *this life!*"

He enveloped me totally with his look and smile; it was as if he were hugging me.

"Girl, I'm finally enjoying life so much, but so much that if there were a place where life were sold I would go there and work like a madman just to get the money to buy more life, to buy more life!"

I felt like falling into his arms in front of everybody. But for all that, I was the opposite of him: to be so happy, so happy as I felt, I wanted to die then and there for fear that the happiness might end.

We passed the celebrated Bom Jesus da Lapa with its church made in a rock cavern; but I didn't visit there because the Captain didn't come down, and we could steal some hours of privacy while the others were taking a walk.

Now, every hour that passed, every quarter hour that the ship's bell sounded meant less time for us to be together. For when we reached Pirapora our company would disembark and go to Belo Horizonte, and he would stay there on his *J. J. Seabra*.

Years later I saw the picture of J. J. Seabra, a politician from Bahia. I cut it out, framed it, and hung it in the corridor; and no one except the Captain understood why I placed it there in the house as though he were a saint—the face of that buck-toothed man with the high collar. Even Estrela and Seu Brandini were surprised; it took some time for them to remember that the name J. J. Seabra evoked remembrance of times past for us.

Ah, the carefree joy of those first three days, that simple enchantment of being together was no longer present; then it wasn't necessary even to touch one another: a glance or a light brush of the hand was enough.

But now, even if that magic hadn't ended, just the thought alone of arriving at Pirapora was a threat.

I didn't ask him what he intended to do afterwards, and he didn't say anything to me about his plans. Perhaps they were still vague and for this reason he didn't talk. Only once he told me that he had sent a large portion of his semiprecious stones to be resold in Teófilo Otôni; it was a secret and risky business, so much so that he urged me not to mention anything about it to anybody—not to anybody, not even to Seu Brandini or Estrela.

The Captain's partner in this business was a Pernambucan who embarked at midday in one port, and disembarked at the next port on the following morning. While he was on the boat, he had dinner with us, after spending a great part of the afternoon on the bridge with the Captain. He also

157

had brought in his pants pocket his little chamois sack full of stones: "It's the prospector's baggage: You never see one without *capanga*—stuffed . . . or even empty, but he is never far from his money bag. For that reason they called us *capangulinos*. We were the pocketbooks for others."

He showed his stones to Estrela and me, and he gave each of us one of the small ones. I received a pale blue aquamarine that I still have today; Estrela's was a topaz, a little larger. Months later when they were in a tight spot, Seu Brandini went to sell it one day and came back furious.

"The Jew said that it wasn't a *precious* stone, but a *semiprecious* one. A big difference and with much lower value!"

Seu Brandini's greatest rage was not knowing by whom he had been cheated: by the Pernambucan who gave the present, or by the jeweler who disparaged the stone in order not to pay its true value!

The Pernambucan—named Vanderlei—the Captain told me was an adventuresome spirit. He had killed someone in his home state and had to flee to Minas. He made his living in the stone business on the banks of the São Francisco, between Minas and Bahia. He left his wife and children in Pernambuco; and for this reason, whenever he was homesick, he came down to Juazeiro, traveled two days on the road to spend a night of fear with his family. The police commissioner was a relative of the murdered man and said all around that he had a dungeon in the jail which he kept vacant—reserved for that assassin, Vanderlei.

In all the fool wasted fifteen days of travel, a week to go and another to return, all for the sake of that one night at home; but he returned comforted, and he always left a crude letter for his enemies: This taste of home was his means of avenging himself.

Very tall and thin, hair with tints of red, with a big stone ring on the little finger of his left hand, Vanderlei talked his head off. His talk was nerve-racking.

At night he joined the poker game with Seu Brandini and Odair. It seems that he lost a fair amount, but he didn't show any displeasure; only upon leaving at Januaria, when Seu Brandini offered his hand and asked "pardon for the bad luck at the poker table" did he say: "No, sir, it isn't necessary to excuse yourself."

He finished with an understanding smile.

"Also, what did I expect when I decided to play poker with a magician?"

On the night of this particular poker game I was as always with the Captain at that little table on the bridge, conversing, while he drank his beer. I took a thimbleful just to keep him company; and in one moment he caught my hand and absent-mindedly began to turn the little gold ring which I wore on the right-hand ring finger—a finely worked antique piece with a little uncut diamond in a rosette at the center.

A present from Laurindo when we were sweethearts, and even Senhora sneered at it; they had told her that Laurindo had received the ring from two bachelor brothers (the people called them "the priests" because they were the sons of old Father Jerônimo) as payment for a survey.

Be that as it may, I liked the ring, and from the day when Laurindo put it on my finger, I had never taken it off; it was as if it were a part of my hand.

Then the Captain began to kiss my fingers, lightly; suddenly he noticed the ring, held my hand up to get a better look at it and said that in Minas one still found works like that, in antique shops.

"Is it a family heirloom?"

Instead of saying yes, it was an inheritance from my grandmother or great-grandmother, I told him the full story without thinking.

"In a certain way it was an inheritance from my husband, a present from Laurindo"—and I told how Senhora found out that it had come from the old priest's gold. . . .

The Captain took the ring slowly from my finger, as if to examine the workmanship more closely. And then, so quickly that I had no warning of his intention, he put the ring in his mouth and crushed it between his teeth; then, without looking, he took the ball of crushed-up gold from his mouth and threw it as far as he could into the river.

I cried out: "Are you crazy?"

Then he looked at me very calmly.

"Don't cry; it isn't worth the trouble. I will give you another—a prettier one. More expensive."

By the way, he never gave me another ring. For him promises weren't important. What he did came suddenly, on impulse. In time he gave me a watch and some earrings with precious stones; and he put a big gold wedding ring on my left hand (so that I could feel married); but he never gave me another gold ring equal to or better than that little antique one.

Whenever I remembered, I was pained about my crushed little ring, thrown to the bottom of the river. I liked it very much, not because it was a remembrance of Laurindo—as if I needed any reminders of him—but I liked the ring for its own sake. I liked to think that once it had been worn on the finger of Padre Jerônimo's mysterious mistress, D. Gloria, who lived hidden in her house, the people saying that they knew she was alive only because every year another baby appeared, which the old priest himself baptized.

But when I tried to speak about this to the Captain, he wouldn't even let me begin. Besides, he dropped a curtain over the subject of the ring as if it were he who forgave me something—some error from the past—which I carried on my finger.

On the eve of the arrival at Pirapora, the company gave a performance on board, "Farewells and Thanks for the Courtesies Received," as Seu Brandini wrote on the black bulletin board of the salon.

It was a simple variety act, because in the open salon there was no way to construct a stage, and the boxes of scenery in the hold weren't accessible.

But from decorations and fantasies which she carried in her hand luggage D. Pepa took out an old curtain of lamé which still lit up at night; and it was used as a backdrop for an improvised stage.

Estrela wore a black dress with fringe and a red rose at the bottom of her low-cut neckline. D. Pepa said that she was not properly dressed to represent a girl from Buenos Aires. Estrela did the apache dance with Seu Brandini. The audience was delirious about that bad apache with the cloth hat and neckerchief, a cigarette butt in the corner of his lips, cuffing his wife and throwing her on the floor, to the rhythm of the concertina's waltz, which Seu Jota had made the accordion player rehearse all afternoon.

In order not to arouse the Captain's jealousy I sang, instead of the piquant duet with Odair which Seu Brandini wanted, my "Maria, It Is Day" number with all the assistance of clapping of hands and audience participation in the chorus.

Odair and Araci performed some magic tricks, using silk handkerchiefs and the Brazilian flag. D. Pepa gave a monologue which was, incidentally, very risqué. Seu Jota do Piano, besides accompanying us with the guitar, played a flute solo.

Of course the performance ended with Seu Brandini, in full glory again, with boots and gaucho trousers, dragging the huge spurs and singing as loud as he could the unfailing Andorinha.

It was a great success; the Andorinha was called for encores three times with the entire company joining in the chorus. Seu Ladislau thought that with a little touching up the same program could be given in Pirapora while we waited for the train to Belo Horizonte. Perhaps it would bring in enough to pay for the boardinghouse, and it wouldn't be necessary to dig into the boxes of scenery.

Seu Jota dedicated his flute number to "the Captain of the ship," who from his armchair in the audience acknowledged his thanks with a wave of his hand.

I saw the scene from behind the curtain, improvised as a dressing room, and I was enraged. I felt so angry with that miserable creature after all that had happened, and here he was still intruding on my Captain. Yes, because I believe there was no one on board who didn't know about how close the Captain and I had become.

While we were cleaning the makeup off our faces—I still had on the little ruffled dress of the Maria act which became me very well and made me look young—the Captain took my arm and led me for a walk on the bridge while waiting for supper. And I, who was still sore at the pianist, on stupid impulse told the Captain everything—about the attack in the boardinghouse room, the bite with which I marked his hand with that bastard's blood in my mouth, even the vomiting!

Well, I still had no clear notion of the Captain's capacity for jealousy and since the least blame wouldn't fall on me I could risk making him jealous. Women are like that; jealousy is a sign of love. Moreover, without being able to avenge myself on the pianist, it was natural that I gave vent to my feelings now.

To my disappointment, the Captain said nothing; I saw, however, that he was pale and bit his lip. He let some instants pass, then he pushed me toward the ladder.

"Let's go, I have to preside at the supper table."

The steward dug up a bottle of Argentine champagne, and one toast followed another, first with champagne and then with beer.

D. Pepa was high and the group made a circle around her, and she then began to tell her anecdotes in that hoarse, vulgar impersonator's voice.

Seu Brandini, full of so much joy and beer, began to bless everyone—above all, the little turtle doves, the little turtle doves! who were the Captain and I—I was so embarrassed.

The Captain drank almost nothing. It is true that in front of the passengers the glass hardly ever reached his mouth; he was firm about it, with a patient smile. From time to time I risked a glance at Seu Jota who was at a table for four together with Odair, his wife, and Seu Ladislau; euphoric, he showed off in a new number: He lined up in front of himself a row of glasses with a graduated quantity of beer in each one: beating on them with a fork he drew out a little marimba music. Everybody in the salon turned to listen, and he finished amidst a round of applause and cries of bis. Seu Jota gave an encore, but I was pleased that the Captain applauded neither the first time nor the second.

The next day we had already landed in Pirapora; it was afternoon, after the rehearsal; and the men of the company, minus Seu Brandini, were having their beer in the bar near the movie house where we were going to give the show.

They were already half drunk, and Seu Jota repeated the number of the little music of the glasses that was so successful the evening before. Just then the Captain entered, accompanied by his steward and first mate (the same ones who were with him the first day I saw him, also in a bar, in Juazeiro da Bahia). They were in civilian clothes, also like the first time.

Odair told me all about it afterwards. He said that the guys from the company received the Captain and his friends with a salvo of applause and made room for them at the table for the three.

They called for beer and Seu Ladislau began the toasts: "To the health of the dear *J.J. Seabra* and its crew! To the health of the Brandini Filho Company. To the health of Velho Chico!"

And then Seu Jota, who must have completely lost his head, took the fullest glass of his musical scale, placing in full view the hand where my teeth marks could still be seen, and toasted: "To the health of the piranha!"

The Captain, continued Odair, seemed to have been drinking before arriving because he was already half high, which couldn't have been possible from those few beers. When Seu Jota ended the toast and drank so fast from the glass that the beer spilled down his neck, the Captain continued looking at him, as if he were waiting for the other to finish drinking; and when Seu Jota finally put the empty .glass on the table, the Captain with the greatest calm extended his arm over the glasses and bottles and gave three slaps on the pianist's face: one with the palm, the others with the back of the hand. Right cheek, left cheek, one and the other, it reminded Odair of movie slaps in gangster films.

"And each one was given with the greatest delicacy, even with care, as if the Captain didn't wish to upset the bottles, as if he were swatting a fly on Seu Jota's face. But the sound of the hand on the face could be heard a long way off."

Seu Jota, with those flaming marks jumping up on the face white as a sheet, got up, carrying his hand to his belt as if he were seeking a weapon; but he had no arms, no one had ever seen him armed. Then he crumpled up again in the chair, dazed.

The Captain didn't take his eyes off him, but he also did nothing else. After a little time had passed, he explained with the greatest tranquility: "I didn't like your toast."

The party was frozen. In that constrained silence Seu Ladislau called the waiter and asked for the bill. But the Captain put his hand on Seu Ladislau's arm.

"The bill is mine!"

Then the others withdrew with Seu Jota; Odair wanted to remain, but he wasn't invited. Seu Jota went in front, walking with his head bowed, no doubt pretending to be more drunk than he was.

The Captain remained alone with his men at the table, his chin stuck out, watching the exit.

In Belo Horizonte we intended to make a layover of two weeks. Our clothes were threadbare, the paper scenery had been spoiled because of the voyage's storms, and there was no money for repairs; the truth is that we of the company were fed up with one another.

Seu Jota was nasty with everybody; he was unhappy because his companions hadn't rallied behind him; instead, they had all put their tails between their legs, fearing that maniac and his bodyguards. The group even began to enjoy the situation and called the pianist Al Capone without much logic: Al Capone was the one who did the slapping, not the one who received it.

Then, one Monday, the afternoon of our day off, I was in my room of the boardinghouse; I had washed my hair and after being in the sun, at the window, until my hair dried, I put on my pajamas and was getting ready to take a siesta.

There was a knock on the door, I thought it was Estrela and said: "Come in!"

The door opened and it was the Captain. My God, I didn't remember how handsome he was. He was standing there looking at me without saying a word, smiling, and slowly opening his arms to me. I fell into his arms almost crying: "I wasn't expecting you, I wasn't expecting you!"

Estrela who had led him to my room and remained in the corridor, laughed upon seeing our embrace and pushed the doorknob as she left.

"People, close the door at least!"

He had fled there for only a night, he would take the return train in the morning.

"Only one night? You are just like Vanderlei!"

I couldn't get enough of caressing him, having him for my very own, to suppress the longing of those sad weeks.

He got up and dressed in a hurry.

"Speaking of Vanderlei, I have important business in the city—that business of the stones. If it turns out well, honey, I will bag a lot of money; and we can blow it all in Rio, at the Casino da Urca!"

164

He knotted his tie and put on his coat. It was the first time that I saw him in a coat and tie, and he seemed even more handsome. At the door he said: "Wait for me for lunch, in town. Do you want to invite Brandini and Estrela?"

In my happiness I shrieked: "No, just us two, just us two!"

The Captain wanted to give me money to pay the pension; I didn't accept. It wasn't necessary. The stay in Belo Horizonte had gone well. Seu Brandini got his foot out of the mud, and after the first week he was already paying us a little on the arrears account.

He shook his head.

"You are my wife; I have the right to keep you."

At that word, *wife*, my heart leaped with joy. I clung to him fiercely.

"Of course I am your wife, but it happens that I am also earning my own living. As long as Seu Brandini can pay, it's best to accept. You know how he is. If he sees me with money, either he won't pay or else he will pay and borrow back. He spends money foolishly and ends up in debt. You don't know Seu Brandini. Look, why not invest what you wish to give me in the business of the stones? It can be my share!"

He said no more but wasn't really convinced. I was already crying with the good-byes, and there wasn't even enough time for him to dry my eyes and console me.

It wasn't pride, it wasn't anything. Or, was it pride? We didn't live together as a married couple, it was one night here, another there, and he giving me money upon leaving. Didn't it seem as if *he were paying me?* My God, and if I could, I would have been giving money to him, cooking, washing and ironing for him, cleaning his shoes, doing the most humble things that I had never done before in my life, not even for myself! I laughed—if Xavinha could hear me—I who at Soledade had a *caboclo* even to wash my hair!

And remembering Xavinha, I again became sharply conscious of the matter of the letter: It was the gall in the midst of my joy.

I had answered the letter in Juazeiro, but up to now nothing had reached me from Soledade. Should I have written directly to Senhora, explaining my fears and recommending prudence? "Pardon if I touch on this subject, but I'm afraid that Delmiro in his madness . . ." No, the whole tragedy had passed between Senhora and me without words: I knew, she knew that I knew, and between what we both knew were the six feet of earth on Laurindo's grave. Whenever one of us might lance the boil, my God, everything would explode. It was one thing for people to talk: it was quite another for people to know. An explosion between her and me could spread that horrible secret to Aroeiras and back, a fireworks of filthy mud. Sad for her and sad for me, because I was certain she had guessed everything in respect to Delmiro.

No, let Senhora be quiet; and by the way she never could be quiet, that wasn't her way. She would invent a way of pouring water on those seething happenings at the cemetery. And it wouldn't be like Senhora to let anyone get near Delmiro.

Ah, she knew what to do, she always knew. At this point I could relax, and trust Senhora.

But why didn't that old magpie Xavinha answer me? She who was so very good at carrying gossip, stirring up a hornet's nest, and stepping calmly aside.

I got dressed and went to look for Seu Ladislau to find out if he had a letter for me. He was in the theater, harassed with some bills. The next day he had to go already to Juiz de Fora to prepare for our stay there.

"I haven't been to the post office for several days now. For me and Seu Brandini, we never have anything but bills. Why don't you take a little skip over there? It's the Central Post Office; ask for General Delivery."

He took out a card "Companhia de Comedias e Burletas Brandini Filho," wrote on it some words of authorization, dated and signed it.

When the girls in the post office saw me, they got excited and called to each other. The woman who took charge of the telegrams declared that up to now she hadn't missed a single one of our performances, nor the repeat performance, and when I signed the receipt for the package of mail, the girl at General Delivery said with shining eyes:

"I'm getting an autograph!"

But she was surprised when she read the signature.

"You aren't Nely Sorel? This is another name: Maria das Dores Miranda . . ."

I had to explain that Nely Sorel was my stage name, but that on documents I had to give my real name. To end the subject, I said: "Give me a card, and I'll give you the autograph of Nely Sorel."

She brought me a postal; the others were envious: each one brought her postal also. I said good-bye half proud, modesty aside, and I even recommended to the girls: "I hope you don't miss my benefit performance on Thursday."

It was the first time I had been asked for an autograph, a big-city custom. In the places where I had performed, the public hadn't begun to do this; at that time we were even annoyed when they recognized us in the street and pointed at us, laughing, as if we were some sort of circus animals.

Oh, a big letter with many pages came; the address in Xavinha's shaky handwriting was the one I had suggested—c/o Companhia Brandini Filho—General Delivery—Belo Horizonte, State of Minas Gerais.

It took discipline, but I didn't open the letter in the street, or on the trolley which took me to the pension. I tore open the envelope only when I was safe in my room, after delivering the rest of the correspondence to Estrela in their room.

"All bills," she said, biting her lip; and I then ran to my room, locked the door, sat on the bed, and opened the letter:

I write these simple lines to give you our news and to ask for yours; here we are doing well, thanks to God. Dorinha, we aren't doing better only because Godmother Senhora has been ill. They think it was only a stroke: The mouth was twisted just a little bit and one arm paralyzed, but it's already straightening out. Dr. Fenelon came and said that the worst was over and that she needed rest. Yes, and he prescribed an injection that the pharmacist comes to give every day. It's D. Dagmar's husband who comes. At the time Godmother Senhora's speech was garbled, but now she's almost talking straight again, thanks to the good Lord. She didn't ask me to tell you anything. She realizes that she isn't supposed to know that I write you; but, Dorinha, it's your mother, won't you come to visit her?

Yes, about those rumors, I haven't answered you sooner because of Godmother Senhora's illness. We were all in anguish here at Soledade, but it was a fuss about nothing because the gravedigger discovered that the sighs which were heard came from an owl with a nest in the chapel of the Leandro Family. Do you remember? It's behind Laurindo's grave. The gravedigger showed the owl's nest to everybody—already two little owls had been born. But those people of Aroeiras are so evil that there are still some who say that Godmother Senhora paid the gravedigger to put the owls there, as if the poor man knew how to make an owl's nest, and even if he had put it there the owls would have rejected it because all creatures reject the nests that others make. How can one imagine such things as these? Evil and more evil.

Yes, about Seu Delmiro, I can say little: We haven't seen him recently. After you went away, he vanished from everybody's sight; but Amador still makes the exchanges which you so strongly recommended; and from time to time he appears, but he doesn't say a word. The other day he spoke and asked if you had died. He had had a bad omen and said that he had dreamed that Dona Dorinha was in heaven with a bouquet of roses in her hand. Every day he gets crazier.

Dorinha, be sure to answer this, say whether you are coming or not, and for the love of God don't say anything to Godmother Senhora about my asking you to come. I hope you are well, and I remain your family friend and obliging servant.

Francisca Xavier Miranda.

So, there were only some owls, only a pair of owls! May God forgive me, but after the sighs were heard, I couldn't deny that I was also scared to death—afraid of those sighs, sighs from one who didn't sigh, I know that. So there were only some owls with their offspring, some owls in that thick marble chapel with a little altar of the dead Lord inside and some colored windows, one of which had been broken ever since I was a child.

Good, it was all explained, wasn't it? The owls, the almost abandoned chapel; the Leandro tribe had practically ended in Aroeiras. Only on All Souls' Day the three old girls who lived in Fortaleza were sent to whitewash, scrub the mosaic, open the door, and pray a mass. The owls must have entered through the broken glass—I can well imagine the people's fear as they listened at nightfall to their *u-u-u!*

I began to laugh. I laughed and laughed, doubling up. I rolled in the bed. *U-u-u-u!* I laughed and laughed until I cried. And then I cried, I sobbed. Happily no one was near, or if they were they gave no sign.

The worst of the crying over, I washed my face (in Belo Horizonte our boardinghouse was among the better ones we had stayed in: I had my own washbasin in my room), ran a comb through my hair, and went to find Estrela.

I knocked lightly on the door, but from outside I already heard the snoring of Seu Brandini, who was taking his siesta (theater people can't so much as look at a bed during the day without falling asleep).

The door opened a little, Estrela's head popped out, and she was tapping her mouth with a finger: I spoke in a low voice: "I know he is sleeping. Come to my room, I want to talk with you."

I had never told Estrela or anyone else what was between Senhora and me; I didn't even tell about the unhappy events of the time just before I left home, or even the old things, which dated from my childhood. I never spoke of Senhora. It would have been easier to let them flay me alive than to open my mouth and bring into the open the bad blood between us.

Xavinha, Xavinha suspected, she had seen too much not to have had some ideas. Whatever she suspected she never mentioned directly. As I think about it, Xavinha, whom everybody found so indiscreet and talkative, never spoke too much when the subject demanded silence.

What Seu Brandini, Estrela, and D. Loura knew was that I didn't get along very well with my mother, that she was a lady of an authoritarian nature, difficult, and that when I became a widow, I had resolved to win my independence.

Moreover, the little bit of money—a fazenda in the *sertão* is not a coffee plantation in São Paulo—a few cattle, a bit of corn and beans and some cotton of the tenants. It only provided a living without anything left over for extras.

And I, still young with lots of life ahead of me, not getting along with my mother, why should I bury myself at Soledade?

It wasn't necessary to explain anything more; everyone thought I was right.

Now I told Estrela about the letter: My mother (and my lips resisted saying that word), my mother seems to have suffered a little indisposition, which moreover had passed and the doctor said that there was no more danger. Did Estrela think I ought to go there?

Estrela looked me straight in the eyes.

"Do you want to go?"

I lowered my head.

"No. If she were ill and called for me, clearly I would go." (No, by God, I didn't want to go there, not even if Senhora had a candle in her hand, nor if she called for me and obliged me to go. But I also wanted Estrela to give me an excuse that Xavinha could give to the people. A good pretext, something reasonable, that wouldn't increase the bad rumors: "What a daughter she is, not to come to the bedside of her sick mother?")

Estrela thought a little, then she spoke slowly: "I'm going to be frank: if you really wish to go, Carleto is going to be desperate. This stay here was the first that we broke even since we began this tour. In Belém, you remember, we hardly covered expenses; in Fortaleza not even that; if it hadn't been for D. Loura, we would have come out deeply in debt; in Recife it was hardly better. And those impromptu performances which we made in the hamlets along the road, you know as well as I: They covered the pension bill and at times not even the passage. Only here has it been good: the daily box office income almost always for a full house.

"If you went away now, I don't see how Carleto could find a substitute for you; even if he made arrangements with another young girl, it would be weeks until she could master the roles and the musical numbers, and rehearse adequately, however quick she might be. Besides,"—here Estrela smiled and touched my face with the tip of her finger—"you already have your public, people who come to the theater just to see you."

I blushed.

"Now, Estrela, I miss my cues badly, and when the time comes to sing, I'm in trouble!"

Estrela wasn't one to praise a person at random.

"It is possible that you still haven't gotten over your shyness, but you are charming and have that charisma of a girl from a good family which the public loves. Since the affair with the Captain, you now have 'it,' or charm, or sex appeal, as they say. It seems that you are glowing with an inner light!"

We both laughed and I said: "Then you think I oughtn't to go?"

"Look, Dôra, it isn't that I think you oughtn't to go—this is another question. I beg you for the love of God not to go. It isn't for myself that I beg, nor for the company: It's only for Carleto, poor thing. He has that gaucho braggadocio way about him, he pretends to be brave, but sometimes at night he awakens me talking to himself. Do you know what he says? He is doing the accounts: 'Five *contos* and fifteen, that scenery was a robbery, twelve *contos* for the hotel . . .' And now, for the first time that he is making some money. . . . Please don't go! If perhaps your mother were very ill . . .'"

I had never heard Estrela speak so much, for such a long time, or with so much passion. She never asked anyone for anything. I put my hand on her shoulder.

"Don't worry, Estralinha. I'm not going."

In order not to have to write, I telegraphed: "Impossible to come now due to responsibilities of work. Greetings."

Seu Ladislau came to speak with Seu Brandini, and I asked him to send the telegram for me. Only after he had gone with the paper did I remember that I hadn't asked about the patient.

End of the Company's Book

171

III
THE CAPTAIN'S BOOK

DERISIVELY, SEU BRANDINI CALLED IT "ESTRELA'S mansion"; actually it was a *vila* house, cutting across Catete Street, with an odd number, house IX.

The *vila* was old; in its early days professionals had lived there—doctors, lawyers, army officials. But with time it was taken over by more modest persons, not yet poor, but almost: taxi drivers, tailors, manicurists; there was even a streetcar conductor.

A German woman, D. Ema, joined together three houses across the street, numbers IV, VI, and VIII to make a boardinghouse for students—more accurately, a house of furnished rooms. D. Ema gave only bed and breakfast, the other meals the boys ate from a lunch pail; almost all got their quick food from the Frenchwoman with a town house on Andrade Pertence Street.

The Brandini couple, to fit the times and their financial condition, had sometimes lived in a ground-floor apartment in Ipanema, other times in a pension on Machado Plaza, or in various other places in the southern or central zones. But one day—about ten years before—a cousin of Estrela's moved to Uberlandia and offered her the rest of that little house IX's lease—an offer which in any other circumstances Seu Brandini would have rejected with disdain. But at that time they were having lean days, and Seu Brandini agreed to live in house IX—for the time being, of course.

The attraction was its modest rent. For this reason when the new company was formed and they went on the circuit, Estrela insisted on taking over the lease of the little old house; it wouldn't be too much of a burden.

"When we return, we'll at least have a roof over our heads; later we can move."

Through their highs and lows and in-betweens the house continued in her possession. The owner of the *vila* had for many years wished to sell the land to a firm that built apartment complexes; therefore he made no improvements: he didn't change a nail with the intent of getting rid of the old tenants who complained even to the point of sending letters to the newspapers about the neglect and abandonment of the house. But in the end nobody left, nobody forsook his corner.

It was all so deteriorated that the German, D. Ema, complained that it had already deteriorated into a *favela* slum; its only advantage was that it wasn't climbing up a hillside. Others spoke of an injunction threat by the Board of Public Health. The tenants themselves did the most urgent repairs: a burst pipe, a gutter on the roof which crossed over the top of an attic or ceiling, the replacement of a broken window; and from year to year one or another tenant gave a coat of paint to his walls, taking advantage of a weekend's leisure.

Be that as it may, Estrela was right to keep the house; with her uncertain pilot controlling the ship the house was a guaranteed port.

When they left to travel, they asked a boy to sleep in the front room in order to discourage thieves and invaders. A closed house in that area—well, we all know what happens: beggars, marginal and slum people install themselves as squatters. Wake up to what's happening and it's already too late to evict them.

The entrance was into the living room, with its sofa, dining table, and a small buffet where Estrela kept the china, flatware, and the glasses. Two bedrooms—and this was the luxury—one for the couple, and a tiny, smaller room with its window opening on the stone quarry behind the house; a bath and the little kitchen, from which one went down two steps to the cement area, where the washtub stood.

I already knew about that house. More than once Estrela had asked for my help in order to send the postal money order to cover the rent.

"I almost always steal the money from Carleto's pocket, but this month his pocket is turned inside out and is empty: dead broke, dead broke!"

So for three months I helped with the payments. Another month it was D. Pepa who helped; yet another it was Seu Ladislau. Estrela joked that she could form a shareholding company for the house rent and nearly all the members of the Brandini Filho Company would own a share. But she noted the debts in her little pocket notebook and paid them back when she could put her hands on some money.

176

* * *

In Juiz de Fora I began thinking about where I ought to try to get a room for myself in Rio, and Estrela said with authority: "You are going to stay with us in the Mansion. We have a second room, isn't that right, Carleto?"

Carleto said there was indeed a room and there would be no further discussion about it. Was he going to let his ingenue stray and be deflowered by the first no-good man who showed up?

Out of politeness I wished to resist, but they didn't have to insist very much to convince me. After all Estrela and Seu Brandini were then the only family I possessed in the world—this was all the more so with the Captain away. Since that night in Belo Horizonte there had been no more news, except for a telegram sent to Juiz de Fora: "All well, many *saudades*."

Estrela's Mansion—when you entered it you left Rio: You wouldn't have had the slightest idea of being in a big city. In that blind alley all was far away, the buildings, city noise; the children played on their scooters on the old pavement and the whole unit seemed similar to that type of row house I was familiar with in Fortaleza, by the side of the public walk: all were joined together, a door and a window shutter, another door, another window, nothing more.

When Seu Brandini, with his mania for playing the grandiose, made a joke about the Mansion, however, Estrela would reply: "I don't know, it's a house, my house, my four walls, my little cave in which to live!"

It still had one luxury which in that time of war was rare: a telephone. Installed during good times when the Light & Power Co., Ltd. put an ad in the newspaper offering a telephone: "THE CHEAPEST MAID IN THE WORLD" as Seu Brandini told it. Since it had been disconnected during their absence, it didn't ring a single time during their first days of return.

The little room which they gave me had in it a student bed, which consisted of a horsehair mattress on top of a bed frame of laths; and some shelves on the wall where Seu Brandini kept his books—I was amazed at so many books, nearly all about the theater, many in French and Spanish.

Seu Brandini was the first person I knew in all my life

177

who was completely wrapped up in books, reading in whatever free moment he had, or even without a free moment, not going to bed without a book to invite sleep, always with a book under his arm, always leaving a book around wherever he went. He bought foreign theater magazines; he had an account (always in arrears) in a bookstore on Carioca Plaza. Perhaps, it is true, he didn't read all the books that he bought; nor did he get to the end of most which he began. Whenever he was "writing" the plays and arrangements, he would redo the dialogue. He always reminded himself: "I must be more colloquial."

On the lower bookshelves, also in my room, were four old trunks holding the remains of decor and props of past seasons—and nothing more.

Then that evening, on the day of our arrival, Estrela went to Catete Street and returned, guiding a Portuguese with a little handcart, and put a tiny wardrobe in the room for me—one of those then in style with a bevel-edged mirror on the door.

"This way the room is more comfortable, and you won't have to keep your clothes in your bag."

Afterwards she dug into the old trunks and found a curtain which she hung at the window to hide the stone wall that was sinister looking. Seu Brandini got rid of those trunks, piling them all up on the tall shelf in their room.

I received these attentions with my heart in my hands, almost wanting to cry; for the first time somebody showed me loving attention—not to forget for a moment the kindnesses of D. Loura, poor thing, who also did everything possible.

"You are our darling!" Seu Brandini said.

Estrela took out of her closet her only linen sheet for me and gave me the best pillow.

"To make up for the student bed's hardness."

I wanted to thank her. I was always wishing to show my gratitude, but Estrela wouldn't let me; instead she took me to the little kitchen where she was making chicken soup.

"Don't you know? It is a tradition. Whenever theater people arrive from anyplace, they ask for chicken soup."

While I washed the chicken, I spoke about payment—after all, all of us had some money. Seu Brandini had almost put in order the daily accounts except some bills which were pending, very old ones, that he tried to forget.

Estrela at first refused.

"Here you are the daughter of the house."

But then she remembered the loans for the Mansion rent and resolved the matter.

"Now I know; I haven't repaid you for the money orders for the rent. So it is you who are giving us hospitality for these months!"

I'm not going to tell about my first weeks in Rio; I was already prepared for the big city. Not only because of the others which I knew—Belém, Fortaleza, Recife, Belo Horizonte—but also because of the movies, magazines, conversations with everybody: Rio is a place to which people feel they are always returning home, although they have never been there.

Moreover, I confess at that time nothing interested me very much: I looked at things only halfway, superficially, keeping back my enthusiasm in order to have a first and fresh impression with the Captain later when he arrived. Ungratefully I refused to make the customary outings— Sugar Loaf, Corcovado, a turn around Tijuca—I even refused to go to the beach at Copacabana. If I accompanied Estrela to one or another pool in Flamengo, it was only on the days when Seu Brandini couldn't go and she claimed my company.

(Senhora had a saying: "Certain women are born to be mistresses in command and others are born to have a master!")

Those two were cariocans by adoption; as soon as they were in the city, they fell into the old life as if they had never gone away. They got up late, bathed in the sea, lunched out of a picnic pail from the pension on Andrade Pertence, took the siesta, and then Seu Brandini would go out for business and friendly chatter in the city while Estrela and I tidied up the house or went to a nearby movie.

At night they ate soup or a bologna sandwich with beer from the little bar and went in search of a theater, to see the news; they paid no entrance fee—Seu Brandini was friend, brother, and godfather of all the impresarios.

I didn't always go with them; I preferred to remain at

home, listening to the programs on Estrela's old radio in the living room. The student who slept there during their absence had moved to a vacancy in D. Ema's pension, and I discovered that as thanks Seu Brandini had paid his first month's rent.

I mended Estrela's and my clothing—she wasn't capable of handling a needle and threw away whatever was torn. I even turned two shirt collars for Seu Brandini. They had the delicacy not to insist when I declined to leave the house—they knew very well that I was reserving all my interest and energy for the Captain's arrival.

And the Brandini Filho Company of Comedies and Musical Farces? Well, now, in Rio it was provisionally dissolved: or it entered into vacation sine die, as it was announced on the bulletin board at the last show. In Rio there was no theater to be rented, nor any hope of one; and even with a theater there would not be an audience for our type of entertainment in a sophisticated city. Seu Brandini spoke of taking the Company to the suburbs: There after all was an untapped audience. But I believe that never in his life had he directed his own company in Rio; or if he had it was long, long ago, and for a short run, taking advantage of a theater on the edge of the city between one tour and another.

The best thing that he could hope for himself on the Rio stage was an actor's contract, perhaps in a revue on Tiradentes Square, including Estrela or not, depending on his luck.

The others of the group were now all scattered: D. Pepa in a married daughter's house in Nilópolis; Seu Ladislau was weighing the chances of and making plans for a new circuit of low comedy for God knew when—but with that war . . . Euclides Contra-Regra found part-time work in the Republic Theater for the season with a Portuguese troupe, and he carried Antenor with him—an able prompter can always be placed in a decent job.

Seu Jota do Piano had gone where the devil might carry him—to his old place as pianist for the lowest-class dance hall in Onze Plaza.

Oh, yes, Odair and Araci with their recent economies of saving penny by penny, even going hungry (Odair had a reputation for being stingy) managed to buy the magician's materials which they still lacked; and a contract was certain for the two of them in a circus, due to open the following month in São Paulo.

And I, the ingenue, with my career interrupted, I, like a bride, I was waiting.

He finally arrived. Stretched out on my hard student bed, his head on my lap, pale and with downcast eyes like someone just recovering from an illness, he was explaining the disaster to me.

"That business of the precious stones in which so many hopes rested didn't succeed with those aquamarines, amethysts, and topazes which you saw in the little chamois bag. I know you aren't going to understand, but the little green, red, blue, and yellow stones are only trifles, of little value. The diamonds have the big value; the tiny ones, the dark ones that are of no use for jewelry; in commerce they carry the name of industrial diamonds, but in the mines, among the prospectors, they are called *xibius* and black or carbon diamonds."

I kissed him and I repeated: "Carbon diamonds—*xibius!*"

"Now, with the war, the carbon diamonds are more in demand than the luxury diamonds. The Germans pay whatever is asked and will take all there are. You see, the munition factories depend on the carbons for precision instruments, to cut steel and glass. For this same reason, through pressure of the North Americans, it is forbidden to sell them: *xibiu* is considered to be war material! To do business with that type of stone demands extreme caution. The contraband stones go to Argentina and from there to Germany. But the government is closing all the exit channels; the inspectors constantly keep their eyes on the diamond prospectors and the ones who pan for gold. They don't let a shipment pass without examining the hands of the diamond buyers. There are always surprise searches during the transport—steamships and boats on the São Francisco, trains, trucks. It all revolves around smuggling."

I was amazed.

"Imagine—how can it be? *Xibiu!* I never thought there could be a diamond that wasn't to be used for a piece of jewelry."

"Ay, the world is big, little girl; there are many things you don't know.

"But our trump card—at least we thought it was—was

that Vanderlei had entered into partnership with a man from Goias, an inspector of precious stones in the exit routes from Minas. Vanderlei made him a partner, and the character seemed trustworthy; he let pass what he wished, and kept for himself what he counted to be his share. He alleged that only contraband compensated for the miserable salaries paid by the government.

"And I, coming down the river twice a month, also had my easy contacts made with the minor diamond buyers (some of them rob the stones from the diamond beds). So I joined as a partner in the shipment which Vanderlei negotiated with a gringo, and that gringo in his turn was an intermediary of people from Buenos Aires in Teófilo Otôni.

"Now the cargo was already arranged and the price agreed upon; the delivery, this time, was to be made in Belo Horizonte; from there the stones would go to São Paulo. From São Paulo by land to Argentina, going by way of Rio Grande do Sul. But just see our bad luck, darling. That route had been working for years; and it had to be now that the American police while tracking the carbon diamonds hit the nail on the head. They got on the trail in Buenos Aires; at the frontier they dovetailed with Brazilian police, went up the Rio Grande to São Paulo, discovering the route of the stones going and coming. From there they saw the gringo coming and nabbed him in Minas. They prepared the trap and caught the unhappy Vanderlei redhanded with the money when he delivered the package and was receiving the money—part in dollars, in accordance with the agreement. Vanderlei is experienced: He underwent an interrogation and beating, and didn't sing; but the gringo was soft, or perhaps the police detectives opened up more with him who had contacts in the foreign countries. Unhappily he knew not only Vanderlei but me too—it was with him that I had the dealings on that trip when I visited you in Belo Horizonte. I went to close the deal because Vanderlei had gone to deliver the rest of the shipment to a client in the north of Goias."

I listened silently, from time to time kissing him, or I hugged him.

"Those miserable police detectives, once the gringo had opened his beak, went to wait for me on board the *J.J. Seabra*—my ship!—at a stop at a steep bank, a bridge of firewood. Of course, I denied everything; but they searched the stateroom (our stateroom!) and they found a package of *xibius* in that little old chamois bag which you know well. Carelessly, I had left that chamois bag in one of the pockets of the trunk! For you to see! The stones were purchased the day before in a port almost at the mouth of the Guaicuí; and I didn't even think about hiding them for I had bought and sold there for years without ever having had any trouble. They brought me to Rio; I was in jail being questioned for three days. Fortunately I had friends here—one case especially, a gaucho, who now is chief of the Special Police Division—you are going to like him, he is Conrado—Chief Conrado as they call him. Formerly he was an associate in the boxing academy where I practiced fighting; there we were bosom friends. One year Conrado made a round trip to Juazeiro on board the *J.J. Seabra* without paying anything, as my guest. An investigator I knew gave me the whereabouts of Conrado; I managed to send a message to him, who came running. By chance he had a friend, who had another friend, and so we went climbing from friend to friend until we reached the cabinet of Chief of Police. This is the situation today: I got out of jail—but I lost command of my ship. Not only did I lose the ship, but I also lost employment with the S. Francisco Company. The captain of the port in Pirapora (that one who lived in a house built like a ship, I showed it to you, remember?) handed down an official report that the Port Authority tolerated much lack of discipline from those river people, but it couldn't tolerate smuggling. An officer of the Merchant Marine, moreover, harming the war effort of our glorious Brazil!''

He had arrived at the house on a Friday at nightfall, beaten down and damned by life. But he was shaved and dressed in a new sports shirt. Well, when they left the police headquarters, Chief Conrado first took him home, gave him the use of his shower and his safety razor and even lent him clothing—the two were the same size.

He also gave the Captain some money because after being imprisoned, he was put into the street with none. The Captain had brought a fair amount of money, but he had used it all up for food, drink, tobacco, and especially tips.

Now he was here, without money and without work, wiped out of all he had saved for the purchase of that cursed lot of *xibius*—my God, what a ridiculous name.

I continued to pass my fingers over his head, through his hair, without saying anything. Finally I tried to cheer him up.

"You have a lot of practical preparation for life. You know about many things, you aren't going to lack work. You can even be the company's leading man."

He laughed and caught my hand, kissing the palm, slowly.

"No, work isn't the problem; Conrado has already promised me a part-time job. What worries me are the lost hopes. I had a princely program for you and me!"

I embraced him.

"Since the prince is with me, of what importance is the program! I'm going to light a candle to Our Lady of Sorrows, my patron saint, in gratitude for you to have escaped so easily. What happened to Vanderlei?"

"Who knows? After the two of us appeared together as witnesses, I haven't seen him again. I understand that they came across his record in Pernambuco, and so that old murder crime was discovered which had never been erased. Still hanging over him, poor thing."

"And now?"

"The probability is that they are going to send him back to Pernambuco. A murder crime has precedence over contraband; they will certainly extradite him so he can pay off his debt to society."

"In the claws of his enemies."

I shivered. Vanderlei, so happy and full of boasts, in a hinterland jail—I knew those jails of the interior—and with enemies outside stalking him.

I began to make plans. At coffee time, Seu Brandini and Estrela had already invited the Captain to continue living with us in the Mansion.

And Seu Brandini offered more.

"Ladislau and I are projecting a new tour—who knows, you may be able to work with us?"

I laughed.

"Didn't I say so? And as the leading man!"

The Captain also found this funny.

"Great! You as the gaucho singing the 'Andorinha,' and I in a sailor suit, singing 'The White Swan.' "

"Sing whatever you like. Just so I don't lose my ingenue."

Then the Captain straightened up in the chair, suddenly
very serious.

"Pardon, Brandini, but Dôra isn't going to work in the
theater again."

Seu Brandini turned red with rage.

"Why not? Are you still living in the Dark Ages when
people on the stage were looked down on? What is there to
be ashamed about in the theater?"

"It isn't shame, but I don't like it. My wife shaking her
hips there on the stage and all the time some man below
with his mouth open. Please understand. For me, no."

"And where did you find Dôra? In some convent?"

"Look, Brandini, I'm most grateful, extremely grateful,
for all you have done for Dôra. I am indeed, I swear it. But
we are going to find you another ingenue."

Seu Brandini was still furious.

"Just listen to you talking. It seems that I am a pimp exploiting your wife!"

The Captain, who was now in a rage also, got up and beat
on the table with his fist.

"Who here is speaking of a pimp? If I thought that, old
dear, you'd already be at the bottom of the São Francisco,
eaten up by the piranhas!"

Estrela and I put ourselves between the two, she saying:
"Carleto, Carleto, are you mad?"

I in my way tried to deflect the furies.

"All this fight over me leads nowhere. I'm very proud,
but I had already made up my mind before this. I'm not
going to work in the theater anymore, Carleto."

"And why not? Tell me, why not?"

"I made up my mind ever since Minas, ask Estrela."

"But why not? Don't you have your good little bank account and your checkbook? When did you have this before?"

I took his arm and spoke with affection.

"But you know that I always performed under pressure. I
never had the knack—and much less the desire. Estrela can
confirm this, and you better than she, for you rehearsed
me. I acted because you pursued me until I agreed. The
people there at home—Senhora principally—said that I

185

couldn't resist persuasive talk; anyone could convince me. I have a weak head, and you are so convincing!''

"Do you wish to say that I forced you to act?''

"No, Carleto, I didn't say 'forced,' I said 'convinced.' But I don't like the stage; I'm shy, every time I begin a scene I'm pressuring myself. Not even when the audience applauds do I like it, and I detest it when they ask for an encore because I have to sing again. I always had my eye on Seu Jota for fear of being out of tune, or my eye on the prompter, for fear I'd forget my lines and pull a boner.''

What I was saying wasn't exactly the truth. On the contrary, I had gotten to like very much that life in the company—the lights, the applause; and even the men's wolf calls, the day replaced by night, and the troupe here today, there tomorrow. It was an adventure that never ceased, and I had always dreamed about taking part in adventures.

But I would be a fool if I tried to balance—on one side the Captain and on the other the company. Even if all ran smoothly in my artist's career before stage lights, what was all that in comparison with him? Nor did it seem a sacrifice for me, it was only a choice between the major and the minor, even though Carleto might not agree with what I thought the major.

Seu Brandini's rage over, he showed only regret.

"A thousand pardons. I thought I had opened new horizons for you, that I had given you a brilliant profession. Just remember that I found you as a 'secretary' for D. Loura, earning your room and board, nothing more. . . .''

I got up out of the chair and embraced my old gaucho.

"No one remembers this more than I nor is there anyone more grateful than I—than both of us, for all that you and Estrela have done for me. Didn't the Captain already say this? But the fact is that I don't even like traveling; I don't like to perform, and admirers mean nothing to me.''

I appealed to Estrela again.

"Isn't that true, Estralinha?''

Estrela lowered her head, agreeing reluctantly.

"I don't know, perhaps. But what I do know is that your head is completely turned by that fellow there. So I don't blame you!''

The Captain looked at Seu Brandini triumphantly. I returned to my seat and he took my hand. Estrela tried to begin the conversation again, but Seu Brandini had lost all his gas.

Finally the Captain said, "Now, how's that! You give me a home and a wife and I'm still complaining. Pardon me, Estrela, I didn't mean to discredit your profession. I respect you too much."

Estrela shrugged her shoulders, half impatiently.

"You think that I also like to be a low-class actress? I work out of necessity. I detest that life of traveling theater."

Seu Brandini seemed like Christ, wounded with a spear in the middle of his heart.

"Estrela!"

"Now, don't lay those eyes on me, Carleto! You have known for a long time that my dream is to have a normal life, something regular every month, how ever little it might be, to live in my own house . . ."

" . . . here in the Mansion?"

"Yes, here in the Mansion, and why not? I am getting old; you also, we need a rest."

Seu Brandini got up, overturned the chair, betrayed and shaken, like the father of the sad Violeta in the play, the one who flees with the traveling salesman. He lacked only the big hat and the high boots. He turned his wounded eyes on the two of us, avoided meeting the Captain's eyes and went out to the kitchen.

Now we were making our plans: a priority, imposed by the Captain, was for me to go with Estrela to the used furniture shop and find a bed in which he could fit.

"For me, not for a dwarf!"

In truth, his legs stuck out over the mattress. Estrela had spoken about buying another student bed.

"Another one of these? No, Estralinha!" The Captain sighed, and then we decided that he and Estrela should go. She was a friend of the Portuguese and could get it cheaper, but the Captain would pay; the money from Chief Conrado was for those first expenses. I had my bank account too, I pointed out.

"You have my savings, you know."

He wished to know how much it was and gave a whistle when I told him and he said: "Then we're going to leave your money there, without disturbing it. Conrado told me that he has a business in mind, and all that is needed is a little capital. Who knows but that it might be the beginning of a new life for us?"

I responded happily, "The money is yours, my dear. The money and the money's owner—the heart, guts, and the gizzard, as Xavinha would say."

In every moment I was touching him, on the hand, in the hair, on his clothing. I lost myself while looking at him, hearing what he was saying, at times only listening to the sound of his voice without paying attention to the words, as one listens to music.

Nor could I believe—he always so distant, at times unsociable, Captain of the *J.J. Seabra*, only giving himself to me during his free time—he was now in my possession, under my hand, all day and all night. May God forgive me but I even blessed Vanderlei's business disaster.

The double bed was bought, the first one we had, and the one which would be with us for the rest of our lives.

The Captain, very restless, wouldn't stay at home; he would talk on the telephone but always in half whispers. Everybody was discreet, including myself. Seu Brandini, who could have asked questions, wasn't the man to interfere in anybody's business.

One day the Captain arrived, saying that he had arranged a part-time job as an instructor in target shooting for PE, the Special Police—something which came through his friend Conrado, of course.

One of the consequences of the new job was that he had to leave the house at nightfall. Not a week passed when he didn't appear in a taxi bringing a sack full of dead pigeons, a by-product of the target shooting.

At first it was a feast. We invited D. Pepa in Nilópolis, and Seu Ladislau (I don't know where he was living) to come lunch with us. The pigeons were roasted and basted with a glassful of Argentine wine which the Captain had also brought.

But within a short time neither Estrela nor I could even look at pigeons, not to speak of cleaning them. Even their smell nauseated us. We began then to distribute pigeons to whomever wanted them: to D. Ema's students, who roasted them on a spit over a little fire made from slats of packing boxes right in the middle of the sidewalk; to D.

Ema herself, who knew how to make an aspic of pigeon conserve—she showed us how and we did it, but it was horrible. Finally we complained so much about that unwelcome glut that from then on the Captain brought us only selected pigeons, the best, the most plump; and he himself plucked them, leaning over the garbage pail because the greatest complaint from us women was the feathers scattered in every corner of the house.

But it wasn't only the dead pigeons he brought. He never entered the house with empty hands; it was a cheese, a sweet, a small bouquet of sweet peas and mimosa, Estrela's favorite. (Today one almost never sees these flowers, sweet peas and mimosa. I wonder why not?)

One day as he was leaving (but this was after Carnival), he asked me to make out a check which amounted to about half of my savings. From this day on the things that he began to bring home were of much greater value: swatches of linen, silk from Hong Kong (until that date I had never heard of Hong Kong), palm-leaf fans, a Japanese tea service—I didn't know from where it all came. And perfumes and drinks, mostly Argentine. It was that business promised by Chief Conrado that was now beginning.

Then the Captain began to talk about renting a house of our own.

"These Brandinis have been angels, but we need a more decent place, including space for a depository and which has a garage because I am thinking about buying a jalopy."

Estrela and Seu Brandini didn't wish to hear us talk about leaving, but I agreed with the Captain; the fact is that the Mansion wasn't suitable for two married couples, everything was so crowded. The room which we occupied had been called "Carleto's study," and this already said everything. When Seu Brandini wished to get a book, he had to ask us permission. There was constant coming and going to the bathroom in the morning. The Captain had no set hour to come for meals, and so most of the time he ate out so as not to bother Estrela.

But it was difficult to find a place to live, chiefly because I imposed the condition of not going very far from Estrela. My dream was an apartment, and very high up, above the tenth floor. Because for me, raised where I was, to live in an apartment was tops, the very essence of living in Rio de Janeiro.

The Captain also had his requirements. So we two spent all our time cutting out ads in the Saturday and Sunday papers, especially Sunday morning; but we never found anything satisfactory. That one was too expensive, this one too small, an apartment just right, however, didn't turn up every day, the Captain would say. There was also the problem of finding someone to stand credit: it was the devil of a job.

When the month of January ended in Catete, it was already as if we were in the midst of Carnival. No night failed when the students working on their *bloco*, their carnival samba and their float, didn't seem like devils filling up the little alley street of the *vila*, beating cans and tambourines until one had to ask for mercy.

The nearby High Life Club was almost inside our house. With the added excitement that it was going to be my first Carnival in Rio. Seu Brandini promised me miracles, even Estrela became enthusiastic.

The Captain laughed when I was making plans; D. Pepa came one afternoon and declared that she had no intention of missing a single one of the four nights at the High Life, with a little boy friend of hers—a new one that no one knew! She planned to bring a roasted chicken to eat inside because the suppers served had highway robbery prices.

In my life Carnival was always a word that others said; in Aroeiras there were the balls into which Senhora never thought of letting me put my foot, not even after I was married. Laurindo went to them, but alone; I only guessed that he had gone to the Carnival ball when the next morning I saw the hammock full of the confetti that he had brought along on his head.

Without fail he returned high, all tanked up, angry and coarse—as Xavinha would say. Dead drunk.

During my time with the company we celebrated a Carnival, but we were making a voyage by ship between Fortaleza and Natal. There was a masked ball on board, but I was so seasick that I paid no attention to it.

D. Pepa complained as usual. Carnival had now degenerated, the fanciful costumes and the procession of the floats were all finished. Rio wasn't the same.

Estrela and I made two dimity dresses, long ones that were in style then, and they seemed more like evening dresses. Each of the men arranged his Carnival shirt—the Captain working with his and whistling out of tune Carmen Miranda's theme song, " . . . He wore his striped shirt and went out there . . ."

Magnificent! I adored all of it, all of it. On Saturday the four of us went out, to check on what was happening on the Avenue. And when we stopped in front of the Opera House that I wanted to see close up because I only knew it from passing by on the streetcar—I was thrilled by those cupolas and facades, and the gold, and bronze, and marble staircase. Estrela joked with Seu Brandini: "Have you already thought about the troupe opening there, Carleto?"

He shrugged his shoulders. He said with disdain that it ought not to be called the Opera House; it ought to be called the Mausoleum. Besides the building was an imitation of the Paris Opera. I was begging him not to shatter my enchantment, and what was wrong with imitating the Paris Opera—when suddenly we saw that the Captain was no longer beside us.

We went into the crowd, searching. But no Captain; I was already beginning to be peeved when finally there he was, very happy and relaxed in the midst of a group of people sitting on a bench under the statue of Marshall Floriano. From there he made gestures, his hands waving, calling to us to join the group.

It was a large family as from the interior: father, mother, and three adolescent girls, in addition to a little boy and girl in Indian costumes. The young girls were dressed up as Hawaiians, but the old man and woman wore their regular clothes, except that the old man wore a sailor's cap and the old lady had a paper rose in her hair.

He was white, she was black or nearly so; the daughters were beautiful and one had green eyes. I took in everything with disdain, the Captain's obvious delight with the girls, chiefly with the one with green eyes whose name was Alice.

Then he pushed me to a place on the bench at his side,

put his arms around me and explained that these people were like his family; they had befriended him when he was young. He held the girls in his arms—of all things! He called the old man "Patron" or "Boss"—Patron Davino.

Estrela, who was listening to the conversation, still standing although one of the girls offered her a seat on the bench, asked me: "Boss of what?"

Everybody laughed and then came the explanations: Patron Davino was boss of a boat; he had worked for the government in a fortress where he lived and had a beach at his door.

"It is like a country house," the Captain recalled.

Then Patron Davino informed us that he was now retired; he had had to move from the house in the fortress's sanctuary. He was now living in his own house in Olaria.

Then the old lady turned to the Captain, and said very softly: "But we haven't given up the tradition of occupying this bench with the family, bringing provisions for the trip four days of every Carnival. Have you forgotten, my son?"

My son! He had forgotten nothing; he brushed this all aside and continued with his hand on my shoulder; I had the impression he would have made the same gesture if I had been an umbrella.

Then came the invitation for a barbecue on Ash Wednesday—a barbecue, no, that meant meat, corrected the old lady—a codfish stew to celebrate the beginning of Lent.

Seu Brandini then attached himself to the group with such enthusiasm and was throwing himself at the young girls, and they responded; be that as it was, he already was explaining that he was an actor and impresario, that he had his own company in which his wife and I worked, and that we had just returned from a tour to the North, including Minas.

Patron Davino was also impressed—and I saw with misgiving that Seu Brandini was stealing the Captain's scene—at this he was a past master. Even Alice lapped up his words; and it wasn't only Carleto who had his eyes on the pretty young adolescent, no doubt with a project of a comedy number in view. Seu Brandini didn't lose any time. The Hawaiian clothing revealed the young girl's body, and it wasn't only her face that was pretty.

Then Estrela interrupted their fun. Besides being angry

with the men, we were wilted from the heat; and Estrela's solution was to continue our walk, our original project. After all, we had come out so they could show me the Carnival samba schools on the Avenue.

But the Captain and Patron Davino had already withdrawn to one side and were deep in conversation, while Seu Brandini was shining in front of the girls and the old lady; I went near the Captain and Patron Davino to overhear what they were saying.

Patron Davino was explaining he had left the fortress but not the sea; he continued to run a boat on his own, and business wasn't bad.

"You might want to try it with me; I have no one I can trust. After all you are a sailor. Who knows, you might like it. Of course a little boat isn't a ship . . ."

The Captain shrugged with that air of false modesty.

"My ship was only a paddle boat, and I am a sailor on rivers, you remember!"

Patron Davino continued in a serious vein, "Water is water, river or sea, and the back of the bay where we work is the still water of a lagoon."

On this high note the Ash Wednesday invitation for codfish stew was already firm between Seu Brandini and the old lady. Estrela repeated her request that we continue our walk; the Captain said to Patron Davino that he hoped they could then close the deal on Ash Wednesday, that perhaps his proposal would be accepted.

The old lady begged pardon for not going with us; but she didn't wish to lose her right to the bench, and besides the girls were expecting some boyfriends. It seems that Carnival for her meant only to remain there, taking charge of the bench, eating bologna sandwiches, coconut molasses candy, and hard-boiled eggs.

Finally the four of us left after fulsome farewells. Alice explained carefully the directions to Olaria and which streetcar to take, but the bus would be better; and you would get off in front of the pharmacy and walk two blocks to the left. You couldn't make a mistake; the house was painted green with "Amada's Home" on the front, written in red letters; and thus I learned the old lady's name was Amada.

Then we were dragged by a huge samba school of celebrants that invaded the whole place, with such a crowd of people accompanying it you could hardly see the costumed people singing inside the circle. They took over the street and the plaza and pushed us to the sidewalk in front of the Amarelinho Cafe. We found ourselves in front of a sidewalk stand where they sold draft beer. Wouldn't you know it? Seu Brandini immediately decided to have some beer and we all joined him; the Captain who had come home tanked up—drinks taken in the street (that day he hadn't shown up for lunch, I don't know where he went). I had noticed that he began to speak louder and pay me little attentions; he was very tight, "breathing fire," as Antônio Amador used to say when Senhora raved at him because he had come from the street drunk, "I'm not drunk, Senhora," and without contradicting Senhora's word, "I'm only breathing a little fire."

The crowd opened up and the samba school advanced singing on the side of the Arches. Another *bloco* then came while we were still drinking our beer, and more than a half-hour passed until we finally left to go toward the Avenue. The Captain and I went arm in arm in front; Estrela and Seu Brandini followed.

A man dead drunk costumed as an angel crossed in front of us and bumped into us. The Captain tapped him on the shoulder with the tip of his finger and declared, "Look where you are going, oddball!"

Then the angel opened his arms and said, "I don't walk, I fly!" and threw himself at my side in his flight.

The Captain (who never failed to have arms on him even when strolling) now reached for his revolver, clearly visible in his belt under his open shirt, spread his left hand on the drunk's chest and put his hand ostensibly on top of the gun and said in a menacing tone, "Go fly far away or you'll get hurt."

Then the angel, who after all wasn't so drunk he didn't understand, smiled acidly and turned to the left.

I, who had also tippled draft beer, found this all very exhilarating and exciting. I continued on, pushing the Captain by the arm and making provocations.

"Look at that one there; he is putting the evil eye on us!"

The Captain went ahead, bumped into the character, let the gun be seen and said abusively, "I find you vile."

I laughed. No one reacted; he was bigger than everybody else, and stronger, and armed—and also crazier.

I never had such a good time. I paid no attention to Estrela's jabs from behind. I felt ever more daring at my protector's side.

Seu Brandini, who didn't relish fights, not even when he had been drinking—anyway a fight for him was only verbal and in the safety of the theater, poor thing—was now desperate.

"You fool, shut up, do you want to go to jail?"

The Captain heard but went to further extremes, and I didn't want to act responsibly. I was finding much delight in the taste of power, provoking everybody who was afraid to respond.

It was the old blood of Senhora surging in my veins. To reach such a climax of evil, wasn't I her true daughter?

Estrela was the most troubled. She finally grabbed me by the arm and managed to guide us to Ouvidor Street; in São Francisco Plaza they got a taxi which, with the million strollers walking along the Tiradentes Plaza and by the Lapa, barely managed to get us home.

I was exhausted by the adventures, fell asleep, and ended up not going to the Saturday night ball. Neither I nor the Captain went, we were sleeping, stretched out on the new bed.

But that dangerous cruising along the Avenue didn't end our Carnival adventures; we still had until Tuesday.

Sunday and Monday we went to the High Life Club, and there we met D. Pepa with her roast chicken and her little boyfriend, a chorus dancer in Tiradentes Plaza. Seu Brandini, who recognized him, said he was a shameless creature exploiting the old woman—but Estrela found excuses: It was money well spent, the poor old thing was happy, happy! Seu Brandini greeted her with the cry: "Long live great Pepa with her two little chickens!"

She as well as the little chickens clapped their hands, applauding Seu Brandini.

We then learned the hits of this current Carnival. All these lyrics were new for me, which if I remember correctly were "On this trip I'm going to Honolulu," "Samba in Berlin," and "With or without tambourine." I don't know if I remember this all too well; I might be confusing them with the Carnival numbers that the troupe did in Belo Horizonte

195

and Juiz de Fora, when the audience ended up singing with us, receiving and returning the streamers which we threw.

But to continue my story: For that final night, Tuesday, we had arranged for a table in the garden (most difficult to arrange); and we were seated there when Seu Brandini suddenly discovered some girls, acquaintances of his, and went into the dance line with them. For a brief interval Estrela and I were alone at our table, because the Captain, despairing of a waiter ever coming to us, had himself gone to get some drinks. Then another of Carleto's acquaintances, who had already spoken to us from his table and whose name I don't know to this day, came to ask for a dance.

I didn't want to refuse so I got up and the two of us went to the part of the garden where there were fewer people; and there he, who of course was in his cups, grabbed my waist and began to exhibit such configurations of the *maxixe* that he must have been a professional dancer.

I was somewhat ill at ease as I danced. You already know that I am shy and besides I didn't know those steps; to my joy the orchestra finally stopped.

But while the character and I were dancing, the Captain had returned with three glasses of beer; and as I approached the table I saw Seu Brandini, who had returned and was serving himself, and the Captain, sitting up straight in his chair, staring at us and livid with rage.

At our arrival the man accompanying me was servile; the Captain got up, pushed his chair slowly away from the table, all the time with his glassy eyes on me and asked in an angry voice: "Should I leave?"

For an instant I was stunned, not comprehending; but suddenly I did understand, pushed away the chair where I was going to sit down and, without caring that the others were looking at me, clung to his neck and whispered to him scornfully, "Don't be an idiot, you devil! How would I know who that clown is! Not even if he were Getulio or even Clark Gable!"

Without realizing that I was raising my voice, fearful of that terrible anger of his, I ended, "You know very well that when it comes to men I am very well serviced!"

Estrela heard and laughed out loud; the dancer had already withdrawn without perceiving directly what he had provoked. The Captain grabbed my waist with both hands and drew me near with such brutality that I was breathless and started dancing with me. With his serious and sulky face he didn't even have the grace to blush.

When we arrived home, almost morning, and I was taking off my clothes, he suddenly seemed to remember the scene. Because he jerked the dress over my head and gave me a slap on the face that was so hard it left the mark of his four fingers.

"This is so you remember never again in your life to dance with another man. Fortunately for the two of you I wasn't armed—in that dive you aren't allowed to carry arms."

Amada's house was painted green all right. It was one of those little bureaucratic houses that at the time were called "decree number six thousand," built by the plan which the prefect furnished—a tiny veranda as an entrance (which D. Amada called "the portico"), a small living room and two other rooms; but as Patron Davino's family enjoyed entertaining their friends and as yet hadn't forgotten the spaciousness of the old house, they covered the little cemented backyard with a tin roof, and it was there that they served the luncheons and held other big parties. As a joke, the girls called it "the Patron's grill" in homage to the Cassino da Urca's Grill which was then the rage with the suburban young girls, and even those not from the suburbs.

The four of us made part of the trip by streetcar, part by bus. It took the greatest of efforts to get there. We were served a lemonade whip, a coconut whip and also a *pitanga* (cherry) whip that was the specialty of the house in past times. Now I don't know how they managed to get the *pitangas*. I found the whip sickening.

The young girls were wearing shorts, which was already daring.

"I don't know why those girls don't go as nudists like the 'Luz del Fuego,' " I whispered to the Captain.

He didn't like it and answered that they were only children. Children, my God; with those children a dozen others could be created.

Yes, but our greatest surprise upon arriving there was to find the old Amada already seated in a canvas chair with a guitar on her lap beginning to sing "The Floor of the Stars." Although born in Algoa, the old Amada had all the wiles of a woman from Bahia and the husband explained: "She learned as a child, when she went to live in Salvador."

Patron Davino, who was little and very skinny, went back and forth between the house and the grill, serving the drinks; on the oil stove of the kitchen, which smelled strongly of burned grease, the codfish stew was cooking in a pot large enough to feed a garrison.

Amada took the guitar and gave the beat; even Estrela felt a part of the group and sang. Seu Brandini, the star of the party, thrashed out all of his repertory, including the Andorinha. Even the Captain joined, out of tune in his bass voice.

I said: "Your voice doesn't go with theirs; it is very low, you have a bass voice."

And he: "Mine is a macho voice. A macho can't sing daintily."

The girls applauded, and he joined their circle, twirling and clapping hands.

After an hour Seu Brandini was so ebullient that he almost forced the Apache's waltz on us, but Estrela declined, saying it was impossible without an orchestra; and I warned him that he might hurt himself on the cement floor.

I didn't sing anything; I said I had a sore throat and a hangover from the ball, that I had come only so as not to offend the friends of . . . (and I was so bad-tempered that I spoke the name I never used) . . . "the friends of Asmodeu."

Wasted venom. Nobody paid any attention. The Captain only looked at me and contrived a twisted smile of understanding.

Finally the codfish stew was served. It must have seemed good to those who liked it swimming in gravy, with an overdose of pepper and lots of Portuguese olive oil (I don't know where they got it in time of war), and the inevitable glass of red wine.

After the dessert of pumpkin and coconut sweets came the coffee. Seu Brandini and the girls returned to the guitar: Estrela, the old Amada, and I dozed in the canvas chairs. Patron Davino took the Captain to the front room, and it was then they must have organized the partnership. When they left the room the Captain was all smiles like a sweetheart who had just asked his girl to marry and said to Patron Davino: "You're going to like him; he's a grand person. We were looking for just such a partner with a boat . . ."

Of course Chief Conrado was the grand person.

While those two were talking, D. Amada with that soft, liquid speech confided complainingly to Estrela and me. "Just imagine our bad luck; Alice, who is charming and has studied shorthand and could have a good job, is now in love with a crazy character who says he is a soccer player, but what he plays only God knows. I'm going to ask Cadet Lucas to intervene; those girls adore him—ever since they have been little things . . ."

"Cadet Lucas? Why *Cadet* Lucas?" I wondered.

"Ah, when he was doing his military service in the fort, he was very young; it was then we met him. Afterwards the friendship developed. Alice was born—he was then no longer a soldier; he never got to be a cadet, but we were already in the habit of calling him that so we continued to call him Cadet Lucas. As a sort of joke the girls picked it up. . . ."

I added one more name to the Captain's others: Cadet Lucas! When I was angry with him this was what I called him now—and I hated the name all the more because my dislike of it never bothered him: He just laughed.

Our first tangible progress was to get a car, a Studebaker. It was black with the paint peeling off and the seat linings worn thin, but the men said the motor was purring.

I have doubts about it now: I don't remember well on what the car ran, where they got the gasoline—wasn't it rationed in time of war? I don't believe that it was even possible then to make synthetic gas. Be that as it may, the Captain never relied on synthetic gas; and he didn't lack fuel for the car, which he called "my little service donkey." The stupid thing was that we had to pay rent for parking in a garage on Pedro Américo Street because cars couldn't enter the *vila*, which even had a bar across the entrance. For the Studebaker to stand on the street it would have had to be on Catete Street, where even standing was forbidden, not to speak of parking.

That lack of shelter for the car made a move even more necessary. All in all no apartments came up, and the two of us were nearly crazy from reading so many ads in the *Jornal do Brasil*.

Carleto scoffed at us and Estrela said that the car aside, and if we wanted to pay for a house, she would charge rent.

But finally, one Monday morning the Captain took out again the last clipping of the day before which we hadn't had the courage to follow up: "SANTA TERESA. Small apartment, ground floor, very picturesque garden, Paula Matos Street, keys in bakery on the corner."

The Captain knew more or less where it was, and we left Estrela to prepare lunch. We went on foot along Santo Amaro and Santa Cristina and from there took the streetcar. You could reach the place by three routes: by the streetcar which went along Neves Plaza; by car, going up Riachuelo Street, turning along all those scary curves; and directly by a stone stairway, climbing up millions of steps to arrive with shaking legs.

In the years that followed I descended those steps many times, but the ascents could be counted on the fingers of my hands; and even then it was only when I was forced to do so, never because I wanted to.

It wasn't exactly an apartment as was advertised; there were some rooms on the backyard. At the front, with an entrance on the other street, was the old mansion, now rented, lower and upper, for two families.

There were also the old rooms for the help, constructed on the ground part of the back, facing the other street which the owner had isolated as an independent apartment. He built a wall which divided the yard, thereby taking advantage of the iron gate in the back which was on the street parallel to that of the streetcar—an old street, still paved with cobblestones. That iron gate served as an entrance to our small apartment: The apartment opened out on a sort of large patio, almost a garden; at the right of whomever should enter were the living quarters—a living room with a window on the street, a bedroom, a tiny corridor with the bath, and finally the kitchen. At the left was a smooth wall and in the back a sort of shed, whose tin roof was attached to the dividing wall which separated our garden from that of the mansion. Our garden had only the trunk of an old fruit tree, some gravel, and in the middle a well with a stone ring that was covered by the remains of an old summer-house or *pergola*.

The iron gate was large enough to give easy entry to a car; it must have been made for the entrance of horse-drawn carriages of the mansion—it was old enough for that.

The Captain was so completely enchanted by the place that he immediately began making plans, a half of the shed would be for the garage, the other half a depository for the merchandise; and he wanted to plant a grape arbor so we could have shade over the summerhouse and we could also have grapes!

The living quarters or the "apartment" left much to be desired, but I wasn't accustomed to luxury; and I had already lost my hopes of having the dream apartment on the twelfth floor. The living room and the bathroom were carpeted, and even a new wooden floor had been recently laid, as the proprietor explained. The rent was cheap because of the climb up the hill and the modest equipment.

It had a gas stove but no water heater—and I must confess that, in that time, I was still afraid of a water heater; the bath and kitchen floors were of cement which the Captain pointed out to the man.

I became anxious that the owner might be offended and send us away because he had explained to us that he had two other serious contenders for the apartment; we were the third. Our good luck was that the other people had children—he preferred a couple without children.

We moved three days later, a modest move because we carried everything to the car; only the bed went by handcart because it didn't fit into the Studebaker, try as hard as we could to get it in.

But after several days the furniture that the Captain had gone to buy with me at the auctions on S. José Street arrived: the table and chairs for the living room, a small buffet, and a wardrobe. I didn't accept the one which Estrela had given me, so as not to deplete the Mansion's furniture. She could use it for her things.

Later we purchased china, flatware, and my beautiful aluminum pots. Bed, table, and bath linens—oh, my linen sheets at Soledade—were ordinary plain cretonne which in the Northeast we called *bramante*, but I loved them as much as if they had been silk and embroidered with silver.

* * *

My birthday fell the week following our move and the Captain brought me a big Irish damask tablecloth—"to begin your trousseau"—the first important gift that he set aside for me from the contraband.

On that day we entertained with a luncheon; the arbor was already planted, but the bower naturally didn't give any shade yet. As luck would have it, it was an overcast day, almost cold; and Seu Brandini, showing off his gaucho arts, made a barbecue, setting up the brazier between four bricks and insisting that the Captain "had to buy" a rotisserie.

We drank vermouth and gin and tonic as an aperitif, and afterwards wine which Chief Conrado brought and everybody enjoyed the treat (they enjoyed Chief's company as well as his wine). He was a tall man such as the Special Police required, and besides he was strong and big as an elephant; he had reddish hair, some large teeth, and enormous hands which reminded me of whales' fins.

The Captain also brought me a present of an American canned ham I had never seen before; and that was the happiest birthday of my life, although that wouldn't be saying much because up to then I had never had any happy anniversaries.

I have mentioned the parties in detail because they were so few and made a big difference in our everyday life, which more and more centered around just the two of us. But it wasn't a prison; it was more like a hedge protecting a garden, which made it fun.

The Captain worked hard and was restless, coming and going at all hours, and I always had the housework—besides keeping him company when he came home; I would sit at the table while he drank his gin and tonic or beer—more often beer—as I embroidered or sewed. It seemed then just like those hours of conversation on the *J.J. Seabra* when we would recall things from the past. That is, he reminisced—the demands made on him when he was a boy in Rio, when he almost lived with Patron Davino, the years he put in on the São Francisco River, first when he was learning to be a pilot and then when he came to command a ship. Now and then he got away from the river and ventured as far as Belo Horizonte and even São Paulo, or came to Rio de Janeiro where he had friends. But he always returned to Velho Chico. Only now had the door been closed in his face; and I, who feared in the depths of my heart that he would be seized by the river madness again and want to go back there, would console him: "Who knows, perhaps when the war has ended . . ."

But he would shake his head, and I saw with misgiving that my poor Captain's eyes were red and running, a thing that happened only after he had opened his third bottle.

As for me, I too told things from the past, mostly from my childhood, sayings of my father which Xavinha had repeated, and one day I mentioned the name of Doralina. He understood at once—this is what made the Captain such a special person, capable of understanding certain things more by intuition than by listening, without demanding explanations.

Then—it wasn't that night but the next morning: when he returned home at noon, the lunch hour, he held in his hand one beautiful red rose bud; and closing my fingers around its long stem, he kissed me on my face and said smiling: "Doralina, my flower."

From then on he called me Doralina, but only in our hours of intimacy and never in front of others, never—exactly as I wished it. I have kept that red rose bud until this very day, and I still have it pressed between the leaves of the dictionary; and even if it turns to dust and disappears, the impression that it made on the pages of the book will never leave.

Who would have believed it! After the deceptions, fears, and financial loss of the Vanderlei adventure, the Captain's business was now going well; at least he always had money and never again did he ask me for any more monies from my savings.

The things in the house multiplied as if by magic, always something unexpected, the most of them unreasonable things like silk pajamas, costume jewelry, perfumes, and bottles of drinks. Also canned things, American war rations which the Captain opened but which I didn't like: I had no taste for any of them.

I became accustomed to see the Studebaker arrive with

the trunk full of cargo. He would enter through the iron gate, lock it, and then would unload all the goods into the little depository room; and many times I even helped to carry the heaviest boxes.

In the beginning I had a mad curiosity to open all the boxes and see what was inside, but the Captain didn't always let me do so for fear the packaging might be damaged, and he would just tell me what was in the boxes. In the end I was no longer interested; the contents varied little and when something special appeared the Captain never failed to set aside a piece—the best and the prettiest—for me or for both of us, as the case might be.

We also gave presents. Estrela said that the Captain suffered from a Santa Claus complex; and she complained that he was obsessed with the mania of giving presents. It was true: That man didn't know how to enter anyone's house with empty hands.

I remember one time when we went to visit Seu Brandini, who was ill, and just at the entrance of the *vila* the Captain discovered that he hadn't brought anything for Carleto; he quickly entered a bakery, and bought an English pastry, one of those concocted by the bakery itself. I only smiled because in these things my Captain was like a child who wanted to do something nice—whatever it might be.

Speaking of the Brandinis: if we were living very well, the same couldn't be said of them. The proceeds from the stay in Minas had already evaporated and the projects for a new company seemed impractical, because Seu Brandini didn't have the economic resources for a theater in Rio; and a circuit in the customary plazas was altogether impossible with the transport difficulties in wartime.

Estrela managed to work, first as a cashier in a beauty salon in Copacabana, but the hours were long and the pay poor. Then a childhood friend, who was now a high officer in an aviation company, hired her to supervise the planes' *comissaria de bordo* or air hostesses, a profession that had its beginning in that time. Estrela was to teach the girls how to dress, wear their hair and make up modestly, how to walk, treat the public, offer drinks, and serve luncheon trays.

"Estrela, you have the manners of an English lady, you are like the Duchess of Windsor!" said the friend in order to convince her, because she, just imagine, had doubts; she was afraid of the responsibility and didn't wish to accept that job which had fallen from the sky. She accepted it only when the man guaranteed that in the beginning she would be on trial; I had no doubts myself and wasn't surprised when she landed the job. I always found that Estrela had the manners of a grande dame, just as her friend said: she knew how to dress with taste and chic, and her body was built like that of an Englishwoman.

Seu Brandini complained about these pro-English remarks, but as a joke, because when Estrela wore a bathing suit she had a lot to show.

Now he, poor thing, was only beating his head against a wall, and I don't know why he didn't get ill from so many disappointments.

At first, he had illusions that being a gaucho he would get work, for in that time only gauchos directed government jobs or at least that was what was said; but he never got a good opportunity. Perhaps the other gauchos didn't take him seriously. The politicians would tap him on the stomach and ask him for free tickets to shows; but the dream of financing for a patriotic show season never came about, only promises.

If it weren't for Estrela with her small but certain pay and the security of the Mansion with the rent that hadn't gone up for fifteen years, I don't know what their life would have been like, I just don't know. Seu Brandini never complained or whined; he always thought up new projects. One day he even arranged a position—well, position wasn't the word, as Estrela explained—it was more a sideline: inspector in casinos and cabarets for a union which protected the rights of authors of musical numbers.

As long as it lasted it was glorious. Seu Brandini went out every night to the most expensive places; he took Estrela sometimes, and he always returned home drunk. He made a collection of new friends, faces that nobody ever saw because they were nighttime people.

But at the end of the year when there were elections the directorate waged a stiff campaign; but it even came out in the newspapers that there had been a big rake-off. Seu Brandini's protector was accused of being the worst of the swindlers; after the elections there was a new directorate and Seu Brandini was through.

Withal, the job lasted nearly a year, and while it lasted he had one big time. Afterwards he never failed to tell about the time when he was an "officer in the financial service of the rights of authors," which was how he said it; and he made it out to have been an important position.

It was already a year since we had moved to the house in Santa Teresa; I finally fixed everything up to my taste, the curtains in the living room and the new coverlet. (It was of Chinese silk, contraband naturally, beautiful, full of dragons and irises; the Captain said that these coverlets were worth plenty, and he told me to choose the prettiest. I took a print of gold and blue, my favorite colors.) The vanity was full of Argentine, American, and even French perfumes—at least so the labels read.

But I concentrated my love on the kitchen. Kitchen for me, ever since I knew what one was, was only the dark domain of old Maria Milagre with her little black girls, the iron-plated stove ("That furnace eats wood like the mouth of hell," complained Senhora when the girls came to tell her that the wood was all gone), and the water in the pots, and those immense clay and iron pots, the rare ones in agate or aluminum hanging on the wall for decorative effect; and the china that was washed in the large, flat clay basin, and the dried orange skins hanging from the rafters of the ceiling, and the salted pork fat curing by smoke over the stove, and the hens entering and leaving willy-nilly and always some woman shouting: "Shoo hen, shoo stupid hens!"

I hardly ever passed by there; when I wanted to grab a sweet or some biscuits, it was from the table of the backyard outside where food was served to the workers. Zeza would light the clay oven in the garden's covered shed, and it took the greatest care for the sweet cake not to settle if the oven was too cold, or for the *sequillos* not to be burned to a crisp if on the other hand the oven was too hot.

I knew nothing of salty food—a girl from a fazenda didn't eat coarse food, that was left for the servants: A young lady ate cakes and fine sweets. And the cheese was Senhora's special secret with her womenfolk in the cheese room.

* * *

Now my kitchen seemed like a dollhouse with its little aluminum pans, only large enough for the two of us, and the gas stove enameled with porcelain which I kept shining like a mirror, and the tile flooring with its blue designs we had installed. The Captain used to joke that my kitchen was sanitary like a pharmacy; but it was obvious that he adored sitting on a chair (also white and enameled!) at my little kitchen table covered with a checked oilcloth, and to eat the omelettes that I had learned to make with Estrela, and the *picadinhos* (minced beef) with olives and rounds of hard-boiled egg the recipe for which was given over the radio. But my specialty, and it was the Captain's favorite dish, I learned from the tavern cook there at the hill's top in the Plaza where we were clients: *caldo verde*—green vegetable soup à la Portuguese.

Even Seu Brandini applauded and also D. Pepa, who as a Spaniard declared herself to be a specialist on *caldo verde* since it is also a specialty of Galicia; they came to visit one night and the Captain insisted that they stay for a supper of my *caldo*. D. Pepa opened her eyes wide when served such a delicacy! Made with good pork fat and with that special Portuguese olive oil which now, because of the war, only the Captain could get.

It was for me a great day, or a great night, I mean to say. We drank real port wine, also from the Captain's smuggling.

Now I was intent on making a *cabidela* (a chicken stew made of giblets, wings, feet, and blood) of the *sertão*; but there was a problem that I didn't tell anyone about: In order to make a *cabidela* it was necessary to kill the chicken, one you bought dead wouldn't do. I didn't have the courage to kill a chicken—I mean kill it with my own hands.

One morning when I was in my kitchen, washing the dishes from morning coffee and thinking about whether I dared to make some croquettes with the meat leftovers from the night before, a boy knocked at the iron gate.

"Telegram!"

I went to the door with my hands wet, signed the receipt with the boy's pencil, and wet the receipt. I remember that I begged pardon and was embarrassed because the messenger had more education than messengers usually had. I

asked him to wait while I got the tip—the Captain insisted
on tipping messengers and was very angry when I forgot.

Only after closing the gate did I read the name on the
telegram—it wasn't for the Captain, it was for me. Who
likes to receive telegrams without warning early in the
morning? So in that mood, already nervous, I opened the
wire with my wet fingers.

"Lament to inform you death of your mother occurred
last night due to cerebral embolism all possible recourses
tried without results interment today sympathy Dr. Fenelon Batista."

I looked at the date. It was the sixteenth, three days ago.
It was sent from Aroeiras. Then all was over by this time
and Senhora was buried in the same grave with Laurindo
and my father.

With my head swirling I sat down on the bed. Senhora,
Senhora with her cat eyes, her white arms, her strong steps,
her shrill voice, her pretty face, her beautiful hair—Senhora, dead.

The Captain had gone out, and I didn't know where he
was; but I needed to talk with someone. I pulled off my
robe, threw on a dress and went to the bakery to telephone
Estrela.

"Estrelinha, Senhora, my mother, she has died."

Estrela didn't understand. "Who died? Who died?"

"My mother—Senhora! I just received a telegram."

"Oh, I'm very sorry! Of what?"

"Suddenly. An embolism."

"Who telegraphed?"

"The doctor. Our doctor, there."

"Ah, poor thing. Where's the Captain?"

"I don't know! He went out. Oh, Estrela!"

"Do you want to spend the day with us, so you won't
have to be there all alone? I should say with me rather than
us. Carleto also went out early today."

"I can't, I have to wait for the Captain." And I repeated:
"Oh, Estrela!"

"Then I will go to you. I'm going to get dressed and take
a taxi. I'll be right there."

I returned home and was still going around in circles between the living room and the kitchen as I waited for Es-

trela, waiting chiefly for the Captain. What was I going to do? What did I have to do?

After all she was dead, buried. Those stupid people—naturally Dr. Fenelon gave the orders. Luckily Antônio Amador was there. He had judgment, accustomed as he was to Senhora's harsh discipline. People said he was a relative of ours, the illegitimate son of my father's brother, Uncle Jacinto, the family black sheep who died from alcoholism. I don't know if this was true, but the child was raised from the time he was very young in my grandmother's home; when my father got married and took charge of the fazenda, he made Amador overseer of Soledade. If he was the son of Uncle Jacinto, his mother must have been black because he had a dark skin although he had "good" hair.

Even if he had our blood he didn't claim it; moreover, after falling into Senhora's clutches he understood the law that she decreed whenever it was said that Fulano or Sicrano (so-and-so) had blood of such and such a family: "A son born in the bushes—an illegitimate child—has no family."

But perhaps what was to be admired most about Amador was that he didn't fear her; he was her friend and did all that she commanded without any discussion. Senhora had confidence in him; she liked him very much, and let Amador choose his cattle from the common lot.

"Separate yours yourself, Amador, but remember the rules: neither the cream nor the skim milk!"

Amador took care of her business in Aroeiras: he sold the cattle and paid the taxes; and at times when Senhora was angry with our lawyer who was lazy and left everything to take care of itself, she would comment: "Amador ought to be my lawyer. But he can only scratch his name!"

Amador would laugh.

"It is bad, bad, *comadre*. On one election day I was so bewildered that instead of signing my name I put down: 'Your obliging servant'!"

Senhora also laughed.

"This proves that you know how to write more than your name."

Amador joined the laughter.

"But it was such a scrawl, *comadre*, that only I myself knew it was 'your obliging servant'!"

The bell rang. It was Estrela, and with her, Seu Brandini.

"Carleto arrived just as I was about to leave and wanted to come also," Estrela explained, as if she were excusing his presence.

Both embraced me without saying anything; they knew that I didn't get on well with Senhora; they sensed that this wasn't an ordinary visit of condolence.

Estrela finally asked, "What was it anyway?"

I showed her the telegram. Estrela read and then passed it over to Carleto. After reading it, he smoothed the paper, folded it back as it was when the messenger delivered it, and put it on top of the table. He looked out of the window and finally sighed.

"That's the way it is. People die!" (I knew he had a horrible fear of death.)

Estrela repeated the question she had asked on the telephone.

"Do you know now what you're going to do? Will you go there?"

I didn't know anything about anything; I was waiting for the Captain. But Seu Brandini objected, somewhat irritated.

"Go, how? How can she go? There's no boat, there isn't anything. The situation hasn't changed since we left Pernambuco. She could go if she could get a priority on the airplane, which is practically impossible. She'd have to wait months."

Just then the iron gate opened—finally the Captain had arrived. He used his own key and brought a package.

"Oh, Estrela and Carleto! So, you guessed: fresh sausage from Minas, just came today! There's enough for everybody, you must lunch with us, you're going to see how delicious it is!"

But then he became aware of our serious faces; he was about to ask a question and Seu Brandini handed him the telegram. He threw the package on the table, unfolded the paper, read out loud, slowly, and repeated. Then he came near me, by my chair, put his hands on my shoulders and said, I don't know if for me or for them: "A mother is a mother."

He ran his hand through my hair, without saying anything more. After a bit he looked at Estrela.

"How did you find out?"

I answered, "I telephoned. I didn't know where you were; I was almost crazy, it was so unexpected."

"You did right." The Captain was silent with his hands on my neck; I touched his fingers with my lips.

Seu Brandini commented, "It was sudden but not altogether a surprise. She had already suffered a stroke, hadn't she? I remember that letter you received in Belo Horizonte."

And Estrela remembered: "But you said she had had a slight stroke . . ."

The Captain left me and sat down.

"What letter? What person? I don't know anything about it."

I put my hand on his arm.

"Xavinha wrote. You were still on board the ship. It seems that it was a blood clot, but it dissolved. Xavinha said in the letter that all was well."

The Captain persisted.

"But I was in Belo Horizonte and you didn't say anything."

"It was because the letter came after your visit. And as Xavinha said, it was only a scare. I forgot to tell you when I saw you next."

Seu Brandini suddenly asked, "And the fazenda? Who owns it now?"

I still hadn't thought about that.

"Well, I do, I suppose. I am her only daughter; she has no other heirs that I know of."

"Is there someone who can take charge in the owner's absence?"

"The overseer. He has already been taking care of everything."

Estrela got up, embraced me.

"You are now with your husband. Go lie down and rest from the shock. Let's go, Carleto."

After they left the Captain sat near me again, looking at me intently, without touching me.

"I find you strange. Oh, the devil, in spite of everything she was your mother. And your way of suffering—not a tear?"

"I'm still half dazed from the shock, dearest."

I paused, trying to find some way to explain myself.

"Moreover, you know that I didn't get along with Senhora."

He shook his head.

"A fight of a mother with a child never goes far. Certainly not to death! I know, many times I fought with my mother. I was damned, I swore I would never put my foot in the house again; and on the first occasion I could I returned and went to receive the blessing from the old lady."

"The disposition of your mother must have been different. Even if I went there a thousand times to receive her blessing, Senhora would continue to ignore me and deny my existence."

Oh, much to the contrary: deny my existence, no! The pleasure that Senhora would have, seeing me arrive at Soledade, hand lifted: "Your blessing, Senhora!" She would humiliate me, that says everything . . . or does it? Or does it? Ever since that accursed night, something warned her that I knew. I don't think she would betray me—but who could swear? And Senhora changed—she was less arrogant—using a sort of ceremony with me.

From then on we exchanged no words that weren't forced; she never again looked me in the eyes.

Only on the day of Laurindo's death, both of us kneeling at the side of him on the ground; even so it was I who looked at her, I who looked her straight in the eyes, I remember. Later, beside the coffin, on the night of the wake, again we two, one on each side. She looked at me on the sly, but when I looked back at her she turned her eyes away.

Later I cannot say she talked with me; she simply gave her orders for the mourning, burial, and mass—in language the people understood. But that wasn't talking—as always, ever since I can remember, she was giving orders.

And finally on the day of my departure without our taking leave of each other, I embraced everybody in the house one by one while she was in the counting room, seated as if she were examining something in her notebook. I came to the door and said: "I'm ready to go."

She didn't reply, got up, and accompanied me slowly. The people of the house certainly thought that we had said our adieus inside the little room. I then got into the car and waved to all. Xavinha cried, Zeza sobbed leaning on the column, and Luzia was wiping her eyes on her apron; Maria Milagre remained by the stove crying, but Senhora stood in the doorway—in silence.

Afterwards, until this very day, not a word: Even the accounting came in Xavinha's letters. Yes, there was one word: written in the margin of that letter from Carmita, Laurindo's sister. But it was the only one.

And now she was dead, and all had ended as it only could end—without a word.

My God, I couldn't explain all that to the Captain or to anyone else in the world, but least of all to him; I had a horror of telling him because I couldn't bear to think of his knowing. I would prefer to die rather than open up the closed wound, the blood and pus in my heart. Yes, I'd rather die, die like her, now free and redeemed. The remorse over, the rage and the pain gone.

Then, overwhelmed by everything, I leaned forward over the table, laid my head on my arms and collapsed in sobs.

He let me cry for some moments; then he drew me from the chair and carried me away clinging to his neck; it was easy because he was so big and I so tiny. He laid me on the bed, lifted the spread and covered me with it and began to caress my head again.

"Cry, my love, cry. Pardon what I said; but I find you are too hard—it is against nature. . . ."

At that word I broke into sobs again. He knew, did he, innocent one, what was against nature . . . against the laws of nature and against all the laws of the world and God.

My loud crying seemed to make up for my other desperate lament, there that night in the moonlight as I in pajamas was seated on the bricks with Delmiro looking at me, as he held the little donkey by the halter. I cried all that I hadn't cried during those months and years; I cried as if a stone were ripping apart my insides and suffocating me. Each sob was a stab of pain which finally gushed out from my throat and mouth.

The Captain lay down on the bed at my side, took me in his arms, pressed my face against his chest, put his lips on my hair, and was lulling me to sleep as if I were a child.

Little by little I quieted down, the sobs spacing themselves out. The danger had passed. He asked me no more
questions—there wasn't anything to ask. My mother had
died. I was lamenting my orphanhood, and he was consoling me. Each one in his own role, just as it should have
been.

By night I was more calm, and we discussed what I had to
do. Well, to go there now was clearly impossible as Seu
Brandini had said.

"That idiot Carleto," commented the Captain, "what a
lack of sentiment, to ask right out about the inheritance at
such a time!"

(Seu Brandini was no fool, what Seu Brandini didn't
know he guessed, and he wasn't a man to lose time. He
may have even asked about the fazenda thinking of the
inheritance—now I was rich, owner of a fazenda, who
knows, I might be able to finance a new incarnation of the
company? I held no rancor against him because of this—it
was his way: I even liked it, with him you didn't have to
pretend anything. I could either talk or remain silent, the
Brandinis understood.)

The Captain continued: "But on one point he is right: a
trip at this time is very difficult. Moreover I can't accompany you, and I won't even discuss your going alone."

He picked up the telegram and reread it.

"How is that Dr. Fenelon Batista?"

"A doctor, his fazenda, Arabia, is next to ours. For many
years Senhora and he had some dispute about the boundaries, but finally one day they made their peace and the old
friendship returned."

(I didn't tell him that Laurindo had been the peacemaker,
with his surveyor measurements; much less did I tell him
that it was Dr. Fenelon who had brought Laurindo to
Soledade for the first time. I never spoke of Laurindo in the
Captain's presence—for the two of us it was as if Laurindo
had never existed in my life, as if he had been dead and
buried for centuries.)

"He is taking charge of things, then? That Dr. Fenelon?"

(I doubted it very much. Imagine! Even dying Senhora
wasn't going to put her business in the hands of an
outsider—Dr. Fenelon, "that evil idiot.")

The overseer, Antônio Amador, must be taking charge of

everything. Senhora had trusted him and—you know—the business of those fazendas isn't that demanding—only a few head of cattle, a bit of cotton, some beans and corn. Senhora, being the mistress of all those lands, was considered rich—and she was the first to think of herself as rich! But the income was small and she had almost no working capital.

"You mean to say that Amador can remain in charge until you can go there?"

"And I still have Xavinha. Xavinha is the boss of all financial matters; whatever goes wrong she will advise, almost too much! She can bore you to death."

We finished drawing up a telegram for Dr. Fenelon. The Captain edited it in his elegant handwriting—I called it English handwriting—of which he was so proud:

Desolate unable to travel immediately due to difficulties of this wartime thanks your assistance advise Amador and Xavinha letters follow for each many thanks Dôra.

I even wrote a long letter. At first it was only for Amador; then I added Xavinha's name on it because at that stage I didn't have the heart to begin another letter for her. I didn't need to pretend much sentiment, because they knew too many things. But I inquired about the details of the illness, and said that I was certain that a letter would come here telling me all about that.

It came, eight pages:

I tell you with the greatest sorrow about the death of my adored Godmother Senhora. As I told you before the deceased already had a warning: She had her mouth half twisted for five days, was talking gibberish, and the left arm was even paralyzed; but afterwards she was completely well, who would say, Jesus, that in so little time. . . . but she wasn't aware of death, she was already in a coma, the priest came but he couldn't confess her, he only gave her Extreme Unction. . . . She was buried in the shroud of Our Lady of Carmo. I put in her hands that rosary which had belonged to her grandmother Amelinha, and I cut off a piece of her hair to keep for myself. Would you believe, Dorinha, she

215

still had almost no white hair? It was beautiful as always. . . . You can imagine that my health isn't good after this horrible shock. . . . Compadre Antônio Amador is taking charge of everything; he says you aren't to worry; it will be just as if the deceased were still alive. All of us are waiting for the new mistress—I hope to God the visit will be soon. We are all very sorry you couldn't be at the funeral or the Mass, but it is God who governs us. I hope that you had a Mass said in Rio. . . .

In my letter to them I recommended that they leave all as it was, that they keep on maintaining the house as usual, that if it were necessary to pay some account they should sell an animal, but probably there was still something left over from Seu Zacarias's cotton.

At the moment it was impossible for me to travel because there were no boats and I couldn't get a seat on an airplane. Moreover it was very expensive; but as soon as I could find a way, I would return.

They shouldn't bother the tenants: Each one should continue with his cleared land as before; God willing, I wouldn't have to delay my arrival there too long and we could then make definite plans.

I thanked Amador very much for the responsibility which he was taking, and I thanked Xavinha even more for everything she was doing.

I showed the letter to the Captain; he approved and took it to mail. He didn't even notice that I hadn't written even once the name of Senhora: I still couldn't, I couldn't dare yet risk writing the name.

From then on the correspondence continued regularly, now Xavinha writing, now Amador having a letter sent for him. He didn't have Xavinha send it; there was jealousy, I do believe.

The Captain wouldn't let me relax; he made me order provisions and acquaint myself with the running of the fazenda; he made me send money to repair the dam which Amador wrote about. When Amador wrote about the hoof-and-mouth epidemic that was attacking the cattle, the Captain himself got the vaccine and sent it by plane, although it arrived there spoiled. As Amador said in a later letter, there was no need to be disgruntled about the serum arriving spoiled because whatever its condition, it had arrived too late: The animals that were going to die had already died—only a few did die—nearly all escaped. What hurt most was that the bull had a bad attack of the disease. His skin had thickened and he got shortness of breath, when he went to the top of the corral he was breathing like an old asthmatic. There was no hope that he would be able to perform his duties any longer.

The Captain spoke a lot about getting a bull in Minas, a humped animal of good breed; but that was a pipe dream. I didn't forget the crossing in the truck over the *sertão* of Pernambuco, and how could that bull have been sent? He agreed it would be difficult, but he could arrange it; he had friends, and then we agreed to let it go until after the war.

And Delmiro? In one of her letters Xavinha said that he hadn't shown himself on the occasion of Senhora's death, but afterwards they told her that he spent three days and three nights singing the hymns of the dead, with a candle burning. Returning from the burial, Luzia thought that it was he who was watching, hidden behind a hedge, but no one could swear that it was really he.

I really had only one concern about our life now: It was that the Captain drank too much and became dangerous; and all the more because of his unfailing custom of going about with a gun.

I would make jokes in order to separate him from his mania: Where I came from no one gained glory from carrying a gun; there it was said that the arm of the macho is cold iron. Why instead of the spectacular gun with which you killed from a distance didn't he use a knife or stiletto to kill close up? A dagger, for example: It could even have a gold handle. I could give him as a present one of those made in Juazeiro, home of Padre Cicero.

But the Captain didn't like the joke; he didn't crack a smile. And he became irritated when I insisted: He boasted of his skill in the use of guns; after all it was no accident that he was made instructor of target shooting.

He couldn't, however, remain the instructor of target shooting in the Special Police, according to Chief Conrado, when it was a question of obtaining a contract. To get this he had to be part of the military establishment—and the Captain wasn't even in the naval reserve, having left the São Francisco Navigation Company under a cloud.

He explained this himself one day when he returned very irritated from the target practice of the Special Police.

But then, weeks later, Chief Conrado became interested and arranged for the Captain a job in an academy of sports and personal defense which met in Estacio Square: also as instructor of target shooting. The class was small, but he always had a regular group formed of policemen—plainclothes detectives—who liked to practice shooting as a sport; and the Captain, all modesty aside, was a famed master, skilled in all types of guns—Chief Conrado would say with pride, "Just give him a gun barrel and a trigger!"

I asked, "Where did you perfect all of this? Were you part of some armed band, or were you in the war?"

And he would laugh.

"You are born with this, it depends on your eyesight and the steadiness of the hand. . . ."

The pay from the academy was small, but as the Captain said, it was a base; at least it guaranteed our house rent. And it helped disguise his undercover operations.

If only it weren't for the drinking, I thought. Handling a gun isn't exactly for one who drinks and, as I said, I was afraid.

Estrela and Seu Brandini felt the same way—not that I told them anything; but they knew from experience that the Captain when drunk was dangerous: He seemed driven, ready at all times to provoke others into action.

I now saw how I had played with fire that Carnival afternoon on the Avenue: My God, how crazy I was. It would never have occurred to me then that he would really pull out the gun; for me it was only showing off among the ruffians—and all in all how easy it would have been, how easy.

Sometimes at night, awake with the insomnia I still suffered, I would feel that latent fear of what he might have done at Carnival; and I would have been the one to blame. And he sleeping there so quietly at my side: although at times he would have nightmares and cry out calling someone, but I never understood who it was; and he would be troubled, breathing heavily, and one day he cried out: "Run, run!"

At these times I would pass my hand over his shoulder, over his arm, in order to awaken him gently, for it is said that it is bad to awaken suddenly someone who is having a nightmare. Then he would ask gruffly: "What was it?"— because he didn't like to be awakened—and I would say:

"You were sleeping badly, a nightmare."

He never asked me what nightmare it was, or how I knew it was a nightmare; he only remembered that he was dreaming and that it must not have been something pleasant.

There was that Sunday when Chief Conrado came to lunch with a group of companions, all in civilian clothes. The pretext was to have a "work bee" to clean our well, which up to then had been of no use, all stopped up with bits of leftover plaster and pieces of brick, I think since they built the wall to separate the two gardens.

The Captain thought that the well would be useful if it were clean since not much water came out of the hydrant on our street; it could be useful for washing the car and watering the plants.

Chief Conrado told him that he knew a lot about wells, that he had once lived in Paraná where they had very deep wells; and on Sunday he came to do the work, bringing his pals. Each man was enormous in size. Conrado wore a pair of the Captain's shorts. He went down into the well and dug there with a shovel and filled the bucket with stones and dirt which the men pulled up vigorously; they put all that plaster and debris into some boxes, and when they left they carried off the rubble in their truck.

But then when the work was done they came to eat the *feiojada* that I had prepared; they drank before and during the meal, and most of them were drunk, except Chief Conrado, who drank almost nothing. In the middle of the drinking, one of them, I don't know which, mentioned target shooting. A very tall, dark boy whom they called Zelito, made up a shooting contest and all agreed to compete; they chose the Captain to be the judge because as a competitor he would have had an advantage over the others.

They made a big paper target which Chief Conrado traced on the bottom of a box, using my plates and saucers to out-

219

line the circles, one within the other, and they set up the target on the wall and the shooting began.

In the middle of the shots a neighbor shouted, damned them all, wanting to know what in the devil all that was about. Just at that moment the Captain was firing to decide a tie: He had hit the bull's-eye. But when the little man put his head over the wall and saw that big character with the gun in his hand, eyes sparkling, the neighbor's mouth hung open, and he was speechless.

The Captain bawled at him: "What are you doing there, cup-head? Do you want a bullet in you?"

The man vanished like a frightened puppet and later we found out that he had complained to the police, but nobody came to subdue the Captain because Chief Conrado had put a stop to the shooting right away.

Now he went about only with that gang. I don't know if the comrades were helping him and Patron Davino in the transport of the smuggled stuff or if they only gave him protection. The fact is that they went hand in glove and began the custom of getting together on Saturdays for beer and vermouth in a bar on Riachuelo Street; they lunched there—if they lunched—and afterwards they drank until nightfall. As the bar wasn't far from the big stairway which led to our house, the Captain, high with his beer, would climb up that stairway: I had real fear that he would fall and roll back down the steps.

I detested those weekly trials: they were for me the worst punishment. In my view he should drink only in his own house under my wing, but I had to accept his drinking; he certainly wouldn't change after age forty.

Then came that Saturday afternoon; about five o'clock one of the companions came to me—it was Zelito, and he wasn't sober by any means, quite the contrary. But he still talked sense and was able to explain what he wanted.

"Dona Dôra, the Captain is impossible with us at the bar. I came to ask you to come get him. I don't know what got into him; he is insulting everybody, saying the most horrible things, about father, mother, cuckold, and everything."

I put my hand on my mouth.

"Oh, my God!"

"We have all been listening with patience—but he is too much. Chief thought of sending for you to come see if you could get him home. Otherwise he is going to keep on saying even worse things, and somebody is going to end up killing him."

I didn't say another word but put on a coat because it was cold. I forgot to close the door; it was the boy who closed the iron gate and took out the key which I put in my coat pocket.

We went running down the stairway toward the bar. Zelito was talking all the time, begging pardon and explaining, the conversation being interrupted by our running.

"He seems to have gone crazy, he has lost all reason . . . and it isn't that his talk is mixed up from drunkenness, he is quite clear, hammering away . . . 'you son of this, that . . .' I can't repeat it all for you . . . and he makes us listen silently, without taking his eyes away, as if he were eating fire. . . . It was then that Manuel Plácido said to Chief that if things continued in this way, we would end up having to kill him. . . . Chief told me to go look for you, and I took advantage of the moment when he was calling Plácido names . . . I left excusing myself to go to the bathroom . . . before he said something worse. . . ."

I didn't answer anything nor did I comment, for fear of crying and making a scene; above all I didn't want to cry. Just imagine if I were to arrive there crying, making a scene, may God deliver me, for that would have been for him the worst insult, his wife coming to look for him making a commotion in the tavern!

For this very reason, arriving at the door of the bar I became timid, and leaned on the wall outside, at least to let myself catch my breath.

Finally I spied him: There he was at a table in the back, seated facing the street, half apart from the others—drunk as a lord. I remembered then the first day I saw him, at Juazeiro da Bahia, also in a bar at a table between two companions.

There were four others there, all drunk, it could be seen at once. They were looking at him with eyes aslant, and he was saying anything that came into his head, with an air of disgust and superiority, but I didn't hear what it was. Fortunately he didn't see me spying from the door; he was

221

so engaged in dressing down his companions, he didn't glance in my direction.

Then I took a deep breath and gathered up my courage— the fat mulatto at the left of the Captain suddenly lowered his oily face, and I had the impression that he was tickling the gun at his hip—and I told Zelito that he should stay hidden. It was better if the Captain didn't know I had been sent for.

Then I crossed to the door, well under the light, and I let him see me. I didn't have to go to the back of the room because as soon as he saw me the Captain leaped out of the chair and came upsetting the empty tables until he reached me. He stopped near me but without touching me.

"Dôra, what are you doing here?"

I raised up my tearful face—I let myself cry without restraint and I invented my story: "Oh, thank God I found you! I didn't know rightly if this was the bar you spoke about . . ."

His patience was short.

"But what do you want, woman? What happened?"

Now I really cried, out of fear, out of anxiety.

"I was at home, alone, preparing dinner. Suddenly a gang of drunks came by; they were singing and leaned against the iron gate and began to joke about shaking loose the iron gate as if they wanted to force the lock." (Days before a gang of teenagers had done this very thing.) "I almost died of fright! I waited a long time, I was terrified, there all alone, without you . . . finally, after centuries it seemed, they left and I didn't want anything more . . . I ran to look for you for fear they might return. If the gate gave way, can you imagine?"

He didn't say anything then, but it seemed to me that he believed me. He looked me in the eyes.

"Drunks, huh, drunks! That's only what it was. They all live there; they're all good for nothing."

He looked back.

"Isn't that so?"

Chief Conrado upon seeing me arrive got up also and came to where we were.

"You came to look for your man?"

He almost spoiled everything, because the Captain trembled and began to stare at me out of the side of that glassy black eye.

222

But I, my face bathed in tears, didn't need to say any more. I only stammered, "No, I was afraid . . . some men, wishing to batter down the iron gate."

The Captain, turning to him, repeated with that disgust: "Drunks!"

Chief Conrado finally caught on.

"Poor little thing, she is frightened. Look, go with the lady, Captain, I'll take care of the bill."

But in such a situation the Captain meant to settle the bill himself; at that time he accepted favors from no one: He put his hand in his pocket and drew out a big bill which he threw to the waiter.

"Keep the change!"

He grabbed me with a force that left red marks on my arms and pushed me toward the street.

We almost collided with Zelito who had remained outside spying, leaning on the wall. Fortunately, the Captain wasn't aware of him; he wasn't paying attention to anything, just looking straight ahead and dragging me along the sidewalk.

I walked toward the stairs, and I perked up my courage for the climb, when suddenly I remembered: what if some of the groups of boys were on the steps, as was their custom on Saturday and Sunday afternoons—and the Captain took it into his head that they might be my drunks?

My body got heavy and I grabbed his arm with both hands.

"Please, darling, call a taxi. I ran down the stairway; my legs are still trembling, and I can't stand the climb now." (It was true!)

It was our good luck that a taxi came by; he gave a short whistle, and the Portuguese driver pulled over.

When we reached home, the Captain without looking at the taxi meter threw another bill at the driver; I believe that he had a pocket full of them. He opened the iron gate with his key, wavering a little, running his eye up and down the street in search of the men.

I murmured, "They have already gone away, it seems. . . ."

He pushed me inside, closed the gate slowly—everything he was doing was done too slowly, too deliberately, as if the least gesture had the greatest importance. He was trying to hide from me how drunk he was, not admitting to himself

223

the idea that he wasn't capable of guarding and protecting me.

I tried to drag him into the house, to see if I could put him in the bed, but he resisted and spoke gruffly.

"I'm going to stay here, on the bench by the well."

We had recently installed a street bench, an old one with iron feet, that the Captain had discovered in a junk shop. We had cleaned, sandpapered, and painted it red, then had set it next to the well under the arbor.

He let himself drop on the bench and leaned his head on the post of the trellis, felt in his pockets and didn't find what he wanted.

"Go get my cigarettes from the dresser. I shall stay here a little while, keeping watch. Let's see if the hoodlums come back."

I brought the cigarettes and gave him one which he lit with a fairly steady hand, but still with that deliberate care, even to blowing out the match and throwing it on the ground. I also sat down on the bench at his side. In the interest of nabbing the hoodlums he seemed to have forgotten about his companions.

I then made coffee but he refused any.

"You think that I'm drunk? I don't need coffee!"

It was for me, I alleged, because I was cold; and he ended up drinking the entire cup. But afterwards he sent me off.

"Go inside, it's really cold. I'll be waiting only a little longer—in a few moments I'll also come in."

In the mood he was in it was better to obey and even give thanks to God—that was what I did.

So I sat on the bed and watched through the window shutters: For some minutes he still held himself rigid, his neck stiff, leaning against the post. Then he began to nod, and stretched out his legs to make himself comfortable on the bench. Finally he dropped his head on his chest and fell asleep.

I didn't trust this first sleep; I waited a bit longer, perhaps a half hour. Then slowly and cautiously, I went near him, took my poor lover by the arm, and urged him to get up, all the while speaking gently, as to a child: "Come, dear, it's cold. Come with me—let's go to bed; for it is late. . . ."

He woke up dazed and asked, "What is it, what is it?"— But he let himself be led, half asleep.

I had already prepared the bed and made him lie down,

even dressed in all his clothes. Afterwards I took off his shoes and socks. I opened his belt and pulled off his pants, lightly, lightly like one robbing. I took off his shirt, I left only his shorts on. He sighed, turned on his side, and buried his head in the pillow. I covered him with a sheet and blanket, even pulling the blanket up under his chin. (I remembered that in times past I had done this same thing for another—but what a difference, what a difference: before out of duty but now out of love.)

I undressed and also sneaked under the blanket. I sighed. His naked shoulder touched mine. I lowered my head on that shoulder which was somewhat cold and kissed it lightly. I fell asleep too.

Yes, after Senhora's death, Soledade and the people of Soledade were constantly part of our daily life—there were letters, now from Xavinha, now from Amador, about the cattle, the work for the new planting. One from Dr. Fenelon about a detail that was not certain in the boundaries "from the time of Dr. Laurindo." A letter from the lawyer ("the lazy good-for-nothing one who lets things take care of themselves"). I got a power of attorney to have the inventory made.

Then I realized we were already in the early days of December, because the Captain's depository was full of Christmas things (the baubles, as he called them); and I helped to separate the lots of presents for the notions stores and other buyers when the postman cried at the door and handed me a letter, a letter from Xavinha.

It was a long letter and a clipping from the Fortaleza newspaper fell out—I recognized it by the type.

A HERMIT'S DEATH

Our correspondent in the county of Aroeiras has communicated to us the "mysterious death" of a *sertão* person by the name of Delmiro so and so, who lived in complete isolation on the land of the Soledade fazenda, whose proprietor also died a short time ago.

No one from there remembers any more the exact date when he came to settle at Soledade, but it must have been more than twenty years ago. The oldest persons on the place affirm that he came from far away,

225

from the south of the state; he appeared at the fazenda ill, badly wounded, and D. Senhora (the deceased proprietor) let him install himself in an old abandoned farmhouse that was on her land.

Delmiro then isolated himself like a hermit, fleeing from people and seeking only the company of birds and plants. He produced his own food and for years he didn't exchange a word with anyone. But last week the fazenda people saw flocks of *urubus* flying over the fence which surrounded the hermit's cabin. Arriving there, they verified that the old man was dead, his body horribly picked to pieces by the vultures. Some of the residents said they had also discovered in the place the tracks of a puma which, according to rumor, generally crosses the Choro woodland for the *serra* Azul in the summer and at times leaves his tracks on the edge of the Soledade dam, where he would stop to drink at night. According to these same informants the puma must have surprised the sick old man, who couldn't fight back and was killed. They further affirm that the lamentable state in which the body was found, torn apart violently, could hardly have been the work of the *urubus'* beaks.

There are also people who suggest that the old Delmiro may have been killed by former enemies, since they suspect that he was at one time a follower of the Prestes Column and later fled the revolutionaries after having betrayed them to the "provisionals" pursuing them. Others say he was a member of a group of bandits who laid waste to our *sertão* during the decade of the 1920s. But it may well be that all these versions are fanciful and that the old eccentric died a victim of natural causes. In any case the police ordered an inquest.

In her letter Xavinha wrote:

. . . As you can see by this Fortaleza newspaper story our dear old Delmiro has met his end in a most horrible manner. As I've said for a long time, he has been growing increasingly worse in judgment, ever more eccentric; he didn't even come anymore to look for the things that Amador left for him; Amador himself carried tobacco and sugar to him—he still had beans left over from the year before. At times we forgot all about him, as it happened when the business of the cattle had already begun, and I was ill with my rheumatism. I didn't even send anyone there to find out what was happening with the old man. Then in the past week the *urubus* rose up over Delmiro's fence and Amador went to investigate; the poor thing was there all in pieces, some say it was a puma. *Compadre* Gonzaga is one who swears that he saw the puma's tracks; but we, we don't know for certain. You know how the people here like to invent things. I have never seen more inventive people. As for me I think he died of a natural illness although there are those who said he died of hunger. The *urubus* made a horrible mess; the men had to carry the bones to the cemetery in a bag . . .

And she ended:

. . . He died a year and two months after the death of Godmother Senhora. All the old people here at Soledade are gone. Only Maria Milagre and I are left. She is like a deer which has shed its antlers, poor old thing, and so blind she needs a guide, worse off than I.

I had sat down on the doorstep to read the letter. I was reading out loud and could hardly continue from the middle to the end for weeping. The Captain stopped his packing and came to sit by me and he finished reading it for me. He knew vaguely about Delmiro's existence.

"What a morbid case! Was he that old man you spoke of who lived alone in the *mato?*"

I then told him about Delmiro's arrival at Soledade, the work it cost me to treat his shoulder wounded by a shot. I told how I, facing up to Senhora, had given him a dwelling in the farmhouse of old João de Deus who used to steal goats and was then no longer at the fazenda. I told about the confession—but I kept secret that name of New Moon. I don't know why, but I didn't even tell the Captain.

I told of his stay with the revolutionaries—(Who could have mentioned the Prestes Column to the journalist? Amador? Old Maria Milagre? But did she know anything about the Prestes Column? Most likely it was Xavinha, flat-

tered to give an interview to the reporter—talking senti-
mentally, having the young man served a sweet and covering her teeth with her left hand. ''I don't like to talk
. . . but people say . . . Godmother Senhora herself was
certain . . .'')

I told the Captain about the bandits and the struggle
against the police. Then about Delmiro's growing eccentricity.

''He had a religious mania, it was what Senhora said. . . .''
And I told about the system of exchanges that he invented to avoid speaking with other people, about the millet and beans that he brought at night.

''But he liked me. He never failed to appear when I called
at the fence. He would bring me presents, flowers, honey,
fruit; one day he gave me a fistful of *jeriquiti* seeds. . . .''
(The moon clear and I filling my hand with the red contents, said while laughing at him: ''Oh, what you won't invent!'' and then the noise of people in Senhora's room and
her voice: ''Go now!'' and the other's voice: ''She took the
medicine . . .'') I laid my face on my knees and burst into
tears again, but when I looked up I saw that he was impatient as if he found so much crying an exaggeration. I continued: ''Delmiro was my friend! I was the only person he
had in the world! . . .''

Still in a bad humor, perhaps because of that inevitable
jealousy of his, he said: ''Yes, I know that you like to
have someone to adore you . . . even that crazy old bandit. . . .''

I kept the letter and newspaper clipping and went to
wash my face; I left the Captain alone with his bundles. It
was lunch time so I began to set the table.

Senhora dead, Delmiro dead. Oh, my poor old man.
Oh—when I used to lean on the fence and he would take off
his crumpled-up straw hat, open up that quick smile under
the mustache, his teeth gleaming; yes, in his dark face under the crisp beard that was like a dry herb growing on his
chin—those bright teeth were a surprise—human teeth was
what I was going to say.

One day I came on foot with Zeza, we were going to get
cactus quills for Xavinha's lace pillow—and he was cleaning
the well from which he drew his water. Down in the hole

one couldn't even see his hat. Just when I was going to call out to him, Zeza put her hand on my arm.

"Listen, Godmother Dorinha."

The old man was singing while he dug, but it was a hymn set to music so sad and despairing that it pained us to listen:

> . . . Let the star guide you to the Newborn, oh my
> pilgrims!
> On the day of the Great Horror!
> On the day of the Great Horror
> All will be seen
> The trees will dry up, oh my pilgrims
> The cold water will boil . . .

Each line ended with a sort of moan. I was going to speak, but Zeza was still afraid and discouraged me.

"Don't speak, Godmother, that old man is crazy, who knows but that he might be digging the well while naked?"

When we reached home, Zeza announced from the porch: "Seu Delmiro is now acting like a devout. He is singing a hymn so horrible that he gives me goose pimples."

Senhora looked at me.

"He's singing hymns, is he? He must certainly be singing to the devil who is his saint."

Well, now Delmiro has realized his day of Great Horror. The secrets which he had, whatever they were, were now safe in heaven and on earth with the *urubus* and with the animals of the land.

Xavinha had made the count—one year and two months between one and the other's death. Now I could return to Soledade.

The men continued the smuggling with impunity; they even got careless, and that couldn't be good. They told me almost nothing about their affairs. I don't believe that the Captain liked to have women mixed up in his business— even if the woman were I.

Just the same Alice showed up at the house one day—he had gone out and I was alone. She was very talkative and lively saying that she was thinking about opening a little shop with her sister, where they could sell the things that

"Cadet Lucas" and her father brought. I asked if it was permitted to set up a store to sell contraband, and she laughed.

"Oh, people buy some legal merchandise as a cover-up and something they can put on a written bill, and if an inspector suspects a cat in the bag, well the person just slips something to him, you know how it is. . . ."

I knew it was stupid to be jealous of Alice; the adoration of the sisters for "Cadet Lucas" was a crush of adolescent girls, more like fans of a film star, given freely without expecting anything in return from him. At that Ash Wednesday lunch, D. Amada had talked to me about the impossible love of Alice for that soccer player.

"She says that he is on the Olaria team. What! A goalie he may be, and this only on practice days; on the days the team plays they don't allow him on the field. . . ."

Alice, after telling about the plans for the little shop (in that time they didn't use the name *boutique* yet), she went into the subject of her love affair with Pequinho—that was his name. Pequinho had invited her to go live with him in São Paulo, where he had an offer of a contract; and what did I think? She was afraid of running risks; moreover, Patron Davino (this is what she called her father), Patron Davino was dangerous when he got angry. But she was mad, mad about Pequinho, anytime she could she went bathing with him on the beach of Flamengo Bay; she never went to the beach of Maria Angu which was close to Olaria; she couldn't imagine going bathing in those mudholes. She was cariocan and went to Vermelha Beach; it was just by accident that she lived in the suburbs now! It would be good, she urged, if I would talk with Cadet Lucas so he could placate Patron Davino. She would take charge of the old lady herself. What the mother didn't like was that Pequinho didn't care how he dressed; the old lady didn't understand today's young people. Just see now if it is chic to wear a straw hat and shoes with pointed toes. This is for actors; a soccer player is a sportsman. He is proud of the pants and shirts the club gives him. . . . For the love of God, Dorhina, speak with Cadet Lucas; Patron Davino adores the ground he walks on. If Cadet Lucas tells him to kill me, he would kill me; and if he speaks a good word for Pequinho, Pequinho will be welcome in our house.

"Oh, for the love of the Virgin, you know, Dorinha, I sometimes want to die; my bad luck is that I'm such a child.

I console myself with stupid things, like this store project; I make plans. I *think* that Pequinho could even get to be an assistant to Patron Davino and Cadet Lucas; I mean to say, when he isn't working, as now, for example, while he's waiting for a contract . . .''

I listened silently to that idiot. A person didn't have to say anything; she monopolized the conversation. That little name of theirs for the Captain—Cadet Lucas here and Cadet Lucas there, just imagine, how cute; it could even be a taunt, for never had he told me that he had been a cadet. A little name of endearment used only by them, a part of him which I didn't possess and didn't know about; but I did know that he adored the name.

So the Captain and his men became careless, even making plans for stores; and I didn't like that. Moreover, they said that their business was as good as a member of the Business League, "as stable as Sugar Loaf Mountain." Patron Davino handled the shipping; the others, I don't know who they were, handled the merchandise; the Captain provided the actual physical work, and Chief Conrado supplied the protection. Could anything be safer?

Yes, the Captain provided the physical labor and ran the risks. He thought that I never sensed the danger like a needle in my bones when he would always arrive home late at night, with all his clothing wet under the sailor jacket, tired, almost dead, and put the car in the garage. Without even eating he would take a drink of cognac. I don't say what my heart guessed because I never guessed, but I didn't like it, I didn't like it.

One day he came home very angry; he came from the academy, sweating as always and went straight to take his bath.

A detective had appeared at the academy and enrolled in the target-shooting course, the Captain's course—a fellow whom he had known in those past days of prison on Relação Street, when he was in the trouble with Vanderlei about the precious stones. The fellow was from the state of Espirito Santo (perhaps from the capital, Vitoria), most unattractive looking, with a bad reputation, and known as Bigode.

Bigode, on the first day of the Captain's imprisonment in Rio, made a proposition that the Captain get some money:

231

With money many doors could be opened. The Captain was very upset: It was the first time he was in one of those prisons, and of course he said that he could arrange the money with some friends in Minas. The fact is, however, that if in that exact moment he had a friend in Minas who could arrange that large sum for him, it would have been a miracle. But he couldn't give himself the luxury of closing that hope, and so he invented the friends in Minas for that Bigode; and it seems that the character got to work and began pulling strings. Three times he spoke with the Captain to say that everything was coming together; the money had only to arrive and then all would be taken care of.

But just then came the blessed appearance of Chief Conrado, and the Captain told him about Bigode's proposition. Chief Conrado said so loud that whoever wished could hear that he had the record of that Bigode, an insolent robber, and that if he showed his face he would throw him out, and that he had better leave his friend alone. All of this Chief Conrado shouted angrily in front of witnesses.

"I have German blood and I'm not afraid of his threats. In the end it may be necessary to have the neck of that big-bellied robber!"

When the Captain was leaving the prison, another detective, who was very nice and had brought him food and cigarettes (he did it for a big price), told him that he should be careful about Bigode: Bigode wouldn't confront Conrado face to face, but he was a very dangerous person.

Now Bigode showed up at the academy and was already enrolled in the course. The secretary of the school told the Captain that he insisted on knowing the name of the instructor of the course before paying the fee.

The Captain pretended that he didn't know him; the character gave his name as Benedito somebody, and when he began the first class and the Captain had to call the students by name, he said: "Mr. Benedito, do you know the parts of a revolver?"

The character smiled and said that he didn't have to call him Benedito, the Captain could call him Bigode like everybody else, as *before*, and he emphasized the *before*.

Afterwards, while the others were practicing at the targets, he stayed on the sidelines making cracks—that he had heard the Captain would return to his ship, that a friend in the Special Police had told him that Chief Conrado very shortly would leave the Morro de Santo Antonio headquarters because he no longer needed that work: He was rich. The Captain pretended not to hear anything although he was boiling inside and wanted to smash the boor's face with a shot.

This happened on a Thursday. The following week the Captain brought home some more news of Bigode.

He entered the academy that day and didn't even bother to take a gun and go to the target shed; he must already have been convinced that he would never be able to hit the mark even at a short distance. He was the worst shot in the world, and he called himself a policeman! He came to the Captain with a proposal—that there were some Red Berets who were abusing this business of protection. They thought they could grab everything for themselves, but there were also many others who wanted to get in on the game . . . people who also had the right, people from the inspection control, people responsible for the surveillance of the entry of illegal merchandise . . .

And then came the worst:

His people had been tipped off on the arrival, a short time earlier, of a big shipment of penicillin; and they demanded their cut. Otherwise they would make arrests.

The Captain was furious, but he pretended to be calm and detached. He said he didn't understand, his business was to teach target shooting; and if he, Bigode, wanted to learn to shoot, very well, for this reason the academy was established, but if not—let him go to the devil.

It was the first time in my life that I had heard of penicillin, and then I learned it was produced only for the American army; and if on occasion one managed to smuggle some, the doctors and hospitals would pay for its weight in gold, or even much more. When it is a question of saving a loved one who is dying of blood poisoning or pneumonia, one doesn't look at the price. The Captain and the others didn't even charge too much, only enough to cover the capital and the risk, and I believed it; I knew that the Captain was never a man to suck anyone's blood: not even in a matter of life or death would he take advantage of anyone. But if Bigode and his partners entered the business, who could know if they might not form an organized gang?

When earlier the Captain had told Chief Conrado about

Bigode's daring to matriculate at the academy, the latter shrugged his shoulders—that was his way; but already this last message didn't sit well with him. This sleazy character must have had a solid gang lined up behind him to get the Captain, just as the Captain thought.

From then on the Captain closed up with me; he told me almost nothing—the fellow must even be becoming dangerous. I found out things in bits, on the days when he was more communicative, or had drunk, or was frightened. Also from the telephone conversations—yes, I forgot to mention, we now had a telephone, a miracle produced by Chief Conrado, although he had promised it long before, but at the time he promised I didn't believe him.

So, as I was saying, the most I could hear were telephone conversations and would put two and two together; when I complained to the Captain that he wasn't telling me anything now, the damned man would say: "Now, don't bother yourself. The less you know the better; and besides we have our firm guarantee."

But then came a night, it must have been the night of the penicillin delivery because the Captain, who had left about six in the evening and returned at dawn, put the Studebaker in the garage and, without even taking off his sailor jacket, tried to unload everything that he had brought. Then another car silently entered the iron gate and this time it was a taxi; the Captain and the taxi driver transferred to the trunk of this car (that I had never seen before) all the packages which had been in the Studebaker. Then the Captain unlocked the depository and also took out everything that was there, piling up the merchandise on the taxi floor—I suppose the trunk was already full. Fortunately there wasn't very much in the depository and so they didn't have to put much on the taxi seats; one had to come close to see it at all.

Upon hearing the noise of the Studebaker, I had turned on the patio light—the electric switch was in our entrance; but the Captain came over and hissed: "Put out that light. Go to bed!"

As I asked, half choking, what this was all about, he repeated irritably: "Go to bed. I'll explain later."

In moments the other car was loaded and the depository cleaned out. The taxi left with no lights on, and the Captain closed the iron gate and pulled the bolt; only then did he come inside and take off his clothes, wet as always.

While he changed and took a warm bath and I was making some coffee and scrambled eggs, he told me the news.

It seems that Bigode's people had set an ambush for them; there was the moment when they nailed the Captain with a flashlight and focused it on his face, and he was certain that they recognized him. I asked: "Was it on the boat?"

"It was of course; but don't ask me anything more, I have already talked too much. In these cases the less you know, the better it is for you. I don't want you mixed up in these intrigues."

Afterwards we went to bed and I, quite naturally, couldn't even get drowsy.

Very early, very early, the Captain telephoned Chief Conrado; they were planning things—but when I came near he ordered me to leave, and I didn't find out what they were talking about.

By eleven o'clock in the morning there was a knocking on the iron gate and I, who was twisting some tendrils of the grape vine around the trellis, went to answer; there were three men, and one, by the description which I had been given, could only have been Bigode. One of them spoke.

"We wish to have a word with Mr. Lucas, commonly known as 'Captain.' "

I closed the door in their faces; they didn't expect that from me. Then the Captain, who was already coming, opened the gate again and said they were speaking with him, that it was he whom they wanted. But he was already angry.

Bigode asked to enter. He declared that he had come with a court order and a search warrant, and it would be better for all if he were received well.

I heard that word "search" spoken and immediately I remembered the revolver; if they got his revolver, I can't even imagine what the Captain might do. I ran to our room and got the cursed gun from the drawer of the bedside table, and I don't know what madness came over me. Looking for a place to hide the gun—the men already entering—I put it on one of the three cement steps which led from the patio to the kitchen door and sat on top of it.

The Captain was now smooth as silk (this then was the very thing agreed upon with Chief Conrado)—he himself opened the door of the depository which was without the padlock—the detectives could see that there wasn't anything inside—only some empty boxes. Yes, they inspected the car, went over everything, lifted up the seats, opened the trunk, and even raised the hood. Nothing.

Then they went to our room, ransacked the wardrobe and the chest of drawers and the Captain said: "You can see that all we have here is our clothes, mine and my wife's."

Bigode, with such insolence that I don't know why the Captain didn't slap his face, said: "But you, being professor of target shooting, must have guns in the house; and this is also among the search items, your permission, please, to look."

At this the Captain didn't answer, he must have been thinking about the revolver in the bedside table, and I couldn't signal him that the revolver was safe; as it happened it was bruising my thighs although I gave no signs of that.

The men looked through everything, happily none of them dared to bother me; they certainly thought that I was terror-stricken, and in fact, I was. From time to time I would put my head on my knees as if I were crying.

I moved away a little when they entered the kitchen, but I didn't get up from the step, and one of them passed close by me saying: "Excuse me, madam."

They rummaged through everything there, even in the oven and the grocery containers, but of course they found nothing.

I don't know if the Captain understood what I was doing with the gun, I think he did; because Bigode insisted that he, being an instructor of target shooting, must have a gun in his home, the Captain answered with the greatest calm that the practice arms belonged to the academy, and he had no need for arms in his house. He even sneered: "I trust the good services of our police."

Then Bigode—I don't know if he was the head of the group, but he spoke for all—said that the order which he brought was not just for a search, but also for arrest; so he

236

invited the Captain to accompany them to headquarters to explain some things.

I wasn't expecting that and the first thing I thought about was that if the Captain was going to jail I'd have to say good-bye to him—actually I felt as if I were nailed to that cement step and that I wouldn't get up unless I was dragged. I began to cry out, sobbing, begging them for the love of God to leave my husband in peace; the Captain drew near me and begged me to be calm, that he was only going to clarify matters, that it was all a mistake.

The men stood aside, waiting, as though they were saying that they might be detectives but that they were also gentlemen and weren't going to be crude with a lady in the middle of an attack of nerves.

Finally the Captain patted me lightly on the head.

"Stop crying, honey, I'll see you later."

I redoubled my cries, and then they left slowly—and only when they had snapped the latch of the iron gate did I get up off that damned gun.

I ran to telephone Chief Conrado, and it took him forever to answer; those barracks must have been like the Vatican. But finally he spoke. I told him in broken sentences what had happened; Chief Conrado asked if the taxi had arrived in time. I answered yes, and that the job had been done. He then calmly recommended: "Don't worry. I'm going to act. It was all a mistake, a conflict of jurisdiction!"

But two days passed and the Captain hadn't returned. I, who at first had had so much courage, was now completely at my wits' end and imagined the most horrible vengeance of that sinister figure, Bigode. I telephoned Estrela, but at this stage I was afraid to say anything on the telephone; besides Chief Conrado had asked me to be careful. Estrela came quickly because she was surprised at my way of talking, and then Carleto arrived; I told everything I could, and they understood. It seems that they had been dreading that such a thing might happen.

They wanted me to go with them to the Mansion, but I was afraid the Captain might return or telephone, and I wouldn't be at home. They then decided to stay with me; I put them in my bed and I slept on the sofa in the living room.

237

Finally, on the night of the second day, the Captain telephoned: He was already in the street talking and was about to take a taxi home. I almost screamed in the telephone, I was so overcome.

He arrived and if I had thought he would come all beaten down, that was my error; no sir, he was highly pleased with himself. All had gone extremely well. His friends functioned like clockwork—the delay was due to the red tape of having to go through "channels."

I didn't understand anything whatsoever, but what did that matter? Perhaps he said that only to tease me. I didn't attach any importance to anything; all I wanted was for him to be home.

Oh, I made a god of that man. That could have been a mistake, I don't know. In the end love is like that: We get a man or a woman just like all others, and endow that creature with everything our heart wishes. Of course he or she cannot be worthy of such blindness, but love wishes to deceive itself. Isn't a mother's love like that? The child can be ugly or bad tempered, but she finds him beautiful and angelic. My little darling, born of my flesh! Well, love is like that, or at least mine is, a unique thing, which takes over my body and my entrails, more so than would a child, and what then?

Yes, for me he was a god: He came as a god, lived like a god, and would die a god; and when he left it was the end of the world for me.

The Captain could appear optimistic and careless, or perhaps it was a show put on only for my eyes. In any event he and the group changed their habits.

Chief Conrado himself came to our house to say that things looked bad; happily, with the returns from that shipment of penicillin, they could stay underground for some months. He gave his jolly fat man's laugh.

"What is has to be. Rome wasn't built in a day. Now we are going to take a vacation."

I turned to good account this idea of a rest or a vacation, and I spoke to Chief about my mother's death and our need to go to Ceará to see about the fazenda that was more or less abandoned, and straighten things out.

238

"If the Captain isn't going to be working, why couldn't we make that trip?"

The Captain raised his hand to stop me. I knew that he hated to have me asking a favor of another man, especially something for him. He broke in.

"Foolishness. Anyhow, I can't go because of the academy."

But Chief Conrado was full of good will.

"The academy isn't a problem. I will speak with the director who is under my charge, and he'll give you a leave—next month?"

There remained still the difficulty of passage, to get the priority for a flight because there was still no travel at all by sea or land—only by airplane.

(I didn't want to think about travel by land, even if it were possible. That would have meant taking the boat part of the way. I knew on what terms the Captain had been with the São Francisco Company. I wouldn't let him expose himself for my sake; there was enough uneasiness in Rio de Janeiro.)

Chief Conrado turned to us.

"Airplane? You aren't afraid of airplanes? Well, I can get you airplane passage; I have a friend in Panair who can arrange it for me. It will not be the first time. As for the priority, I'll speak with our captain. I'll say you are a friend of the house, that he knows you. I still have those good pals at headquarters, if you have problems. You can count on the plane tickets."

So the journey to Ceará was settled in this way. We didn't have to make many preparations for the trip. The depository was empty; the Studebaker could stay in the garage. I would leave the house key with Estrela so she could get in to water the plants once a week. Suddenly the Captain had an idea.

"Why don't they spend a little vacation here at our house, to relieve the monotony of Catete—for them it would be the same as going to the country."

Seu Brandini was so attracted to novelty that he accepted the invitation then and there.

Even so the trip was still delayed for almost a month—certainly the priority wasn't as easy to obtain as Chief Con-

239

rado had said. But one evening the Captain came home with two tickets in an envelope, and an authorization sealed and stamped for a flight on the plane for Monday, four days off.

I wanted to show him Soledade; and I was shocked and disappointed when the Captain told me positively: He thought it better that he not go this first time.

"They would be scandalized, when if the first time you return there after your mother's death, you arrive with a man at your side. . . . They could also think that I am interested in the inheritance. . . ."

He paused (and then he made his point).

"Moreover, it is as if I were putting myself into the dead man's nest—his clothing might still be in the drawers . . . everything there must still be smelling of Laurindo. . . . No, ma'am, I stay right here in Fortaleza, and only if you run into some complications and phone me shall I go."

I protested, and I wasn't just pretending because I really hated being separated from him; but as I thought about it I knew it would be better to go alone. With all that was there, without my knowing how things were—Laurindo, Delmiro, Senhora—the less the Captain knew, the better for my tranquillity. All this persuaded me the Captain should wait. Let me first speak with the people there, get a foothold in Soledade. . . . How many years and how many changes! But would the dammed-up waters flow again, the secrets unfold themselves?

We surprised D. Loura when we arrived at her house. She already knew about the Captain in my life; when we moved to Santa Teresa I had written that I was married, but didn't offer any details. I was a widow, I could marry; I didn't feel I had to explain he was legally separated.

I couldn't mention marriage to the fazenda people because certainly the inventory documents passed through many hands: It was enough for one of them to read and then everybody else would know. In them I had to declare as in the power of attorney: "Jane Doe, Brazilian, widow, etc."

It was obvious that the Captain made an immediate conquest of D. Loura, Osvaldina, and even the telegraph operator; when the Captain exerted himself to be friendly he was invincible. He hastened to open our trunks, took out the gifts, and was giving them out as if he were an old buddy—even a bottle of wine for the telegraph operator, who, although he didn't drink, accepted it and went quickly to put it away in the closet of his room.

The Captain handed out the parcels and said, "These are only mine; Dôra will give you hers!"

I went to get my presents. We had also to give detailed news of Estrela and Seu Brandini, those ingrates who never wrote; and now with the Company disbanded, no one knew anything about them!

I told about the highs and lows, and that poor Seu Brandini still had his diabetes. Estrela was doing well training her air hostesses.

Speaking of air hostesses, it reminded me that I was still nauseated from the plane trip: I had been terrified, I had suffered from the takeoff in Rio to the landing in Ceará, I had even wished the airplane would fall en route just so I could put my feet on terra firma—and everybody laughed at me.

D. Loura voiced again what she always said—she could die of an airplane disaster, but only if the airplane fell on top of her. To go up in one—may God deliver her—never. Then we talked in the manner of people just arrived who like each other very much and are happy to see each other again—I say to see each other again even with respect to the Captain, because he was the perfect "old friend."

We spent a week in Fortaleza sight-seeing. I showed him the city; it was a honeymoon.

At times Osvaldina went out with us. All they talked about there was the American air base; American money was all over the place; even the shoeshine boy in Ferreira Plaza charged in dollars! The people there were proud of the tiny dirigibles stationed on the outskirts of the city on the landing fields, and they really were pretty.

But at the end of the week the Captain took me at dawn to the train; I hung on his neck because I was terrified to go alone. He kissed me in front of the passengers, which caused astonishment because that wasn't done in public in that provincial corner. He reminded me to telegraph him as soon as I arrived at Aroeiras and to telegraph again for any other reason.

241

The train left and I said good-bye at the window, crying like a fool; and he was laughing and making signs to me. It was the first time that we were separating, and then I remembered how many times he had already seen me crying, I who formerly had the reputation of being the girl who never cried. Maria Milagre once said that behind each eye a person had a bag of tears and during his lifetime he would have to cry them out. Without a doubt I was emptying mine! After the sack was empty one never cried anymore.

The entire world might change, but that train line never changed. . . . Every station was the same as it had been when I was a child. Look at the dried-banana stand at Siqueira!

In Baturité the baskets of oranges and tangerines, the tiny baskets of grapes, the church of Putiú all white next to the river with the green *serra* in the background.

The only thing new was that there was no longer a lunch stop at Itaúna; now there was a dining car attached to the train; but it was full of men drinking beer and talking loudly so a lone woman wouldn't venture there. I ate fruit, dried bananas, and sweet millet pastry that a woman sold all rolled up in a banana leaf on a tray covered with a very white cloth.

Running alongside the track was the highway of the pilgrims who went to Canindé. Then we passed the big bridge of the Choró which my grandfather had worked on—and I recalled that when I was a child I had speculated about which iron girders, which pieces of that big skeleton my grandfather had made; and I was so proud. It was as if that bridge were a little piece of my inheritance.

At long last the conductor, walking along the aisle, announced the station of Aroeiras. The train stopped and I got off.

Awaiting me at the station was Amador, more gray, still thin and dry in his Sunday-go-to-meeting clothes. He had a rented car—a new luxury, and I even recognized the car: It was Dr. Nilo's old Dodge—Amador explained that the driver had received the car as an inheritance; Dr. Nilo had put it in the will. Now he was in the plaza earning a living as its new owner—when he could get the gasoline.

We waited for the luggage. The station agent was new

and didn't know me; only the owner of the tavern on the other side of the tracks came over to welcome me.

We left the station and went down the street. Further on after the bridge we continued by the old royal highway; the new thing now was that the highway, instead of running through open fields as before, was closed in by wire fences. Amador, who rode beside the chauffeur and was constantly turning around to point out something, called my attention to it.

"Now it is all fenced in. He who doesn't have a wire enclosure is at a disadvantage. Like us at Soledade. People now put their land under wire and let their cattle roam on the grounds of those who don't have fencing."

That highway: if I said that I had crossed it a thousand times, I would not be lying—perhaps a thousand times would be too little. Ever since I was a youngster, I went over it by horse, by cabriolet, by open carriage, at the pommel of my father's saddle and afterwards at Antônio Amador's. In Senhora's lap, so they told me, when I was scarcely forty days old, she on horseback sidesaddle, dressed in her familiar gorgeous raw linen riding habit; I was coughing, dying of whooping cough which hit me right after I was born.

Over that highway I rode as a secondary school girl on my little strawberry roan horse named Chuvisco, mounted like a man in my father's English saddle. Senhora wanted to forbid that, but I refused to obey her; the long pleated skirt of the nuns' school uniform covered me up completely. I dreamed about wearing riding breeches and puttees like girls in the movies. But I was only to have these later, when I practically governed myself, and Senhora didn't have the will to stop me.

In Dr. Fenelon's new car I had cut across the highway dressed as a bride. Going, I rode next to Dr. Fenelon himself, who was my godfather; returning, I had a bouquet in my hands and a smile in my eyes, sitting beside Laurindo, my husband, who was wearing a white three-piece linen suit with a mottled carnation in his lapel.

Across it I had passed as a widow, dressed in black; and across it I had passed again, but without the black clothes, in my light blue suit, ten days after Laurindo's burial, defying the people's tongues and Senhora's orders, thinking I would never return.

So, aside from the new fences, the highway didn't seem to have changed much. The wild mimosa on both sides, the tenant houses like little bird nests with their backyards, and in the windows the flower pots of common caladium.

The railway tracks which crossed the highway twice and the little bridge over the Carcará Creek; it was forded below because the main bridge was only for the train track.

Finally, on top of the long knoll the old house of Soledade stood with its entrance porch, its high property line side walls, at the left the long warehouse, at the right the weather vane and the dam.

The big *mulungu* tree in front was almost leafless and seemed dead; and everything else seemed dead, the house, the patio of scorched ground. The only thing alive in that sad place was the little flock of goats grazing on the large flat rock surface with the little goats bleating plaintively as they climbed up and down the stones.

The car honked as it pulled over and a head appeared in the kitchen window.

I was already on the porch, the baggage taken down, and Amador had said good-bye to the man, when finally Xavinha came out with Luzia and—my God how she had aged—Xavinha, I mean—Luzia was pregnant. I found out later that it was due to bad luck; the man had skipped town when he found out about the child. I asked about Zeza—she had married Luis Namorado, Laurindo's former "secretary," and they no longer lived at the fazenda.

The house was swept and clean. Amador had even had some whitewash put on—but even so it smelled like an old church full of bats.

Xavinha, Luzia, and the girls still had their old rooms off the dining room; the front was all locked up, uninhabited.

Xavinha cried and blessed me. I also cried. I could now cry more easily than several years back. She led me to the hammock she had set up in my old room, the *alcova*. The spool bed had been taken down because the rats had eaten the mattress.

But only that—Xavinha pointed out—only that had been damaged; everything else was kept in the trunks and closets as during the time of Godmother Senhora.

Xavinha repeated this with pride, going from place to

place, hobbling with her rheumatism, opening drawers and doors with the ring of keys—Senhora's keys, keys which in the hands of the deceased never rusted: They were always polished like silver. (She would explain condescendingly that it was something in her sweat or blood—and it was true, haven't I already said so? Metal objects she used were always shiny and bright like new.)

Xavinha explained ten times that those keys were only brought out today, for my arrival. They stayed in a bag, the bag in a box, and the box under some clothing, at the bottom of the cedar chest; and the chest remained in the trunk room that had no window but only a door closed with lock and key.

It seemed to me that Xavinha now had a sort of new sweetness, that age had softened her bossiness of former times; she was now as dependent on "Compadre Amador" as earlier on Senhora. And repeating the name of Senhora, she began to cry, as old people cry: only the eyes filling up with water and the lips opening. She said these words that I would never forget: "For me, when Godmother Senhora died, the light of my world went out."

And if Senhora were aware of it she would chide her: "Stop puling." Would Xavinha still be puling? All the same I believe that her tears were sincere.

I lay down in the hammock and sent Luzia to open the trunks. She brought in first the presents which were on top—the lace mantilla for Xavinha to wear to church, and the cut of white dimity cloth also for her; the felt hat—for Amador and more cuts of printed cloth, costume jewelry, earrings, and brooches for his grandsons and granddaughters, who now were all over the place, everyone washed and combed beside the hammock receiving the blessing from me. And the rosary of gilt metal beads for Comadre Jesa, Amador's wife, and also a wool shawl for her to use on chilly mornings. In the old times Comadre Jesa never came to the fazenda—Senhora, who didn't like her, used to say she was always "breeding or whelping."

As I went on explaining the use of each item, the girls gave squeals of joy and tried on the earrings; and then one of them who took Zeza's place came in with the tray of coffee, and she also got her present. The sadness of my arrival finally turned into an occasion of happiness, embraces, and

245

receiving the blessing; and nobody cried for Senhora anymore.

Then I remembered Maria Milagre.
"And my dear old *nega*? What has happened to her?"
Xavinha broke into tears.
"Completely blind, my dear, completely blind! She
doesn't leave her room anymore; she refuses to have a
guide."
I got up and went running to Maria Milagre's room, the
last one after the kitchen—dark, without a window. I remembered it well. On the wall were the old lady's portraits of saints with faded ribbon bows and palms which
had been blessed on Palm Sunday. In the middle of the
room was the blue hammock, and seated in the hammock, the form of the ancient woman who lifted her head
at my entrance.
"What is it?"
With a heavy heart I put my hands on her tiny shoulders.
"Can it be possible? Nobody told you I was coming?"
The old black felt for my hand on her shoulder and gave
that little half ferocious smile of hers.
"Ah, you have already arrived? You came to take charge
of what is yours? It's about time."
Xavinha complained, "Scold this batty old person,
Dorinha. She won't accept a guide; she spends the whole
day in her hammock. When she wishes to leave the room,
she goes groping along the walls; and if one of the girls
comes close to offer her a hand, she beats the girl with a
stick."
Maria Milagre mumbled her ya-ya: "Those dumbbells.
I have been going about this house for more than eighty
years—don't I know all the corners and nooks? It's enough
for them to take out the stool so I can sun myself on the
patio!"
I continued to embrace her shoulders.
"I missed you, darling. Look, I brought you a bed cover
for a present—and a pipe, such as they use in Rio . . ."
The old lady glided her hand over the entire pipe carefully, tried the stem in her mouth.
"And tobacco? I still have my old pipe. What I don't have
is tobacco."

246

Xavinha interrupted again.

"Come, come, Maria! I just gave you money to buy some tobacco yesterday!"

The blind one lifted her little stick into the air.

"That Xavinha doesn't change a bit! On the Virgin Mary, I do believe she will always be just an old maid. Those little pinches of yesterday's tobacco are already used up."

"Don't worry; I'll have Amador bring you tobacco."

Luzia came to the door.

"Godmother Dorinha, don't you want to take your bath? It is ready."

I embraced old Maria again; she and I, we two who always understood each other. In former times she was the only one who had the courage to stand up to Senhora. Now she was saying good-bye to me with the new pipe in her mouth, staring out vacantly: "I knew you would come. Your time had arrived!"

I took my warm bath from the gourd, drawn from Senhora's private pot with the large mouth. It seemed to me the smell of Senhora's soap was still in the air, in that bathroom with the cement floor from which she left, red, perfumed, twisting her golden hair, stopping to change her *tamancos* or clogs for the bedroom slippers left outside the door.

I lunched on a lamb which Antônio Amador had slaughtered for me. It was so good that I promised myself I would give the Captain such a lunch of lamb: the boiled skin and back bones, the *sarapatel*, the liver, the haunches roasted in the oven. And the next day, the *buchada*. I also promised such a luncheon for Carleto. Another time I would bring both of them, I swore this to myself.

Around four o'clock I woke up from the siesta. I was still half asleep and gradually became aware that Xavinha was standing next to the ropes of the hammock; when she saw me awake, she looked around mysteriously and lowered her head close to mine.

"I was waiting until everybody was outside to give you the money; I didn't want to open the secret drawer in front of anyone."

She showed me a small key, separated by a little metal chain from the others on the ring—the key to my father's secretary, "the wallet," as Senhora called it.

247

"Let me rinse my mouth and eyes first, Xavinha."

She waited next to the lavatory. Then she took me solemnly into the office and put the key in my hand.

The lock rang that well-known little bell which from the time I was small had made me run from wherever I was to see Senhora open and close "the wallet."

Xavinha pointed out the two little secret drawers, hidden between the pigeonholes at the right and at the left.

"In this one are the jewels. I never looked into it. And there is the one with the money. That one I opened and counted the cash: It had ninety-five cruzeiros and a handful of little coins. Amador wanted to spend it on the day of the funeral, but I wouldn't let him. He found some other way. . . ."

"He sold an ox: He wrote me."

"Well, that's it. But I didn't mix into any of that—what Senhora had on hand is accounted for."

In the middle pigeonhole I saw a roll of papers. Xavinha explained: "Those are the death certificate, the receipt from the cemetery, the receipts from Dr. Fenelon, and the pharmacy bills. Amador has already paid them. Here is the inventory document which the lawyer wrote."

In the large pigeonhole were the land deeds—in the place where they always were. I remembered: the yellow paper with the faded writing, tied with a little ribbon frayed at the ends.

Under the deeds was a notebook, the kind schoolchildren use—I didn't remember its having been there.

Xavinha insisted that I read the papers—I looked them over and paused on the lawyer's notations:

DATA FOR SENHORA'S INVENTORY

Fazenda Soledade, a half league of lands in front with a league in the back giving on the river.

The fazenda house and its improvements: storage house for meal, other storehouses, warehouses, shops, etc.

12 mud huts for the tenants.

The dam.

Corrals, cattle chutes, enclosures, planted fields, cleared lands.

Orchard below the dam.

132 head of cattle, including the bulls, freshened heifers, and calves.

2 field horses and their trappings [the old Violeiro had died, the saddle was there].

1 female donkey and 6 asses with 5 saddle frames for cargo.

205 head of sheep and goats.

Senhora's gold jewels

2 gold rings.

4 gold chains.

1 gold brooch with pearls.

1 same in silver, rose shaped.

1 gold cross with a diamond.

1 pair of earrings of coral and diamonds.

1 silver thimble with garnets.

1 soup ladle, 6 forks, 7 silver spoons [all locked away in the cedar chest].

1 Belgium lamp with pull chain.

1 set of English china, pieces missing.

2 French crystal compotes.

1 set of white metal flatware, pieces missing.

The Furniture

1 double bed with turned spools.

2 cedar wardrobes.

2 chests of drawers, *idem*.

1 Austrian sofa and six chairs.

2 consoles.

1 radio, old model, with batteries.

1 secretary [my father's].

1 dining room table and 10 chairs.

1 china closet with a marble back.

1 buffet, *idem*.

1 oratory with all its saints.

1 little silver lamp in the oratory.

1 prie-dieu.

1 Singer sewing machine, used.

2 single iron beds.

Small tables, stools, chaises, an old gramophone [broken], etc.

1 trunk of hammocks.

Bed and table linens.

(Senhora's everyday clothes had been distributed to the poor in accordance with her orders; they had been given away after the first attack of her illness.)

The rest, old household goods, large copper pans, kitchen utensils and utensils for cheese-making, everyday china, iron and metal flatware.

A random piece of foolscap paper, and on it was set down the inventory of everything Senhora owned: her treasures, and her lands.

It was Laurindo's price. For this he had married me! In the end he got nothing. Death had cheated him.

Later I got the notebook, the one next to the roll of deeds, leases, and other documents about the land. It couldn't be the expense accounts—these were kept in a hardcover account book in the drawer. I knew them well.

On the first nine pages nothing was written, as if the person wished to give the impression that the notebook was blank. But from the tenth page on were notations in pencil. A sort of diary—in Senhora's handwriting.

The years weren't noted and often there was no indication of the month. It began suddenly, like this:

June 18—Monday:
They went to bed early. She didn't pray.
19—They went horseback riding. At lunch he almost choked on a fishbone and she did nothing.
20—Nothing. I didn't see them all day. They ate little for supper, went to bed. Quarrels?

At times two or three days or an entire week were missing without any explanation.

26—(Monday.) He went out at dawn on Violeiro with Luis Namorado. Let's see if this is going to work out. She cooked eggs on the alcohol stove. I loaned L. 50 milreis.
30—Three days' vacation. Dora eats, sleeps, reads, and embroiders. Very calm.
July 2—L. returned yesterday; played piano—Waltz of the Flowers—very pretty.

The notations covered a large part of the time of our marriage. There were big interruptions—more than months at

times—without any explanation. By months I tried to identify the years, taking as a basis some important fact, as
when I lost the baby and went to Fortaleza. Months before,
in the middle of that routine procedure—she had written:
she ate, she didn't eat, she went out, etc. Then came the following note:

May 25—Pregnant? She was nauseated. She denied it
and said that something she ate made her ill. It must be
so.

But farther on, already in June:

12—Yes, pregnant. MD ordered eggshell cambric for
maternity shirts. She is very yellow and thin but
doesn't show.

A month followed with day-to-day notes. New loans to
"L.": 30 milreis—80 milreis.

July 2—Mundica came from Aroeiras—brought MD's
order of diapers. I wanted to pay; she said she had her
own money.

From then on more days noted; she only wrote about L
and, funny thing, if I remember this was a time when I was
very ill.
She said nothing of my illness except that on the day I
made the trip—I don't remember the day for certain anymore—she said:

19—Trip to Fortaleza. (Nothing more)

and

30—Return. She lost the child.

MD withdraws more and more every day—she only appears to relate to L—indirectly:

They quarreled. L. went to play the piano; then he
left alone.

251

I had thought she hadn't noticed the nights of drinking, but there it was:

. . . arrived drunk, 2 o'clock. He had to be put to bed. MD told me nothing.
. . . L. is drinking a lot. There have been five Saturdays of this in a row, without exception. I don't think he has any more money.

There was a short note about the trip to Maranhão, a copy of the telegram calling him. Then:

. . . MD wanted to go. Just for the trip, I think. But who is going to take care of the expenses? It seems to me that she is sulking. L. cried a lot.

Ten days without any notes. Finally:

He returned, very sensitive. He says he lost weight, but it doesn't seem so to me. MD had a turkey killed. Peace made.

The notes continued as usual, without any variation. The "loans" continued (I hadn't known about them). But the writing ended the third of July—twelve days before Laurindo's death on July fifteenth.

As I was deep in the notebook I saw Xavinha's excited eyes on me. Had she read the diary? I skimmed over the first pages and found out what they were about—however, the notes didn't make sense—I closed the notebook, and put it back in the same place, under the property documents.

But that night, after Xavinha had gone to bed, I went to the secretary, unlocked it very slowly in order to deaden the sound of the little bell, took out the notebook, and went to read it again in my room by candlelight.

I read, I reread—I still couldn't understand it. I don't understand it to this day and I still have the cursed notebook in my possession. I tried to see if there were some pages torn out—the last two fatal days, perhaps. But if this were true the job had been well done. If someone had torn out pages, it had been done from the stitching and the corresponding pages of the other side had also been removed.

In the morning I returned the notebook to its place. I was tempted to carry it away with me to study the notes slowly, but I didn't want the Captain to see it; and I couldn't hide anything from him.

On the next day I went to visit Delmiro's place. Nothing remained any longer, only the pitchforks which belonged to the *tapera*. Amador had taken away the roof tiles and the rest fell in on itself. No one went by there; the people passed it from a distance. If the place already had a bad reputation from the time of the old João de Deus, what would it be like now?

I spent four days at Soledade. I approved everything that had been done, without examining very much. Xavinha and Antônio Amador obliged me to take with me at least the jewelry and the silver flatware—it was too much of a responsibility for them.

The Captain was restless in Fortaleza. I suppose that he regretted having allowed me to go alone. D. Loura joked, saying that he didn't take his eyes off the door.

"The man is madly in love, Dôra!"

Hearing that, I was dancing on clouds. The Captain wasn't one of those who hides love or is ashamed to love.

"If you speak of traveling again, I'll give you a spanking."

I told him all about Soledade. That desolation, the house half shut up, it seemed as if time had stopped.

"But I don't think anything remains there of Laurindo; he passed like a shadow. Didn't I already tell you that in my childhood, my greatest difficulty was to find any sign of my father's presence? No, in Soledade there was only Senhora's mark. The people there speak of her as if she were still alive, as if she had gone on a long trip and hadn't returned."

Estrela and Carleto met us at the airport and the latter declared that he was thinking seriously about not leaving the

Santa Teresa house. Whatever will be will be. On the other hand it did have that devilish steep street and they couldn't be ungrateful about the Mansion, their friend in lean times. (Now it was he who felt warmest about the Mansion; Seu Brandini was like that: all the time that he had hopes of a better place, for example, an apartment in Leblon which for a while was a mania of his—ah, then the Mansion was an animal's den, a chicken coop. But now that he knew himself to be a prisoner there without any hope of leaving, he began to appreciate it and to boast about it; and anyone hearing him talking about living in Catete would think that the old gaucho lived in a palace right beside Getulio.)

As "payment" for rent, they left us a finch in a cage that was like a wire bungalow with a swinging perch and a birdbath. The Captain was delighted, but I, no, I didn't like it; I never liked to see a bird imprisoned—neither Delmiro nor I.

The academy paid the salary for the month of vacation, and the next month the director called the Captain and offered him the position of head of the Department of Sports and Hunting—shooting, yachting, fishing, camping—which the academy people called the Department of Boy Scouts. It meant an increase in pay and less time for him to devote to the business with Chief Conrado and Patron Davino.

We settled down to routine living and, if that wasn't happiness, I don't know what was.

Speaking of Chief Conrado, one afternoon he came to the house to welcome us back, and I don't know how the conversation turned to that awful day of the Captain's arrest, and I told him about the episode of the gun—I seated on top of it, glued to the step, bellowing to distract the men.

Both laughed until they doubled up and finally Chief Conrado said with a careless air: "That Bigode! Poor thing, he ended up bad, did you hear?"

If the Captain knew he gave no sign of it and Chief Conrado continued: "He vanished, he had been missing for more than a week; finally his body was fished from the bay and identified; it was he all right; besides they almost couldn't make the identification, the body was all eaten up by the siri crabs."

The Captain commented, half choking, "What an awful thing!"

And Chief Conrado: "You knew also, didn't you? He made his living by robbing the people of the numbers game in the *morro* of S. Carlos. One day the gang got fed up and ended it."

Carleto and Estrela, who were present, didn't put two and two together. But I was frightened; and as soon as the visitors had crossed the door step, I tried to make the Captain confess.

"My dear, was it really the bookies who finished off Bigode?"

He shrugged his shoulders, laughing.

"Certainly you don't think we did it. We don't have enough pull for that sort of thing—even though the *canaille* deserved it."

"And you found out only today? You don't seem much surprised."

He didn't get angry about my suspicions.

"Who is surprised when one such as he gets what he deserves? Don't you read the papers? There is a war on in the numbers game. Bigode was up to his neck in this, and he paid for his excesses."

He drew the bolt on the iron gate, and walked in front of me, and after a bit he turned around.

"If you throw too many stones one will hit you on the head. . . . Remember I was in Ceará."

He was so meek. Wouldn't it have been more natural for him to be irritated by my questioning?

But I didn't insist, didn't touch on the subject again with him or with Chief Conrado. That Bigode—it was difficult to imagine a more disgusting creature; perhaps his mother liked him when she gave birth to him—but only because a mother is a mother.

Now it happened that the Captain became friends with a customer who bought liquor from him, a man very much linked to the government people of Catete, a four-flusher who had even sent to Buenos Aires for a French girl to come live with him.

His name was Dr. Valdevino. He said he was gaucho, but the Captain suspected he was from Uruguay—or Par-

255

aguay; but it was more likely he was from Paraguay because he was crazy about *guarani* things—doesn't that make sense?

Whenever the Captain went to Dr. Valdevino's apartment carrying merchandise, he would invite him to have a drink and joked: "Come try out some of your poison. I want to see if you will risk your life!"

They kept on doing business in a hot gaucho manner. There were always other fellows there, and at times the Captain would join the poker group that met regularly on Tuesdays.

One afternoon Valdevino invited the Captain to go to the horse races at the Jockey Club, and he insisted that I come also.

"Don't fail to bring your wife along!"

I ended up renting a hat—Estrela told me where I could get it; it was Havana straw, matching my millet-colored crepe dress. The Captain thought I looked like one of the Muses; actually I acted like a baby chick just out of the shell! I don't think I put anybody to shame.

I bet on a horse that finished in fifth place—I didn't do so badly. I strolled along the turf while Dr. Valdevino showed me everything. I found it charming when he called me "Senhora" in the gaucho manner: "Look, Senhora, what a beautiful horse." "Good night, Senhora, I hope you enjoyed everything."

This even made me nostalgic for the stage, because in many of Seu Brandini's plays this was the way that the cavaliers addressed the ladies. (Or was it because it was my mother's title which I so coveted? "Senhora"?)

But when I told Carleto, he said that this was a Castilian custom, that people in Rio Grande didn't talk like that—only stupid people from the vicinity of Rio de la Plata rather than from our area.

The Frenchwoman didn't go along, but she did go the day we had the launch trip to the bay. She was no longer a young girl. I even think she was closer to rather than farther from the awful side of the forties; for that matter, neither was Dr. Valdevino any young kid, with that paunch of his and double chin. Besides there were those thick eyeglasses, the slicked-down hair, the big ring with the red stone on the little finger, and the pearl stickpin in his tie, and once he wore spats—the Captain told me that, I didn't see them my-self.

Seu Brandini, who had been introduced to him by the Captain in a bar on the beach, said that this guy wasn't real. He was a stage type.

"I'll bet we are going to find all that false, with that stom-ach, head of hair, and big nose . . ."

But as I was saying, the Frenchwoman went with us on the boat trip. She was a woman whose best days were past; she had a rather leathery neck and spoke a mixture of Portu-guese and Spanish, jumbled up with French. But she could make herself understood, and she seemed to be polite. As she was cold natured, she rolled herself up in a gabardine coat. The legs under the shorts were not what they might have been, and also there were the freckles: on the nose, on the neck, on the arms, even on the shinbones and the thighs. Her name was Francine. She could have been a woman from the Buenos Aires "zone" or whatever they call the red-light district in that country. (In the end the Captain and I never did take our dreamed-of trip to Buenos Aires, which he had promised me for so long.) But she seemed like a lady, with good manners, and an amiable smile.

Self-consciously the Captain was talking to "Madame Francine" and she smiled and said, "I prefer that you call me Francine; but if you insist on the 'Madame,' then call me Madame Gonçalves, which is the surname of Valdevino."

The Captain was sore and when we left he said to me, "Did you notice that French whore putting on airs?"

But I liked his not making a scene.

On this same trip to the bay they handed over the direc-tion of the launch to the Captain, and they put on his head the pilot's cap and—oh, my God—what a reminder of the time when he was indeed the Captain, in his own right. In his hand the launch seemed like a horse under the reins of a master picador, like a bird flying on top of the water; and he was like a prince, looking straight ahead, his hand resting lightly on the wheel, his movements easy. At times when the foam splashed on his face he wiped it dry with the back of his left hand, in a rapid gesture—oh, I can only repeat that he was like a prince.

But the invitations for me came only from time to time, and I believe just out of politeness. I don't know, but I think

Dr. Valdevino had his eye on the Captain for something special, some foolish and risky adventure—I said just this to the Captain and he was peeved.

"Nonsense, woman; he's a good customer, nothing more."

However, I feared that my suspicions were correct and Carleto, who had already found out something about the character, agreed with me.

"They say he is a man very much involved in shady business and likes to hire daring people . . . with the Captain's history of having brushed with the law, his sallies into the area of contraband—I wouldn't be surprised."

Well, the day came when Dr. Valdevino indeed sounded out the Captain about a business of automobiles to be brought from Miami and unloaded in French Guiana, and taken from there to Belém—they could make a fortune!

But when the Captain told me about it I was stunned, for this was no longer contraband with baubles: It was business with a smuggling ring. Even he was frightened and pretended he didn't understand the man.

Fortunately there wasn't time for Dr. Valdevino to insist on his proposal because Getulio killed himself at that time, and Lieutenant Gregório was put in jail; and all those with a foot in the Catete racket vanished.

I speak of a foot in the Catete, but it was their feet; the Captain's importance never reached these heights, thank God, as he himself explained to Seu Brandini, who asked him if he weren't afraid of being involved in the purge. The Captain laughed.

"Why afraid? I was never in on the big deals nor did I get anything big—I only got the crumbs. I only peeped at what they had—just licked the honey jar on the outside!"

Suddenly it got hot for them. Dr. Valdevino decided to take a trip south, and before doing so he married Francine. He was a widower, at least that is what he told us. Between us, we thought he must have put everything that he owned in her name; the marriage was one with a separation of goods. We didn't attend the wedding, celebrated half secretly; but we went to their apartment the following day, and Francine seemed to have been rejuvenated; her blue eyes shining and her hair, the color of the freckles, loose on her shoulders.

We went there because Dr. Valdevino telephoned requesting us to visit; he wanted to make a proposition. Horrified that it might again concern something similar to that of the automobiles of French Guiana, I insisted on going with him. Since I took the message I told the Captain that Francine had insisted that I go also—it wasn't exactly like that but I said it.

The proposal actually had nothing to do with automobiles; it was something else very special.

Dr. Valdevino didn't wish to rent his apartment which was full of many valuable furnishings—Persian carpets, silk draperies, silverware, china, and crystal. Yet he didn't wish to leave the apartment closed up with nobody in it. He said he was afraid of thieves, but I think he didn't wish to attract the attention of the new government—at least this was what could be understood.

For this reason he proposed that we stay in the apartment, sort of like caretakers, until things quieted down.

At that word "caretakers" the Captain curled his lips, and was perhaps going to respond negatively; but Francine understood, because she interrupted very quickly in her Spanish jargon that I am translating because I don't know how to reproduce it correctly: "You stay here as the house owners. Use our guest room, spend some time on the beach. Copacabana is beautiful, isn't it, Dôra?"

I agreed at once for fear that the Captain might refuse. Dr. Valdevino added that we could use the garage, in the space left vacant by his car, inasmuch as they were going to travel overland because Francine adored car trips. As for myself, I got the idea that they wanted to avoid the airport or maritime police in those dangerous days.

The apartment was large, in the vicinity of Posto Quatro, the front overlooking the sea. It had a drawing room and three bedrooms. I told Francine that we would stay, but on one condition: that she keep everything of theirs in the closets, even the carpets and the curtains, because I didn't have help and couldn't take care of everything all alone.

I had the impression that Francine liked my idea; perhaps she hadn't suggested it herself for fear of offending us.

As they were in a hurry, I stayed there the rest of the day, helping with the packing. Francine had discharged the maid, who talked too much. Only the cook who was going south with them—on the bus, I think—remained.

Then I thought to ask for the help of Estrela, whom they already knew—that is, Dr. Valdevino had met her one afternoon in our house when he came for some whiskey, and they had hit it off together.

Estrela came and began packing and rolling up the rugs. The Captain went about with a notebook, making an inventory of everything. Estrela said to me under her breath: "I don't envy them because I am not envious, but that gringo surely knows how to take care of himself!"

I, too, envied nothing; for me all of those things were illusory, and the silk draperies were already fading from the sun. If I were to envy something, it would be the silver trays; but truthfully why would I want such huge trays, the monogrammed silver, or the two sets of porcelain wrapped up, which filled an entire enormous closet in the dining room?

Where would I use them?—then why wish for those things? I recalled an old crackpot who lived in Aroeiras. He begged for everything on which he laid his eyes, a spoon, one shoe of a pair, a doll—and if people asked: "But Mané Doido, why do you want this?"

"Just to possess."

For me Francine's things were the same as those which Mané Doido asked for—where could I have put all of that luxury in our Santa Teresa rooms?

So I didn't envy anything; I didn't even wish to use any of their things. I preferred to see everything of theirs under lock and key to save us from responsibility.

I believe that Francine also liked my approach, when I said I was going to bring my own table and bed linens; but I would use her china in the pantry—it is said that all French-women are stingy and Francine badly covered up this trait.

The Captain didn't like my modesty—he took me aside to the balcony as if he wished to show me something in the sea and said with irritation: "Don't put on that modesty act, for I didn't come here as an employee of those gringos! *Caretakers*, wasn't that what he said? Caretakers, his slaves. I came only to do him a favor; I don't need anyone's apartment!"

I explained to him that I feared it would be too much work; I would be relieved if the things were put away. I quieted his irritation with another Soledade story, that of the woman who insisted on living alone with her children in a house with just one room, "because it took less work to sweep."

Within a few days I was as accustomed to living in that apartment as if I had been born there. By luck the classes of the academy were in the afternoon; hence we had the mornings free. We hardly jumped out of bed when I put on my bathing suit and he his shorts; it was in this outfit that he went to buy the bread, newspaper, milk, and meat. I would quickly make some coffee and we would set off for the beach until lunchtime.

On Saturdays and Sundays it was the beach almost all day long. Estrela and Carleto would come, and one Sunday when the Captain invited the members of the Patron Davino household, the old lady and the other daughter, Aldira, came. Alice had finally married the soccer player. (She ran off with him to São Paulo and, incredible as it seems, he even got a place on the reserve team. I don't know if it was on the S. Paulo or the Corinthian team; I do know it was a first-rate club. When anyone spoke about this, the old lady, Amada, would say she would believe it only when she saw Pequinho on the field with her own eyes.) Aldira was less excitable than Alice, and as soon as she arrived she headed for the beach. She had already made plans to meet some little friends of hers there, and we saw her again only when it was time for them to go home.

The old Amada had brought a package of *acarajés*—bean cakes cooked in African palm oil—which she had made; Estrela (who also came) adored them, but I couldn't give an opinion since the pepper made it impossible for me to taste anything. Accompanying them was a sauce which the old lady brought in a deep metal pot; one was supposed to open the *acarajé* and put on it that sauce which burned like liquefied lead. The Captain ate countless *acarajés,* and the old lady laid her bold eyes on him and smiled.

"Ah, you don't change at all, Cadet Lucas!"

I hated her.

Amusing, how quickly people adjust to new situations. The elevator, doorman, people living over and under us, and we ourselves perched on the seventh floor. But I didn't forget my own little house. I made the Captain take me there in the Studebaker once or twice a week when I would

261

sweep the patio, water the grape arbor, and dust the furniture. The birds (that first cage with the finch from Carleto had now increased to three) we had taken to the apartment, and it seemed to me that they found the sea smell strange after the tide went out.

One night some of Chief Conrado's men came, the same ones who used to get together with the Captain in the bar on Riachuelo Street, including Zelito, the one who had come to call me that awful afternoon when the Captain was so impossible.

I don't know what it was, I suppose that it was the presence of those men who made a profession of beating, imprisoning, attending meetings and conferences—swaggering in their offices, as Carleto would say—their presence fanned I don't know what repressed sparks in the Captain's breast. Who knows if perchance he wanted to be one of them also? Who knows if he suspected that in a certain way, the comrades looked down upon him because in fact they did have the official position, the uniform, the police billy, and the red beret, while he was called Captain only out of courtesy, almost as if it were a nickname. . . . I don't know, ah, I don't know.

I know that he drank, that they all drank, and that our alcohol had run out. The Captain opened Dr. Valdevino's bar and took out two more bottles of whiskey and I was terrified. Holy Mother, he was using Dr. Valdevino's property; but neither did I dare say anything, for he was already well lit up, and when he was in his cups he was invariably wild.

One of them, one Pamplona, suddenly pointed to a picture on the wall—a portrait of D. João VI in a hand-kissing ceremony in the palace—and asked whose face it was. The Captain became irritated, berated Pamplona for being ignorant—how is it that illiterate didn't recognize the face of D. João VI, King of Portugal and Brazil?

Pamplona said, "No, I never heard that Brazil had a King, only the Emperor."

The Captain, angry and drinking continuously—and the more he drank the more he dwelt on that subject of the king—ended up beating on his chest and saying, "Emperor of Brazil and King of the World!" And he bragged about the devil Asmodeu, his patron saint, who if he wished would protect him and give him all the power of the earth.

"You have heard of a devil's pact?"

He said these crazy things with a ferocious face, his eyes bloodshot; and I don't know what caused me more pain, fear or shame. As luck would have it the others—every one of them—were also on a drunken spree. Each one sang his own praises, and I think I was the Captain's only listener.

I never forgot: "Emperor of Brazil and King of the World." Days later after the drunk was over, I recalled the phrase to the Captain and asked him where he had gotten it. He was embarrassed, smiled, and said that it was a joke from his childhood.

That night didn't end without its brawl; one of the guests vomited out of the window and the doorman came to complain that it had fallen on the balcony of the fifth floor; the neighbors on the eighth floor also complained about the noise of the victrola because, of course, the Captain and his friends had put on the victrola, playing as loud as possible—roaringly—that collection of Dr. Valdevino's *guarani* records. I thanked God that he and Francine hadn't left those luxurious rugs on the floor.

Those days of vacation in Copacabana lasted four months. One day a telegram from Dr. Valdevino came, saying we would be visited by a lawyer (we already knew him) who would bring a letter with instructions.

The man came and the letter explained that the apartment with everything in it had been sold to an Argentine diplomat and that this and that was to be handed over less the things on a listing that Francine was sending me: clothing, some pictures, and a service of French crystal.

I found it very sensitive on Francine's part that she ordered I should have for myself, as a remembrance of her, a music box which played "J'attendrai" with a ballerina turning on her toe while the music played, which I had admired while we were packing. What I found most touching was that Francine had remembered this from a past day filled with much confusion. Today I still have that little music box but the ballerina doesn't dance anymore. However, the music plays, tinkle, tinkle, and I can rarely stand to listen because it brings back too much nostalgia of all that has passed forever.

* * *

Everything came full circle, the snake bit its tail: I ended by returning to Soledade.

I returned alone, returned for good and all. This time it was different. When I came before, just shortly after Senhora's death, the sense of her presence still spread over the house and the land, like a body's warmth or a voice's echo—the shadow of Senhora continued to control everything, the animals and the people.

Now I perceived that this was all fading away. I had hardly arrived when I sensed that Senhora's ashes were cold. Wounded and bruised as I was, I no longer needed to efface myself; I could take comfort in the old embers without fear of the live coals.

All the people there, freed from her heavy hand, began to deteriorate very, very slowly.

Xavinha had sunk into her hammock, no usefulness left as a custodian or watchdog. The hens had made their nests in the rooms; the pigeons lived in the cheese house.

Luzia and her child now occupied the room next to Xavinha's, which earlier had been the sewing room but was now in disarray with lines of diapers hanging up, hammocks still tied up in the middle of the day, a baby's bottle with sour milk standing on top of the Singer machine, the replacement for the old New Home.

Zeza was missing. After many moves she was now living with her husband, Luis Namorado, in a house far away, on the border of Arabia, keeping watch over the gate to the highway.

I went to receive the blessing of Maria Milagre in her dark room. She remained seated in the hammock, rocking, the stick in her hand. She made me come close, felt my face, shoulders, and arms to find out if I were a little fatter.

"What, the same slender reed comes back! It seems that those lands where you went don't have food!"

Amador was also getting old; he had always had his drunk spells, but now it wasn't a spell anymore; now he drank constantly and spent most of the day on his porch without stirring, sleeping half because of old age and half because of the firewater, chewing on a wad of tobacco. Comadre Jesa now emerged with new force, taking care of the most urgent things, curing the swollen stomach of the cow Jacana, the navel of the little calf; it was she who had raised on a bottle the two lambs rejected by their mother. Amador hardly concerned himself anymore with anything. If it hadn't been for his son who acted as foreman, I don't know what would have happened.

The cattle had also dwindled—by sale, death, or theft. The past year had been a shambles, the sheep were reduced to almost nothing, the goats even less. Of the horses, only one was left for me.

The warehouses were almost empty, the cotton income proceeds from Seu Zacarias were next to nothing, and the few cotton roots in the fields in their second growth.

To tell the truth, the fazenda Soledade was going under, almost the same as Xavinha, who had been its keeper and overseer. Poor Xavinha, hardly able to get up out of the hammock, indifferent to almost everything, all day long braying for Luzia to bring the coals for the pipe, water to wash her feet, the lemon-herb tea, a clean glass, the mug of water. Luzia, angry, pretended that she didn't hear most of the demands and then the old woman would shake a cowbell she had got from Antônio Amador, and which resounded throughout the empty house like the bell of an animal that had gone astray. Xavinha was worse off than Maria Milagre.

But it was mine. It was the only place from Pará to Rio de Janeiro that was mine. My house, with the whitewash on the walls dark from the mud of the preceding winter, mine the corral with fences begging for repair, mine the sparse amount of cattle and newly born animals.

Alone in this world I knew, alone and more than alone—with that band of useless old people at my side—but at least I wasn't among strangers as I had been in those last months in Rio, oh my God, those last months in Rio.

In the mornings I had the pitcher of milk drawn from my cow, or for lunch the remains of the bean crop from my barn, the chickens and eggs, the fish from the pond; eating in poverty, but eating what was mine.

Estrela and Carleto didn't understand. In that widowhood of poverty in which I found myself so suddenly, they could only imagine me beginning everything all over again in the city, to sell the fazenda, to start a new company—just imagine, to return to the stage after all those years—when in the first instance I had become part of the company as a last resort, by what miracle I don't even know myself.

Seu Brandini was even peeved when I refused.

"You are crazy to bury yourself in those backlands; you won't be able to stand it for even two months!"

He didn't understand—Estrela perhaps understood a little—that I felt buried, suffocated, entombed among strangers, with nothing of mine around me, all alone in the midst of people, alone from one day to the next, alone for breakfast and alone for lunch, alone in the afternoon, alone in my room and in the street, alone at night in the dark, alone in the midst of human beings. This he didn't understand.

At the fazenda I was also alone, but it was a type of peopled solitude, a solitude with which I was familiar, an ancient solitude which I carried in my blood.

The Captain had understood—and this was his genius; he always used to understand me, guessed what I was going to do, as if it had been written down in a book for him.

The moment I took the thermometer I bit my lips with misgiving upon seeing how high the fever was; the Captain smiled feebly, freeing me from lying; he said as if one thing didn't have anything to do with the other: "After all of this you'll return to Soledade, won't you?"

Those words pained me like a knife in my breast and I repeated, dazed, "After what?"

And with his speech already weak, he said half irritably, "After what? My death, of course."

I fixed on him my eyes which burned with pain and insomnia.

"If you die before me, I will bury myself with you in your grave."

He passed the tip of his finger, lightly, on my hand which gripped the bed cover.

"Nonsense, nonsense."

Yes, nonsense. I didn't bury myself in his grave or anyplace else. People don't bury themselves in anyone's grave. I kept on staying in our house, sleeping alone, eating alone, walking aimlessly in the midst of others, floating on the current like a dry husk.

After the worst days of the shock had passed, I looked at all around me as if I saw houses and people of a strange city; and I heard the language of the people as a foreign language. My instinct pleaded with me to go away, to return to that faraway place where the pain which could hurt me was a pain which I knew, not this pain of abandonment in this place that had meaning for me only with him, only with him and nothing more.

In no hour in Rio had I lived without him, because even during the time of waiting, when we arrived and I was with Estrela and Carleto in the Mansion, in a certain sense I was already with him, reserving myself with everything suspended, waiting for him.

Carleto thought I was frightened because of the lack of money in Rio. It could be that I was frightened, but that wasn't the main thing. I knew that to earn enough to support myself wouldn't be impossible. I could even continue selling the Captain's baubles. He had left me notes and addresses, telephone numbers, and the preferences of all his clientele—and I knew persons from whom I could get new merchandise. I also knew how to cook: I could sell ready-cooked food. The lease of the house was still good for two years—it wasn't even seven weeks that it had been renewed by the Captain.

But above all I had developed a general hatred of the place—if not, well, hatred, it was antipathy, indifference, even nausea. Why then should I stay?

In the final analysis I was Senhora's daughter and had her example to follow—her house, her land, I could follow in her footsteps. Without her at Soledade to stop me and bar my entrance to all doors open to me—without her there—that was my place.

A king dead is a king deposed. The Sinhá Dona had died and I had arrived—I don't wish to say the new Sinhá, because then, at that time, I was nothing of a Sinhá Dona: beaten down and wounded, thin and with downcast eyes I seemed more like a Delmiro who had fallen unconscious from his donkey than a Dona of the land who returned to her kingdom to rule.

But it was mine. I didn't have to compete with anyone—it was mine—and above all, I was at home. There wasn't a leaf of the *mato* or an animal, an insect, a bird, or a fish that was strange to me—none with which I would not feel comfortable. The old ones growing weak were mine to watch over, to put up with and accompany to their hour of death. The daughters of the old servants were my new servants. The people received me as if there had been no absence; they merged one time with another, and the years of separation were forgotten.

He had a little life insurance: This I discovered only when I investigated the papers in the Captain's drawer: a policy of which I was the beneficiary. With this I paid the debts, the immediate expenses, and I even had something left over for the trip. I didn't waste any money on return passage. Chief Conrado arranged to get another free ticket from Panair, and he even sent all my baggage overland in a truck. I gave him the Studebaker as a gift; it had no sale value, it was just a souvenir.

Seu Brandini put an ad in the *Jornal do Brasil:* "Person who is moving wishes to sell all the furnishings of her residence"; and I spent two days there in the house, haggling over the bed, chest of drawers, stove, table, chairs, and everything I couldn't carry with me. I took the house linens, china, and some pans—my beautiful pans for making our meals, his and mine.

Carleto wanted to sell the birds, but I didn't let him; I gave the three cages to D. Amada, who in those most dreadful days best understood me. She didn't try to console me in any way, but remained alongside in silence, looking out of the window; at times she brought me a glass of milk or a cup of tea, and one of those times when I pushed away her hand she said: "Drink, it is liquid. So you can have water in your eyes with which to cry."

She didn't mention the Captain's name; she didn't lament like the others—"Poor thing, so young, still so strong!"—she received the few visitors; she left me in peace. It was this that was most precious about her—she left me in peace.

In Rio I had not worn mourning, but going to Soledade I remembered that I had to buy black clothing. In the *sertão* I found wearing black obligatory. It was my badge of widowhood, or even more than this; that black clothing was the marriage certificate I signed for the Captain.

There mourning was still a passport of widowhood; it guaranteed me the right to live alone without anyone bothering me about anything, to command and countermand in my small earldom, so ugly and decadent. Senhora's earldom—I now being the Senhora.

But the black dress was the only concession I made. The rest of the adornments of widowhood, the picture frame on the bedside table, the two rings on the left hand, his reminders enshrined and exhibited—for this I didn't have the stomach.

I couldn't. I couldn't live the life of a widow—as Senhora lived it. Widowhood was painful for me. It was an active misfortune, accursed.

Senhora used to make fun of a friend of hers.

"Many a woman has made of widowhood a new start in life. . . ."

I suppose it was so. Perhaps at the time of the death they suffered pain. But it is that very pain which marks the beginning of the new life—it is like the pain of childbirth. Instead of the living husband to make life meaningful, they now had the dead which gave them a new role with its attending rites: the eternal mourning, the photographs of the deceased, the monthly and yearly masses, the flowers in the cemetery, the wreaths with candles for All Souls' Day. Senhora's friend would say: "He died thirty years ago, and it seems to me as if it were only yesterday!"

And Senhora: "Pray to God for a few more years of life, and you may yet celebrate your golden anniversary."

Senhora could speak harshly of that other widow, but she herself took advantage of her widowhood as a natural way of life, with problems but full of compensations: The authority and independence gained made up for the shortcomings and she didn't hide that fact.

But I—no, ah, I—no. For me there was only that horrible solitude, the emptiness, and the despair; a nothingness in which I felt myself to be reeling about, finding no bottom. My flayed flesh bleeding.

269

I still lived so full of him and so overwhelmed by the lack of him that the pain of that lack gnawed at me constantly like the hunger of one who is starving. Instead of consoling myself with memories and in a certain way enjoying my sorrow, I was driven to find some free moments for thought, to get away from the pain of him, to soothe my mental and physical aches so as not to have to run madly screaming.

The worst, the most horrible, the principal thing was the breakup of our unity of two, of our sharing. From one moment to another I saw myself alone, cut off from any communication whatever. Nothing that I might do, nothing—not crying, lacerating myself, going mad and beating my head against the wall, or cutting my veins—nothing was capable of provoking any reaction whatsoever or any reply whatever, even a most distant one. One moment he was there, he mine and I his—and the next he was gone, and it was as if he had never existed.

That part of him for me had ended: all, all! and without any preparation or warning. Only silence and endless distance remained.

And I couldn't do anything about it—if I were lord of the world or if I were the Pope I couldn't change things. No magic, miracle, or power could help.

So then what consolation and compensation could I have? Even if I covered myself with mourning veils as Senhora wanted for Laurindo and which I refused (now my attitude in that remote time seems of such little importance) and filled up the house with his portraits, the furniture and the walls with his objects—what then?

Now one vast nothing. All now could only be of my invention, pretense, and imagination. Of what use to me would his personal effects be: his glass, watch, eyeglasses, and clothing, if the important and most precious thing of all—his body, flesh, hands, his very substance!—had had been destroyed and ended by death. Oh, my God—his hands, mouth, eyes, all gone. Now only all skeleton and skull—so it is said, God takes these morbid thoughts away.

I put everything that was his into a trunk and threw away the key. To this day I have never opened it and I have no intention of opening or looking into it. This holds true for the most cruel of all—the photos. That face—and we say that *it is indeed he*—it *was* he and he exists no more! In no corner of the world, not in heaven or on earth or in the water, nothing more of him which shows in that photo exists. He is finished. Neither flesh, color, nor form; and, more than all, the expression: how he smiled and the sound of his voice and the light in his eyes—these things that by their very nature are already elusive, that when one is alive come and go and never repeat themselves in exactly the same way, it is what the photo in that moment immobilizes—after death what will it then say?

If the girl I was more than twenty years ago which the photo recorded, is today gone, buried in time as in death—yes, what about someone who is really dead?

Work was my salvation. Everything had to be started all over again: The dirty, deteriorated house had to be repaired and whitewashed, the fallen-down fences mended, and the clearings again opened up. To put the men to work, to demand three days of work per week, a custom they had dropped since Senhora died. To replenish the cattle, exchange the old cows for young heifers, arrange for a bull, sell the barren cattle, and in addition sell everything that could be turned into ready cash. To arrange a loan for the cotton farmer Seu Zacarias to replant the cotton: There was still the old clearing with cotton roots dating from before Laurindo's death.

Rarely was there a foot of fence still up, rare the tenant's house that wasn't about to cave in. Even the dam needed careful checking, the orchard was a forest, the sugarcane planting abandoned after the third cutting was now hidden in the brush and uncared for.

The money brought from Rio, raised by Carleto from the sale of my possessions, was being spent for those expenses which I couldn't postpone; but at least I didn't have to think about the little needed to take care of myself and my people, a sizable number. I would kill a sheep, I would kill a goat, I had Xavinha's chickens, the ducks, the eggs, and the milk. I ordered that a cassava manioc be dug out which by a miracle Amador had left standing from the previous year—I had manioc meal made and flour was guaranteed for six months.

I tried in every situation to remember how Senhora had done it; and all was repeated now as in her time because

271

even if I might have wished to do anything differently I didn't know how. Hence it was her law that continued to govern us.

Little by little I steeled myself in the armor of my black clothing. My sweetheart kept occupying less and less place in my heart, and I opened up the prison only at night when all alone. Only at night did I dream and remember, whether I wished to or not. Sleeping, awake, tossing in the bed—my old bed with a new mattress—where I, widowed, stretched myself across it . . . alone.

Sleeping, awake, dreaming.

In those hours when I was all alone I relived, retold to myself, and remembered what I couldn't stifle.

Things which I hadn't even told to D. Loura, not because I didn't want to but because I couldn't, I was so choked and grief-stricken. She in amazement exclaimed: "But a man so strong, still young! He seemed like a bull!"

A bull, a thoroughbred racehorse, a big fish of the sea . . .

I embraced D. Loura, crying so much I couldn't talk.

She kissed me, put me to bed, gave me some tea. She consoled me, cuddled me, and spoke no more.

Worst of all, I had at first thought it was only the flu. It seemed like the flu. How was I to know it wasn't?

He often had an attack of that sneaky, crippling flu during every year. Body weakness and headache, pain in every bone of the body. He refused food—but this was natural for him. The drinking stopped at last, and he never had a cigarette. How was I to know?

He could have complained but said he felt nothing serious, just the weakness, the weakness! It would pass away. That devilish flu—wasn't I now used to it?

Moreover a flu epidemic had been going around the city; more than ever he had been wrapped up in his business trips to the back of the bay; Patron Davino's launch had been seized, and it had been another ship which spawned merchandise on the banks of the Mage and Surui. At times the old Studebaker had been unable to get to these places with difficult access, and then they took the bus. And withal, fewer goods—new times, different men, uncertain

272

protection—the game had been no longer worth the candle. At times he had told me so.

"Today we do this more for the sport of it."

Sport! Hadn't the academy with its regular pay at the end of the month been enough? Wasn't that enough for us to live on?

Then that morning, already ill with the flu as I thought, he went out feverish, very weak. He returned late at night and went straight to bed without eating or even taking a bath. He lay down in all his clothes and when I went to take them off, I realized his skin was blazing like live coals: He was burning up with fever.

I attacked the matter obliquely, I knew his reactions.

"Your body is warm, it seems like a fever. May I try out on you my little gold thermometer I got on Christmas Day?"

He growled and I went to get the thermometer, a gift from him which I hadn't had any chance to use before. (I also put it away in the trunk of the lost key.)

I almost had to make him let me place the thermometer and hold his arm for two minutes; but when I took it to the light to read my sight blurred. I don't know why I didn't pass out—the mercury was way up at forty degrees centigrade.

Even so I had the strength to pretend, and I didn't even need to fake because he wasn't interested in knowing anything. He only complained about the headache. I wrapped him up well—the cover slipped from my hands, they were trembling so—and I slipped out to the hall where the telephone was.

Forty degrees—never in my life had I seen a thermometer at forty degrees. Making a mistake with the numbers, dialing, and beginning over again, I finally got the line to Estrela. The phone rang and rang with no answer and only then did I remember that Estrela and Carleto had gone to spend the weekend in Saquarema. I next got a line to Chief Conrado and this time God favored me—he answered on the third ring.

I told about the Captain's illness, the flu, the fever. Did he know a doctor? Estrela had once brought a doctor, an acquaintance of hers—but I didn't know his telephone number or even the right name of the man. . . .

Chief Conrado laughed at that: "You all don't have a doctor? That's what good health means!"

But I was in no mood for jokes.

"Estrela is away. . . . Do you think I ought to get just any doctor from the telephone directory? I am so foolish, Chief Conrado, so worried. . . . Just imagine, he has a fever of forty degrees!"

Chief Conrado then promised to help at once.

"Now, be calm, Dorinha. Why the big fuss? I'll dig up a doctor. You stay by his side and I'll be there right away."

The Captain moaned just then and I let the receiver hang as I went to look in on him; I returned to the hall and put the phone back on the hook; fortunately Chief Conrado had already hung up.

Oh, what a horrible wait! At every instant I wanted to use the thermometer again, to see if the fever was still climbing, but I didn't have the nerve. How much above forty could a fever climb? My hand on his head told me he was hotter. Was it going to forty-one, forty-two? And where is the limit before death comes?

Perhaps two hours had passed when finally Chief Conrado arrived with an old man who had a thin face and frightened eyes, his collar open and no tie; and he begged pardon for his attire.

"Conrado pulled me out of bed."

The old man was the doctor. Chief Conrado called me to a corner and told how he had tried to get his family doctor, but he couldn't locate the cursed man—nobody knew how to reach him, perhaps he was in Petrópolis! Then he tried to find someone else he knew who lived in Botafogo—but that one was on duty in his hospital.

The doctor took some steps in our direction and Chief Conrado spoke out loud: "Luckily I remembered my old friend, Dr. Nogueira, who worked in our ambulance unit until he retired, and fortunately he still works in his clinic. And just imagine, very near here on Rachuelo Street. As he said, I got him out of bed."

Dr. Nogueira entered the bedroom, examined the Captain for a very long time, listened, probed, looked at his tongue, the whites of his eyes, took his temperature, and checked his blood pressure without saying anything. The

274

Captain, who hated to be manipulated by doctors, was so weak he couldn't protest.

At last the doctor went to the living room and sat down at the table to write out the prescription; and I asked what could it be with the fever so high, and he interrupted me.

"I can't tell you anything positive, my lady, when it is that high. It may be the flu, a very bad case. It can be something else. All these infections act the same in the early stage. We have to wait until it develops."

The following day Dr. Nogueira returned in the afternoon. The fever was still high, the situation hadn't changed. The doctor repeated his routine: He probed, listened, took his temperature, checked the blood pressure. Finally he tied a rubber band on the Captain's arm and drew a little blood. He ordered me to give the patient cold baths if the fever went up any more—but then he looked at me with a smile.

"He is so big and you are so tiny, it is going to be difficult to carry him to the bathtub. It will be enough to wrap him up in a sheet soaked in cold water."

"What do you call a very high fever, doctor? Above what?"

"Anything above forty. Take his temperature often."

I took his temperature every hour on the hour. For the second time the column rose a bit higher than the forty degrees—more than a tenth.

I covered the bed with a rubberized sheet and a cheap spread, then, as Dr. Nogueira instructed—it was very difficult—I rolled a wet sheet around the Captain. I did this with fear—all my *sertão* blood rebelled against the idea of treating fever with cold water.

But the fever came down. When I was drying him and changing his clothes, he ran his hand over his face which was hairy with three days' growth and asked me to shave him.

"If I'm going to die, I want to die handsome."

On the third day Dr. Nogueira arrived, this time in the company of Chief Conrado, who hadn't returned since the first night; because of the pressure of work, he had only telephoned.

275

After examining him the doctor took the two of us out to the living room.

"Ma'am, everything makes me believe that it is typhoid. We must remove your husband to isolation."

"Where?"

"S. Sebastião Hospital, in the Caju."

"He won't want to go. He hates hospitals!" Chief Conrado interrupted.

"Let me talk with him. I know how to convince the character."

The news that the Captain's illness was typhoid and on top of that the order to take him to the hospital for isolation made me even more despondent. I felt my heart sink, I was speechless. Typhoid! I couldn't hide my tears from the men and I ran to the kitchen.

Finally I washed my face, returned to the room, and found the Captain half sitting up in the bed, fighting mad.

"I won't go! I shall treat myself in my own house, next to my wife! I know S. Sebastião, that shithouse."

Chief Conrado began to joke, cajole, reason, and almost plead. But the Captain only bit his lips, getting angrier all the time.

"I won't go! Not even if you use force!"

Until the doctor lost his patience and smiled.

"Listen, my friend, a patient has no choice. If you continue to resist, I'll give you an injection, you will go to sleep and we will carry you sleeping in an ambulance. . . ."

The Captain half closed his eyes, reached into the drawer of the bedside table, and took out his gun.

"Oh, you will, will you? I would just like to see some S.O.B. come close to me to give me an injection . . . I will shoot!"

Dr. Nogueira recoiled a step; behind him Chief Conrado began to laugh. I knelt at the side of the bed, put my arm around the chest of my darling patient, succeeded in laying him down again and passed my hand over his head and face. I kissed him lightly on the face and slowly I took the revolver out of his hand. He let his head drop on the pillow and breathed heavily, exhausted. But still furious.

I whispered in his ear, "I am going to speak with the doctor. I won't let them take you away from here, this never! Be calm, my dear. Be calm."

In the living room, Dr. Nogueira was very much upset

and only said, "Incredible! Incredible! This I have never seen before."

And I asked, "Dr. Nogueira, what hospital is that? Can you give me a guarantee?"

The doctor shrugged his shoulders.

"It is a public hospital. Isolation. What do you wish me to guarantee?"

I begged, "Dr. Nogueira, please. Isolation is necessary so that the disease won't be spread, I know. But here we are alone in the house, just the two of us—he and I! And this house is also isolated; it even has this patio separating us from the street. . . . No neighbors enter here, nor do I know—"

But the doctor protested, "In cases of typhoid I am obliged by law to notify the Department of Public Health."

I persisted, "Listen, Dr. Nogueira, I am frightened by his reaction. I don't know what he is capable of if you try to carry him by force. . . ."

Chief Conrado laughed again.

"We had a sample! . . . The animal is even crazy. Listen, Nogueira, old man, what if we keep it a secret? As the lady says, they live here alone, there is no risk of the disease being spread . . . even you can't add any more treatment, how can they do any more in the hospital?"

Dr. Nogueira hesitated (I could see that Chief Conrado had some influence over him). "All of this is most irregular. . . ."

In that instant, to carry him off to the hospital was for me the greatest threat. To think of him far away, in an infirmary, in the midst of other contagious patients, without being able to say anything. And furious, desperate, feeling himself betrayed, capable of some madness. . . .

"Can I guarantee you that nothing here will be lacking in the treatment?" insisted Chief Conrado. "I will even bring a nurse. . . ."

Dr. Nogueira cut the air with a gesture of his hand. "No, if we aren't going to notify the authorities, it is better not to have any nurse mixed up in this. For now, at least. . . . Perhaps he will respond to the medication. . . ."

Again he sat down at the table, opened his briefcase, and took out his prescription pad. The Captain called to me from his room and asked for water.

I gave him the water and quieted him.

277

"They aren't going to take you away, no, my love. I fixed it so that I will keep on nursing you right here at home."

Dr. Nogueira returned shortly to the room carrying the prescription. He explained to me the dosage of the medicines, the correct times to give them, and the diet. He insisted on the cold compresses. Chief Conrado said that he himself was going to get the medication.

I continued to give the medicines which controlled the fever and applied the wet compresses all by myself. Estrela hadn't returned and I didn't know their address in Saquarema. They wouldn't return until Thursday. I could have called someone at Patron Davino's, but I was afraid to break the secret, to know in whom to confide. Chief Conrado came as often as he could. The hardest thing for me to do was to put the wet towels around his body which was burning up with fever, his eyes crossed—but I forced myself, obeying blindly the cursed old man; I would have even put the Captain in fire if with this they might promise me to save him.

On the morning of the fourth day the Captain seemed to be a little better. He called me to come beside him in the bed. I knelt down on the rug, as I always did and leaned over him, stroking his hair with my hand. He lifted my hand to his mouth, in that old gesture of his, and I felt the heat of his fever burning my fingers. He began to speak in the voice that he reserved for me only, and at those special times, he was almost timid, low voiced, and tender.

"Take off your clothes, come to bed, I want you here, with me."

I was frightened.

"But darling, you are ill . . . this is madness . . . afterwards you will get worse."

He insisted, drew me near and with his uncertain hand tried to unbutton my dress. I caught his fingers and he murmured sadly, "I must be repugnant . . . smelling of fever and medicine. . . ."

I kissed the hand which I held, quickly undressed, lay on the other side of the bed and helped my poor lover to undress also. When we embraced, his skin disturbingly burned on mine; he was ablaze. His mouth smelled strongly of the medicine, and he had a humble little smile.

278

"Ah, today only you . . . Today I don't have strength for anything. . . ."

I did all that he wished—I alone, as he said. When it was finished, he remained for a long time with his head back, eyes closed and breathing deeply, as if he had come from under water. I didn't move; I continued to keep my arms around him until his breathing returned to normal. Then I wiped away the sweat which bathed him again, put his pajamas on, and covered him. Only then I dressed and left him so I could cry in secret.

On the sixth day the Captain began to complain of strong pains. Dr. Nogueira, who had come late at night, late for the visit, began to probe.
"Here in the abdomen?"
"Yes, in the stomach. It hurts a lot."
The old man took me again to the living room, and spoke in a low voice. "I don't like these abdominal pains. It can be intestinal perforation. Early tomorrow I am going to bring a colleague for a consultation. Tomorrow very early."
All the time the devilish old man was making me more and more afraid. Consultation? From what I remembered, consultation was a sign that the patient was given up as incurable. "They already had a consultation. . . ."
Holy Mother, what could that be—was an intestinal perforation serious?

In the morning the doctors came for the consultation. The other doctor was a stranger. I didn't even know his name, they must have said it, but it didn't register; he was a young man in a white hospital uniform. They said nothing to me; they talked in a low voice. I only heard Dr. Nogueira say, "Of course, of course. Immediately. I had considered that."
They went to the telephone, it seems that they couldn't find whom they wanted. Dr. Nogueira proposed, "It is better for me to go."
But the other one spoke, half uncertain, "Perhaps it is better if I go too . . . who knows, they might create some difficulties for you. . . ."
They said they would return in a little while—a half hour, at the most—and left.

279

But I didn't need to see the doctor's worry to discover how much worse the patient was. Everything told me this— his lost look, total weakness, stretched out in the bed as if he were dead, his body burning.

The time came to give him the medicine; I looked in distress at the watch; the half hour promised had already passed and no one had come. I resolved to give the pill even so, they hadn't told me to suspend it. I came with a glass of water and managed to speak in a natural voice.

"Your medicine, dearest. . . ."

He even half opened his mouth, but didn't try to swallow. He whispered, "Cold . . . cold . . ."

He was swimming in sweat, his forehead wet, his face, as if he were crying. I took his hands which were cold as ice. I insisted on the medicine, bringing the pill to his lips again. But his head fell back on his chest, in a faint. I clung to him, wiped the sweat from his head and face and rubbed his wrists as I stared at him and only then did I understand that he was already dead.

But he still had the warmth of life. Yet kneeling, I leaned over the side of the bed and laid my face on his, and took him in my arms. I could still feel his body warmth, it was as if a little bit of life remained.

But he was already pale, pale, pale, as if a yellow wave were sweeping over his skin. I knelt there until he got cold all over. I arranged the bedclothes and ran my hands lightly over his eyelids; I closed his eyes as I had seen Senhora do with Laurindo.

The doctors were ringing the bell and I went to open the iron gate.

In the midday sun a cowboy all dressed in leather crossed the patio, passed by the foot of the *mulungu* tree, leading a red cow with her calf.

It was Zé Amador, on horseback and in his father's clothes; from a distance he took off his hat to me and received the blessing.

Antônio Amador came to me on the porch, coming from

his post at the kitchen window, and invited me to go to the corral to see the cow which had just given birth.

"She went to hide the calf in the old clearing of the deceased Delmiro. She is a heifer with her firstborn; you have to give her a name. Since she is also red, why not Garapu? She might be the granddaughter of that other Garapu—that one which the now deceased Senhora bought from your herd, don't you remember?"

And we went out into the hot sun to see the new Garapu who was mooing angrily because she didn't want to go through the open gate.

End of the Captain's Book